The *Sonata*

Chance S

Fractured Sonata

Beautiful Sonata

Pagan Sonata

Dark Sonata

Missing Sonata

*For Jackie, with memories of early morning lattes
and edible underwear*

Temporary cover illustration by the author © 2023

Tattoo designs Copyright © Weygang Designs 2020

Gustav Holst – *The Planets Suite, Op. 32*

Felix Mendelssohn – *Piano trio No. 2 in C minor, Op. 66*

Gabriel Fauré – *Piano trio in D minor, Op. 120*

Franz Schubert – *Piano Trio No 2 in E flat major, Op. 100*

Felix Mendelssohn – *Wedding March in C major from the incidental music to* A Midsummer Night's Dream, *Op. 61*

Pyotr Ilyich Tchaikovsky – *Piano Trio in A minor, Op.50*

Bedřich Smetana – *Fantasy on a Bohemian Song* I Sowed Millet *for violin and piano in F minor, JB 1:12*

Franz Liszt – *La Campanella for piano solo, No 3 from* Six Grandes Études de Paganini *in G# minor, S. 141*

Gabriel Fauré – *Élégie in C minor for cello and piano, Op. 24*

Gustav Mahler – *Lieder eines fahrenden Gesellen*

Ludwig van Beethoven – *Cello Sonata No. 3 in A major, Op.69*

Bedřich Smetana – *Prodaná nevěsta (The Bartered Bride)*

Johannes Brahms – *Wiegenlied Op. 49 No. 4 (Lullaby)*

Gustav Holst – *The Planets Suite, Op.32*

It was nearly the end of November 1983 and Kathy looked round the kitchen of her Earl's Court home thinking she had seldom seen so many people at the table in that house. The musicians had all gathered as they had their one rehearsal for *The Planets* tomorrow and Kathy was sure she could feel the anticipation and excitement almost as a physical force in the atmosphere of the room. Piers was actually at home for once when there was an invasion of musicians as his shifts meant he wasn't needed to fly Concorde for four days and he had just come off a twelve hour on-call without being paged. Thinking he may be asked to fly anywhere in the world he had spent most of the twelve hours resting so he was at his amusing best at that lunch. Emma had arrived at the house not long before they all sat down to eat and this time wasn't fazed by having Danny Tarling sitting at the table with her.

Danny himself had flown in from Los Angeles as he was currently in negotiations with the film company who had made him famous as the assassin Alan McKenna and wanted to tie him into a contract for at least another three films. He didn't have a problem with that and was more than happy to sign a multi-million dollar contract with them, but he was also negotiating to be able to work for another studio on the story of Speedbird 446, a dramatization of the crime thriller of the same name by Kerryanne McDowell which had already shot to the top of the bestseller lists on both sides of the Atlantic and in other countries of the world as well.

There had been a flurry of revived interest in something that had happened nearly four years ago and the three flight crew whose names were now public knowledge spent a lot of time avoiding press interest and demands for TV interviews. That was part of the agreements they had signed; they were not to give any interviews until the film was made and released. The three didn't mind. They were being paid handsomely for their silence. Piers and Mick were still working together as part of a regular crew and couldn't help wondering if Dacre wasn't a bit miffed that he hadn't been their third for that memorable landing. The cabin crew would now tell them that once the names of the flight crew were known to the passengers there was always a buzz of conversation in the cabin.

It was inevitable really that after the musicians had had their meal and managed the washing up between them they would amble into the music room at the front of the house and settle down to having a run-through of some piano quintets.

Jean-Guy was impressed. He was pleased that Emma had suggested to Kathy she should take the first violin part and there was no doubting they also had one of the best viola players on the circuit. Their pianist had been putting in the hours and altogether they made one impressive quintet. Listening to the sounds, he realised the string quartet they had didn't have the panache of the Stretto Quartet that both Kathy and Danny used to play with but they were certainly a very well-matched group and he began to make plans in his mind.

Kathy was equally impressed. She had been quite surprised when Emma had told her to take the first violin part but when she thought about it, it did make more sense as Emma wasn't playing much these days and certainly hadn't had any professional engagements for nearly two years. The pay for the musicians performing in *The Planets* barely covered expenses, but the prestige of taking part in the performance was reward enough. They all had to go to the Guildhall School tomorrow for the orchestral rehearsal then the musicians wouldn't meet again until the rehearsal with the choir in early December. Kathy couldn't see Piers very well from where she was sitting but from what she had seen at the lunch table he was certainly in a much better place than he had been two years ago. He had settled into an odd lifestyle that Kathy knew wouldn't suit her where he split his time between flying aeroplanes, playing piano trios and still doing some modelling work for House of Viola.

The modelling work had been quiet for a several months but was due to start again in the new year when Annette was shooting her winter collection not due for release for nearly a year. She had wanted to find a suitably atmospheric location in the UK so Kathy had half-seriously suggested she should use the rambling and rather run-down stately home in Somerset where Emma now lived with her husband, children and parents-in-law. So a scout from Viola had gone to have a look, had loved what they found and the restoration fund had received a substantial boost from the fashion house with a hefty location fee. The family hadn't had a clue what they could charge but Viola admin and legal teams knew what a fair and going rate was and that was what had been agreed on. Emma had been a bit disappointed that Danny wouldn't be one of the models but had been immensely cheered to learn that Kathy, Jean-Guy and Piers were all booked for the shoot along with Annette's new discovery, Ria. They hadn't met Ria yet but according to Annette she was a very beautiful young woman from Sierra Leone and, unlike Kathy who was a tiny five foot two, was only two inches shorter than Piers who, at six foot one, was the tallest of any of them in the quintet.

The four who were rehearsing tomorrow didn't want to spend more than an hour or so playing quintets so by three o'clock the two women were in the kitchen with coffee and shortbread biscuits. They could hear Piers had moved his piano practice upstairs and the other two were still in the music room no doubt embroiled in some discussion or another about playing.

"Almost like old times," Emma mused as she dunked her biscuit.

"Almost," Kathy agreed, thinking rather uncharitably that she now felt the upper hand was hers as she was the better-known musician, was the one playing the Guarnerius, and also Emma was now a guest in her house rather than her being a sub-let in Emma's.

"Penny for them?" Emma asked and Kathy realised she had been a bit quiet.

"Not really worth the penny," she replied and smiled. "I was just trying to remember the last time we shared a gig."

Emma suddenly thought that maybe Kath wouldn't want to remember those times and tried to be diplomatic about it. "Goodness, must be quite a while ago. You came to live with me in Hogarth Road when?"

Kathy silently blessed her friend for being discreet and not mentioning all the times the two had conspired to share concerts so they could talk. Not that Emma had ever managed to persuade her oldest friend to get out of the relationship Emma could see was abusive even if she, in the middle of confusing control and cruelty with love and affection couldn't or wouldn't. "Summer of 78?" she hazarded. "I ran away in the May of 77 so yes, must have been about then."

Emma skirted dredging up Kath's past horrors. "True. Not long before the time of this film that's being made. Weird to think you knew Piers then but didn't know you knew him, if you see what I mean. It must be even weirder for Danny playing a character who's a friend of his."

Kathy was just glad the whole sordid topic wasn't going to be raked over again. "I think the two of them find it quite hilarious from what I can gather. Apparently Piers is going to take Danny with him to Heathrow and has got permission to give him a guided tour of the flight deck of a VC-10 before he goes back to Sweden this time so at least he looks as though he knows what he's doing. As I understand it, they've made up a pretty realistic studio set for the actual filming but as it's way over in California it's not likely Danny can return the favour."

"Not letting him loose on the real thing then?"

"No chance. But the best bit is that Piers and Mick and Dutchman are going to be doing tiny cameo roles in the film. It's not in the book but Kerryanne put it in the screen play that there's a bit of a conversation between crews before flight 446 leaves and the pretend crew are going to tell the real crew that they'll be OK as the storm isn't going that fast according to the weather reports. So the pretend crew go off and then the real crew are told that their flight has been cancelled because the weather is so bad. One of them has to say the line 'Good luck to flight 446 in that case, glad it's not me flying it' and then propose they all go back to their hotel and go to the bar as nobody's going to be flying anywhere until the storm has passed over."

Emma caught the joke. "Which one of them gets to say the line?"

"Piers and Mick voted for Dutchman, who was quite happy to do it as it means he gets a mention in the credits."

"He's a funny bloke, isn't he, your Piers?"

Kathy half snorted. "He's not mine. Not sure he's anybody's half the time in spite of that chunk of platinum he wears on his finger. And what do you mean, he's funny?"

Emma looked a bit ashamed. "Well, um, I kind of propositioned him earlier."

Somehow Kathy wasn't surprised, bearing in mind Emma's past history. She felt an odd sense of disappointment that Emma had done just what Piers had talked about when they had had that conversation in the lay-by. She conveniently wouldn't think of her own appalling behaviour towards him. "Why would you do that? You're married and so is he."

"I know that. I've cleaned up my act beyond all recognition since I got engaged so Derek's got nothing to worry about. Then this morning I found known musician of the two of them to deputy section leader. The two sat side-by-side as dictated by the seating plan, and didn't say a word to each other for the whole rehearsal. Kathy had a feeling that the younger of the two brothers was either going to complain to the organisers or quit.

Everybody in the orchestra had played the piece at least once in their musical career and the standard of playing was so high it was little more than a run-through with the rehearsal conductor and they were finished early in the afternoon. The four from Earl's Court weren't surprised that Danny lit a cigarette even before they were outside the rehearsal hall.

"Were you expecting Donald to be there?" Kathy asked sympathetically.

"No," came the curt response. "One of us will have to quit as we can't play together."

"Can't, or won't?" Jean-Guy asked. He had heard the front desk of the viola section in that rehearsal and had been very impressed indeed.

Danny took a long drag on the cigarette when they were in the street and spoke through an impressive exhalation of smoke. "Can't. Sorry, but it's all very sub judice right now." He glared up the road to where his half-brother was just getting in a taxi. "Basically that bastard, not literally unfortunately, is suing me for my viola. Giles Delaney has taken on the case and it's throwing up so much mud it looks like it'll drag on for years."

They all knew Danny had inherited his famous uncle's viola but it was Jean-Guy who asked, "So how come it was you who got the viola and not your brother who is the better known player?"

myself alone in the sitting room with
unbelievably good-looking hunk of deliciousnes
just kind of thought out loud and he heard me. \
was so embarrassing, you have no idea." She sr
"Anyway, he was very nice about it and didn
huffy or anything, but the answer was a definite
I got the distinct impression it's something he's l
deal with a lot in his life. Downside of lookin{
that I suppose. But we're OK about it now. V
agreed that I'll keep my smutty thoughts to n
and he won't tell anyone what I said."

Kathy leaned towards her friend and tri
hard not to laugh. "Go on, tell me. What did
say?"

As soon as Emma whispered it to her, it \
lost battle and the other three all heard the shrie
laughter coming out of the kitchen.

It had been a long time since Kathy
played in a full orchestra and it felt decidedly o{
be sitting in the front desk of the second violins
Emma beside her. They hadn't sat like that since
had been at school and then Emma had been se{
leader with Kathy as her deputy. She didn't recog
the woman sitting on her right as deputy leade1
several of the faces were known to her from
various ensembles she had played in over the y
There had hardly been any murmurings when D{
Tarling and Jean-Guy Dechaume had turned u
play but then there were some seriously illustr
musicians in that orchestra including Danny's l
brother Donald, who was clearly put out whei
learned it was his own relative who had usurped
principal viola's chair and demoted the much be

"That was the term of Uncle David's Will. Either his eldest child or, if he didn't have any kids, his brother's eldest child. I was thirteen when he was killed in that car crash and the viola came to me. Donald wasn't even born. He didn't find out for over twenty years that I'd got it as it had been put out at the time that the instrument was destroyed in the crash. When he handed it over at the time, my father said it was to stop people trying to buy it off me so I couldn't trade it for hard currency. I don't know whether that was true or not. Main problem is by the time Donald did find out, my mother had long ago committed suicide and my father had married Donald's mother soon after that and certainly before Donald was born, which made him the legitimate heir. So confusing all these names beginning with D. You really don't want to hear all this."

"Yes we do," the other three assured him and escorted him to the nearest café so he could continue his narrative over a round of drinks.

"Right, this goes no further, OK? Well, I guess maybe we should tell Piers but it's not common knowledge as any biography of David Tarling was written before Donald started his lawsuit. When Donald started getting well known, I was still the rank amateur so he decided he'd help himself to Uncle David's viola. I'd guess our father told him the instrument hadn't been destroyed in the crash after all. No idea why, unless it was to deliberately set him against me as has now happened. So his argument is that our father and my mother were never married which made me the bastard of the family, literally this time, so not in line for the inheritance. Fortunately before I handed over the viola I'd told it all to Annette one very drunken evening and she told Giles who was round at my flat while I still had the hangover and took on my case. Then we hit problems. There was certainly no marriage certificate for my parents, which was the basis of Donald's claim, but there was no birth certificate for me to be found. No school records as I was taught at home, no medical records as I never went to see a doctor even when my hand was being so systematically smashed up. In fact, until I joined up at the age of seventeen, I basically didn't exist. My mother had taken her own life when I was thirteen, within weeks of Uncle David's crash, and yes the two incidents are related but I'm not going into that now, so nobody could check with her and Donald very cleverly didn't start proceedings until our father was so far gone with alcohol-induced dementia there was no chance he could offer a rational explanation. And so the case rumbles on and until it's resolved Donald and I aren't allowed to share bookings or communicate in any way. I guess he didn't expect me to apply for this band, never mind get in it. So I guess I'd better be the one to quit."

The others howled their protests and said it should be Donald who quitted. Danny was quite touched when the other three said that if he quit or got asked to leave then they would go too. They finished their drinks, three of them still with their minds full of what Danny had just told them and returned to Earl's Court on the Tube. The afternoon was turning to evening by the time they got back but it wasn't fully dark although the street lamps were on and there were welcoming lights shining out from the house.

They filed past the Aston Martin in the car port and Kathy let them in to the kitchen, then they stopped in a group as they heard the piano being practised in the music room at the front of the house.

"Is that him or a recording?" Emma whispered to Kathy.

"Well, if it's a recording he'll have to have bought a record player. I knew he was getting good but that's pretty incredible."

Jean-Guy was the last one in and guessed the pianist either had his ears plugged or simply hadn't heard their arrival above the volume of the music. He remembered the hours the Prof had put in, patiently cajoling this pianist to play much more loudly than he had ever been allowed to do when he was the background accompanist to his talented sister. "It's true what your father says, Emma, that Piers really is the laziest pianist he has ever come across and doesn't try at all hard when he is playing with us. On his own he will play like that, but never when he thinks we can hear." He shut the side door rather loudly and the playing stopped. "Now he knows he has an audience. Wait for it." As Jean-Guy had predicted, the brilliant Shostakovich was replaced by a much more restrained performance of the piano part to the Chopin cello sonata for a few minutes.

Kathy clattered the kettle on to the top of the Aga and Piers timed it perfectly so he arrived in the kitchen just as the kettle boiled. "Good rehearsal?" he asked.

"Very odd," Kathy told him as she made a pot of tea and guessed it wouldn't be a good idea to pass on what Danny had told them just yet. "I can't remember the last time Emma and I sat together in an orchestra. Probably when we were at school. Except this time we had to behave ourselves, no silly giggling until the music teacher told us off for the umpteenth time."

Danny had gone out into the garden so he could have a cigarette. "I can beat that," he offered. "That's the first time I've ever played in a professional orchestra."

"How the hell did you get through college?" Jean-Guy asked him.

"Never went. I was like Piers, straight into the armed forces at the age of seventeen, then into driving. My hand was too bad in those days for me to earn a living at music. I did a few amateur orchestras just to keep playing but the first proper orchestra I played in was when I went on that course in Scotland year before last. And I still don't know why I ever thought that would be a good idea."

"Were you in the RAF too?" Emma asked curiously, realising just how little she knew about the man who had taught her oldest friend to drive even though Kathy had admitted they had crossed the professional boundaries with a short but very steamy relationship at the time.

He laughed and stubbed out the cigarette in a pot with a lavender bush in it. "You joking? That's for the posh boys. I was in the Army; never made it beyond Corporal, trained as a marksman and did several tours of duty in Northern Ireland."

Kathy glanced across at Piers but he had just put the habitual cold water in his tea and was testing the temperature of it. "Don't suppose you went to Drumahoe, did you?" she asked.

"Did actually. It's not far from Londonderry and it's a beautiful part of the world. I liked Ireland. I've promised myself I'll go back when we've stopped blowing each other up out there. Why do you ask?"

She smiled. "We all know someone who was born there. And I'm surprised he's let you get away with calling it Londonderry. We're all under strict instructions to call it Derry, with no London in it."

"Forgotten you're Irish. Sorry."

"And apparently I'm also posh," Piers remarked and didn't sound best pleased.

"Oh, shit," Danny remembered. "Also forgot about the Wing Commander crack from Kathy. Were you really a Wing Commander?"

"That was the last rank I held," he admitted guardedly. "And, yes, I am Irish as I won't let these two forget."

"So what happened to your Irish accent?"

Piers did smile then. "Got drummed out of me when I got my commission."

Danny was thoughtful for a while. "Can I hear your Irish accent? It might be interesting to play you as Irish in the film."

The accent stayed firmly Home Counties. "No chance. The author would fire you."

Danny came into the kitchen closing the back door behind him and got the coffee machine going as he didn't drink tea. "True. Did I tell you I got the script just before I came across here? Haven't really looked at it yet but I'm guessing the conversations between you and your crew and the control tower in Greenland are pretty authentic transcripts?"

"Haven't seen it," Piers had to admit. "The three of us got put under contract as alleged technical advisors, although none of us has yet been asked to advise on anything, which meant we signed away the rights to anything we said during that flight or landing. We have no say whatsoever in the script."

"That seems a bit mean," Emma sympathised as she checked there really weren't any chocolate biscuits left in the tin. "I mean, it's your story in a way."

"It was. It's Hollywood's now. Anyone fancy cooking tonight or shall we go out?"

"Out!" they all chorused and then started a heated debate about where they should go. In the end Piers finished up having his first ever Lebanese meal and, following the chef's recommendations, found it didn't upset him at all. He wished he'd tried it years ago.

Kathy and Jean-Guy went back to Suffolk the next day and Emma returned to Somerset leaving Danny in the house for another day so he could get a lift into Heathrow in the morning to have his look round the VC-10 before flying back to Los Angeles while Piers went off to New York on the afternoon line for once.

Jean-Guy was busy at that time of year with many concert halls putting out extra shows building up to Christmas and he was also now in demand as a tutor at a couple of the main London music colleges. To the disgust of his agent he was also forever turning down offers to give talks or to play at private functions. Although he didn't mind teaching cello masterclasses, he didn't like the idea of giving talks, especially if it was likely to involve his personal history, and he didn't want to play at private functions without his chosen accompanist and Piers simply would not accept such bookings. Jean-Guy didn't know why, but if Piers wouldn't do them, then nor would he.

"What we need to do," he said to Kathy as she opened the first door of her Advent calendar as December began, "is nail Piers' behind to a piano stool and get him to make studio recordings with us. I've done several now with orchestras but I don't want to record with any other accompanist so of course Jane is now nagging me to book a recording session with someone else."

"It's one of his funny things, isn't it?" she mused. "He's clearly reluctant to go into the recording studio and his thing about the penguin suit is frankly getting rather ridiculous. I can understand that the piano playing represented everything horrible about the way he grew up, and I know we're all glad we made him see it could actually be quite a nice thing to do. I can even understand, in a way why he doesn't want to do the private functions as he does have this enormous chip on his shoulder about the privileged classes. But the penguin suit? Can't think of any reason for that. It's almost as though he's scared of something. Definitely signs of panic under that bloody-minded refusal."

The Prof had often thought that too, and wasn't surprised that Kathy should be so sensitive to the feelings of their pianist. He had been sitting with them in the kitchen although he had long finished his breakfast before they even got downstairs. "Have you thought of asking Roisin? We all forget that from the age of sixteen until we adopted him nearly thirty years later, Piers didn't touch a piano. So whatever makes him not want to record or dress up is something that goes back to his childhood."

"Just phone her up and ask?" Kathy questioned.

"Why not? She has asked you all to keep in touch and you are genuinely concerned about her brother so I'm sure she will be pleased to explain. It may help solve a lot of issues with your trio which really isn't getting as established as it should be by now."

"It's him. It's always him," Jean-Guy protested. "Kathy has got him to write up the calendars so we know when he's flying but that's maybe a couple of months ahead. He used to be nice about it and make charming excuses, not always very good ones but he was being pleasant about it. Then I found out he was saying he was working on certain days and it was before the rotas were even released so he could have worked round my dates. Now he doesn't even try but just gives me one of his black looks and tells me to go away but not so politely."

"Talk to Roisin. Write to her if you don't want to phone her," was the Prof's sage advice.

"And if that doesn't work," Jean-Guy told Kathy, "get him half drunk on frozen vodka and flirt with him like you do until he tells you."

"I do not flirt with him!" Kathy squeaked indignantly although she knew at the back of her mind that she and Piers could flirt with each other like a couple of old tarts.

"Yes you do," the other two told her.

"And he is as bad as you," Jean-Guy added, feeling safe in his teasing now at least Kathy had agreed to marry him even if that was as far as they had got. "I just try not to let it bother me any more."

"Very magnanimous of you," the Prof remarked drily and he looked directly at Kathy as if wanting to know her feelings on the matter.

Kathy felt herself smile at the man who was a second father to her. "You've got nothing to worry about. I told Jean-Guy I'll marry him. And, OK, maybe it's taking me a bit of a while to get round to firming up any plans but Piers and I definitely don't have that kind of relationship. There is no way he would do anything to jeopardise what he has with Sarah and the kids. I mean, your lot threw Kerryanne at him not so long ago and he walked away from that so what chance would I stand with him even if I wanted to?"

Jean-Guy thought that was so sweet, and rather unexpectedly naïve. "He told me the first time he ever saw you in the grocery shop in Earl's Court you were buying eggs and milk and you were wearing your blue coat that makes him think of Paddington Bear. You didn't even notice him among the tins of beans or whatever it was he was buying but he said it was very strange as he thought you were really attractive and he wanted to talk to you but you looked as though you would run away if he did."

"He told you something that personal?" Kathy asked incredulously.

"Yes. It was one evening in Earl's Court when you were out at a gig and he was getting towards the end of an on-call waiting for his pager to go off and we were sitting in the living room and talking to keep us both awake as much as anything. So he found out that I have slept with over twenty women and he, for all his looks and job, has only ever slept with five, including my sister although I don't feel she should count as it wasn't his idea. There was nobody for four years between Chantal and Sarah. Which I must admit I found so hard to understand how he could cope."

Kathy had a feeling that Jean-Guy was on some kind of a mission, trying to find out why she wouldn't commit to him and agree a date. So far she hadn't even been able to agree to go shopping for rings with him. She thought she was over what had happened to her the last time but even now, over five years later, she was realising just how deep the wounds and the memories were. Sometimes she thought it would be kinder to Jean-Guy just to say she had changed her mind and couldn't marry him. But then he would never understand how she could do that and not love him as much as she did. He had challenged her about her feelings for Piers enough times and the memories of the conversations in New York earlier in the year still hurt. All the words in the English language seemed to have deserted her and she wasn't sure what to say.

"You surprise me," the Prof said bluntly with his eyes on the woman who had become his second daughter. He could only imagine what was in her mind but her face was certainly troubled.

"He's had many offers," Jean-Guy continued, looking hard at Kathy who was staring at him as if he had started speaking to her in Czech. "Of course he has with looks like he has. And at least four unfounded accusations of sexual misconduct from frustrated colleagues in his various jobs, but he is not a stupid man and he has learned to make sure he is never alone with women he doesn't know and trust. Truthfully, I think he is scared to even say anything to a woman sometimes in case she thinks it is an invitation."

Kathy knew she had to speak now. "He told me, remember? When we were on our way to visit Sarah. He told me that he had been accused of the most horrible thing possible. I felt quite ashamed of my sex and told him so. But why are you raking all this up now? I've told you I'll marry you. You know what a bad time it was for me last time I was engaged. So just give me a bit of time and space to get used to the idea."

Jean-Guy felt his face flush as he realised he had perhaps pushed things too far with her again. Sometimes he felt he was tiptoeing round her when those ghosts of her past still haunted her. "I'm sorry," he said genuinely. "I suppose I can't believe I have been so lucky that you chose me and I am frightened of losing you."

"You won't," Kathy reassured him. "You have to trust me and Piers. We honestly are just friends. I don't want anything more and nor does he." She found an ironic smile from somewhere. "In fact, I have a feeling that if ever he and I did, well, you know, get physical, it would ruin our friendship and I'm not risking that. I wonder if he still gets the unwelcome offers he used to get. I mean, he's what? At least forty six and still looks about thirty."

The relief Jean-Guy felt was overwhelming and he could hear it in his voice. "Not nearly so much now he wears a wedding ring and his friends Mick and Dacre have put out the news that he also has eight children. And he has taken Sarah out to Heathrow now so many of his colleagues have met his wife."

"So that's why he took her out there," Kathy acknowledged. "I did think it was a bit of an odd thing to do when you've got the whole of London to choose from. Well I still think it was mean of those women to do that to him. And I told him so when he explained it all to me. You know I'm his official bodyguard, right?"

"It is the downside of his looks," Jean-Guy explained, laughing inside at the very idea of the petite Kathy sticking up for the man who was nearly a foot taller than her. "It's like a beautiful woman will always have the men after her. He is a very beautiful man and the women all want him and assume that he will take them simply because he is a man." He smiled at the woman he loved. "I used to wish I was more handsome and not losing my hair since ten years ago and getting fat round the waist but now I know maybe looks aren't a blessing for a man." He paused and took her hands. "You have made me very happy and said you will be my wife but now we are stuck again and have got nowhere with our plans. It worried me that perhaps you are still a little in love with Piers the wrong way so I talked to him recently and he has told me many things and I can understand why he is happy to keep you as his annoying little sister as he calls you."

Kathy gave him a hug. "You're plenty handsome enough for me," she told him and meant it. "Poor Piers. He found it so hard to tell me about the women who did nasty things to him because he was afraid Alison was going to do something like that so she could ban him from seeing his children. He wanted me to know as he suspected Alison would come to me and Sarah to tell us what he had done to her and ask one of us to go to the police with her. She hasn't done it yet but I know he really doesn't trust her." She paused as she realised how close she had come to breaking that fragile trust Piers had in her as a woman and she was thankful their friendship had survived her indiscretions. So far as she knew, Piers had never told Jean-Guy about her clumsy advances towards him in Sweden and she hadn't mentioned it either. Mostly because the memories were too painfully embarrassing and she didn't want to think about it.

Kathy looked at the older man in the room with them and realised Piers had probably told the Prof what she had done as he knew there were certain records on him that had to be maintained with the utmost truth, no matter how cringingly embarrassing it was. "Did you know about this?" was the most diplomatic way she could think of putting it.

"Yes," the Prof had to admit. "Piers was very thoroughly vetted before he was allowed to work for the security services. He has a past littered with stories like that which I am sure is why he chooses his lovers so carefully. Yes, it is true he can have problems with his joints as he has told us but that is controlled and I think he uses it as an excuse for his lack of trust in women."

Kathy was sure now that Piers had told the Prof about the times she had propositioned him but managed to sound more offended than anything else. "Are you saying he doesn't trust me?"

The Prof smiled to see the indignation on her face but he knew what she really wanted to know. "When he first saw you, almost certainly not. Now he has decided you can be trusted but he has left it too late. I think maybe he regrets that but, if I am honest, I am glad you chose this one."

Kathy looked up into the dark eyes of the man who had his arms round her by now and cuddled against him as she told the truth. "Oh, I stick by what I said all that long time ago. Piers is way out of my league. It's exhausting just trying to keep up with him half the time. But I do remember the first time I saw him. I hadn't been sharing with Emma all that long and I hadn't got used to the idea of sharing the food in the kitchen so I didn't like to eat her food and went to buy something to eat after a concert. Until I really talked to him years later I thought he was a policeman. I was just making sure the eggs were OK before I bought them and he had to pass me to get to the tins of stuff further down the shop. He just said 'excuse me' as you do and I said sorry for being in his way and that was it. But it was odd. I felt as though I was going to be safe now. I was living with Emma not on my own any more and ... this is going to sound ridiculous." The other two waited. "I saw this policeman in the corner shop and felt as though I'd met a guardian angel. I hadn't even spoken to him." Her thoughts flicked briefly to that time in the ticket queue at Liverpool Street when she had seen the man who looked so much like Piers.

"And what did you feel when you saw me at Ipswich station?" Jean-Guy asked lightly, hoping he hadn't been too heavy with her just now. To his relief she gave him her happiest smile and kissed his cheek.

"I saw you all skinny and sneezy and knew my dreams had come true."

"You say all the right things," he told her fondly and would have said more but was interrupted by Audrey streaking out of the living room and hurling herself at the back door, yowling and chirruping loudly as she then raced round and round the table.

"That only ever means one thing," the Prof announced. "I hope he hasn't been standing outside the door for the last ten minutes listening to us."

"No, it's OK," Kathy said. "I can just hear the Land Rover now. And I think this year I may send Roisin a Christmas card."

They listened and heard the Land Rover stopping outside the house and the brakes squeaked as they always did. Audrey continued circling and yowling but nobody came in.

"That's not right," Jean-Guy said for all of them.

The Prof got to his feet. "One for me, I'm guessing. Kathy, make him some coffee, please. You seem to do it the way he likes it."

Kathy and Jean-Guy waited in the kitchen for what seemed like ages then the Prof came in carrying Piers' bag for him, followed by Piers himself walking quite badly and with a visible frame round his neck and from the lumps under his clothes it was protecting his spine as well.

"What the hell happened to you?" Jean-Guy said first.

He managed to smile. "Crashed the Aston. Got whiplash thanks to my bendy back and couldn't get out of the bloody Land Rover until the Prof came and gave me a hand. Now I'm signed off for six weeks."

"How did you crash it?" Kathy asked anxiously and handed him a mug of coffee.

"Ice on the M4 coming home after a late-arriving afternoon flight. Bit of a pile-up and fortunately I finished up at the edge of it. Aston's a write off so that'll be an insurance job." He sat at the table and thankfully sipped the coffee. "That must be the only time I ever wished I'd been driving the Land Rover."

The others were amazed he should be so calm about it all but then realised it was all part of his years of training. His rationality told him it was an accident, he hadn't been badly injured and things like that didn't affect him the same as they did a lot of other people.

"Oh, your poor car," Kathy sympathised.

"It did me proud. I opened the driver's door and walked away from it. Well, OK, hobbled away from it. Plenty of people involved not so lucky."

"You're sure it's a write off?" Kathy asked, remembering the time she had driven that car across London to take Piers to hospital.

"Fraid so. The passenger door was half way across the seat and the boot had a jack-knifed articulated lorry in it last time I saw it."

"Someone was looking after you when that happened."

"Would have been a lot worse but the lorry driver behind me was well back and could see ahead better than me. I wondered why he was hooting and flashing his lights. Saw the red lights ahead of me so braked just a bit, then realised I was on black ice and smacked into the edge of the crash sideways. Good bit of driving by the lorry driver though even if the poor bastard couldn't quite stop before he hit me, so all credit to him."

"How long are you in the frame for?" Jean-Guy asked while his mind processed just how lucky the other man had been. Either that or he was one hell of a driver.

"Couple of weeks. Then just see how it goes. Really wish you had a shower in this place though as I'm sure I won't be able to get in and out of the bath for a good few days." He gave Kathy one of his roguish smiles. "And, no, Piglet. Thanks for the offer but I won't need your help."

Kathy briefly revisited the memories of her behaviour in Sweden and was grateful this man could make remarks like that. He had moved on and she knew she had to do the same. "Surprised you didn't stay in Earl's Court," she remarked, not unkindly.

He wrinkled his nose. "Too many bloody stairs in that place. That and it's due to be invaded by Strettos some time next week and even if Olga won't be around, I thought life would be a lot more peaceful out here."

"Do you charge them rent?" the Prof asked curiously.

"Of course. Had to have liability insurance and I'm not paying that out of my wages. I charge them even more if they're being residential, which they are this time. I'm not a total push-over. Danny's got a key now as he's there so much with his London work and he's in charge of them this time as he's staying in London for a while so he'll still be there when you two go down next week for the full rehearsal. Then I guess he and Emma will be up here for the actual gig. Main problem is I'm now down to one car so if it's OK with you lot I'll have to come with you in the Land Rover to the gig. Danny has said

I can share his lodgings after it as they've put him somewhere on his own in a hotel."

"Should you even be driving?" Kathy wanted to know, thinking but not saying it was now getting to be glaringly obvious Danny didn't want to be in Sweden with his wife any more than he could possibly avoid.

"Probably not. Half killed me getting out here. But I'm sure either you or Danny can drive us all to Ely if I'm not up to it. Anyway, if you'll excuse me, I'm going to go and find a floor to lie on for a while and try and get myself straight again."

"Not the floor," the Prof recommended. "You may not get up again, and I'm pretty sure none of us could lift you. Go and lie on your bed."

"Oh, God," Piers grumbled. "More bloody stairs."

"Not as many as you have at home," the Prof told him smartly. "Off you go. Just this once I'll bring your bag up for you. And you can tell me how this injury will affect your work."

Kathy and Jean-Guy didn't say anything, but they were pretty sure the Prof wasn't bothered about Piers' airline duties when he made that last remark.

Piers seemed much brighter by the afternoon and agreed to have a go at playing the piano for them so they could do some more work on the Mendelssohn. Jane had managed to secure a booking for the trio at the Barbican at the end of January as part of a "Winter Proms" season there and Jean-Guy had been adamant that it was time they got beyond their habitual *Dumky* and Mozart and stretched not only themselves but their audience as well. The Prof didn't try to take Piers' medication away this time as all he had been prescribed were some very strong painkillers to take when it got too bad and he took some after lunch which seemed to help.

The Scherzo movement of the piece still gave them a few issues, mostly because Piers set such a cracking pace the other two couldn't keep up. So he would just laugh at them and call them a hopeless bunch of amateurs. But they had been practising and both the Scherzo and the frantic finale fairly raced along. The top of the piano was down to accommodate Audrey but Piers had learned to use his wrists and arms to full effect and although it made his physical style less subtle it meant he could get an impressive fortissimo out of the old Broadwood until the Prof, listening from his study, seriously began to wonder if the instrument wasn't about to break under the strain as it hadn't been played like that for a long time.

"That is so in the Barbican programme!" Jean-Guy declared as the trio stormed to a magnificent close. "Anyway, Piers. Barbican. Very formal."

"And?"

"And I want to see you dressed as a penguin. I will concede with the shoes."

"No bloody chance."

"Can't you tell us why?" Kathy cajoled as winningly as she thought she could.

He idly rubbed Audrey's head and she purred at him. "No, I can't tell you. Well, I could, but I won't." He sounded almost sad, a bit wistful, but quite resolute. "You'll just think I'm being ridiculous."

"You have told us so much else," Jean-Guy put in kindly.

"I have bared my soul to you both over the years, as the saying puts it. But this is deeper than the soul. It goes beyond my very bones and, oh shit, I really can't think straight."

"Feed him some vodka," Kathy told Jean-Guy lightly. "He's half off his head now on Paracetamol."

"I wish. They've got me on some bloody strong codeine with an emergency back-up of morphine which I don't want to get on but that's all that works when my joints are giving me hell like this. And you wouldn't hit me when I'm down, would you?"

Jean-Guy looked at him shrewdly. "No, we wouldn't. But I will find out the story even if I have to ask Roisin to tell it to me. If you could only tell us why then maybe I would understand enough not to keep asking you. We have talked about so much together. What can be so dark and bad that you won't speak of it?"

"Think about it. How much do you know of me when I was Ciaran Maloney? Practically nothing. And that's what I won't speak of. So drop it, back off and basically butt out of that part of my life or I promise you I will shut the lid of this piano right now and never play another note."

Kathy looked at Jean-Guy. "So, full black at the Barbican it is then?"

"Guess so. But as punishment for keeping silent you must now learn Mendelssohn's second trio. And that is much worse than the first."

"Do you know what? I'm so far gone on codeine I really don't care. Where's the music?"

"In the brown envelope under your cat's behind. I ordered it by post and it only arrived this morning so we can all sight read it together. I must admit, it's one that even I haven't played. May I suggest we start with the slow movement as there's no way we're going to read this one all the way through."

As they had known would happen, the Prof heard them playing a piece that wasn't in their usual repertoire and came silently in to sit on the piano stool and help Piers out by turning pages so he could see what was going on and also make playing easier for the other man. He just sat and turned page after page and was stunned to hear the sounds those three were able to make. Kathy was now playing a Guarnerius, Jean-Guy's talent seemed to have no limits to it and Piers was one heck of a pianist when he was half stoned on codeine. The teacher in the older man saw how the three were able to flick glances between each other to keep the musicality and somehow each instinctively knew which part had to dominate and the other two would let that part sing out before the three met again as a whole. The Prof had to agree with Jean-Guy that when they played like that it really was as though they breathed as one.

He applauded at the end. "Bravo! I look forward to reviewing that one on record. Put the two Mendelssohn trios together and it will be perfect."

They waited but nothing was said by the pianist.

"Good idea," Jean-Guy tried. "It's about time we did some recording work."

Piers turned back a few pages and made a couple of pencil marks on his score. "Well, my diary's now a public document on the calendar so just let me know. Where will you do it?"

"I think that will be one for your agent to set up," the Prof advised. "Anyway well done you three. I shall now go and do what I always do at this time of day and make tea. How's the backache?"

"What backache? Oh, shit. I really am stoned on codeine." Piers started to run through his end-of-practice exercises and Audrey got off the piano. "And in case you're wondering, it's since I heard that bloody tape Kerryanne got from somewhere. Nothing is sacred any more. So let's get some of this crap on disc and let it haunt us for ever."

Kathy had a sudden insight. "You recorded with Roisin, didn't you? Is that what this is all about?" She saw Piers take hold of the lid of the piano as though to close it. "Sorry," she said quickly. "I was just curious."

He left the lid up and got stiffly to his feet. "Well, don't be. I'll help make the tea, I need to move or I'll get stuck."

Jean-Guy watched the other two men leave the room. "I am glad it was you who said that. I think if it had been me we would have lost our pianist permanently."

"I know what his problem is," Kathy realised.

"Oh?"

"Just occurred to me. But you mustn't ever tell him I've worked it out. The Prof has got a couple of recordings Roisin did when she was about sixteen, so Piers would have been what? Eleven? Twelve? One of the tracks is Stravinsky's *Four Russian Songs* and there's a slight mistake in the piano part as it was a live recording."

Jean-Guy had talked to Piers enough to realise what that meant. "Shit. That was one kid who went to bed that night bruised and hungry. Probably also explains why he doesn't like more modern pieces." He looked at Kathy who obviously didn't know whether she was more angry or upset. "He'll be fine. Lots of nice words and flattery and we'll get him back in the recording studio."

Roisin sent a reciprocal Christmas card with a short note in it saying that it was lovely to hear from them and she was looking forward to their concert in Ely cathedral. She would have loved to have been in the choir but a diary clash meant she couldn't make the rehearsal so she wasn't allowed to join the performance. So they were none the wiser but now knew the sister was not going to tell her brother's secrets.

As Donald Tarling had pulled out of the concert following advice from his legal team, Danny and Emma both arrived at the farmhouse the day before the concert at Ely and Professor Mihaly finally got to meet David Tarling's unknown nephew. It was soon obvious to the academic that Danny, like Piers, didn't have good memories of his musical childhood but, unlike Piers, seemed to have been ruthlessly trained by his uncle but never put on the concert platform. Even more of a puzzle to the older man was why David Tarling would coach the child so brutally and then, when he got to be about twelve, systematically smash up his left hand. David had died in a car crash when his nephew had been thirteen but

Danny had no doubt that the ultimate aim of his uncle had been to make sure he never played a viola in public. It was, he told the Prof, some kind of irony that he still had some use in his hand when he had been bequeathed the very instrument his uncle had never wanted him to play.

Sleeping arrangements for that night were a bit confusing as Emma, back in her childhood home, had been put in the small front bedroom on her own and the famous actor and model found himself sharing not just a room but a bed with the man he was going to have to pretend to be when he shot his scenes for the film in the new year. It didn't help that his room-mate was still in a back frame as he had done as he had been told and gone to the physio follow-up appointment and they had said his neck was fine but his spine was still a bit out of kilter so they had shut him in a more restricting brace and told him to wear it twenty four hours a day for ten days and then go back for another physio session.

Danny had brought the film script with him on this trip and the five musicians spent a very relaxed evening before the concert day all allegedly helping Danny learn his lines but in reality shrieking with laughter over the script. Kathy had thought she would never stop laughing as Danny and Jean-Guy did a perfect parody of the conversation between Speedbird 446 and Narsarsuaq control while Emma took the parts of Dutchman and Mick in the background and portrayed them as getting ever more hysterical and then they all started improvising lines. The three were in a row on the sofa while Kathy and Piers were in the armchairs and the five all went to their rooms that night feeling rather light-headed and exhausted from laughing so much.

The atmosphere was still full of fun and jollity the next day and the musicians had a brief run through of some piano quintet music in the morning with the Prof quite blatantly in the sitting room with them so he could hear David Tarling's viola being played; an instrument he hadn't heard live for over twenty years.
They had all nominated Danny as driver of the Land Rover and they set off in high spirits to Ely with Kathy between Emma and Jean-Guy on the back seat.
Emma was very quiet at the beginning but about an hour into the journey she whispered in Kathy's ear. "Is this really happening?"
"What?" Kathy muttered back.
"Me in a car with you lot going to play at Ely cathedral?"
"Very true," Jean-Guy told her and was amused to see her look embarrassed. "Anyway, Danny and Emma, I would like to speak to you both about playing as a more permanent quintet or quartet."
"Sounds promising," Danny offered. "But I don't have a lot of time these days."
"I was thinking more as we have done here. We are all good musicians and don't need to have lots of rehearsals. If we have a booking as a group, we can have one initial meet to decide on the programme, all practise on our own and just have one or two runs-through before the gig. Then it doesn't matter if two

of you live in Stockholm and Somerset and another is half his life in New York."

"Got a gig in mind?" Danny asked.

"Not really. But if you two are happy in principle I will look into dates."

"Well don't book me into anything until this film is released. It's already in production and I'll get my part done in a couple of weeks then editing work. It's being premiered in London as it's about a British plane even though it's an American production. I hope you're all going to come?"

"A film premiere?" Emma gulped, sounding like someone who had stepped into fairyland.

"Sure. Full-on glamour from all of you and you'll all be walking the red carpet. I've got Annette working on the outfits so she'll be grabbing you for measuring, Emma, when the shoot's at your house. When is that? Next month?"

"Hang on a minute," Kathy had to laugh. "Are you seriously expecting us to all troop along the red carpet at your film premiere?"

"Why not? It'll be in the first week of May. Anyone got any problems with that?"

"But there are so many of us," Emma protested although inside getting madly excited. "Are you allowed to bring such a mob?"

Danny caught her eye in the mirror. "I'm one of the stars, I can bring as many as I like." He nudged the man in the passenger seat. "You'll be there, won't you?"

"Three-line whip for me, Mick and Dutchman. Airline says we've got to go in uniform with shoes and medals polished as a publicity opportunity. We're negotiating on that one. Irony is we've all been head-hunted by the opposition."

"What do you mean?" Kathy asked.

"Virgin Atlantic. Starting up in direct competition next year."

"Wow. Are you going to jump ship?"

"I'm sure Dutchman will as he's not getting the captaincy he wants and Virgin have offered it to him. Mick and I are sticking with Concorde. We decided we'd never cope with taking seven hours to get to New York. We can get there and back in the time it takes them to go one way." He wasn't particularly interested in discussing a job offer from a rival airline. "I hope you're walking down the carpet with Kerryanne and fuelling the rumours I've been hearing of your affair," he told Danny.

Danny didn't look at all pleased. "Olga's heard those rumours too. That was not a pleasant conversation I had to have with her. And I wouldn't go near Kerryanne if you paid me. She'd eat me for breakfast. Mind you, her kid's kind of fun. She had to bring him to a meeting as her child care had let her down. Got the distinct impression her child carer has now been fired if not imprisoned."

"She has a child?" Kathy exclaimed. "I would never have expected that of her. Always seemed so career driven."

"Yeah. Bobby she was calling him. Walking and talking and into everything so I guess he's about two. I found it bloody amazing she let anyone get close enough to get her pregnant. Or more likely she went to a sperm bank. He's a bright kid and good-looking too so I guess it cost her a lot of money."

Kathy waited for a comment from Piers but none came and she suddenly guessed what the massive secret was with Piers and Kerryanne and, as he silently shot her a warning glare across the unknowing Emma, she realised Jean-Guy had worked it out too.

"So tell me," Danny innocently asked the man sitting next to him. "How the hell do you and your wife cope with eight?"

"Quite easily," he laughed. "I'm hardly ever there."

Kathy could feel the magic in the air by the time the orchestra had gathered backstage and she was standing in a group with Emma, Danny and Jean-Guy waiting for the nod to take up their seats in front of the choir who were just filing in now.

"I have so missed this," Emma breathed. "Why did I ever think I'd settle for plastering walls and producing babies in Somerset?"

"I'm sure you'll be happy to go back there," Kathy assured her. "And we're all coming to visit you in February anyway so you can laugh at us in our silly designer clothes."

The call came and they all filed on. As the cathedral was lit by hundreds of candles, it was surprisingly warm and the audience was in sufficient darkness for Kathy not to be able to see who was sitting where. She knew Piers was somewhere with Roisin as the seats weren't numbered and brother and sister had arranged to meet up before the concert started so they could sit together.

Kathy had always loved *The Planets* and to be playing it by candlelight with the composer's daughter conducting it was one of the memorable experiences of her life. Imogen Holst had met the musicians briefly in the afternoon and had taken about an hour's rehearsal but they all knew she was not in the best of health and realised what a privilege it was to play under her direction.

Aware of her oldest friend next to her and conscious that Danny and Jean-Guy were also physically close to her made the whole evening one of those perfect musical occasions for Kathy and it was with a sense of loss that she sat motionless next to Emma as the last notes of *Neptune: the Mystic* died away, sung so beautifully by the choir. There was that brief moment of shattering silence and then the applause started and Miss Holst indicated to the orchestra that they were to stand to acknowledge the appreciation of the audience. Kathy and Emma exchanged a glance and then the two looked across at Danny and Jean-Guy who looked as tired and euphoric as they felt.

The four players somehow found Piers and Roisin in the crowds outside the cathedral and those who hadn't met before were introduced to Roisin's husband and daughter and then there was a lot of giggling and chatter as they went first of all to drop Emma and Kathy off at their B and B. The landlady was still up and waiting for them and asked if their friends would like to come in for coffee so they all finished up in a large room with two big beds in it and all getting very silly over a pot of coffee and a plate of biscuits. Kathy vaguely thought that it was always a good idea to turn up with an international film star in tow if you wanted to impress your landlady and get given coffee and biscuits at gone midnight. Slowly the chatter got more sporadic and Jean-Guy said something once about he probably should be finding his way to his own digs but by that time Piers had fallen asleep stretched out on the floor to keep his back straight and Danny couldn't stop yawning.

"Lightweights," Danny yawned again and settled down on the bed next to Emma. "Give me five minutes and we'll go and crank up the Land Rover. Mind you, I reckon that one's out for the count on the floor."

"Five minutes," Jean-Guy agreed and settled down next to Kathy.

Two minutes later and Emma and Kathy were trying not to splutter with laughter as they realised they were the only two left awake in the room. Without disturbing the sleepers they got ready for bed and fell asleep next to the men who weren't supposed to be in the room at all.

It was another quiet Christmas in the farmhouse that year. Piers was still on sick leave after his car accident so he made up his Yule garland on the twenty first again and this year's one had pine cones in it as well as dried orange rings. Christmas Eve morning the other three sat quietly with him while he remembered the anniversary and he spent the night with his family again, coming back to the farmhouse for his Christmas lunch. Kathy had noticed that this time, more so than any other, Piers was impatient to get back to his flying and was almost feeling imprisoned in the farmhouse although it had been his sanctuary so often in the past.

By the turn of the year he had replaced the doomed Aston Martin with another one but this one was very shiny and black and a year younger than the maroon one. It was delivered to the farmhouse by the dealership and its new owner was clearly glad to be mobile again. Kathy wasn't sorry as it meant she had more access to the Land Rover, but she did miss the old Aston which had, just once, taken her so swiftly through the London traffic. She guessed that unless there was another emergency there was no way she was going to be allowed to drive the new one.

Sitting at the supper table on New Years' Eve, she was startled to be handed an envelope by Piers.

"What's this?" she asked.

"Open it," he told her. "You should have had it for Christmas but I couldn't get out to get it until I had a car. So Happy New Year instead. A little something for you to be getting on with in 1984."

Kathy opened the envelope wondering why the other three were watching her so intently.

"Oh!" she exclaimed. "I thought you'd given up on that idea."

"No chance," Piers told her and the other two gave her a round of applause. "Your first ten flying lessons, paid up front, and first one booked for the tenth."

"You'll need this too," Jean-Guy told her and handed across a gift bag. "Your first pilot's log book."

Felix Mendelssohn – *Piano trio No 2 in C minor, Op. 66*

It was the second day of 1984, a week until her first flying lesson, and Kathy was deeply puzzled. She could hear Jean-Guy was practising upstairs and she could see the Prof was at his desk but there was no sign of Piers. She had looked in the sitting room but he wasn't at the piano or in one of the chairs in front of the fire and she had even gone upstairs to check if he was in his room. His coat was still in the hallway so she hoped he hadn't gone out in the bitter rain. It was Audrey who gave him away by wandering out of the kitchen into the sitting room and chirruping loudly. She only ever greeted one person like that, so Kathy followed the cat and there she found Audrey's owner.

He was sitting quietly on the wide window ledge, out of sight from the door, with his back propped up on the wall and his legs outstretched. He had pulled the cuffs of his brown and grey striped sweater over his hands as though seeking some kind of comfort from the soft wool and Kathy had to admit he could actually carry off such a horrible mix of colours and make it look somehow homely and cosy rather just than a handknit sweater that was at least two sizes too large in spite of her best efforts with tension and stitch count. It was a lovely yarn and not as scratchy as she had been expecting but the colours really were two shades of mud. He was leaning his head on the window and his eyes were unfocussed and dreaming out beyond the raindrops streaming down the glass. Kathy looked at him and had to smile to herself to think he didn't look much like a multi-millionaire who still flew Concorde because he liked it.

Hearing her step in the doorway, he turned towards her and offered her an absent smile. "Sorry, not often I get the chance to sit and dream."

"You carry on dreaming," she told him. "So long as they're nice dreams. And you're not in any pain."

"No, I'm fine." He tucked his legs up so she could join him on the windowsill, "Bit self-indulgent really. I was just feeling old and thinking of Kyne. Today would have been his birthday too. Born first, bigger and stronger than me but he only lived for three hours."

Kathy was appalled she had known him so long and hadn't realised. "It's your birthday? Why have you never told us?"

"When you've had as many as I have you tend to try to forget them."

Kathy did her maths. "You're forty eight. That's not old." She remembered where she had heard that name before. It had been during a wedding service when both the bride and groom had identified themselves with their full names. "Didn't you take Kyne as your middle name?"

"Yes. My twin was named Kyne Pearse and I was Ciaran Seoirse. So I kind of helped myself to his name."

"And Buchanan?"

There was some warmth in his smile at last. "Was the name of a block of flats opposite the stop in Derry where you caught the bus to Drumahoe. I stood looking at that name dozens of times in the rain."

"I often wondered how you came to choose your name. Must be weird choosing what to call yourself."

"Was a bit. Anyway I'm sure you didn't come wandering in here just to share my birthday blues."

"Forgotten why I did come in here now. So you were born on January second which is why you call yourself a snow-baby. When was Roisin born?"

"She did way better than me. She's a leapling."

"A what?"

"Leapling. Born on the twenty ninth of February. She'll be thirteen this year."

Kathy realised that the man on the windowsill had tried to end his life on what had been his forty sixth birthday, the day before his triplet daughters had been born. She wasn't quite sure whether that made her happy or sad so she didn't try to analyse it. "I hope she's having a party." Kathy gently slapped his legs. "Well, I'm now going to make you a birthday cake. And don't pull that face at me and say you don't eat cake. You'll just have to tell Annette you need an elastic waist in your trousers for the next outing of Samildánach. When is that going to be anyway?"

"No idea. Our next gig with her is at Emma's in February. And that's just a shoot, so with any luck I keep all my clothes on this time. No wandering about in biker jeans and wings. You know her legal team have put a block on Sammy's real identity being known, don't you? Total copyright on the whole look so nobody else can use it for anything, which suits me fine."

"I still can't believe nobody has twigged Sammy is you yet."

"I can. You can hide a lot behind a pair of red eyes and a stripey face. Can you imagine the stick I'd get at work if that ever got out?"

Kathy had to laugh. "Dacre would never let you live it down."

"If Dacre has seen any of the photos, he knows already. He was in the hospital with me when they got the soaked clothes off to put the gown on so he's seen the back tattoo. Probably seen a lot more than that, no dignity in those bloody hospitals. And Angela is just the kind of woman to look at fashion show photos in the Sunday supplements. So I wouldn't mind betting I've been rumbled in their household."

Kathy had got up to go and make a cake but instead she sat back on the windowsill, wrapped her arms round his tucked-up legs and put her chin on his knee so she could look at him. "And he's never said anything?"

"Oh, he'll be plotting so he can let it out just when it'll embarrass me the most. Hope he doesn't or he'll have the Viola legal team onto him." He turned his attention back to the rain. "He's had since last March to out my alter ego and he still hasn't done it."

"Perhaps he's not going to."

"Problem is if I warn him off then I've admitted to being Sammy so if he doesn't know now he will then. So complicated."

There was a dull flatness to his voice which she didn't like so she hugged his legs just a bit tighter and kissed his knees. "Please don't go back to that dark place."

He turned to look at her then and gave her a faint smile. "Don't do that. And I'm not."

"Truthfully?"

"Almost. Do you remember how your ex was like a shadow in your life? Sometimes it was just something niggling at the back of your mind and other times it was so strong it was like someone had turned all the lights off?"

She looked at him and felt just a bit scared. "I never told you that. Did Jean-Guy tell you?"

"Nobody told me. When you live with your own shadow you can see other people's. That's why you're currently trying to break my legs because you can see just how close my shadow is today." He acknowledged the little cat who had draped herself over his shoulder a while ago. "You and Audrey." He shifted on the windowsill to ease his back but carried on looking at the rain, rather than at her. "Am I the reason you won't marry Jean-Guy?"

"What? No. Don't flatter yourself. You've got a wife and eight children and I've never fancied you like that in all the time I've known you. Not even when you let me have the custard creams."

He gave her one of his lovely smiles. "What? Not even when I stood at the end of that runway and you got all overheated?"

Kathy had a bad feeling her indiscretions in Sweden were hanging in the air between them but she wasn't going to let any of that impinge on this conversation.

"And you've pointed out that was only Annette's marketing so it doesn't count."

"Well if it's not me, then it's your ex. Something is stopping you. And you know I don't mean I'm flattering myself you fancy me. I mean you're worried about me even though it's been two years and you really don't have to be."

Kathy leaned her cheek on his knees and the two looked out at the rain together. "I don't know what it is. I sometimes think maybe it's the memory of what happened last time I was supposed to be getting married but Jean-Guy and I have been sleeping together for ages now so it can't be that. Then I think maybe it's all tied up with having babies and seeing Emma almost giving up her playing so she can be a mother but Sarah and Alison have said many times they can soak up any of mine into your army if I need any child care. And it's not as though Jean-Guy and I often have gigs together so we could easily manage a child between us. He keeps suggesting dates and something always makes me not want to do it."

Neither noticed Jean-Guy had arrived in the doorway and had seen them sitting so cosily on the windowsill his first instinct was to go and pull them apart but then they were silent, just looking at the rain and something warned him not to interrupt.

"Are you scared of committing to him? Is there something, I don't know, maybe even going back to your parents that means you don't want to say you'll stick with one person for the rest of your life?"

No, I don't think so. I love him so much and I can see it's hurting him that I won't agree to a date."

"You won't even let the poor sod buy you an engagement ring."

"I had one of those once before," Kathy said and felt the silent tears slide from her eyes.

Jean-Guy watched with something between fascination and extreme envy as Piers dropped his legs down and Kathy stretched out so he held her close on top of him while she wept hot tears on his neck and Audrey's fur.

"Just speak to me, Piglet," he encouraged gently.

"I can't," she gulped rather inelegantly.

"Can't what?"

"Go through all that again. All that fuss and argument over flowers and dresses and churches and whether we're having gold or platinum. I want what you had. No fuss at all. Just you and Sarah and half a dozen of us. You didn't even have a suit on. And Sarah was in that awful floral dress that she's had nearly as long as I've known her. I think it's the only dress she owns."

"Have you said this to Jean-Guy?"

"Yes. But he thinks I'm just trying to save him money as he's not as rich as you."

"Just forget about me," he said rather impatiently. "This is about you and Jean-Guy. So just tell me, exactly, what your perfect wedding is?"

Kathy nestled her head on his shoulder and let his comforting embrace soothe her as they both watched the rain drumming on the already soaked garden. "I used to think I'd like to be a winter bride but then Emma pinched that so maybe something like late summer when the trees are getting just a bit blowsy and the fields are ripe. Anything except the spring. And that's not because you pinched that, it's because it's what my ex told me I was going to have. Autumn I find a sad time of year so, yes, late summer. I always thought it would be lovely if the Prof could be the one to give me away. I always feel he's more like a father to me than my own dad is."

"You don't have to have your family there at all if you don't want to," came the soft assurance. "You can surround yourself with friends and cats if that's what you want."

"I don't, do I?" she realised and sighed once. "In that case, the Prof can give me away. You will be Jean-Guy's best man and the two of you will be in those lovely woodland shades that suit him so much. All russet browns and dark reds. You'll have to wear the red, brown really isn't your colour. I think I'll have a midnight blue dress and maybe make the cloak the colour of a night sky without stars. And I'll have a hood instead of a veil so when we've taken our vows, Jean-Guy can put the hood back and then he'll see I've got sparkly things in my hair like you have when you're being Sammy. And I'd really love a copper wedding ring even though I know it'll send my fingers green after a time."

"You could always go for rose gold. If they get the mix right that can look quite coppery."

Kathy caught her breath, finally able to see it in her mind's eye. "Yes. Perfect. Rose gold. I don't want a boring conventional plain band. Maybe something a bit Celtic. Or with leaves on it. I quite like your ring even though I know you hate it."

He didn't rise to that comment. "And what about the engagement ring? Rose gold as well?"

"Oh, can you imagine it? Rose gold, and the stones of late summer like emeralds and amethyst. Pearls, I love pearls."

Jean-Guy felt he ought to be making notes and there was no way now he was going to move and let them know he had overheard everything. He was surprised Piers hadn't shown any sign of knowing he was there as he couldn't believe the man with such acute hearing hadn't heard him.

"Piglet, it sounds perfect. Why don't you set the date while you're planning your summer wedding in the January rain? Make Jean-Guy very happy as he asked you to."

To Jean-Guy's fascination, the woman who was talking about her perfect wedding to him quite calmly pushed up another man's sweater and shirt enough to expose part of the raven tattoo on his ribs.

Kathy gently traced the outline of the raven. "Do you think Sammy would come to my wedding?"

Piers lifted her hand away and pulled his clothes down again. "Not if you have it in a church," he told her. "For one thing you would offend his Pagan sensibilities and for another his wings would drop off with the cold."

"Oh, no," Kathy was quick to reassure. "He would have a coat. Raven black with a dark red lining and a trim of black feathers." She sighed. "I don't know that I want a church wedding. Yours was absolutely lovely but you married a Christian. Jean-Guy has told me several times that he's an atheist and I think your faith all tied up with nature sounds so much lovelier than Christianity. Which is another reason I can't settle and agree to anything. If you had done the wedding planning and not Sarah, what would you have done?"

"Doesn't matter. The wedding is the woman's choice. So you pick what you want and I'm sure Jean-Guy will be so happy just to be able to marry you he really won't care too much. Just remember he wants to marry you before we all go to Prague in September so don't leave it too late in the year as he'll be cramming in practice sessions by then."

Kathy felt unbearably sad at the thought of getting married. She pulled the ring off Piers' finger and looked at it. "Do you regret marrying Sarah?"

"No. Why should I?"

"Because she made you marry against your beliefs."

"Can I have my ring back, please?"

Kathy closed her fingers round the metal that was warm from his hand. "Isn't this what marriage is all about?" she asked suddenly. "Giving in? My ex made me give in to all his demands and you gave in to all of Sarah's. The only difference between us is that I ran away and you went through with it." She held up her closed fist and it was all clear to her now. "You wear this symbol of the complete and total suppression of your beliefs and your wishes. She trapped you in the place of worship of a faith that destroyed yours nearly two thousand years ago and she forced you to wear this as the ultimate control." She hurled the ring across the room without thinking about it. "And that, I have realised, is why I don't want to get married."

Jean-Guy saw all his dreams crumbling. His only hope now was that this woman would forgive him enough to allow him to carry on as her lover, even if never as her husband. He then began to realise he had seriously underestimated the other man.

"Piglet, listen to me for one minute. Answer me one question. Do you think Sarah and I love each other? No, don't look at me as though I've finally lost it. Just answer the question."

"Well, yes, you do now. I'm not sure you did then."

"Thank you. Now, another question for you. Do you think I'm a complete idiot?"

She was feeling a bit foolish now. "Um, you have your moments."

"Let you get away with that one. So you're telling me that my marriage is a big mistake on my part? That I've given up on all my own wishes and my own beliefs? Has it ever occurred to you that I wanted to be with Sarah even way back then? OK, the way we went about it at first was wrong and truthfully it shouldn't have happened that quickly as we both had a hell of a lot of adjusting to do to get used to the idea of each other. But I found I had fallen in love with a warm and loving woman who accepts me for what I am. A broken human being who can't believe in her God. All Jean-Guy is asking you to do is be his friend and his companion. His, what was his word? His sputnik. Walking side by side and facing whatever gets thrown at you. It's not about one of you bending your will and giving in to the other. It's not about control. And if that's what you learned from your first engagement, then I'm sorry for you."

Kathy was silent. She watched the rain falling on the garden and rested her hand on his chest, feeling the rise and fall of his breath as though it was the raven breathing under her touch. His eloquence had surprised her, his words had made her think, and she really wished she hadn't thrown his ring across the room like that.

He let her think for a while then planted a kiss on the top of her head. "Tell you what. Why not go for Lughnasadh? Lugh is Sammy's name and so it's his day. First of August, also known as Lammas. You can't get much more late summer than that as it's the first of the harvest celebrations."

Kathy got her thoughts back into order. "Isn't that a bit pagan for a church wedding?"

"Do you want a church wedding?"

"Not really. I just always assumed I would. Can you even have a pagan wedding in this country?"

"You can have a register office and then go for a handfasting. I tried so hard to get Sarah to agree to a handfasting but she wasn't having any. But I keep trying. Haven't given up yet." He turned his gaze out to the rain again and idly rubbed her back. "If the two of you marry in the local register office you could have the handfasting anywhere. On the beach, in the garden, doesn't matter. Gisela is a pagan celebrant and she can do the handfasting for you if you like."

Suddenly it all felt so right and she was glad he had been with her and helped her sort it all out in her mind. "So I can marry Jean-Guy in the garden here? Under the big old crabapple tree?"

"If that's what will make you happy. But make him happy too and have the register office bit first." This time he did look straight across to the doorway where Jean-Guy was loitering not wanting to break whatever enchantment was in that room.

"Perfect," Kathy sighed.

"Will you tell him?"

"He knows already doesn't he? How long has he been standing there?"

"Long enough to listen to your doubts and I hope long enough to see where the hell that ring went or Sarah is not going to be happy. Even if I did pay for it myself. Jean-Guy, please tell me you saw where it went?"

Kathy kissed his cheek feeling light-hearted and relieved that her mind was now so much clearer on the whole matter. "Come and help me give the birthday boy a pull," she invited Jean-Guy. "Then I'm going to make him a cake." She gave Piers her best glare, "And don't you dare tell me you're not going to eat any. You still have your reputation when it comes to chocolate."

"I was going to give it up," he tried valiantly but knew the others wouldn't believe him for a minute.

Jean-Guy was crawling round the floor, peering under the furniture. "I'm sorry, I can't see it anywhere. You'd better have a look, your eyesight is better than mine. It will be easier with a torch." He stood up and watched as the other man got so stiffly off the windowsill. He had to smile. "I think I owe you many thanks for saving my marriage before it has even started. Kathy, you are to have what you want. I will be very happy not to marry in a church and I like the idea of a marriage in the garden on Samildánach's day. But it seems now we have lots of wedding plans to organise. Where the hell are we going to find a ring such as you described?"

"Well, in the summer when the tourist season is going, we would go round all the local craft fairs and find ourselves a jewellery maker and put in a commission. Or I suppose we could look in the yellow pages or ask in the library for any information on local makers," Kathy suggested. "I'm sorry," she said to Piers. "Here, let me have a look." She could feel the panic setting in as there was no sign of that platinum ring anywhere. "Oh no, I really am so sorry. I'll tell Sarah it's all my fault. I'll borrow the Prof's big torch and get a magnet or something. It can't have gone far. I heard it hit something and then fall so it must have bounced off the bookcase. We'll find it."

"You'd bloody better," was all he said as the Prof came in to ask if anyone wanted coffee and saw Kathy and Jean-Guy were both crawling round the floor, looking under the furniture. "What has happened?" he asked.

"Well, the good news is, I've chosen my wedding day," Kathy told him. "It'll be on Lammas which is the first of August. Register office in the morning and a proper pagan handfasting in the garden in the afternoon. The bad news is I've managed to lose Piers' wedding ring for him."

The Prof was faintly baffled by that but he was getting used to these young people now and nothing surprised him any more. "I'll get my big torch out after coffee. Don't worry, Piers, it can't have gone far."

Jean-Guy was starting to feel a bit guilty too and he hadn't been the one who had thrown the ring. "Do you have any idea where we can get an engagement ring made? I have promised Kathy she can have whatever she wants and I think it will have to be specially made."

"Why don't you just ask Sarah's mother?" the Prof suggested mildly. "There can't be much going on round here she doesn't know."

"And let me know what she says," Piers requested. "In case I have to get a duplicate made before Sarah finds out."

Kathy drove into the village the next morning so Piers could spend the triplets' second birthday with them and none of them really felt like walking as the weather was still bitterly cold. Kathy and Jean-Guy went into the shop promising to join in the birthday party as soon as they could and they were relieved to find the shop was quiet so they could ask their question without too many nosy villagers listening on the side lines.

Sarah's mother had to think about that for a few minutes. "Daisy," she said in the end. "Now what's her surname? She was Daisy Ginger until she got married and moved out Wenhaston way a long time ago now. But her marriage split up after the children had left home. I think I heard they've gone to live in America, or Canada or somewhere. But Daisy inherited what had been her parents' cottage when they died, oh a while ago now, and she keeps it on as more of a holiday cottage. But she's in the village quite a lot for someone who works in London. Bit like Piers really I suppose. I'll have to ask Mrs Alexander. Daisy's her mother's cousin's third child. But she definitely used to make jewellery." She thought about that a bit more while she served another customer in the shop. "Daisy Hollinger. Or Dillinger. No, I'm sure it was Hollinger. When she was a young mother with not much money she used to make things and we'd sell a few in the shop. Called herself Daisy Chain which I thought was quite clever. All sorts of pretty things from the sea glass she'd found on the beach. So talented." She looked towards the door as someone came in. "There she is now. Gwen, does your Daisy still make jewellery?"

Mrs Alexander looked faintly surprised to be so accosted as soon as she had set foot in the shop. "Yes, but she's in London now and she's very upmarket. Sells her pieces for hundreds of pounds. She's come on a long way from making bracelets from sea glass when that rat of a husband of hers kept leaving her. So he was in the Merchant Navy. I bet he'd been cheating on her the whole time."

Sarah's mum had heard Gwen Alexander's rants too many times to want to hear it all over again. She looked at the young couple in front of her. "Sorry, loves. Looks like it's yes and no."

Jean-Guy hung on his nicest smile. "Mrs Alexander, do you suppose there is any chance Daisy would accept the commission to make a ring for Kathy? We both like the idea of using a local maker rather than spending money in the big shops on the high street."

The older women looked at them. It was Sarah's mother who knew them better who dared ask what the whole village had been wanting to know for over a year. "Does that mean you two…?"

"Are getting married," Jean-Guy confirmed. "August the first. It'll be a register office wedding."

"Oh," said Sarah's mother. "What's wrong with the church like Sarah had?"

"Nothing," Kathy put in quickly. "It's just that neither of us has that strong a faith."

"Hmm," said Sarah's mum, unconvinced. "Would you like to see if Daisy can ring you at the farmhouse? Sarah's got the number somewhere."

Kathy hoped the Prof wouldn't mind someone else knowing the farmhouse phone number, but he did seem a lot more relaxed about that these days since the others had started living with him. "Yes. Thank you," she replied feeling that somehow they had now upset the two ladies.

"What sort of ring do you want?" Sarah's mother asked although the others were all quite aware it wasn't really anything to do with her.

Kathy decided to make amends. "I'm looking for an engagement ring and then we'll need two wedding rings. We want to go for rose gold but as coppery as it can be made. And I was hoping for emeralds or pearls or something like that in the engagement ring."

The older ladies looked even more suspicious. "Not diamonds and platinum like Sarah has?" her mother asked almost anxiously.

It was on the tip of Kathy's tongue to say she didn't want anything straight from the shops but realised in time that wouldn't sound good however she said it so she just smiled and said, "I want summer colours. I do like Sarah's diamonds though. But they're really not me."

Sarah's mum didn't quite sniff dismissively but she unsubtly changed the topic. "Has Piers gone next door for the party?" was the next enquiry.

"Oh, yes. I think he was almost looking forward to it in a funny kind of way."

Sarah's mother still didn't look very happy. "You know he refused to join us for Christmas lunch don't you? Just told us he doesn't do Christmas and off he went like he always does. But Sarah told him he's stopping with us for the lunch this year. He's got two families now and he's got to learn to share us."

"It's been a funny visit this Christmas as he's hurt his back," Kathy defended her friend before

Sarah's mother really got going. "I'm sure he told you he was in a car crash a few weeks ago and got whiplash so he hasn't been very mobile. But he's getting a lot better now," she continued trying to avoid upsetting the woman who knew people who knew jewellery makers and probably had lots of other useful contacts. "He's had a new car delivered so at least he's mobile again." She thought it would probably be rather indiscreet to say Piers hated having to sleep in Sarah's bed and found his one at the farmhouse so much more comfortable for his back. He had offered to buy her a new mattress and Sarah had been quite offended, pointing out there was nothing wrong with the one she had and he had known not to push the matter.

"Yes, he told us about the car crash and his back." Sarah's mum shrugged. "It looks plausible as he's in that frame thing but I don't know why he won't stay more often especially as Alison's away for the holiday again. Are you buying anything today or did you just want to ask about the rings?"

Guilt made Kathy and Jean-Guy buy some fruit and a bar of fruit and nut chocolate then they went to join the mayhem of the party next door. The triplets were all up on their feet and toddling by this time but the quins hadn't got to that stage even though they could all now stand up to watch what was going on around them. The visitors to the house soon found out that eight children could make a heck of a noise and none of them could genuinely have said they were sorry when the tea was eaten and it was time they could take a respectable leave.

"What did Sarah say about your wedding ring?" Kathy asked as the three got into the Land Rover

"Oh, um, well I just told her I'd taken it off while doing some mucky jobs in the garden and she believed me. Just make sure you find the bloody thing before I see her again because even she won't take the same excuse twice."

"How are things with you and Sarah?" Kathy asked.

"We're OK, just so long as that bloody Alison isn't around." He shrugged. "I've not been in the best of moods since that crash and I don't like to go to her when I'm feeling like this as she picks up on it and it makes her tap into something in her ancestors that scares the crap out of her. I don't know when her family converted to Christianity but it wasn't more than four generations ago."

Kathy remembered the way Piers and Sarah had looked at each other when she had introduced them and they had touched hands for the first time. They had something old and deep in common which they had realised with that first physical contact and it didn't matter that she was a shop girl and he flew a supersonic jet. Two ancient lines had come together and that was all they needed to know.

"Got you some fruit and nut in the shop," was all she said. "Got any space in your tummy after that birthday feast?"

Piers almost laughed. "Thank you," he said. "You two know my weakness. Really shouldn't eat it though as it has got milk in it, but what the hell. I suppose you want to do some work on the bloody Mendelssohn when we get home?"

To Kathy's surprise, Daisy Hollinger rang the farmhouse that evening and the two women talked for quite a while about rose gold rings. Daisy promised to sketch out some designs and post them to the Earl's Court address as they would get there more quickly and, if there was anything Kathy liked, they could meet at her studio as she wasn't far away in Notting Hill.

Kathy went back into the living room where the piano and cello were playing a slightly lopsided Mendelssohn. She wasn't quite sure how to ask what she wanted to know but Jean-Guy spared her having to start the conversation.

"Have you bankrupted me now?"

"Well, I could if you'd let me."

"Oh? I've not long settled the bill for your hot coals ring. What have you in mind now?"

Kathy looked at her beloved ruby ring on her right hand. "Um, Daisy loved the idea of the harvest colours and suggested a fairly simple band and she can put yellow diamond, emerald and even rubies in it if we like. They'd only be tiny, not much more than chips so not as expensive as it sounds. She's going to post me some designs to Earl's Court."

Jean-Guy was delighted that they seemed to be making progress at last. "Good. We'll see what she comes up with. Did you like her?"

"Yes, but I think she only got in touch so fast as Gwen Alexander told her that you and I have done modelling for Viola and I think she's going to try to get at least the engagement ring finished in time for the shoot next month so it can be shown off."

Piers glanced at the clock. "You'd better ring Annette about that one or Daisy may find she's run foul of a few copyright laws. I can't imagine Annette will want to showcase someone else's work with her collection. Have you got her number?"

"In the back of my diary. Do you think I should ring her tonight?"

"I would, before Daisy gets carried away designing things that can't be advertised as she would like."

Kathy had to smile. "You're still the sensible one, aren't you?"

"Maybe. Or perhaps it's just that I've had more tangles with Annette than you have. I'm not allowed the wedding ring as she didn't design it, not for any aesthetic reasons. She said I could have a plain band but I couldn't see the point in getting one just for her photos. Which reminds me, I must run the hoover over the carpet to see if that picks it up."

"Still not found it then?" Kathy asked and the guilt started to come back again.

"Nope. Think it's gone to join that thing Sarah gave me when we got engaged."

"Maybe you should have gone for the finger tattoo she offered you," Kathy replied, looking round the room hoping to catch a glimpse of platinum somewhere on the floor. "I could ask Daisy to design you something if we don't find yours. I'll pay for it as it's my fault it's lost."

"I'll try the hoovering first. I think Sarah might get a bit upset if I change wedding rings. I've just got that one nicely bashed and worn in. Go and phone Annette."

"Bully."

"You need it. Go on, hop it."

Kathy realised Piers was still cross with her, just trying his hardest not to show it. She wished she had thought of doing the hoovering that morning. She hadn't expected to catch Annette at home on the Berkshire number but she didn't have a London number for her except her offices. It turned out the designer was at home that evening and listened to Kathy's explanation about Daisy and the engagement ring.

"Do you have a number for Daisy?" she asked.

Kathy hadn't been expecting such a practical response and gave her the London number for the jewellery maker.

"I'll give her a ring. I'd like to go more into jewellery but it's not really my forte. I might see if she'd like to collaborate on the collection. I like the idea of an independent woman designer." She was thoughtful for a few moments. "Do you think Jean-Guy would wear an earring like Danny does?"

"I have no idea," Kathy admitted honestly. "I can't see it somehow, it's not really what classical cellists do, is it? I'll ask him."

"Mm, please do. It's a pity Piers' job won't let him." Suddenly the fashion designer snorted with laughter. "I wonder if he'd consider a nose ring? He's made a couple of cracks about it before now and he did only say his employers don't allow earrings."

"Now you're being silly," Kathy decided.

"I know. But I'm half way through a bottle of chilled rosé and stuck on what to do with poor old Sammy after next month's shoot and the rest of the collection isn't doing much better."

Kathy was delighted to learn Piers was going to be in the full costume again and remembered what she had dreamed up for her wedding day. "Maybe it would be easier if he didn't have feathers on his arms? Can you put the wings more on his back even if it's over the clothes? Or maybe Sammy can tuck his wings in and wear ordinary clothes? I asked Piers if he'd come to my wedding all dressed like that but he said he'd be too cold so I said he'd have to wear a black coat with a red lining and a feather trim. I mean it's the make up and jewellery that make him Sammy isn't it?"

"Yes! Kathy, I love you! I can get that coat idea in next month with a few tweaks. Want me to design your wedding dress to say thank you? If you let me run it out as part of my collection then you can keep it after the shoot and I won't charge you. But, yes, the wings on the arms were the problem I was having and I can't keep the poor bloke half naked every time I use him, can I?"

"Well you could, but I think he might have something to say about that," Kathy laughed. But already the excitement was starting to course through her at the very idea of a Viola design wedding dress. "But if you're serious, that would be lovely. Thank you. Only I don't want to have a white dress or anything so traditional. I always said I'd have a hooded cloak rather than a veil and I wanted inky blues and summer night colours."

"Sleeves in the dress? Or strapless under the cloak?"

"I don't know. I haven't got that far. But strapless does sound as though it'll be more fun for Jean-Guy when he finds out."

"Do you know what? You have such a sweet and innocent face and the soul of a slut. Sorry, got to go. You've taken me from total designer block to idea overload. Are you in London again soon?"

"Yes. Piers is travelling up tomorrow in his new car and Jean-Guy and I will be about two days behind him."

"Good. I'll call round some time with a portfolio."

Kathy went back into the sitting room where the other two were having one of their discussions over timing and dynamics with neither giving way. "Annette wants to know if you'll wear an earring," she said abruptly to Jean-Guy.

He looked faintly astonished. "Why the hell would I want to do that?"

"I don't know. She just asked me to ask you. And you can't say your job won't let you." She turned to Piers who was looking almost smug. "And it's no good you thinking you've got away with it. You only said your job doesn't allow earrings. She's got her sights set on your nose."

To the surprise of the other two this seemed to amuse him no end. "Interesting concept. I wonder what they'd say. Oh well, it's not going to happen anyway." He closed the lid of the piano and picked Audrey up for a cuddle. "Going to miss this crazy cat. Maybe I should take her back to London."

Audrey clambered up and settled herself round his neck as she so often did and purred loudly.

"Maybe you should just come here more often?" Kathy asked.

He ran his hand along the closed lid of the old Broadwood piano that was finally starting to show its age. "Nah, got a better piano back home. This one's getting a bit worn out now."

"Go and make us some tea, you ratbag," Kathy told him. "When are you next airborne?"

He sighed happily. "Medical check first thing Tuesday morning. Can't see why they won't pass me, I feel OK now. So with any luck back to Concorde next week. And you," he told her sternly, "need to get that bloody hoover out."

Gabriel Fauré – *Piano Trio in D minor, Op. 120*

The recital at the Barbican was another unequivocal success for the Dodman Trio. Even the three who played in it were overwhelmed by how well they rattled off two Mendelssohn trios and then, just when the audience thought the exhausted musicians had had enough, they brought the house down with Fauré's Opus 120 for an encore. The audience wouldn't let them off the stage for a full five minutes after they had played their last note but made such a racket of applause and cheers and foot-stamping that the three began to wonder if their audience had been listening to something else through headphones as all that noise couldn't be for them.

Jean-Guy got quite emotional in the dressing room backstage and the other two thought he was going to full-on burst into tears at one point. So Piers discreetly went out into the corridor and left Kathy to calm Jean-Guy down before they joined him with the happily exhausted cellist looking much more relaxed.

Kathy gave the weary Piers a smile and hooked her hand through his arm. "Home?" she asked him.

"Definitely. I need to be in bed before midnight or I won't get enough sleep in before tomorrow's charter flight."

"Going anywhere nice?"

"Just one of our Bay of Biscay trips." He had to smile. "You've got to admire these charter passengers. They're flying Concorde for the love of it and the thrill of going supersonic, unlike the more blasé regulars to New York. Quite a party atmosphere and we take bets on how much of the crockery they're going to nick."

The other two laughed with him as they went to where the Aston Martin was parked. "Seriously?" Kathy asked.

"Oh, yes. I think the airline factors missing souvenirs into the cost of the tickets. The crew all really enjoy them as it makes a change and it's only a short trip for us. Puts money in the airline's coffers too so it's winners all round."

"You'll have to nick some crockery for us," Kathy told him jokingly as she climbed into the back seat while Jean-Guy loaded his cello into the boot.

"Oh, no," Piers told her and sounded quite shocked. "That's cheating. You have to nick your own."

"Hm, like I'm going to be going on that aeroplane again any time soon."

Piers drove them back to the house in Earl's Court where Kathy made them a post-concert meal of scrambled egg which was interrupted by Piers' pager going off which confused all of them as he wasn't on-call. He reluctantly went up the stairs from the kitchen to the phone in the living room to see what was going on.

He was back in less than five minutes and not looking best pleased. "Seems I'm going to miss the Biscay party tomorrow. We've had a captain literally fall off a horse so now I have to take a business charter out to San Francisco instead. Going to be a long one as I'm full captain and need to get the flight plan logged and paperwork sorted. Even longer as we have to cross the States subsonic, silly bastards seem to think we'll break all their windows if we don't. So

I am now off to bed with my alarm set for seven in the morning and I'll see you all sometime the day after tomorrow. God knows when."

He went wearily back up the stairs and the other two looked at each other.

Jean-Guy shrugged. "Glad I'm not an airline pilot. He wasn't even on-call."

"Yes, but we all know the airline like him as he lives so close to the airport."

Jean-Guy pulled a wry face. "Still it also suits us so I'm not going to suggest he moves. When do you think would be a good time to tell him tonight's concert was recorded for a commercial disc?"

"Probably some time before he sees the reviews in the music papers."

"True. Well that's our landlord going off for a couple of days so shall we leave the washing up for the morning and go to bed?"

Kathy took the hand he held out to her. "Good idea."

The postman had so much mail for the three of them the next morning he had to ring the bell at the street door as it wouldn't fit through the letter box. Kathy had just about got downstairs and switched the coffee machine on so she didn't bother going upstairs again but sat at the table to look through the designs that had been sent to her by Daisy Hollinger. There was a letter in with the sheets of drawings.

Dear Kathy

Here are my preliminary ideas for your rings. I hope you like at least one of them, but if not, I will be happy to discuss any changes with you.

I can't thank you enough for putting Annette Delaney in touch with me. We had a lovely long chat and she has commissioned me to make some jewellery for her fashion shoot next month. I'm going to have my work cut out to get finished in time especially as a lot of it is to be suitable for men which isn't something I do much of.

If you are able to decide on a ring fairly soon I promise I will sit up night and day to get it done so you can wear it next month! I have rose gold in stock and have put a tiny sample in for you so you can see the colour of it. It is very coppery so I think will suit you.

Brightest blessings
Daisy H

Jean-Guy wondered where his coffee had got to so he went down the stairs and found Kathy in the kitchen with silent tears pouring down her face and sheets of drawings spread all over the table.

"Kathy? What the hell's the matter?"

She sniffed rather inelegantly and wiped her nose on a piece of kitchen paper. "It's Daisy's designs. Look."

So Jean-Guy looked at the one she pointed out to him and saw a delicate design with tiny stones in shades of yellow, orange, red and green. It was certainly unlike anything he had ever seen before.

"I liked that one first," Kathy told him and looked at him with enormous blue eyes still swimming with tears of happiness. "And then I saw this one which is pearls and now I don't know which one I prefer. She's designed wedding rings to go with the engagement rings. Would you wear any of these?"

Jean-Guy was more of a traditionalist and had always thought a simple gold band would be what he wore as a wedding ring but he dutifully looked at the designs that were somewhere between Celtic and Art Nouveau and wasn't sure what to say.

"Would you like my opinion?" he asked softly and sat at the table with her.

"Yes, please."

"Then, for you, I would choose the pearls. It reminds me of waves on the beach and you like the sea and all things watery. But it is totally your choice."

She studied the pearl design and saw what he meant. "Yes, you're right." She shuffled the sheets of paper round a little. "She suggests this one as the wedding band to go with the pearls. What do you think?"

"That's the one you like is it?" he asked.

He thought she had never looked more beautiful than she did when she smiled at him then.

"It's as though every dream I have ever had since I was a child has come true," she said to him barely above a whisper.

"Then I will help make that dream come true for you," he told her and kissed her. "You'd better phone Daisy and let her know." He looked at the designs too. "And if you were serious about replacing the one for Piers, I think you should get this one. The pattern on it looks like clouds."

"Can we wait until the Prof has finished looking? I know the hoovering didn't find it, but it's got to be somewhere in there. I'm still hoping it turns up as Sarah will never understand why I was throwing her husband's ring across the room in the first place."

"Truthfully," Jean-Guy admitted, "I don't know why you did that either."

Kathy was slowly coming back down to earth. "In the meantime, he's out there with no wedding ring on and probably getting chatted up by all the women. But you're right, the clouds ring would look lovely on his hands, and I suppose that thanks to Annette's fees I could just about afford platinum which is what I threw away." Rather than let the guilt gnaw away at her, she pulled out the letters that were under the drawings on the table. "The postman also brought all three of us letters from the Foreign Office. What do you suppose that is all about?"

Jean-Guy had come to learn that Kathy tended to have a totally different idea of priorities from him. He grabbed his letter and ripped the envelope open. "Oh, it is good news. They have given permission for me to go to East Germany in April and to Prague in the autumn so I just have to go to the embassies to sort out visas and work permits. I expect you and Piers have got the same letter too."

Kathy stopped dreaming of wedding rings for two minutes and checked her letter. It was identical to the one Jean-Guy had received so they put the one for Piers in the toast rack which was where they always left his post when he was away and she flung joyous arms round Jean-Guy's neck. "Oh! It's almost too good," she told him. "But I mustn't say that in case I jinx something. I can't believe I'm going to get a special ring made just for me." She gave her fiancé a loving snog. "You really are just too totally adorable to spoil me like that."

"I'm guessing your first ring wasn't a special order," Jean-Guy said then wished he hadn't as Kathy never liked to be reminded she had done this before.

Just for once, she was too happy to care. "Nothing like. He did the whole cheesy thing of hiding the ring in my dinner in a really posh restaurant then he got down on one knee and proposed in a very loud voice in front of a lot of people. It was a really expensive ring too, a huge diamond cluster that looked ridiculous on my fingers. I left it in the kitchen for him when I ran away. But at the time I didn't feel I could refuse. I actually thought it was quite romantic really but as soon as I told Emma she literally cringed and told me it was just another way he was bullying me into doing what he wanted me to do. Backing me into a corner so I wouldn't say no."

He was pleased she had been able to speak about it and she was still hugging him hard so he guessed he had been forgiven for saying what he had. "Oh dear," he said sympathetically. "And I asked you in front of witnesses too."

"No you didn't, not really. We'd already done our broomstick-jumping in Sweden. You just asked me to make it legal. And it was only Piers and the Prof and, do you know what, I'm glad they were there to witness it. We're all one big family and it was lovely to have included them."

Jean-Guy felt as though he was letting his breath out. He seemed to have done the right thing by default and he wasn't going to argue with her.

By lunch time Kathy was practically dancing round the kitchen as she had spoken to Daisy and knew her engagement ring was going to be ready within a week. Daisy had sent a ring gauge measure with her drawings as well as the sample of the gold which was as coppery as she could get in rose gold and Kathy still couldn't believe one of her dearest dreams was going to come true. She was in the kitchen making lunch and heard the phone ring upstairs but as Jean-Guy was up there anyway crashed out on the sofa she let him answer it.

He came into the kitchen a few minutes later and Kathy took one look at his face and felt her euphoria draining away.

"What's happened?" she asked. "Please don't tell me there's been a plane crash?"

Jean-Guy was faintly startled and gave her a reassuring hug. "No, nothing like that. That was the Prof on the phone. He still gets copies of our letters from the Foreign Office and he said the one for Piers has refused him permission to travel to East Germany and Czechoslovakia." He sat at the table. "So that's it. If we are to go as a trio then we have to find another pianist. Accompanists not so hard as our host countries can provide me with one. But I don't know what to do."

"Why have they refused?" Kathy asked and sat with him.

"Because he is ex-military, flies the most advanced passenger plane on the planet and, the Prof said although apparently the letter doesn't, he has worked not only for the British Intelligence but of course has also been involved with the CIA when he worked with Kerryanne, but there is nothing official to bind him except the secrecy agreements over the work he has already done. And they won't trust him unless it's official."

"So no way round it?"

"None. He can't even get round it using his Irish passport as there is also a letter in his envelope from the Irish Embassy in London also refusing him permission to travel to those countries."

"Oh dear. Someone's going to be in a filthy mood when he reads his letter. What do you want to do?"

Jean-Guy shrugged. "I have no idea," he admitted. "I think the Prof is going to see if there is anything that can be done, but it's not looking good."

A thought occurred to Kathy that wouldn't remain unspoken. "Do you think there's something sinister going on? Someone, somewhere is blocking his application? But why? He signed all their agreements a couple of years ago."

"I don't know," Jean-Guy admitted. "I am never going to be free of it, am I? Even now when I have my British citizenship and can travel wherever I want. Always there is something in the background holding me back."

"We don't know that. It all sounds perfectly plausible so let's just wait until Piers gets back tomorrow and see if he has any bright ideas."

"He is the sensible one, remember? If he has been told officially not to cross the iron curtain then he won't."

"He flew straight in to East Germany to get your sister."

"No, he flew to an Allied air base and didn't leave it. She was at the air base waiting for him and from what the Prof said at the time that was all he was allowed to do. There was no sightseeing for him on that trip."

"Well, I'm just a violinist from Wimbledon. It's all way beyond me. So I'm going to eat my lunch and then go and put in some practice as I have a couple of gigs coming up and haven't even looked at the music." She paused. "I don't suppose the Prof has found that ring yet?"

"Oh, yes, good news. He said it must have hit the bookcase and bounced back across the room. It actually turned up in the log basket. He was making up the fire yesterday morning and found it at the bottom of the basket."

Kathy felt as though she was letting her breath out. "Thank goodness for that."

"Yes, he said he won't risk posting it so Piers will get it back next time he's down there."

"Almost a pity, I really like that design with the clouds on it."

Piers got back to Earl's Court late in the afternoon of the next day. It was already dark and the other two were beginning to think he would be out for another night when they heard the rumble of the Aston being backed into the car port. They shot out to the kitchen from the music room and by the time their third came in through the side door there was a mug of tea at just the right temperature waiting for him on the table.

He thankfully gulped the tea down but remained standing leaning on the Aga. "Should have been back a couple of hours ago but there was a message for me at the airport and I've had to come home via Whitehall for an interview. I daresay you've heard?"

"Yes, the Prof told us," Kathy replied. "What did the monsters in Whitehall have to add?"

Piers filled up his empty tea mug with water from the tap and drank that too. "Nothing I'm allowed to tell you. They were very apologetic about it but said there was no way I would ever get permission to travel to Soviet Europe unless it was on official business. Apparently playing music doesn't count."

"So that's it then?"

"Well, no."

The other two waited.

Piers sighed. "These bloody secrecy agreements. We've negotiated and reached an agreement. And I can't say any more than that. Sorry. Any food in the house? I'm starving."

"Didn't you eat on the flight?" Kathy asked as she went to see what was in the fridge and the pantry.

"Nah. Can't stand airline food."

"So when the hell did you last eat?" Jean-Guy demanded.

Piers looked at the floor. "Um, some time in San Francisco between sleep and paperwork."

Kathy couldn't keep the impatience out of her voice. "You know you've been told to eat regularly so you don't build up a load of stomach acid and burn yourself again. How much does it hurt?"

"Quite a bit," he admitted knowing it was no good trying to hide things from these two.

"You bloody idiot," Jean-Guy almost shouted at him.

Kathy was ahead of him. She shoved a badly made sandwich into his hands. "Here, peanut butter and grape jelly. Your favourite. Now eat it or I'm taking you to hospital. And you don't want to go back there, do you?"

"You little life-saver," he grinned.

Kathy and Jean-Guy had forgotten just how fast a hungry Piers would eat. Two more mugs of water and he scraped spilled jam off his uniform jacket with his finger which he then licked clean.

"OK, off to bed for a few hours. See you when I do."

"Oh!" Kathy remembered as he headed for the stairs. "Good news for you. The Prof found your ring in the log basket."

He didn't seem as pleased at the news as she had thought he would. "Oh, OK. Gets it off your conscience at least."

Kathy looked at the closed door of the box staircase after Piers had gone. "That is not what I was expecting him to say at all. Thought he'd be happy."

"I'm guessing he has just been told he is going to get recruited by the security services after years of avoiding them. I think he is more annoyed about that than he is happy the ring is found. He always hated that ring anyway."

Kathy was too busy looking forward to seeing Emma again to worry about Piers, and her excitement levels escalated all through February. She didn't even care that she had to drive the Land Rover all the way to Somerset with Jean-Guy in the passenger seat and Piers about five hours behind them as he had been told to report to the security services to learn more about what would be happening in East Germany and Czechoslovakia. He still hadn't committed to doing anything until he knew what was involved and the other two just hoped he would accept whatever was offered.

Emma was waiting at the foot of the drive to the house she now called home and hopped into the back seat of the Land Rover as soon as it got to the half fallen-off gates.

"Show me!" she demanded almost before she had shut the door and she leaned forward to admire the rose gold hoop of pearls on Kathy's hand on the wheel. "Oh! That is just so adorable! How much did that cost you?"

"Absolutely nothing," Kathy laughed. "Daisy made it for me as a thank you for getting her jewellery in on this photo shoot."

"I remember her when she used to make sea glass jewellery for the shop. How is she?"

"She's pretty incredible. So talented, her work is just amazing." Kathy had been expecting someone young when she went to meet Daisy Hollinger at her studio and had been surprised to be greeted by a woman in her early sixties with long grey hair which she wore loose down her back and very bohemian clothes. She had entrusted Kathy with all the items of jewellery for the photo shoot and they were still carefully wrapped in the Daisy Chain box on the back seat of the Land Rover.

Emma looked round the car. "And talking of adorable, where is His Deliciousness?"

"He's been held up at work. Will probably get away from London late tonight and expects to get here about three o'clock in the morning. He said please can you leave a door open for him to save him having to sleep in his car."

"But I've got a room sorted out for him and everything," Emma complained.

"Don't tell me, next to yours with a shared bathroom and no lock on the door so you can catch him in the shower," Kathy laughed.

Emma shivered. "Oh, don't. That's just too delicious to contemplate. Seriously, how will he know where to go to sleep?"

"He probably won't sleep. He has no body clock whatsoever. Either that or you'll find him happily snoring on the first sofa he comes across."

Emma joined in the joke against herself. "That would be better then I can pretend he's Sleeping Beauty and kiss him awake. I would offer to sit up and let him in but there's no way I'll still be awake at 3am."

Kathy hadn't been to the house in Somerset before although she had seen photos of it and was impressed with the way Derek's family were restoring it one room at the time so they had started out with a kitchen, a bathroom and two other rooms for living and sleeping in but had now managed a drawing room and three bedrooms as well as the original kitchen and bathroom. As they were expecting three overnight guests they had managed to get a second bathroom usable and also a couple of bedrooms although one of them was very small. House of Viola had asked to use the ballroom, a vast room that ran the whole length of one side of the house with a spectacular view over what would one day be a terrace and a formal garden but right now was a lot of broken paving and a riot of brambles. They were also hiring a side room which had a water supply and someone from Viola had already been down and set up the make-up stations and there were racks of garments there with locked covers over them.

"It's something we'd never thought of doing," Emma admitted. "But now we've had all sorts asking if they can hire the place for a studio or film set. It's amazing how much they'll pay too. Ron's hoping to get a lot more done by the end of this year but then as Sue pointed out it's because it's in such a state people want to hire it for the atmospherics. So he said well at least get the roof mended so it's not so wet inside."

"How are you finding it living with the parents-in-law?"

"It's like being at home but better," Emma laughed. "Anyway, back to the kitchen. I expect Sue's got supper well under way by now and it's early bed tonight as we'll have Piers arriving at three, and the rest of the shoot at about six ready to start at eight. Apparently they're expecting Piers to be in make-up for over an hour. Wouldn't have thought he needed that much doing."

"Yes," Kathy told her with a wicked smile on her face. "Annette's giving him another outing as Samildánach."

"You mean in nothing but tattoos and leather jeans and half a dozen black feathers?"

"That's the one."

"Oh, God," Emma groaned. "Tie me down now."

Kathy slept better than she had thought she would in a rather cold and damp bedroom on a very soft feather bed but the weather in the morning was clear and bright. She could see from her bedroom window that there was a black Aston Martin parked outside and already the vehicles that accompanied one of Annette's fashion shoots were being skilfully unloaded.

A quick wash and dress later and she went downstairs to find out what was happening. The first person she met was Annette who grinned hugely and motioned her to silence.

Curious, Kathy followed the other woman to what had become the family drawing room and there, on a cushioned window seat was Piers apparently fast asleep with a hen standing on his right leg. She managed not to laugh out loud and signed to Annette to ask if she had taken a photo. To her great delight Annette indicated back that several photos had been taken. At that moment the hen started making crooning noises and woke the man asleep on the window seat.

He sat upright and looked at the bird in total bewilderment. "What the hell?" he started then heard the shouts of laughter in the doorway and looked across at Kathy and Annette. "Did you plant that chicken there?"

"Wish I had," Kathy told him.

He just sighed and put the hen on the floor so he could get off the seat. "And good morning to you too. Where do we find breakfast in this place?"

"Kitchen," Kathy told him. "What time did you get here?"

"About half past two. Found a way in through the French windows and helped myself to somewhere to sleep."

Annette took hold of the striped sweater he was wearing. "What the hell do you call that?"

"Warm," he told her. "And don't you go getting snotty about it, Piglet made it for me."

"How many times do I have to tell you never to wear that kind of knitwear? It really doesn't suit you."

In the kitchen they met Ria who had travelled down with Annette and Kathy thought that the designer had been quite right. Ria was a very beautiful young woman and she smiled cheerfully when introduced to the man she was going to have to pose with.

Annette looked at the two of them as they exchanged a few pleasantries and didn't look happy. "It's no good," she announced.

"What isn't?" Kathy asked.

"It's not going to work. What the hell is it with you?" she asked Piers.

He looked faintly surprised. "I have no idea what you're talking about."

"I put you with the best looking women I can find and nothing suits you. What is it about you that works so much better when you're on your own? Oh well, never mind. You're just an awkward customer."

Breakfast was a rushed affair and then Emma, children, husband and in-laws were banned from the ballroom and the preparation room so they didn't see any of the clothes being used in the shoot.

Kathy always quite liked being sat in the make-up chair with her newly-washed hair in a towel while the make-up ladies worked on her and then the hairdressers got hold of her and eventually she was passed over to the dressers who could whisk clothes on and off her faster than she had ever thought possible. Jean-Guy had thought long and hard about the earring idea then had said he would try it on the understanding that if he didn't like it he could take it out again so Kathy wasn't surprised to see there was a body piercer as part of the crew who had set up his sterilising equipment and had a ferocious set of needles wrapped in sterile packaging. She thought it was a lot of fuss for one infinitely nibbleable ear but put it out of her mind as she chatted idly with the young woman doing her make up.

She couldn't see the others but knew Annette was having Piers turned into Samildánach as the wig was a bit of a give-away. Except this time the only coloured streaks in it were different shades of red from a deep crimson to a brighter ox-blood but nothing lighter than that and there were no glittery gems in it this time. The whole thing was darker and Kathy wondered what the finished look was going to be.

The styling room was quiet as the stylists worked, chatting in low tones with their clients and they all jumped when the concentration was broken by what was unmistakeably a very annoyed Piers.

"Ow! Did you just pierce my nose? You cow. I told you not to."

As the make-up lady had paused in her work, Kathy risked looking across the room in time to see Annette slap Piers on the wrist. "Don't touch it. We'll take it out at the end of the session."

"You'd bloody better."

"Oh, shut up. You're just the overpaid model. The design I wanted wouldn't work as a clip-on. Just be thankful I'm not getting your tits done as well."

"At least I could hide that. No. Don't you dare."

"You just gave consent."

"No I bloody didn't."

Clearly Annette wasn't taking any arguing from the model. "Left side only," she gave the order. "There's too much ink on the right. And, you, not another word, or some other bits of you get done too."

Kathy, Jean-Guy and Ria were finished with make-up and hair and Annette joined them to supervise the first set of outfits. It was a winter collection she was shooting that day and Kathy's first session was with a deep red dress that Annette called daywear but which Kathy privately thought wasn't what she would wear to go to Sainsbury's. Annette put her with Jean-Guy and arranged them so Kathy's left hand with its Daisy Chain rose gold ring was artistically posed on Jean-Guy's back and his head, now with its left ear ornamented with a subtle Daisy Chain stud and small hoop, was towards her with such amusement in his dark eyes she wondered what the joke was.

"What's so funny?" Annette wanted to know. "You're supposed to be looking in love not as though she's telling you dirty jokes."

"Sorry," he said. "I've just seen what's being dressed in the corner. It doesn't look happy."

Annette glanced across too. "I'm not paying it to look happy. I'm paying it to look so hot all the middle-aged men in Christendom will want to look like that too. No, I want all the wives and mistresses of middle-aged men to want to buy the look for their men. Hmm. Having seen the look it's definitely one the mistresses will be buying. I can't imagine any wife would want her husband to look that hot. Oi, Grumpy. Over here a minute."

Kathy gave in to temptation and let go of Jean-Guy so she could turn and join the others watching a foul-tempered Piers crossing the ballroom to join them. Samildánach looked as though he would cheerfully hurl a few thunderbolts given half the chance and Kathy wasn't surprised to hear the camera's motor drive going off to capture that walk across the room. From the red-streaked hair to the bare feet, he was giving off a cold, controlled fury that scared even Kathy and she was used to it. She wasn't surprised to see Ria physically take a couple of steps backwards.

Piers arrived next to Kathy and the scary red eyes glowered. "What?"

Standing next to him, Kathy could see that Annette had had the septum of his nose pierced and not one nostril as she had expected. The open ring was a dull pewter with silver tracery and dark red stones on its ends so she could see what Annette had meant about it not working with a clip-on. The ring on his chest was the same twisted metal design, again with red stones on its ends. She looked down past the missing fluff and wasn't surprised to see the tickly ring was back on his toe. She almost felt sorry for him.

"Nothing," Annette told him and smiled. "Just wanted to make you stomp across the room so we could get some action photos of you."

He sighed. "I'm putting my fees up."

Annette tugged the long black coat around a bit so the dark red lining showed and then physically positioned Kathy hard against him and pulled the coat round her too. To keep her balance, Kathy put a steadying hand on Piers' chest just above the ring and wasn't surprised to feel his skin was unusually hot as he was in such a mood. It was an extraordinary feeling to be touching that beautiful figure who had so bewitched her when he had stood at the end of the runway in New York. Just for a brief moment she nearly forgot it was Piers until she heard him swearing under his breath as Annette's positioning of her models threatened to put the two of them off balance. Annette leaned Kathy backwards until she thought she was going to overbalance and was glad to feel Piers put an arm round her as her feet slipped in their skyscraper heels on the wooden floor. He looked at her but she really couldn't tell whether he was smiling or not. But oddly enough that ring in his nose was one heck of a turn-on for her.

"Hang on, Piglet," he said as the motor drive went off again.

"Trying!" she exclaimed, and forgot just how hot he was as her feet started slipping. "Not used to these heels."

"You're hurting my back," was about all he managed to say before her feet went from under her and the two of them were in a laughing heap on the floor.

Annette took her fashion shoots very seriously and those two were in danger of making their make-up run as they just sat there giggling and she could hear Jean-Guy and Ria weren't much better behind her.

"Oh, for pity's sake!" she berated them. "Stop behaving like a pair of infants. Sort yourselves out and just get up."

That was easier said than done as one was in six-inch heels and the other was in rather well-fitting leather trousers but they managed it eventually with a bit of help from Jean-Guy, and Annette had to send the two of them off to have their make-up repaired.

She sighed and looked at Ria and Jean-Guy. "Ria, take your shoes off, please and the pair of you go and stand in front of the mirrors."

Not quite chastened but at least no longer weeping with laughter, the two newly released from make-up wandered back across the ballroom with Kathy hanging on tight to Piers' arm to watch Jean-Guy and Ria making such a lovely couple so long as the photographer could find a way to disguise the fact Jean-Guy was the shorter of the two by about three inches. Annette had almost forgotten the other two as she dealt so ruthlessly with the models under the lights and Kathy and Piers watched quite happily as the two were put through at least three outfits each.

"That one's nice," Kathy remarked as her fiancé was dressed in a chestnut brown suit with a pale cream shirt and stood next to Ria who was sitting half curled up on the windowsill in a mustard yellow dress that suited her dark skin so well.

"Think we're last year's fashion, don't you?" he asked.

"I think we're just in trouble." She looked up at him wondering if seeing the two on the windowsill had brought back memories of Chantal so she decided to distract him any way she could. "I love that nose ring on you. Please don't take it out until your bosses say you have to."

His smile reassured her that his memories were a long way away that day. "Hm. You might not say that when I haven't got a striped face and red eyes."

"Does it hurt?"

"No, but it tickles like hell."

Annette didn't even turn round. "Kathy, go and get dressed first in the blue. I've done with you in the red. Piers, I'll want you with the full wings on after the next shot."

"I'm still putting my fee up," he called across to the designer.

She turned and looked at the magnificent figure of Samildánach with the petite Kathy on his arm like some kind of naiad. "Darling, look like that and I'll double them."

"Did you just call me Darling?"

"I'd like to call you something else but there are ladies present."

The dressers were ready for them and Kathy knew Annette had put her in her wedding dress. It was a beautiful midnight blue with a laced front that really was laced, there were no zips in this one and a full skirt with even more petticoats under it than she had had for her Smugglers' Race dress. Over that they put a cloak of inky blue trimmed with feathers and a few quick tweaks of make-up and hair and she had dark blue drop earrings, a coppery choker and sparkles in her hair.

Thankful the heels of her shoes were lower than the skyscrapers that had made her overbalance, she looked across at Piers standing patiently as the dressers got him sorted out. The wig had been changed for one much plainer, shot through with a shimmering iridescence, the heavy jewellery round his throat and wrists either looked a dull black or shone like spilled petrol depending on the lights and a different, more tailored black coat was just thrown over his shoulders so his shirt could be seen and Sammy's wings had clearly been tucked away for this shot.

"I really need Emma to see you with the wings on," she told him as the two waited at the side of the ballroom together while Annette finished with Ria and Jean-Guy then sent them off to get out of her clothes. "Any chance they're going to put in an appearance soon?"

"After this outfit, she said. But in the meantime I'm going to make the most of being fully dressed for once."

Annette turned to see what the other two were up to and even she, so used to working with beautiful people, caught her breath. The violinist and the airline pilot were quietly standing together as though they had stepped out of another world. Her inky blues and his iridescence were perfect together and there was a peace and serenity about them as she had leaned very slightly against him and he had one arm on her shoulder nearer to him so the cuff of his coat fell on her breast as the dresser had put the cloak back over her shoulders and the strapless dress was quite low on her front. It didn't matter that she looked tiny next to him. It didn't matter one iota that he was supposed to have been posed with the taller Ria. It just didn't matter as Annette felt something in her soul that she had never known before. Something deep in her bones. She didn't notice that Jean-Guy and Ria had wandered out in their own clothes and were standing behind her just looking at those two, waiting quietly side-by-side.

"My God," she heard Ria breathe. "Are those two even real?"

Jean-Guy didn't trust himself to speak. He couldn't believe that the figure standing in front of him was the woman who would come to him in their bed and he would feel the heat of her body against his own. She had never looked more beautiful, more vulnerable and he saw a fragility to her beauty as she stood protected by the raven. He wished he would look half as impressive with a stripe down his face and a ring in his nose, but had a feeling he would just look faintly ridiculous.

"Are you ready for us yet?" Piers wanted to know. "I'm bloody sweating buckets in this coat."

Annette scrabbled her senses back together. "Yes. Sorry, miles away. Let's get on with it."

Kathy thought she'd try her luck. "If I swear Emma to eternal secrecy, please can she come and see Piers when he gets his wings on? Please?"

"Oh, go on then. Jean-Guy you can go and get Emma. Just Emma mind you, nobody else."

So Emma watched as her oldest friend got very cosy with the spirit of an Irish god and a photographer took images of them. After the blue dress there was a gorgeous dark green ballgown and finally an elegant black sheath dress that was iridescent like the wings of the raven. And how Kathy managed to walk in those skyscraper heels Emma had no idea. To her great delight, as Kathy's outfits got more extreme, so those of the man being photographed with her got more minimal and he ended up as she had dreamed of him too often. With leather trousers that fitted him so well and his top half wearing nothing more than jewellery and black feathers. Emma could barely remember she was looking at two of her best friends as she gazed at the final shot. The two of them on the crumbling windowsill with his raven's wings enfolding her and she cuddled trustingly against him with her head on his shoulder as they looked out together at the world beyond.

"That's a wrap!" Annette shouted. "Brilliant. Thank you all of you. Amazing session. And you two on the windowsill, I meant it, I've just doubled your fees. Kathy, you're on the runway with him."

"What?!"

"You. Runway. Him."

"Are you joking?"

"Ask Danny and he will tell you I have no sense of humour."

"But I'm only five foot two."

"And you are absolutely beautiful when you look like that. By the way, in case you hadn't guessed, that was your wedding outfit you were wearing earlier. Look after it because I'm not making another one. And you, keep that thing in your nose. You can afford to get fired now."

"It does suit you," Kathy tried. "At least wear it until they tell you it's the nose ring or your job."

"It'll be gone by seven o'clock Tuesday morning then," was all he said.

The fashion shoot was skilfully packed up and had gone by the time Kathy and Piers rejoined Jean-Guy in the ballroom, all three thankful to have had their make-up removed, had showered and got dressed in their own clothes. Only Annette and Ria were left when the three wandered into the back hall where the designer and her latest model were waiting to leave when they had said their goodbyes. Annette wasn't best pleased to see Piers was back in that awful striped thing Kathy had knitted but at least he still had a ring in his nose. There was a round of hugs and kisses then the two going back to Berkshire that day left the house and the three who were staying on until tomorrow went along to the kitchen hoping to find a late lunch as there hadn't been any refreshments all day.

To their profound relief, Derek's mother had already got a pot of tea on the table as well as a pile of sandwiches.

"Thought you'd be hungry," she told them. "You've been working hard all morning." She looked a bit puzzled when one of them took his tea black and added some cold water to it but she had no complaints about the way the three of them totally demolished the sandwiches and gratefully thanked her for the unexpected food.

"Got something for you," Kathy told Piers when her hunger pangs were satisfied.

He looked at her, mildly curious. "Is it contagious?"

"Not yet," she laughed. "Hold out your hand. No, not that one. The left one."

Jean-Guy just managed not to say anything as he watched the woman who now wore his engagement ring slip a wedding ring onto the finger of another man. It felt so wrong to him. But worryingly it looked so right.

Piers didn't quite scowl as he looked at that hated chunk of platinum now back where it belonged and he wiggled his fingers trying to make it more comfortable. It had been very disconcerting to have Kathy do that to him and he deliberately wouldn't look at Jean-Guy. "Thank you. I think," was all he said.

Kathy totally missed the feelings of the two men. "And I promise not to throw it anywhere ever again," she told him with a smile.

"What have you been throwing?" Emma asked as she joined them with Derek and their sons and they all bunched up along the benches at the kitchen table to accommodate them as well.

"Doesn't matter," Kathy said rather than have to try to explain.

Emma saw the ring that had been missing that morning was now back on Piers' finger but she didn't say anything. One day she would find out what had been going on. But it seemed the deliciously handsome man was still married.

"Busy day?" Derek asked.

"Knackering," Kathy replied with a weary smile, thinking how much nicer Derek looked now he spent his time in scruffy clothes restoring what had become his inheritance, rather than wearing a suit and sitting behind a desk all day.

"Well you three, if you've got any energy left, Emma and I would like to show you something. It's a bit of a hike."

Kathy shot an enquiring look at Emma but she just grinned hugely and said, "You have no idea how hard it's been for me not to tell you. Come on."

So the mystified three followed the two residents up the back staircase, along a corridor at the top of the stairs, through a sequence of rooms each smelling appallingly of damp and then into a long gallery with a series of doors leading off it on the left and a lot of windows on the right.

"Exercise area for the Georgian residents," Emma explained. "I have a feeling the boys will be riding bikes along it as soon as they're old enough. Anyway, when the Georgians got bored and didn't fancy walking up and down, they had plenty of books to read." She flung open the first door and the others could see there was a very fusty-smelling library in there. "And, if they didn't fancy reading then they made music." With an unmistakeably triumphant flourish she opened the second door and the three visitors just stopped in a stupefied bunch in the doorway.

"Bloody hell!" Jean-Guy said first. "What the hell have you got in here?"

Emma was delighted her little drama had worked so well. "What do you three all reckon?"

Kathy had to laugh out loud. "I reckon I don't know how you could keep quiet about it for so long."

"Oh, it hasn't been all that long. I mean we had a quick look everywhere when we took it over but all we could see in here were the keyboard instruments. It wasn't until a few months ago that Derek and I were up here looking through the music when he tried to take a book down and we realised it was just painted onto a panel. So we poked about a bit and it turned out to be a secret cupboard and there they all were. Three violins and a couple of cellos. Ron's played it by the book as they weren't on the original inventory and Derek's sorted out all the legal stuff and, basically, we would like to give you a violin and a cello as a wedding gift. Which we can do now you're officially getting married and the tax man has said it's OK."

Derek felt a bit sorry for the three who had just had this sprung on them. "We had to get in an expert to assess them and she said the violins are two Strads and a Guarnerius and the cellos are another Strad and a Rugieri. The valuer said that they're certainly genuine but she guessed they were either unnamed or ones that had dropped off the radar a long time ago. She went away and did some research but there were bills of sale to match them so they got declared to the tax man and that was the end of it. Emma's already helped herself to one of the Strads so, please, choose which of the other two you would like."

"It needs to go for repair which we can't afford at the moment." Emma explained. "Go on, you two. Go pick. They're not in the best state any of them and the ones you don't want will have to go to auction."

Kathy and Jean-Guy wandered into the room. There were two cellos on their sides on the floor and the violins were on top of the piano in the middle of the room. There was also, Kathy noticed, a very handsome wooden music stand next to the piano but she guessed that wasn't on offer.

Emma watched the two of them as they stood there like children in a sweet shop. She smiled indulgently and said to Piers, "The piano is a Bösendorfer and that little thing in the corner is a harpsichord with no maker's name on it that we can find and Derek's got half a mind to take it on as a restoration project. I don't know if you're interested in the piano? Dad says the one at the farmhouse is getting a bit clapped out now as it's been working so hard."

He was still standing in the doorway, looking at the other two who were now both on the floor with all four instruments and inspecting them very closely but still too stunned to speak.

"Tell you what," Derek suggested to Piers, "Just check it out for us, huh? Let us know if you think it's worth restoring."

So the pianist of the group lifted the top of the piano and nearly laughed. "Well, your first problem is you've had mice in it." He lifted the lid and they could see the keys were discoloured and some of the veneers had come loose. "It's in a bit of a state," was the best he could offer, then had a good look round it. "Yup, definitely a Bösendorfer. I'd put it at late nineteenth century. Truthfully in this mess it's firewood. But, the frame looks salvageable and it'll need a total rebuild."

Emma looked a bit miffed at his rather brutal assessment. "Is it worth restoring?"

"Well, I would if I'd inherited something like this. I mean the thousands you spend on rebuilding it will improve the value by tens of thousands but unless you're going to use it you may as well sell it in this state and let the new owner restore it."

"I was thinking of sending it to Dad at the farmhouse and he can pension off the Broadwood. I mean legally it's my piano so if I choose to store it in Suffolk then I haven't gifted it and it'll be there for you and Dad to play."

Piers experimentally tapped a few of the keys and smiled. "That is between you and your father."

Emma saw the smile. "But if it was your choice?"

"I'd go for the Bösendorfer any day of the week and fully restored this one will be a beauty. But he can get the Broadwood sorted out much more cheaply."

"I'll talk to Dad. He has been saying the Broadwood needs some attention for a while now. He may decide it's worth spending money on this one instead."

Emma, Derek and Piers looked at the other two who were still sitting on the floor.

"Can I make a suggestion?" Piers asked.

"Please do," Emma requested. "Or they are going to be there for a week."

"Can we take the whole lot back to London with us and let these two try them out? Then if you tell me which auction house you want to use I'll arrange for the others to be sold."

Emma smiled. "Kath is quite right. You really are the sensible one."

He nearly laughed. "Tell that to my bosses if I turn up on Tuesday with this thing in my nose."

"I love that thing in your nose. It really suits you. And even if they get that one off you at least you'll know there's still another one hidden away. Which I'm guessing will appeal to your sense of humour."

"You're getting to know me too well." He sighed as he looked at Kathy and Jean-Guy. "Come on, you two, get your new toys packed up and see if you can borrow some blankets to wrap them in. We're taking the whole lot away and then you can choose.

And, as my contribution to the wedding gift I'll pay any restoration costs on whichever ones you pick."

To Emma and Derek's disbelief Kathy and Jean-Guy dashed over to their third and enveloped him in a hug before they both kissed his cheeks. She could never have imagined the traumatised Kath who had crawled away from that messy relationship would ever behave like that again and it was so good to see the old Kath re-emerging from that fragile shell.

Jean-Guy and Derek took a cello each and Kathy clung possessively to the violins as they set off back to the inhabited part of the house.

"There was a whole pile of music too but we've brought that down to the sitting room," Emma told Piers who was still looking at the old Bösendorfer. "Most of it's all wrinkled with damp but you might like to look through it. Loads of cello stuff which is no use to me and loads of quartets and I think a few trios. Anyway, it must be nearly supper time so you can have a look at it all this evening." She saw the way he cast a final glance at the ruined Bösendorfer and hung back a bit so they could walk behind the others. "You like the piano, huh?"

"I learned to play on a Bösendorfer like that," he said quietly. "Best piano I ever played. And do you know what, I have no idea what happened to it. It's probably been destroyed."

"Oh? What makes you think that?"

"Well, assuming it stayed in my father's house after Roisin and I left, it would have been there when the house got blown up. Incendiary bomb. Nothing left except one outside wall and a walnut tree in the garden. Unfortunately he wasn't at home so whoever set the bomb wasted their time."

"Do you know who set it?" Emma asked.

He was a bit surprised his revelation hadn't shocked her, but then he remembered who her father was. "Most probably the Loyalists. Might have been the Brits. Didn't matter, he got picked off by a sniper just a few weeks later and rumour at the time said it was the Brits getting rid of a troublemaker."

Emma looked ahead but the others were chatting and laughing as they went down the stairs. "Did my dad ever tell you how he came to leave Czechoslovakia?"

"You mean your mother? Yes, he did. Soon after we first met. He and I have had several long conversations over the years." He noticed for the first time that Emma looked a lot like her father. She had the height and the dark hair already shot with more grey than he had although she was only Kathy's age, but her eyes were a kind of hazel green unlike her father's dark brown.

"He told me about you after I'd been so horrible to you and made you go flying. No, shut up and let me finish. All he wanted me to do was understand that you aren't a man to be messed with. But you're like him. Everyone thinks he's just this easy-going academic and he looks it now his hair and his beard are so white but people knew he wasn't to be messed with either and probably if he hadn't got out when he did then he would have been picked off by a sniper too."

"Sorry, didn't mean to bring back memories."

"Oh, you didn't. I was just about a year old when we came here and I have no memories whatsoever of Czechoslovakia or my mum. I think it's been me who's stirred up unhappy thoughts from your past. But we could spend the next hour apologising to each other and I don't think either of us wants that. So if having a Bösendorfer back in your life would upset you then forget we ever offered it."

He smiled then, quite touched by her concern. "I've played many kinds of piano over the years and playing a Bösendorfer again wouldn't upset me. So if you want your Dad to have it then go ahead and ask him if you can store it in Suffolk. And as he's helped me so much since I've known him, if he wants the piano then I'll pay the restoration costs on it. After Annette's paid me for today I can afford it. And chuck your Strad into the pile and I'll pay your restoration bill too."

The three on the stairs paused and looked back when they heard Emma's shriek and were just in time to see her fling her arms round Piers' neck and give him a full-on kiss on the lips. Kathy looked quickly at Derek but he seemed amused if anything.

"I love you!" Emma declared happily. "Please can I dump my husband and run away with you?"

"Oi!" Derek yelled cheerfully at her. "Leave the guests alone, you little tart! Come on, we've got to find some blankets and it's my turn to cook tonight." He shook his head and remarked to Kathy and Jean-Guy, "Mad woman. Hormones in overdrive again but we're hoping it'll be a girl this time."

Piers laughingly refused to let Kathy drive the Aston Martin the next morning so they could get back to London more quickly but he helped them carefully load the blanket-wrapped bundles in the back of the

Land Rover before roaring away from the house and leaving them to follow more slowly.

Piers had been up in his room when he heard the other two arrive and wasn't surprised that even before they brought their bags up they were in the music room raiding their supplies of spare strings and bridges. He went down two flights of stairs and stopped off at the kitchen to make coffee for the three of them then went into the music room and sat on the piano stool to listen to what would happen next. He knew the brown plaid bundle on top of the piano was Emma's chosen Stradivarius and wasn't too surprised to see Kathy had already got strings on the dark violin. Jean-Guy was still winding strings onto the amber-coloured cello although he had already sorted out the more chestnut coloured one which was now on its side on the floor.

"Here goes," Kathy remarked more to herself than anyone else and launched straight into a Kreutzer study.

The two men looked at each other as Kathy took that violin from its lowest register right up into notes so high they thought her wrist would break to play them.

"Beautiful sound," Jean-Guy commented. "Which one is that?"

Kathy thought she had maybe left the mortal world of Earl's Court and was somewhere in music heaven. "The Guarnerius," she said dreamily. "I've never heard a violin like it. It's perfect. It doesn't even need any restoration work on it. I could put it in my case and take it with me to my gig tomorrow."

"I'd insure it first if I were you," Piers told her practically. "Not sure you'd get away with claiming for it on the Juilliard's policy for the other one."

"Will you stop being so sensible, just for once?" she laughed. "I didn't mean it literally."

"Me? Sensible? I'm the one who's clocking in to fly Concorde on Tuesday with this thing stuck in my nose. And right now the bloody thing really is stuck. How sensible is that?"

"Not at all," she had to agree. "But I bet you don't get beyond check-in."

"I probably won't get beyond the car park. Come on, Jean-Guy, let's hear what you brought home."

Franz Schubert – *Piano Trio No 2 in E flat major, Op. 100*

Kathy and Jean-Guy both had engagements on the Tuesday evening Piers was due back from New York after a same-day turnaround so they weren't in the house when he got back and he had obviously gone to his room by the time they got in within half an hour of each other and had settled in the kitchen to make themselves post-concert tea.

"So, what do you reckon?" Kathy asked. "How far did the nose ring get?"

Jean-Guy had to smile. "I would bet he sat in his room here and took it out before he even drove to the airport."

"I think you're probably right. Pity, I really liked it on him. Anyway, have you decided yet?"

"Almost. I like that the Stradivarius is, like the Guarnerius you chose, ready to play now but unless we pay to have the Rugieri restored I won't know which I prefer. And even though Piers is now annoyingly rich and can afford the restoration work, I don't like to ask him and then decide I don't want to play it."

"Which one spoke to your soul?"

"Now you are going all mystic on me. I am thinking purely of tone and range."

"Then tomorrow you must just sit with them both and think with your soul. Remember to listen to the silence."

He smiled at her fondly. "You are such a strange woman."

"Thank you. I shall take that as a compliment."

Jean-Guy finished his tea. "Well, I'm off to bed. Got a teaching job at ten tomorrow morning and need my beauty sleep."

"Be right with you. I must just go and say goodnight to my very own personal Guarnerius. I hope I'll hear from my insurers tomorrow so I can start to play it out. Thank goodness for Annette and her ridiculous fees so at least I can afford it."

Kathy heard the rattle of the letterbox in the morning and, as she was awake anyway, went down the stairs hoping to find out if her new violin was insured. There weren't many letters but the one she wanted was included and she read it through while the coffee machine slowly woke up beside her. She felt a huge smile cross her face as she read that her cheque had now cleared so she was insured to play the Guarnerius anywhere in the world. She was still smiling when Piers wandered sleepily in to the kitchen.

"Can't sleep, huh?" she asked him.

"Not a good night," he admitted.

"You've still got the nose thing in."

"It was very odd. Apart from some sarky comments about bogies from Dacre and Mick, nobody said a word. All the way through check-in, security, flying there and back, not one word was said."

"Going to leave it in?"

"No. I've got the name and address of the piercer from Annette and I'm going to see him this morning to get it taken out. I tried yesterday before I left but I couldn't get either of the ends off which is how I'd have guessed it went in, and didn't like to cut it in case Annette wants it back at some point. Tried to turn the bloody thing upside down so at least it didn't show but that lasted about five minutes and I sneezed it straight back down again."

Kathy wanted to laugh but Piers didn't seem the slightest bit amused that he still had a bit of metal stuck in his nose. "Jean-Guy I were convinced you'd get it out even if you had to break it. But, yes, I can see you were being sensible about Annette's property. Anyway, you've got a letter from the airline. With any luck it'll be offering you a pay rise."

"Hmm, unlikely," he said and took the letter from her.

Kathy got on with making the coffees and didn't pay him much attention.

"You absolute bastards!" he announced and sounded as cross as he had when he had had a needle put through his nose.

"You been fired?" Kathy asked and felt quite worried on his behalf.

"Not quite. Written warning for breaching the uniform code and they're fining me two hundred pounds. If I turn up with the ring again then the fine goes up to five hundred."

"Wow. Harsh."

"Why? Why the hell did they let me work all of yesterday and then send a sodding letter in the post? Any one of half a dozen people could have spoken to me yesterday and told me to take the bloody thing out. Mick or Dacre would have got the wire-cutters out and done some minor surgery if necessary." He put the letter down and took the mug of coffee from her. "It's that kind of thing that just makes me want to quit. Why the hell am I spending my time conforming to their rules when I don't need to?"

"I don't know," she said gently. "Why are you?"

He thought about that before replying. "Mainly because I just love flying. And there is no way on this earth I could fly something like Concorde on a private licence. Annette's fees, generous as they are, won't last much longer. Maybe a year or two. She's told me right from the start that I was never going to be with her long-term. As long as I'm bringing in the money for her she'll keep me on her books but, let's face it, in two years' time I'll be fifty and I don't think I'll want to be doing her work at that age. I think I'm pushing it now. Yes, put bluntly, I have enough in the bank to see me out for the rest of my life quite comfortably if not extravagantly even if I am also building up the trust funds for the kids. But, you know me, I've worked since I was seven years old. What the hell would I do all day?"

Kathy was briefly envious of his financial independence until it occurred to her for the first time that, thanks to Annette too, her bank balance was the healthiest it had ever been. But she could also understand his feelings. What would she do all day if she didn't have music to play? "So for the sake of a silly nose ring, no matter how much it suits you, get it taken out, and stick with the airline for a bit longer. It may be we could get the trio going and then you could play music like we do? It wouldn't take long." She looked at him and knew she felt sorry for him in a way. "But then, as you say, you'd have to give up flying. No, maybe you'd do better to stay as you are."

"Or stick two fingers up to them and put myself on the market as an accompanist and ensemble player. Do you know what? I get a headache just thinking about it."

"Then don't think about it," was her advice. "Go and sort your nose out."

"After breakfast, the bloke doesn't even open until ten. Has Jean-Guy decided if he wants that cello restored yet? Only I thought while I'm going out that way I can drop off Emma's violin."

"He can't decide because he can only play one of them."

"Good point. I'll take it anyway. I'm guessing it's the one without the strings on it?"

"It's the one with the broken sound post rattling about inside it and the horrible noise when you tap it as there's a split in it somewhere. It's in a bit of a state, poor thing."

"So you want him to adopt it?"

She smiled then, glad to see his mood had cleared. "Of course. Just like you wish you could have adopted that poor bashed up Bösendorfer with the mouse nest in it."

"So long as they left the mice behind," he laughed and put his letter on the table. "Much as I don't mind small rodents, I don't really want one running about inside my piano."

Jean-Guy heard the click of the front door at about nine thirty that morning and thought it was probably Kathy going shopping but then he heard the Aston Martin driving out from the car port and was a bit confused as Piers never got up and went out that early if he wasn't working.

He went downstairs to find the kitchen and music room were both empty but Kathy had thoughtfully propped a note up against the coffee machine to let him know she had gone with Piers to take Emma's violin and the cello to the restorer. There was also a letter on the table and he had read half of it while the machine made him some coffee before he realised it was one hell of a stinking letter and it was addressed to Piers anyway. Like the recipient, he couldn't understand why it had had to be a formal written warning and a fine rather than a discreet word at the time. Thankful he was a freelance musician and could pick and choose when and where he worked, he took his coffee back upstairs and got ready to go and do a hard day's teaching at Trinity College. He hoped the Rugieri wouldn't be long at the restorer's as he really, really wanted to play it.

The three all met up again at the supper table that evening which was unusual as more often than not at least one of them had work to go to. But instead they all sat in the kitchen eating the pasta dish Jean-Guy had made.

"I liked the ring in your nose," he told Piers conversationally and was a bit baffled when the other two exchanged a look and a smile. "What? Where is it?"

"Upstairs," Kathy told him. "Have a closer look."

So Jean-Guy looked but couldn't see anything. "What am I looking at?"

"It's worked!" Kathy declared delightedly. "We went to see the piercer who worked with Annette and told him the whole story which he found incredibly funny. Just to keep Annette happy, there's a retaining bar in there which you can hardly see as the ends are much smaller and hidden up his nose, which will be fine as it didn't make him sneeze this time. And the ring, once you've got it sussed, is easy as all you need to do is get the knack of turning one of the ends what seems to be backwards as it's screwed the opposite way to most things to stop it unwinding itself. No pliers needed. He said to leave the hidden bar in there for a good six weeks and let it heal properly then Piers can just whip the ring in and out as Annette wants him to. Give it a few months and he won't need the bar at all. And he's had the last laugh over the airline too."

"Two hundred pound fine still gets me," he pointed out. "Direct deduction from salary too so I can't even get out of it. I'm not laughing about that."

"You on call tonight?" Jean-Guy asked.

"Not tonight. Mid-day to midnight tomorrow. And it can only be a short-haul because of my JFK lines."

"Good. I spent some time going through all that music we brought back from Somerset and there is the Schubert Opus 100 among it. We didn't have that one and I think it will be a good one for us to try tonight."

The two looked at a beaming Kathy. "Time to play with the new toy again," Jean-Guy agreed.

"What will you do with the other Guarnerius?" Piers asked curiously as he stacked the plates as it was his turn to wash up.

"Give it back, I suppose," she realised. "I only seem to have had it five minutes."

"Well I can save you postage," he offered, "and take it with me when I go to New York any time. Just tell Judy or someone to meet me at the airport and collect it."

"You're so useful," she told him fondly.

They played the Schubert that night and found it great fun. And once they had run through that, Jean-Guy quite calmly informed Piers that the recording of their Barbican concert was scheduled for release next month and they needed to get some publicity photos done. To the relief of the other two, he just smiled and asked laughingly, "Do you want me to wear the stripey woolly or a pair of wings?"

"I am so tempted to say penguin suit but I think our concert full black will do. I'll get Jane to organise something."

Piers just flicked back through his music. "Can we have another go at the Scherzo, please? There's some odd fingering there I need to work out."

If anyone at the airline ever noticed that one of their captains had a metal bar tucked up his nose then nothing was said or written and the bitter winter slowly warmed into March as the Dodman Trio polished up the works they wanted to take on their visit to Germany in April. None of them could quite believe it had been two years since they had been there last. It wasn't a long visit, and they were only due to be away for a week with concerts in Cologne and Hamburg as well as the contentious ones in East Berlin and Leipzig. But Piers had got his clearance and had even agreed that they could fly for this trip as it was all short hops starting with the flights taking them from Gatwick to Berlin via Amsterdam in the second week of April. In the first week of April the very well-behaved Concorde captain took a valuable violin back to New York and was given lunch at the Juilliard as a thank you for its return. He even took his equally well-behaved first officer with him as Dacre Forsyth had long been curious to see inside the school where his elder daughter had won a place to study as a pianist but had never made it after an inexplicable failure in her A Levels had sent her on the downward spiral that nobody had been able to stop.

The captain of Concorde made a perfect landing at Heathrow which was just as well as they had several senior members of the royal family on board. The three flight crew joined the cabin crew to say their goodbyes to their illustrious passengers and the Irish captain didn't even have the slightest of ironic smiles on his face as he dutifully made his perfectly correct bow.

Post-landing checks completed, the flight crew went to the men's room in the crew area of the airport where the impeccable captain changed into a scruffy pair of jeans and swapped uniform shirt for an unironed blue Chambray then finished off the whole disreputable outfit with a brown and grey striped sweater that would have looked terrible on anyone else. Uniform packed away in a small case he gave his fellow flight crew a wicked smile and fiddled with his nose before finishing up with a silver-coloured open ring in his septum.

"Will I do?" he asked.

"Well, you're not in uniform so they can't say anything," Dacre agreed. "But you do look a mess. And why the hell have you put that thing back in your nose? And how come you can get away with it when it would look ridiculous on anyone else?"

Piers didn't answer the question but ruffled his hair into disorder and pulled the fringe down over his forehead so it was nearly in his eyes then pushed a pair of tatty dark brown boots onto his bare feet. "OK, that's me done. Time for two weeks' leave and I'll see you all when I get back."

"Going somewhere nice?" Mick asked as he came out of one of the cubicles.

"Just back to Suffolk for a while. Probably about time I reminded the wife what I look like."

The three walked out into the main concourse of the airport and weren't paying much attention to the passengers and crew all bustling about until they were stopped by a couple of men.

"Are you the crew of that flight 446?" one of them asked in an accent that was definitely from the other side of the Atlantic.

"Nothing to do with me," Dacre laughed truthfully.

The men ignored the one in the striped sweater. "What about you?"

Mick looked faintly startled. "Sorry, gents. Even if I were there's a total news block on that one until the film is released next month."

"Seems word has gotten round," one of them commented. "Nobody will say anything. OK, sorry to have stopped you."

The three walked on to catch the official transport out to the staff car park. "I will be so glad when that bloody film is released," Mick muttered. "Then I get my pay-off and I can go."

The other two looked at him. "Go where?" Dacre asked.

Mick grinned then. "Nowhere probably. I couldn't just do nothing all day but it's nice to know that I could."

The three parted ways in the car park and Piers was thoughtful as he set out in the Aston to the first of his stop-offs. They had all known there was a lot of interest in the forthcoming film about flight 446 but all staff had been bound to silence until the release and weren't even allowed to speculate so he was thankful he hadn't been crossing the concourse in the uniform of a captain with the telltale medal ribbon below the wings. But it hadn't occurred to him that maybe he would lose Mick as a flight engineer. He hoped not. They had all got so used to each other now it would be a pity if any of them broke up the regular crew. He slotted the Aston into the airport traffic and started to follow the signs that would take him into the city.

Kathy and Jean-Guy were not expecting Piers to travel to Suffolk and then go all the way back through London again to get to Gatwick for their flights out to East Germany. They went into the farmhouse through the back door as they always did and were a bit surprised to find the Prof in the middle of preparing the evening meal and for him to greet them with, "So, back to Germany in a few days. The other one not with you?"

"I didn't think he was coming here," Jean-Guy replied. "He said he has a few things to do in London and I assumed he meant it wasn't worth driving all the way out here just to go all the way back again in a couple of days."

The Prof paused, clearly not expecting that reply. "Oh, I was sure he would come here for these few days. Perhaps he will, we never know with him do we? Well the surprise is in the sitting room. Want to go and see it or would you rather have a cup of tea?" He spoke to empty air and the other two were in the doorway to the sitting room already.

"Wow," Kathy said. "That is one hell of a piano."

"Yes it is," Jean-Guy agreed. "I can't wait to hear it played. I really hope Piers does drop in as the Prof seems to think he will."

They went back to the kitchen and Kathy tried to keep out of the way as best she could while making tea. "What happened to the Broadwood?" she asked.

"It's gone to the music school out at Snape. Bit of minor restoration work after the hammering it's had recently but otherwise perfectly good."

"Sorry to see it go?"

"Not really. I don't get attached to material things any more. I am curious to hear what this one sounds like though. I have tried it, of course, but I don't have the same touch."

Kathy and Jean-Guy realised the Prof must have known something as they were only half way through their mugs of tea when Audrey set off the three-minute warning by chasing out to the kitchen and jumping on and off the table a few times before hurling herself at the door with the impeccable timing which meant she landed perfectly on Piers' shoulder as he came in.

"You are one crazy cat," he told her fondly and picked her off so he could give her a cuddle.

"Your cello's on the passenger seat, Jean-Guy. I don't have enough hands to carry everything and I had a feeling I was going to get assaulted by a cat."

If a fire-bell had been rung, Jean-Guy couldn't have gone out of that kitchen any quicker.

"Everything accomplished?" the Professor asked, not sure if he was expecting a reply. He looked at the other man as he picked up his mug of tea. "You got your ring back then."

Piers glanced at the platinum ring with a wry smile. "Oh, yes. Never thought I'd be glad to get it back but you have no idea how many sympathetic people asked me if I'd separated from my wife." He took off his grey jacket and the other two saw he now had a handgun in a belt holster that had been perfectly hidden under the jacket. "Licenced and legal," he told them.

"How are you going to carry that on a public aeroplane?" Kathy asked.

"Because I have a small book of documentation with me that gives me permission to carry it as Jean-Guy's official minder, and we're taking Interflug flights throughout, apart from the hops to Amsterdam which the Prof's lot have dealt with, so the airlines have been informed in advance. All paperwork checked and cleared with them." He put what looked like the oddest British passport Kathy had ever seen on the table. "I'm travelling on diplomatic papers for this trip and also for the one to Czechoslovakia so no questions asked at any airport."

The Professor picked up the paperwork and looked at it almost sadly. "So they got you in the end?"

"Yes," came the desolate admission. "After years of asking, bullying and flat-out threatening, they finally got me. Just one minor victory as technically I'm freelance and I name my own fee."

"Is that sensible?" the Professor asked. "That gives you no back up or security."

Piers shrugged and put the papers in his jacket pocket. "It's the only way I'll do it for them. And I've made sure I'm so bloody expensive they won't want to use me that often. In fact, if I'm lucky, I'll price myself out of the market."

"I think you'll find they know your worth and you won't get away with extortion."

Piers was unrepentant. "Probably not, but I'll enjoy trying."

Kathy knew what was going on and she didn't like it. She was acutely aware of things rumbling in the background that were totally alien to violinists from Wimbledon. Things that made her feel as though someone had taken her comfort blanket away. "So," she said lightly, to turn the conversation, "what did you say to all those dozens of women who asked if you were separated?"

He treated her to his most wicked smile. "I told them the dog had eaten the ring and I was waiting for it to come out the other end."

"Your dog must have the slowest digestive tract on the planet."

"True, but it wasn't a line they wanted to pursue. And at least Sarah never found out. It felt very strange not wearing it for so long." He looked at the ring now back where it belonged. "Still don't like it though."

"But you have to admit it keeps all those hundreds of voracious women off you."

"Hang on a minute. First it was dozens and now it's hundreds. If you must know, three people genuinely thought my marriage was on the rocks and were concerned about it and only two were hopefuls."

"And they all got told about the dog?"

"I think I may have turned it into a snake at one point."

The Prof shook his head and thought again how much two of those three, although content together, were only complete when their third was with them.

A delighted Jean-Guy lugged a quilt-wrapped bundle in through the back door and didn't even seem to notice that their pianist was now armed.

"Come on, we don't eat for half an hour yet. I want to hear what this one sounds like."

After supper, the Prof again came and sat with them and thought to himself that it hardly seemed like the same three who had first started playing together in that very room just three years ago. The rebuilt Bösendorfer had a rich tone that made it the perfect match for Kathy's own Guarnerius and Jean-Guy's Rugieri and their run-through of Mendelssohn's second trio warmed his cynical heart. He sat on the piano stool as he had done so many times before and quietly turned the pages as they were needed as the exquisite music poured through the old house.

"I have nothing to say," he admitted when the music ended. "I cannot fault your playing or your musicianship. I hope the Germans realise just how privileged they are to be able to welcome you."

They flew from Gatwick to Amsterdam on the first leg of their journey and passed through all parts of check-in without incident. In Holland they switched airlines and the Interflug crew were pleased to welcome someone as distinguished as Jean-Guy Dechaume to their flight. They were travelling first class and Kathy wondered what all the fuss had been about as Piers sat quietly in his aisle seat and read a book for the whole flight to Berlin. Although she couldn't fail to notice he politely refused any refreshments on offer.

To Jean-Guy's delight, his parents had come to Schönefeld Airport to meet them and he didn't care if it was a public place and there were some very serious-looking gentlemen waiting to escort them to their hotel. He just flung his arms round his mother's neck and very nearly burst into tears. She hugged him back and it was left to his father to move round them so he could talk to the other two travellers.

"So delighted to meet you both at last," he greeted them warmly and they all shook hands. "Jean-Guy has written so much about you both in his letters. And now, Kathy, tell me when you and Jean-Guy are getting married?"

"First of August. I think I've kept him waiting long enough."

"You've certainly made his mother very happy. Anyway, I see your guides are waiting for you. We'll see you later on and we have permission to travel with you to Leipzig tomorrow so we will be with you for the first two days. Then you go back to the West and we return to Moscow. I hope you have lots of space in your suitcase as his mother has prepared a lot of tea for him."

Jean-Guy parted reluctantly from his mother and the three musicians were taken by car to their hotel which wasn't far from the concert hall where they were to play that evening. They went to the hall in the afternoon to test the acoustics and for Piers to get to know the piano which turned out to be a new Steinway with a very stiff sustaining pedal. Jean-Guy's parents were at their hotel when they got back from the run-through and accepted that they would have to stay in the hotel foyer to have tea with their son and future daughter-in-law and then take an evening meal in the hotel restaurant so they weren't alone with them in a room where they couldn't be monitored. Piers excused himself and said he was going to go up to his room to ring his wife and let her know he had arrived safely.

Kathy liked Jean-Guy's parents as, unlike hers, they were knowledgeable and interested in the kind of music she played so the conversation was easy and they didn't notice how time was passing until the hotel manager came across to let them know their table was ready for their evening meal and would Mr Buchanan be joining them?

"Oh, I bet he's gone to sleep upstairs," Kathy exclaimed. "He really needs to reset his body clock. Shall I go and get him?"

"Let them ring the room for him," Jean-Guy advised and Kathy realised how easy it would be for them to get split up if they weren't all careful.

The manager duly rang the room for Mr Buchanan and was able to assure the rest of the party that he had indeed fallen asleep upstairs and would join them presently at their table.

A slightly breathless and very apologetic Piers joined them a few seconds after they had sat down. He was sitting next to Kathy at the table and she caught a slight scent on his clothes as though he had been outside with someone who had been smoking cigarettes. She had a feeling she knew what kind of a deal had been brokered between him and those who had the authority to stop him travelling and guessed he had been out and about on some errand or another so she didn't say anything.

They all chatted so long over their meal it was a rush to get to the concert hall in time. Kathy had chosen the dark red dress Sarah's mother had made for her but realised too much of the Prof's cooking was finally beginning to take its toll as the dress was definitely a much snugger fit than it had been back at Snape Maltings. She thought the men looked very smart in their full black but this time they had dinner jackets over their shirts to hide the fact one of them was still travelling armed even on a concert platform. As always she waited off-stage next to Piers with Jean-Guy slightly in front and he gave her a very odd look.

"What?" she hissed softly.

Before he could reply they were called on to the stage and there was a very polite round of applause from the audience. As always, most eyes were on the cellist and very few people noticed what the pianist was doing with his shoes especially as Kathy always positioned her chair as he had once asked her to so he was mostly hidden from view. The two string players could tell just how much their pianist was hating that piano with its stiff pedal although its tone was a clear, bright sound which was quite a contrast to his Blüthner they were used to hearing.

Thirty minutes of Mendelssohn and fifteen minutes of *Trio Élégaique* brought them to the interval and the audience was much noisier as they cheered the musicians off the platform.

"Going well," Jean-Guy commented as he and Kathy drank coffee while Piers poured himself some iced water. "How is Sarah?"

"Oh, OK. Couldn't say much."

Kathy and Jean-Guy knew when the shutters were coming down. The brief reply made them realise that perhaps they were being listened to even as they chatted in the interval of their concert and Kathy hated that there were so many secrets now. It reminded her of their first few months together when it had looked so much as though Piers would slip away from them and go back to the military. He had come back to them, but she couldn't help wondering how much longer they would be able to keep him now he had been caught up in this life of lies.

They played their other Mendelssohn in the second half then finished off with the Suk *Elegy* and were still surprised to get a standing ovation. Concert over, they weren't at all surprised when Jean-Guy's parents invaded the dressing room and there were more hugs and kisses for the son they missed so much. Out of politeness to Kathy and Piers they started by speaking English and the chat was all about his visit to Prague in the autumn where he was giving four concerts in five days. The first was a trio concert, then there were two recitals with just the piano, and the last was a concert with the City Orchestra. Kathy got the distinct impression his parents were looking forward to the cello and piano recitals far more than hearing him as part of a trio. She felt she ought to be offended but his parents were far too nice.

She joined Piers who was sitting on a table in the dressing room while Jean-Guy and his parents gossiped now rather loudly in Czech as though they would never stop. "Wish I got on so well with my parents," she said and sounded more bitter than she intended. "I'm dreading my sister's wedding next month."

"Are you pregnant?" he asked bluntly.

"What? God, no. Whatever gave you that idea? You know yourself how lethal the Prof's cooking is and now Jean-Guy and I are living with him so much it's not doing our waistlines any favours."

"Have you taken a test?"

"Don't need to. My little visitors are turning up as they always do. And I feel absolutely fine."

"They do sometimes. I suggest you take a test just in case."

"Don't be silly. And don't you dare mention anything to Jean-Guy. I'm not raising his hopes just to dash them again."

He looked hard into her eyes. "Take the test," was all he said then he hopped off the table. "Come on, you lot. Our escort will be waiting for us and I'm in need of food."

Jean-Guy wasn't so full of euphoria at the wonderful concert and meeting his parents that he didn't notice Kathy was in a funny mood when they went to bed.

"What's the problem?" he asked eventually once it was obvious he was out of luck.

"What problem?"

"I don't know. You tell me."

Kathy bit at her lower lip. "Piers thinks I'm pregnant."

She didn't sound at all pleased and Jean-Guy thought that was a very odd way of putting it so he suppressed the joy and excitement that were starting inside and asked as calmly as he could, "Do you think you are?"

"I know I'm not. And it's kind of annoyed me as it means I'm getting fat and I've never been fat in my life."

Hope dashed, Jean-Guy could sympathise with her disappointment. "I think we have to face the fact that we are eating much too much. I sometimes wish the Prof wasn't such a good cook. And then Alison keeps feeding us leftover cake. Our waistlines don't stand a chance. Don't forget it got to the point where Sarah told Piers he was getting, what was it?"

"Pudgy," Kathy remembered and her mood lifted. "I am so going to remind him about that if he dares to make one fat remark at me again."

She watched Piers very carefully at breakfast and noticed that while she and Jean-Guy happily munched their way through quite a few hundred calories, he just had a bowl of fruit and one cup of espresso coffee then a glass of iced water.

"Slimming?" she asked slightly more cattily than she had meant to.

His eyes laughed at her over the rim of his glass of water. "Always. I'm not getting called pudgy ever again. That hurt."

"Don't you get hungry? I don't think I could live on fruit and water like you do."

"I crave cake and bowls of chips. Sometimes together in one meal. I hate drinking black tea and not having a biscuit with it. I sit here and hate you two for scoffing your way through that lot and I get half a melon and a couple of peach slices. I can't remember the last time I ate dessert."

"Tell you what," Jean-Guy laughed. "When we get home give yourself a night off and eat the whole contents of the pantry."

Piers poured himself a second glass of iced water. "Wish I could but I've learned over the last few years that if I eat too much in one go I make myself sick and that doesn't end too well these days."

"Even now?" Kathy asked sympathetically and forgave him for being so grumpy.

"Even now." He finished the glass of water. "At the last endoscopy they said I've got to accept the damage is irreparable and permanent. Anyway, I'm in the mood to explore Berlin for an hour or so before we have to go to the airport and I doubt if I'll ever come here again so eat up, you two and we can go and see what's what."

"Really?" Kathy asked. "Can't we just have a morning off? We've only got a couple of hours before we have to go to the airport."

"And that's another reason you two are getting fat. No enough exercise. Come on, you can't come to Berlin and not go and see the wall. There can't be many from our part of the world who'll see it from this side."

To Jean-Guy's relief he could see from the hotel breakfast room that his parents had arrived in the foyer. "Ah, my rescue party. I'll be OK if you two want to go exploring."

Piers and Kathy stood side by side and looked across the barbed wire and concrete at the huge grey edifice that was the eastern side of the Berlin Wall.

"Well," Kathy offered. "It's not what I was expecting at all, but I think I'm glad I've seen it. Pity we can't see it from the other side as well."

They lapsed into silence. There were a few other people either looking at the wall or standing in groups and chatting but as neither of them spoke German they had no idea what the others were saying.

A young blonde woman interrupted them by asking in perfect English, "Excuse me, but does either of you have the time, please? My watch seems to have stopped at half past twelve."

"Hope not," Piers replied. "I've a plane to catch at eleven." He looked at his watch. "It's just gone nine."

Kathy thought that was an odd thing for him to say. As a pilot he habitually said 'aeroplane' or 'flight' never 'plane', and she began to wonder.

The woman smiled her thanks and, with continental politeness, briefly shook his hand in farewell. Then she walked away without looking back.

Piers shoved his hands into his coat pockets. "OK, seen enough wall now. Let's be on our way."

Kathy didn't say anything but somehow she wasn't surprised when Piers stopped at a news-stand and bought a magazine, putting the change into his coat pocket when he had paid for it.

"Here you go," he told her with a smile. "German knitting patterns. I'll ask Kerryanne to translate them some time as she understands knitting-speak."

She hooked her hand through his arm and didn't ask any questions. "Do you have to walk so fast?" she begged, feeling herself getting out of breath at his cracking pace.

"You're the one saying you're eating too much. I'm just helping you burn calories. Not that it'll make you any thinner no matter how fast you walk."

"What the hell are you talking about?" She pulled on his arm and forced him to slow his pace.

"You. Carrying a passenger."

Kathy rounded on him in her annoyance. "Will you just shut up about me being pregnant? It's not like we haven't been trying and, quite frankly, it's a bit insulting that you just make jokes about something I'm starting to think will never happen. Just because Jean-Guy isn't as prolific as you is no reason to be such a bloody smartarse about it all. Especially after what I told you."

He stopped walking and she, not expecting that, crashed into him from behind. "Sorry, Piglet," he said genuinely and gave her a hug. "You're right. But I am worried about you so, please, just to make an old man happy, get yourself a test? And for pity's sake, tell Jean-Guy before I feel obliged to do it for you."

Kathy didn't want to think right now how she would ever go about doing that. "Yes, alright," she said a bit snappily. "When we're home again. But I still say it's just the Prof's cooking that's done it." She lifted her head. "Speaking of which, can you smell chocolate?"

"Hey, I hear and see well. My sense of smell isn't the best in the world."

Kathy looked round and saw a shop over the road. "There. Come on, I'm in the mood for chocolate."

"You just ate half of Berlin's food ration for breakfast. This is the Russian sector, people don't have things like chocolate."

They crossed the road and stood outside the shop which seemed to be a takeaway only café and the menu was all in German.

"Can't understand a word of it," Kathy said. "What's the German for chocolate?"

There was a young man behind the counter and as the shop was very small he was able to call across to them in English with a strong American accent.

"Hi, guys. What can I get you? Do come on in, I don't bite."

The two stood back to let a couple of women leave the shop and then they went in and Kathy looked at the few cakes on offer.

"I thought I smelled chocolate," she said, realising that it wasn't the cakes that had brought her over the road.

"Sure. Hot chocolates to go. Two?"

"Just one, please," Kathy replied. "He can't drink milk."

"No problem, sir. I can make it with soy milk, coconut milk or almond milk. Which would you like to try?"

"What?" Piers asked, never having been offered such a choice. Even Alison had only ever had soy. "How the hell do you get stuff like that out here?"

"It helps to be an American in Russian Berlin. I can get all sorts of things that the locals can't. Do you like Bounty bars?"

"Well, yes. Used to."

"OK, I'll make you a coconut. It'll be quite sweet."

"Not too hot, please," Kathy requested and got her purse out of her bag. She gave Piers a nudge with her elbow. "Come on, indulge yourself. My treat."

"Oh, go on then," he agreed, feeling a bit mean for having made the pregnancy comments earlier. "Thank you."

The young man grinned hugely and presently handed across a disposable cup with a drink in it that smelled slightly of Bounty bars. He and Kathy both watched intently as Piers took his first sip of this unknown phenomenon.

"Well?" Kathy asked.

A smile lit up his face. "Better than sex," he told her. "Way better than sex."

They happily drank chocolate and ambled the grey, uninspired streets of East Berlin, with a quick excursion to Checkpoint Charlie just so they could say they'd seen it, then back to their hotel where Jean-Guy and his parents were still talking in the foyer.

"Don't they ever stop?" Piers asked.

"Doesn't look like it. You wait and see, I'll meet up with my parents at Gayle's wedding and it'll be 'hello, how are you?' and that's all we'll say to each other all day." She remembered something. "Sorry, you're not invited are you? It was for 'plus one' not 'plus two'."

Jean-Guy saw the rest of the trio had come back. "How was the wall?"

"Still standing," Piers assured him.

"You'd better all get packed and ready to go," Jean-Guy's father reminded them. "We'll meet up with you at the airport but we don't have the advantage of diplomatic transport as you do."

Jean-Guy followed Kathy into their room and shut the door behind them. "Just what is Piers up to?"

She was genuinely confused. "I have no idea what you're talking about."

"The Prof told us in no uncertain terms that we weren't to be split up for an instant and already he has left me twice and you once." He paused as he remembered something. "Is he…?"

Kathy clapped her hand over his mouth before he finished that sentence. "He's just going exploring. He has a curious mind. And we found a hot chocolate he can drink as it was made with coconut milk."

Jean-Guy finally understood that she was signing to him to imply their room was probably bugged and he felt a bit of an idiot for not realising it sooner. "Coconut milk?" he asked instead. "Never heard of it."

"Nor had I. Seems a funny thing to find in the heart of the GDR but there it was. A little takeaway café on the streets of East Berlin run by an American.

He suggested we try the Asian shops back home as they use a lot of coconut milk in their cooking."

They deliberately chatted about banal things as they packed then it was off to the airport and a few hours later they had left Berlin behind and were on their way to Leipzig.

Felix Mendelssohn – *Wedding March in C major from incidental music to* A Midsummer Night's Dream, *Op. 61*

The Dodman Trio concluded their short German tour with a sell-out concert in Hamburg to an audience that demanded two encores and in a concert venue that promptly booked them back annually for the next three years. Their flight brought them back to Gatwick on a warm and breezy day, and only a few days after their return the whole trip seemed like a dream. Except they had all found the Asian shops round Earl's Court and there was now a plentiful supply of coconut milk in the house.

Kathy was quite sorry that Piers so diligently flipped the retaining bar up his nose when he was in uniform but she guessed a two hundred pound fine and the threat of increased penalties was enough to make any pilot do as he was told. The crew of flight 446 also lost the negotiations over the film premiere and all the air crew able to attend had to go to in their uniforms.

The premiere was on a mild evening in late May and Kathy, Jean-Guy and Emma weren't in the forefront of the media frenzy so they could watch with amusement as the press finally got to see what the real people looked like and pose them with the actors pretending to be them. Kathy wasn't the only one who thought the real Captain Buchanan and First Officer Hollander were actually much better-looking than their acting counterparts. The group she liked best was when the media called for the author to be posed with Danny and Piers and all three were in a bunch with Kerryanne in the middle with her arms across the men's shoulders and they had tight hold of her round the waist. She looked even more stunning than usual that night in her long white dress and heels that put her as tall as the men either side of her. Her smile had never been wider and her honey-blonde hair had never been as flicked as it was in front of the dozens of flash guns going off that night.

Kathy wasn't quite sure how it happened, but she found herself seated between Jean-Guy and Piers with Danny directly behind her next to Kerryanne and with Emma on Jean-Guy's other side. Piers had Jake Hollander and Mick Belmont on his right side and the three were laughing quietly about something as the film started. To the surprise of the cynical Kathy the film wasn't as lightweight as she had been expecting. Mick Belmont was first shown visiting his mother in a care home, Jake Hollander leaving a night club in the small hours of the morning, disgusted at having to be sober, and Piers Buchanan taking the pager call that put him on the return flight he wasn't supposed to be part of in the first place. The characters of the passengers were skilfully drawn although there were the clichés of the nervous first-timer and the know-it-all who was depicted as an ex-serving US Air Force officer who reckoned he knew more than the crew did.

Kathy wasn't expecting to enjoy the film as much as she did, but the main plotline was about four of the passengers on the plane and she could tell a pilot had written it as although it was a tense thriller there were no unnecessary dramatics that would have been impossible on a civilian airliner.

The audience watched attentively as the action built up to the landing with hero and villain both convinced they weren't going to survive and the whole cinema fell spontaneously silent when Captain B asked for silence so he could hear what the aircraft was saying. There was a quick scene with the nervous passenger whimpering in his seat and the USAF officer declaring loudly it was a load of crap but he was hushed by the calmly efficient cabin crew. Kathy thought Kerryanne had shown so well how the captain had had the courage to make that decision not to put out the mayday and try to run for Reykjavik, almost certain they wouldn't make it, but to land a broken plane in a blizzard at one of the most treacherous airports on the planet. Which also meant the main characters survived the arrival in Greenland so the story could conclude in the airport terminal.

The actual landing was a spectacular example of special effects and Kathy was reminded of Mick's description of the ground-level aurora borealis in the snow in the way it was shown on the screen. The set of the cockpit made it look very dramatic with the scoured, opaque windscreen battered by the relentless snow and ash, and warning lights and sounds going off all over the place. To Kathy's admiration, Kerryanne had even found out the theme of the child of bickering parents being bought a teddy bear at the start of the journey when all he really wanted was his old bear and for his parents to settle their differences. Believing they were facing certain death, the parents did indeed make up and the child without regret gave the unwanted teddy bear to the pilot. The consumption of Greenland vodka was kept to a minimum and the film ended with original footage of the genuine aircraft being brought safely back home to land at Heathrow in the rain. Over that footage it was put on the screen that Captain Buchanan had been awarded the Queen's Gallantry Medal and First Officer Hollander and Flight Engineer Belmont had received Queen's Commendations for their actions that day and that all three were still working for the airline. The audience were also informed that rapid advances in weather forecasting and aviation safety in general, meant that today no flight would ever be exposed to such risk. The whole film was dedicated to the memory of Mabel Belmont who had passed away just a few months before the film had been released.

The house lights came on and Kathy wasn't surprised when the entire audience gave a standing ovation to the crew of the flight whose part in the story they had just been watching. She was also not surprised that there was even more of a media frenzy when the subjects and stars of the film left the cinema and she was glad that she and Jean-Guy could slip away with Emma and catch the Tube back to Earl's Court while Piers was dragged off to some kind of after-party with Kerryanne hanging possessively onto his arm and, Kathy had no doubt, profoundly relieved to have his wedding ring back on again.

She was half-woken by the rattle of a key in the lock at 2am and the muted chatter of Piers and Danny on the stairs but just rolled over and went back to sleep again, knowing that neither she nor Jean-Guy were working that day and the two of them and Emma had a lazy morning half planned before Emma had to catch her train back to Somerset in the early afternoon.

Danny went back to Los Angeles the next day to start his rounds of publicity for the US release of the film scheduled for the middle of June. Kathy and Jean-Guy didn't see much of Piers over the next few days as with the media restrictions lifted, the air crew were in heavy demand for TV and print interviews and the piano in the music room sat untouched for several evenings.

Kathy yawned and stretched lazily in her bed, feeling the familiarity of Jean-Guy beside her.

"Fidget," muttered his sleepy voice. "What time do we have to be in Wimbledon?"

"Oh, God," she groaned and snuggled against him. "It's Gayle's wedding day, isn't it?"

"Yes, it is. Come on, you'll be fine. Shall I go and wake up the coffee machine?"

"No, I'll do it. I'm more awake than you anyway." She was not expecting to find Piers in the kitchen, wrapped in the bathrobe he had bought when his house had been invaded by lodgers and other guests, standing beside the coffee machine and yawning as he waited for it to wake up.

"Good morning," she greeted him. "Have you just come in or are you on your way out?"

"Just woken up. Kind of." He handed her the first mug of coffee from the machine. "What time do we have to be in Wimbledon?"

She took a gulp of coffee and could feel the elation soaring within her. "You're not invited," she told him lightly.

"Weddings are public events. We'd have had half the village at ours if Sarah hadn't told them all to stay away. They can't stop me going into the church.

So I don't get the meal but I'm sure you can smuggle me in to the after-party if you're staying for it. I've had such a peculiar few days. What day is it?"

"Saturday."

He added the habitual water and downed his espresso in one go as he always did then refilled his mug from the tap. "OK. So I have three days then it's back to Concorde. Some kind of normality at last."

"And I bet if you turned up on Tuesday with your nose ring on display they'd let you get away with it this time after all the good publicity you've given that rotten airline."

He just looked at her with his eyes peeping through his fringe of hair that had grown quite long. "Hmm. Don't think I'll risk it. But, guess what, I've had at least three publishers wanting me to write an autobiography. Offering me lots of money for it too."

"Going to do it?"

"Not a chance in hell. Jean-Guy awake?"

"Almost. I'll take him up some coffee."

"And I'm going to hit the shower down here. Then if he's awake I guess I can do some piano practice without disturbing him."

Kathy allowed herself the delicious image of Piers having his shower then just padding dripping wet and naked across to the piano. "You probably should. That poor piano thinks you don't love it any more. Anyway, the wedding is at three and it's straight down the District Line then we can hop on the bus or walk from the station. So I suppose we'll leave about a quarter to two."

"I'm sorry. I thought for one minute you said strange words like 'District Line' and 'bus'."

"Seriously? You're going to drive to Wimbledon? It'll be quicker on the Tube."

"I don't do public transport, you know that. Then you can wear your six-inch heels and pull me over on the dance floor again."

She kissed his unshaven cheek. "Missed you," she told him happily. "Enjoy your naked piano practice."

"My what?!" he yelled after her as she, laughing, went up the stairs.

The first person Kathy saw when she got out of the Aston Martin was her mother. Then she saw who she was talking to. "Jesus!" she exclaimed and backed into Jean-Guy, not even noticing she had stabbed his foot with her heel.

He saw what she had seen. "Shit. I was not expecting that."

Piers locked the car and arrived on her other side. "Isn't that…?"

"Yes," Jean-Guy hissed. "That is her ex. What the hell is he doing here?"

Piers pushed his sunglasses on top of his head. "Well, as he's in the morning suit I'm guessing he's something like best man." He dropped the glasses down again as the sunlight was really very bright for eyes that were sore from television studio lights and lack of sleep over the last few days. "No, Piglet. Stop backing away. He can't hurt you now."

"Yes he can. He always can." Kathy could feel the panic rising in her and she just prayed Richard wouldn't see her before she had got back in the car. He turned just as she had spoken and looked straight at her as she stood there in her floral dress, flanked by two men, neither of whom was as tall or as wide as him. There was a slight smile on his face as he excused himself from Kathy's mother and walked across to them.

Kathy just whimpered a bit and backed up as far as she could, feeling Jean-Guy's arm coming snug round her waist as her back bumped into the car. She hoped Piers was carrying his gun under that suit jacket, although common sense told her he wouldn't be. This was Wimbledon after all, not East Germany.

"Kathy!" Richard exclaimed. "Lovely to see you as always. Hope you're going to save a dance for me?"

Before any of them could say anything a group of about half a dozen wedding guests, who had been looking very hard at the group beside the Aston Martin in the car park, interrupted them.

One of the women who Kathy remembered vaguely as one of Gayle's work colleagues put on her brightest smile and asked flirtatiously, "Sorry to interrupt, but aren't you Captain Buchanan? You landed that plane in Greenland? Been all over the telly recently."

Kathy couldn't believe the look on Richard's face as the man standing next to her just smiled and replied with frosty politeness, "Only when I'm working and today is definitely a day off." The other guests got the message and walked on but still chattering about not expecting to see anyone famous at Gayle's wedding. Piers was in full Wing Commander mode as he nudged Richard to one side. "Excuse us, but I think Kathy would like to meet up with her family now."

Kathy wasn't surprised when her mother came to meet them as her two companions almost bodily carried her towards the church. She could feel they both had a tight hold of her and she was convinced her feet weren't quite on the ground.

Her parents had never been physically demonstrative and Mrs Fairbanks didn't hug her elder daughter.

"You're looking well," was the oddly formal maternal greeting. "Aren't you going to introduce me?"

"Yes, sorry. This is Jean-Guy, my fiancé as I now have to call him. And this is Piers. Sorry, he wasn't on the guest list but he's not planning on staying for the meal."

Her mother had the manners to shake hands with the two men, but didn't make any comments about the one who had been on the TV recently.

"Have you chosen a wedding date?" Kathy's mother asked politely. "I know Gayle had awful trouble as the church was booked solid for over a year."

"Yes," Kathy said almost defiantly. "August the first, and it'll be in the register office in Woodbridge. Just a quiet wedding with a few friends, that's all we want." She thought it would be a very bad idea to mention a Pagan handfasting.

Her mother was clearly horrified. "You aren't coming home to get married? And on such short notice too. I hope you haven't been up to any nonsense," she reprimanded her daughter as though she was a teenager who had stayed out all night.

Kathy was close enough to the other two to feel that Piers was in extreme danger of laughing but with superb self-control he kept his face straight and told the ruffled parent, "No nonsense at all, Mrs Fairbanks. I'm her landlord as well as a friend, and, trust me, I know exactly what goes on in my house."

He had the years and the gravitas to get away with the comment, even if he did have a ring in his nose, and Kathy wasn't surprised to see her mother looked a bit happier. "Oh, all right then. And how are Emma and her father?"

"Oh, they're fine," Kathy managed. "I don't see much of Emma now."

Richard walked up to the group but still couldn't get physically near Kathy. "You need to go inside," he told them sharply. "Gayle and her father are due to be here in a few minutes."

The three went into the church, politely informed the young child doing the ushering that they were on the bride's side and were shown to a pew that already had some people in it.

Piers looked round and realised he was going to have to take his glasses off in that gloomy church. "We'll take the one behind, if it's all the same to you," he remarked and went in first with Kathy next and Jean-Guy on her other side in the middle of the pew.

"What was all that about?" Jean-Guy asked as he picked up the Order of Service from the ledge in front of him.

Piers nodded towards the side aisle which he was now next to. "Quicker exit," he replied but wasn't smiling. "And you're safer stuck in the middle of a pew."

"Safer from what?" Jean-Guy hissed. "This isn't Eastern Germany any more."

"Safer from some bloke who must be about six foot four and weigh best part of twenty stone. I bet you two looked ridiculous together."

"But he can come down the side aisle," Jean-Guy said, speaking out loud what Kathy was thinking to herself.

"Nah, he's best man. His duties will keep him safely in the main aisle." He looked at the Order of Service. "Jeez. Three hymns and a sermon? My back will never survive." He loosened his shirt collar under his tie. "Wake me up when it's over," he remarked with a smile and for a moment Kathy genuinely thought he was planning on snoozing through the whole service.

The organ blasted out Mendelssohn's *Wedding March* and the three joined the congregation in standing to welcome the bride as she entered the church on her father's arm.

"Corny," Piers whispered in Kathy's ear. "Guess your sister has the musical soul of an amoeba?"

Feeling a lot safer at the back of the church with her ex occupied at the front and her guardian angels protecting her, Kathy fondly tapped him on the arm. "Now you're just insulting amoebas."

With the skilful help of Jean-Guy who wouldn't leave her side, Kathy was nowhere near Richard in any of the photographs when they were taken outside the church. She couldn't help noticing that a lot of people wanted to engage Piers in conversation but, back out in the light, he had his sunglasses on again and was clearly just being his distant, polite self that he did so well.

She was quite relieved when her mother came fussing up to her and said, "I've managed to find space for your friend at the meal as Aunt Jen said she couldn't come at the last minute so I've popped a couple of cousins on different tables and he can sit with you and Jean-Guy. I wish you'd told me you were bringing him too. I'd have put you nearer the top table."

"It's fine, Mum, really. He wasn't expecting to be invited to the meal. But thank you for accommodating him."

"Have you spoken to Richard yet?"

"Um, we've kind of said hello."

"Good. Such a polite young man. I don't know why you never married him all those years ago. At least he wouldn't drag you all round the world like a gypsy."

Kathy couldn't believe her mother would be so insulting. She tried not to lose her temper and spoil her sister's wedding day. "We had some differences," she said rather formally. "And I couldn't see a way round them. And I like going all round the world. I met Jean-Guy's parents in Berlin and they're really nice people."

She jumped when Piers arrived silently beside her and casually draped an arm across her shoulders. "Hey, Piglet. Heard the news? I've been allowed to gatecrash the dinner." He gave Kathy's mother his most devastating smile. "Very good of you, Mrs Fairbanks. I wasn't expecting to be fed. It's just that your daughter has told us so much about you, I was curious to meet you all and as I'm not working again until Tuesday the opportunity seemed too good to miss."

Kathy had no idea her own mother could be so silly and giggly. "You're very welcome, I'm sure," she managed to say. "Anyway, it's time to move to the church hall now so we can get you all sorted out as the caterers want to start serving at five."

To Kathy's relief, she was seated between Jean-Guy and Piers at a table towards the back of the hall and they were sharing with two of Gayle's school friends who she hadn't seen since they had been about sixteen and one of them was there with her husband. Richard, as best man, was well out of the way at the top table. It was a full-on three course meal and she felt so sorry for Piers who had to make do with carefully easing the lettuce leaves out of the prawn cocktail which was heavily laced with cayenne and could only pick the vegetables out of the main meal as the chicken was served covered in a very creamy sauce. She had had hopes for the dessert but the fresh fruit salad had had cinnamon added to its syrup and just to finish him off, the coffee came ready served with cream.

The other three at their table had been disinclined to chat but whether that was because they were overawed by the company or had been told by Gayle that her elder sister was dating a foreigner, she didn't know. The food had been really nice and she had quite enjoyed her meal but could see that a few lettuce leaves and a handful of green beans weren't going to sustain Piers for very long.

"We don't need to stay for the party, if you're hungry," she told him softly.

"I could eat the table. What happened to lunch?"

"You ate it before we left, remember? The ham sandwich?"

"Oh, yes," he said vaguely as the best man got to his feet and smartly rapped a spoon on the table so he could start off the speeches.

Kathy was miles away dreaming of a handfasting in the garden of the old farmhouse by the time the speeches were all over and the cake was brought out for the happy couple to cut.

Jean-Guy leaned across her and said quite sharply to Piers, "Are you feeling OK? You never have much colour and now you are matching the tablecloth."

"Hungry," he replied. "But I'll survive."

"In pain?" Jean-Guy persisted.

"Not that much. Let's not spoil the wedding, huh?"

The cake was cut, more toasts were drunk and then the caterers skilfully started bringing round pieces of cake for all the guests.

Kathy inspected it first. "You're in luck," she told Piers. "Gayle never did like fruit cake so she's blessed you with a plain old madeira."

The other three at the table were a bit surprised when the rather silent but very handsome man, who looked vaguely familiar, had eaten hardly anything of the meal but then bolted down three pieces of cake so fast they doubted he even chewed them.

"Better?" Kathy asked.

"Much," Piers assured her and finished off his third glass of water.

People were leaving their tables and beginning to circulate as the music started, the bride and groom had their first dance, and Gayle's friends made their excuses and went off to talk to some more sociable guests.

Piers started systematically crunching up the sugared almonds from the little baskets of favours on the table. "You kids can go and dance if you want," he offered. "I really don't mind."

Jean-Guy looked at Kathy. "Want to?"

"Why not." Kathy didn't think she and Jean-Guy had ever danced together and it was rather pleasant to rest in his arms and just let the music wash over her as they moved to the beat.

Piers was on the last few almonds when he was joined at the table by the bride and groom. He wasn't surprised. They were being good hosts and going round all the tables.

"Hi," Gayle began. "I don't think we've been introduced. "I'm Gayle," she told him quite unnecessarily and offered her hand in greeting. "And this, in case you hadn't gathered is Colin."

He accepted the handshakes while thinking that Kathy had been quite right and Gayle looked nothing like her. "Good wedding," he told Gayle without giving his name. "Very traditional."

She could see he was wearing a wedding ring that seemed to have been in place for quite a while. "Did you bring your wife today?"

"No, she's at home with the kids. It's hard to find a babysitter when you've got eight of them."

"Eight," Gayle was surprised. "You don't look old enough."

He just smiled and finished off the almonds. "Where are you going for your honeymoon?"

"Oh, nowhere very exciting," Gayle replied trying to work out how this man was familiar to her. "Cornwall."

He thought about that for a while. "Do you know, I don't think I've ever been to Cornwall. And I'm sure if you're on honeymoon it'll be more than exciting enough for you both."

She smiled back, rather liking this man with his lovely smile and quiet, diffident manner. "Have you known Kathy long? I'm assuming that's her boyfriend on the dance floor with her."

"Yes. I suppose we first met each other about six, maybe seven years ago. She's a nice kid but she wasn't expecting to see her ex here."

"We work together," Colin explained. "Been mates for a long time. He kept in touch with Gayle's family after Kathy went as he was trying to find her for them." He gave his new wife a loving smile. "He was the one who introduced us, actually."

"Are you really the bloke who flew that aeroplane?" Gayle asked curiously, having finally worked out how she knew who he was.

Piers kept things light and conversational. "I work as a pilot, if that's what you mean."

"No, I saw you on the telly the other evening," she persisted. "You were on a chat show and I was only half listening but they said something about you crashed a plane in Greenland and it got made into a film. How on earth did Kathy ever get to meet you?"

"The aeroplane didn't crash. It was just an unexpected landing. And we both use the same grocery store."

"I never really understood why she suddenly went off," Gayle put in sounding a bit regretful. "One minute she was engaged to Richard then he turned up at Colin's house in an awful state and said she'd gone running off without giving him a reason. And then she spent the next year or so moving all over the place and we didn't even know where she was half the time. Still, at least Richard kept in touch with us and did his best to find her and we'd give him her address if we knew it. But she just kept on running. None of us has any idea why. Did she ever tell you why she did such a thing?"

Reflecting this wasn't at all how he had heard the tale, but did explain how Richard had managed to keep up with Kathy, Piers was prepared to be entertained. "Not really. She was free and single when I first met her. And that was it? She just bolted with nothing said at all?"

"Nothing," Gayle confirmed. "And she never said anything to you?"

"I've heard her side of the story," was all he was willing to say, not wanting to upset the bride on her wedding day. "Anyway, I've kept you long enough, you've got other people to go round."

"True," Gayle admitted. "Well, it's been nice to meet you. Try to get her to keep in touch in future."

The very idea made Piers smile. "I don't flatter myself I've got any say over what that one gets up to."

The newlyweds moved on and Piers sat quietly for a few moments waiting for the room to stop whirling in circles and hoping he wouldn't be sick as he could taste the blood in his mouth.

Kathy turned her head on Jean-Guy's shoulder. "I think Piers needs rescuing. He doesn't look at all well. You go and make sure he's not going to pass out and I'll go and chat up the caterers."

Not so long ago, she thought to herself, she would never have dared approach a team of professional caterers and ask if she could have some food for someone who hadn't been able to eat most of their meal as he had food allergies. She picked a sympathetic-looking woman to ask and the initial response was a rather brusque,

"Is that the one who was on the telly the other night? I noticed he didn't eat much. I was starting to think he wasn't very impressed with our twenty pound a head meal. It's the most expensive meal we offer and I don't think he even touched most of it."

Kathy wished she'd chosen someone else to ask. "Oh, no. Nothing like that, honestly. He said the food looked delicious but he can't eat spices or dairy. And he was a last-minute change of plan so we couldn't let you know in time."

The woman was mollified. She gave Kathy her business card and said, "Give me a minute. I'll see what I can do."

"And could I have some of the ice too, please?" Kathy asked, seeing a whole tub full of ice and champagne bottles on one of the work surfaces, and deciding to push her luck. There was no reply to that so she waited patiently but with one wary eye on the room, trying to see what her ex was up to. He seemed to be engrossed in conversation with another small, blonde woman so she hoped he would leave her well alone until she and her companions could get away.

"Here you are, love," said a voice next to her and she jumped. "Sorry, didn't mean to startle you."

Kathy gratefully took a plate of chicken and vegetables with no sauce on it, yet more cake and an apple from the smiling lady and could barely manage the cup of ice as well. "Thank you," she said. "He'll be very grateful."

To her relief she was back at the table before her ex had noticed she had been in the room on her own.

Piers just gave her a smile and stuffed a few ice cubes in his mouth but Kathy noticed he still looked a bit sick. He swallowed the ice and pulled the most awful face Kathy had ever seen him make.

"Sorry," he said. "Mouth full of blood, didn't taste very nice. Didn't dare speak in case I dribbled."

"You put it so nicely," Kathy told him fondly. "Here, eat chicken instead."

The chicken disappeared in record time, but Piers gave the cake to Jean-Guy and Kathy as he had eaten theirs.

"Thanks, Piglet. Has that ex of yours spoken to you yet? He's been circling the room and chatting up all the blonde women he can find."

"He gives me the creeps," she admitted. "In a way I'm glad he hasn't made any attempt to get near me but he's in the same room as me and the fact he hasn't done anything makes it worse as I'm just waiting for it to happen."

"Mind games, Piglet. Once you've spotted them then they're easier to resist." He bit into the apple and gave her one of his lovely smiles. "Now, if only we were in East Germany and I was armed I could take him out into the car park and shoot him for you."

"Just eat your apple and don't be silly," she told him but silently grateful for his humour. "Would you really shoot him?"

"Whoa, where did that come from?" he half-laughed.

"I would," Jean-Guy put in. "But I'm not the one who knows how to use a gun."

"Can we stop talking about shooting people, please?" Piers asked. "No matter how frivolous you two are being. Just remember bullets are traceable and that gun is registered with the police."

Kathy remembered a throwaway remark her former driving instructor had made. "I bet Danny would do it. I never knew he'd trained as a marksman."

"Piglet, behave. The only rifle Danny uses now is a replica in a film."

She thought about it for a few moments. "He's got the perfect cover hasn't he? His modelling takes him all over the world and nobody would ever suspect someone who spends his days dressing up in designer clothes would ever be able to shoot someone." Neither of the men said anything in response to her flight of fancy and their silence made her realise that the three of them were on the brink of a very peculiar world and she really hoped none of them would ever topple into it.

She saw her parents were now making the rounds of the tables and her heart sank to realise they were both the worse for drink. Her father was definitely more drunk than her mother and she really, really wished she hadn't come.

"What did you say to Richard?" was her mother's rather abrupt greeting. "I hope you haven't upset him again."

"Not at all," she replied vaguely, trying not to think about the conversation they had just had about shooting him.

"Good, you treated him shamelessly. Anyway, how have you been? We haven't seen you for a while."

"I know, I've been busy recently. But I will try to write more often." She wondered if she dared flout convention and suggest they leave while the bride and groom were still dancing.

Her father stared drunkenly at the young man who had won the heart of his elder daughter. "Did you have to pick yourself a foreigner?" he asked rudely.

Kathy took Jean-Guy's hand under the table. "I didn't do it to spite you," she protested hotly. "And I'm not going to apologise for the man I love. We're getting married in August and then in September we'll be honeymooning in Prague where he's giving a series of concerts and probably having some kind of celebration there as his parents are so happy for us."

Her father belched. "I don't know what's got into you these days. You used to be so polite and now you're rude and aggressive. There was no need to speak to us like that."

Jean-Guy didn't like to see Kathy look so upset and his grasp of English was getting a lot better even when the speaker was slurring his words. "No, she is not rude. She has learned to live on her own and she is not the dependent mouse she was before. She is a strong woman now and I am proud of her."

"Well we're not," Kathy's mother said disgustedly. "We never taught her to behave like that. Strong woman, what kind of nonsense is that? All that poor Richard ever wanted to do was spoil you rotten. We spent a lot of money on that wedding and you just ran off with no word of explanation."

Kathy could bite back her temper no longer. She had never, ever been so ashamed of and angered by her parents before. "If it's about the money, I'll pay it back to you. But I've got no regrets that I dumped that bully and now I'm making my own way in life with the support of my two best friends."

"No need to shout at us," Kathy's father said very loudly even though his daughter hadn't raised her voice. "Bloody foreigners teaching you their manners and you bringing them to your sister's wedding of all places." He nodded towards the other man who had been trained, and finally learned over the years, never to lose his temper in public. "Why couldn't you have picked someone English like this one?"

Piers realised that what Kathy had said about her father was true and he was genuinely appalled that anyone could be so offensive. He had been surprised that Jean-Guy had managed to follow the fast, slurred speech of the man who would be his father-in-law in the summer and could see this had the potential to escalate into something quite hostile.

Kathy's love for the raven who guarded her made her want to weep when he set himself up as a target to take her father's venom away from her betrothed.

"I'm not English. The RAF taught me to sound like this but I was born and raised in Ireland.

Jean-Guy may have a French name and Prague as his place of birth on his passport but he's naturalised British now. Which makes him less of a foreigner than me as I travel on Irish papers."

Kathy's father didn't like being wrong-footed and was annoyed at being caught out. "You bloody foreigners always stick together. I've always found the Irish to be such a feckless lot."

Piers suddenly missed his wife. Sarah always felt so soft and warm in his arms and she didn't have a malicious bone in her body. She would never have said anything like that. He didn't think she was even capable of thinking something so hateful. A stab of homesickness for Suffolk and his wife and children caught him by surprise.

"Yes, I suppose we can be," he said thoughtfully and looked across to the other two. "Let's all be Irish and feckless. Let's get into the Aston and drive to Suffolk. Right now. In all our wedding finery."

"I don't even have a pair of clean knickers with me," Kathy laughed, glad to see he was seeing the funny side of her parents' frankly rather mortifying behaviour.

"Nor do I. And no cheating when we get there and changing into stuff you have there as I hardly have anything and it wouldn't be fair."

"And I don't have a violin with me. And Jean-Guy doesn't have a cello."

"And none of us is working before Tuesday so let's just go. We'll walk the beach in totally unsuitable clothing and eat too much cake in Alison's café."

"The Prof isn't even expecting us. He'll have locked up and gone to bed by the time we get there."

"So we'll break in." Piers got to his feet. "Please give our apologies to Gayle and Colin," he said to the bride's parents. "But I'm going to be true to type and do something completely feckless for the first time in I don't know how long."

The other two caught his mood. Kathy picked up her clutch bag. "Well, I'm up for being completely feckless too. How about it, Jean-Guy?"

"I'm sure I would if I knew what it meant," he said, still not sure what was going on, and the three went out of the stuffy church hall into the cool freshness of the May night.

Kathy inhaled the night air and looked round at the church and the church hall that were within walking distance of the house where she had grown up.

"That's it, isn't it?" she said out loud.

"Yes," Jean-Guy agreed. "It's all over now. Your parents will probably never speak to you again. And if that was my fault then I apologise. So, I need some lessons please."

"I think I owe the pair of you one big apology for my dreadful parents. And what do you need lessons in anyway?"

"Being feckly."

"Feckless," she corrected with a fond laugh. "You're going to learn how to be feckless."

"No, Piers is the feckless one so, as I am what he is not, I must now be feckly."

Pyotr Ilyich Tchaikovsky - *Piano Trio in A minor, Op.50*

Sarah woke slowly in the morning to realise she was comfortably settled against her husband and he was looking at her with dreamy blue eyes full of love for her.

"Hi," he said softly and traced one finger round the outline of her face. "Sleep well?"

She leaned into him and inhaled the scent of their night together. "I thought I'd dreamed it," she murmured and let him touch her in that way he had which had made her realise what seemed like a long time ago now that he was the man who could make her dreams come true. She had been fast asleep next to Alison when what had started out as a rather carnal dream about her husband had turned into the realisation that he was kneeling next to the bed and kissing her awake. Before she could speak he had motioned her to silence, helped her out of the bed and handed across her dressing gown. They had slunk down the stairs without disturbing any of the sleeping adults or children.

"What's the matter?" she had asked softly once they were in the hall.

He had just taken her hand and she had gone with him, naked under her dressing gown and his car was outside with the engine running. It had been like an extension of her dream as he had brought her to the haunted old farmhouse and taken her to his bed and there she had woken up. Without a stitch on her and all her clothes back home in her parents' house.

In the room at the front of the house, Kathy and Jean-Guy were just stirring too. "What was all that about?" Kathy whispered to the man she loved.

"I have no idea. I think that's what happens when the sensible one decides he really doesn't want to be sensible any more."

She snuggled against him. "I love it when he's not sensible. The Prof's going to be a bit baffled when he goes downstairs."

Petr Mihaly was indeed mystified. Parked outside the farmhouse was a black Aston Martin. There was no sign of a ramshackle Land Rover but he couldn't think of any reason Piers would travel to Suffolk on his own unless there was some kind of crisis and if there had been a crisis he wouldn't have parked his car and then, presumably, gone to bed. There was no sign of a violin or a cello in the sitting room but Audrey was nowhere to be seen which meant Piers was in the house and she was with him in his room, so he hadn't parked his car at the farmhouse then walked a mile in the dark into the village to spend the night with Sarah. He knew the three of them had gone to Kathy's sister's wedding yesterday but he couldn't think of any connection between that and Piers arriving in Suffolk. He went out to check the other man wasn't asleep in his car as that was another missing piece in the puzzle. The house had been locked and bolted last night as it always was but clearly Piers had somehow managed to get inside. The only open window was the fanlight in the bathroom upstairs and there was no way a middle-aged man of six foot one would squeeze in through that no matter how double-jointed he was in his spine.

He put the kettle on to boil and had one of the frights of his recent life when Kathy's voice spoke brightly behind him.

"Morning! Hope we didn't disturb you last night."

He was genuinely delighted to see her and gave her a hug of greeting. "Not at all. I didn't even hear you arrive, which is not a good thing, but I am always happy to see you, you know that. But how did you get in? I may need to look at my security now."

Kathy laughed. "Piers and Jean-Guy climbed on the old patio table, then Jean-Guy got on Piers' shoulders as he's lighter and I climbed up the pair of them and got in through the bathroom window then went downstairs and let them in through the back door. It was all totally unplanned. We just ran away from my sister's wedding and came straight here. We have no instruments, no luggage, nothing. And today we are going to go for a walk in our unsuitable clothes and eat too much cake at Alison's café."

He caught some of the joy of her mood and was secretly rather impressed with their ingenuity. But he would definitely have to look into making the house totally secure. "Not like you at all."

She laughed. "It was Piers. My parents had just been unbelievably rude to all three of us and he got an impetuous fit in his head and off we all went. So unlike him, but such fun."

Piers himself came into the kitchen at that point. He was wearing nothing but his smart trousers from yesterday so all the tattoos and rings were on show. He smiled to realise Kathy had just thrown her dress on and had no underwear on whatsoever.

"Morning," he greeted them. "Um, can any of you suggest anything Sarah can wear please? I kind of abducted her in her dressing gown and she hasn't got any clothes with her."

Kathy could feel the laughter bubbling up inside. "You did what?"

"Abducted Sarah. In her dressing gown. Which doesn't really go round her properly as it's quite old and she'd like to come down for breakfast. I've given her my shirt to wear but she'd like to cover up her bottom half a bit."

Kathy and the Prof really wanted to laugh at the idea of poor Sarah stranded upstairs in the scary house with nothing to wear except her husband's shirt, but thought that wouldn't be very diplomatic.

"You're welcome to go through what I have," the Prof offered. "Shall we celebrate with some very unseasonal porridge?"

Breakfast was late that day. Sarah eventually came down the stairs in Piers' shirt and a skirt she had somehow cobbled together out of two dressing gowns and her husband was still happily wandering about half naked. Kathy hadn't bothered with underwear and Jean-Guy was the most presentable of all of them as he had put on both shirt and trousers from the day before. The five of them sat round the breakfast table for best part of an hour just talking and laughing with Kathy and Jean-Guy chattering nineteen to the dozen about film premieres and stuffy English weddings and the married couple exchanging quiet nothings in a way they hadn't done for a very long time. Then they all set out in their unsuitable clothes to go and eat cakes at Alison's café.

Sarah couldn't believe they were going to make her walk along the coast path in her husband's shirt and two dressing gowns with wellies on her feet as that was all there was for her but the others looked just as crazy so she went along with it. Kathy had to borrow wellies too as she drew the line at walking the coast path in four-inch heels and the men decided to let her off. Jean-Guy still looked the most presentable of any of them and Piers was told that borrowing a shirt from the Prof was cheating so he pointed out he was covered in copyrighted tattoos and they agreed he could put a shabby old T shirt under his jacket, which looked terrible but suited the occasion.

Sarah was excused the dress code and was told she could go and get a skirt to wear but that was all she was allowed and had to keep the shirt and the wellies. She felt a bit guilty as it meant her parents had to manage the shop and the children between them, but there was no way she was going to miss out on the cake eating at the café.

Alison looked a bit surprised when the ill-dressed quartet came into her café but they all looked so happy she didn't have the heart to reprimand any of them. It was quite obvious to her eye that Kathy wasn't wearing underwear so she gave herself a bit of a treat too.

"What happened to you last night?" she asked Sarah who was wearing a man's shirt, her husband's Alison guessed looking at the state of him, and a tatty old skirt with a pair of pink wellies.

Sarah didn't care that Alison was clearly a bit cross with her as she was cuddled into her husband's arms. "I got abducted," she giggled as he kissed her on the neck.

"I like your nose ring," Alison told Piers, while thinking her partner was in a very strange mood that day. "Is it new?"

"Oh, there's an even better one," Sarah laughed and pulled her husband's jacket open but he snatched it closed again before she could hitch up his T shirt. "Do you think I should get pierced to match?"

Alison got the idea of where the other piercing was and privately thought she should but didn't like to say so in a public café. "What do you all want?" she asked. Then wished she hadn't as all four suddenly started howling with laughter. "What has got into you all today?" she wanted to know.

"I have no idea," Kathy admitted. "But I rather like it."

The four gave her their orders then settled at one of the inside tables with their coffees and cakes. Piers watched Alison skilfully making the coffees for her queue of customers for a while then suddenly went up to the counter and spoke to her. The other three didn't hear what he said but they heard Alison's roar of laughter.

"You? Want to learn how to use a coffee machine?"

"Uh-huh."

"Well, I've just got this new one so don't break it. Come on then, round you come and put a pinny on. Pay attention while I make this lot and then I'll teach you your cappuccinos from your lattes. Oh, and according to my cousin out in New Zealand there's a new coffee on the block. It's called a flat white and you get to draw pictures on it."

Kathy saw Sarah was watching her husband with a loving smile on her face. "He's full of surprises, isn't he?" she asked.

"He is incredible," Sarah agreed. "Just when I think I've got to know him he goes and does something like that and he's off again in another direction." Her smile became a little rueful. "I sometimes think we've only stayed together as we have because we don't see that much of each other. He wears me out after about three days as it's like living with a bundle of pure energy and I can't keep up. I mean does he ever stop and just read a book?"

"He does," Kathy had to admit. "But not usually for long and he always has lots of books on the go at the same time as he gets bored with most of them after a few pages."

They were quite surprised when Alison came across to join them what seemed like only a few minutes later, calling over her shoulder as she came. "OK, Steph and Amanda will look after you while I take a break for a few minutes. And don't fiddle with the controls again, it's not the flight deck of the Concorde."

"Concorde doesn't have a 'the' in it," came the instinctive, but not unkind, correction from the man working the coffee machine not very quickly but apparently knowing what he was doing.

Alison sat next to Sarah and remarked to the other three at the table, "Well, if everyone picked up that machine so quickly I could retire. He's pretty bright, isn't he? Listens to instructions and remembers them."

Kathy couldn't help but think of Marianne's comment about Piers learning to fly an American fighter jet after one lesson and thought to herself that the coffee machine must be like a child's toy after that.

Sarah watched her husband for a while as he got his own rhythm going on the coffee machine. "Now, that's what I thought I would finish up with."

"What do you mean?" Alison asked curiously.

"Just someone who would work with me in the shop like Dad does with Mum. I knew I would cope with the right man to give me children and it never occurred to me that I'd get anything other than what I'm used to. Ordinary people doing an ordinary job."

Alison watched Piers as well but slightly more critically in case he started adjusting her new machine again. "He's going to ruin that jacket. Can't you pop home and borrow something of your dad's for him to put on? I don't think he'd be too impressed if I told him to take the jacket off as you've pinched his shirt. And that T shirt he's wearing looks as though it's older than I am so I don't want that on show either."

Kathy wanted to laugh at the idea of Piers working in the café in just an apron and smart trousers. "Oh, I think you'd find all the women in the village suddenly arrived at your counter if they knew you'd got him working here topless."

They were still laughing at the image when the object of their mirth returned to the table and gave Alison back the apron. "Had enough of that now," he announced.

"Well, I'd give you a job for your coffees but then I'd fire you for your lack of commitment," Alison told him.

"I don't want a job. I'm thinking of buying a new coffee machine as my one at home is on its last legs."

"In that case come back when I close and I'll teach you how to clean it. These machines aren't for the fainthearted and why on earth would you want an industrial coffee machine in your house?"

"I don't want one that big, there's only three of us living there. Just wanted to suss it out."

Jean-Guy couldn't eat any more cake. "So now that is sussed. What do we do next while we're being feckless this weekend?"

Piers looked at Sarah and said rather regretfully, "I suppose your folks are expecting you back in the shop?"

"Yes. I should have been behind that till by six this morning."

"OK, you're excused. But when I've had my cleaning lesson at five o'clock I'm coming to get you again. So pack yourself some knickers this time."

"What are you going to do?" Sarah asked as she got reluctantly to her feet.

"Well, it's the right weather for it so I think I may just go for a walk." He exchanged a lazy kiss with his wife and watched her go back across the road.

"How far do you want to walk?" Kathy asked.

He gave her a smile. "Further than you would want to go. So if you two want to be excused too, I won't mind. I think I may just head north up the coast path, leave you two and my half-decent shoes at the farmhouse then carry on and see where it goes."

"If you had all day it would take you to Lowestoft in the end," Alison told him. "There's a local campaign going on to get the path open all along the coast from Lowestoft to the Thames. Do you like walking then?"

"It's what I used to do before these two distracted me. I spend my working life sitting on my backside going all over the world so when I had time at home I'd pack a rucksack and just go walking. Stayed in cheap accommodation if I found any, never booked anything, or else just slept out in the open." He smiled as though at a distant memory. "I suppose on a good day I'd clock up thirty miles or so. Always been an ambition of mine to walk a thousand miles in one month but haven't managed it yet. One year I will."

Another riddle was explained. "No wonder you walk so fast," Kathy remarked. "And keep so fit. But is it sensible to go off without your shoes?"

"I always walk barefoot if I can, especially if I'm on one of the old tracks. I like to feel the history of it as well as look at the scenery."

Kathy knew what he meant. "Well, don't let us stop you if that's what you want to do. Personally I think I'm going back to the farmhouse and as we can't play music I'm going to dig out some knitting. Just don't cut your feet to bits."

"Oh, they'll cope. They have for years."

"Are you wearing your watch?" Jean-Guy checked with Piers.

"Yes, why?"

"Today I am the sensible one so I will tell you to be home in time for tea at four."

"And," Kathy told him perfectly seriously, "you have to bring me back a piece of sea glass, a stone with a hole in it and a seagull feather."

"Hmm, for some kind of weird Satanic ritual no doubt?"

"Something like that. Go on, go and be barefoot and feckless. You've earned it."

They returned to Earl's Court on the Monday afternoon all feeling refreshed and thankful for their time away but glad to be able to shower and change their clothes at last. Clean and a little calmer now work was beckoning them all tomorrow they sat at the kitchen table eating the chicken and rice Piers had made for them. The other two had noticed that his culinary style often had Caribbean or Chinese influences to it, Jean-Guy was definitely more European and Kathy was very English and liked to cook roasts. So between them they tended to manage a fairly well-balanced rota of meals.

Piers had already taken the nose ring out and slotted in the hidden retainer although he wasn't sure he still needed it and the other two thought he was rather quiet at the supper table.

"You OK?" Kathy checked. "Missing Sarah?"

He smiled. "And that brood of kids of ours. No, I was just thinking tomorrow is going to be my first flight since that film came out. Same for Mick so far as I know."

"Is that going to be a problem?" Kathy asked.

"I have a bad feeling that Dacre is going to do something very embarrassing to the pair of us, that's all."

"Nothing more than you deserve," Jean-Guy said and almost laughed at the thought of it. "Right, I shall wash up tomorrow as I have a free day so let us go and make music. What would you all like to play?"

"Something we haven't done before," Kathy decided. "Let's just have a few last hours of fecklessness before we all have to take our metaphorical nose rings out and behave ourselves again. Anything come back from Emma's we haven't looked at?"

"There's the Tchaikovsky," Jean-Guy remembered. "We've been putting that one off as it's so long and not the easiest in the world to play."

The other two looked at each other. "Tchaikovsky it is then," Kathy agreed.

Kathy wasn't really surprised when Piers got back home quite late after his first flight since the film premiere.

"How did it go?" she asked and gave him his mug of tea. "Did Dacre get you and Mick?"

"He did. Jean-Guy gone for his gig?"

"Yes, should be back any minute. Come on, what did he do?"

Piers took a couple of mouthfuls of tea and had to smile. He took a black feather out of the breast pocket of his shirt and gave it to her. "I thought I'd get in his good books and took him in another bottle of single malt since he said he liked the last one so much. And the sod let me think I'd got away with it.

He'd stuck up a film poster in the rest area and written slightly rude things on it but Mick and I could cope with that. Then in the briefing he gave Mick a trophy he'd made out of toilet roll tubes to look something like an Oscar."

Kathy could well imagine that little ceremony taking place and smiled too. "So far so good, and by this time you're getting really worried?"

"Just a bit. No, he waited until we were crossing the passenger lounge. He let me and Mick walk on ahead then a bit too loudly asked me if I'd checked the weather forecast for the flight. So I said 'yes' and he asked if I'd made sure there wasn't any snow. By this time all the passengers were looking at us clearly thinking they were about to be piloted by a pair of lunatics."

Kathy really wanted to laugh now. "At what point did he ask if the plane was broken?"

"Oh, he's not going to scare the passengers, even he wouldn't go that far. No he just asks the nearest passengers if they've seen the film. Which, unfortunately for me and Mick they had so that was us well and truly identified."

"Well, that's not so bad."

"No, but just as I thought that was going to be it, the bastard stops and looks as though he's picking something up from the floor and in front of all the passengers and crew gives me that feather and says with his innocent face on: 'I think you've dropped something. Or are you moulting?'."

"Classic!" Kathy hooted. "How did you get out of that one?"

"Not very well. Told him I'd been cleaning out the parrot's cage. But he was ready for that and said I must have got over my allergy then as my eyes weren't red any more."

"Met your match there. Did anyone say anything?"

"Only one lady passenger who asked me if I'd got any tattoos. So I lied and said 'no' then did my Wing Commander bit as you call it and told Dacre and Mick we had to be getting on or we'd lose our flight path."

"Mean. You could have let Dacre have his fun."

"He had his fun for the next four hours don't you worry. But at least it meant I could warn him off going public before he got into trouble with Annette's legal team and fortunately he took the hint. But I was still glad to get rid of him and go and crash out in my room at the hotel."

"No Kerryanne this time?"

Piers put his mug in the sink. "No, not this time. I don't expect to see much of her now she's bled me for a novel plot. Where is Jean-Guy playing tonight?"

Kathy looked at the calendar. "Queen Elizabeth Hall. Why?"

"No reason. Anyway, I'm off to bed now. Got to turn the pager on at midday."

"Didn't think you were on-call tomorrow."

He laughed without humour. "Oh, I've been well and truly caught now. Apparently I'm going to be called in to go … to somewhere." He stopped. "Sorry, can't say. But I'm sure you can work it out. My on-call shifts have now been extended so basically that sodding pager is permanently switched on." He turned and looked out of the kitchen window to the garden now lit only by the street lights and Kathy had never heard him sound so bitter. "It seems I'm now very useful as although those in the game check the passengers arriving if they're a bit suspicious, nobody ever thinks to check the crew. And I can expect to be called in for quite a lot of safety pilot work to take me to where they want me to be without exceeding my flying hours."

"I'm sorry."

"So am I. But as soon as our trip to Prague is over and done with then that's it. I'm out. I'll have played to their rules and done what they wanted for quite long enough."

"Just look after yourself."

He kissed her cheek as he went to the stairs. "Nah, I'll let you do that. Good night."

By the end of June the story of Speedbird 446 had had its US premiere and all the stars and crew turned out again as they had been either told or paid to do, as did the author, and the film again received critical acclaim before it was released nationwide.

All Kathy and Jean-Guy knew was that the now very well-known Captain B seemed to be in increasingly foul moods as the summer wore on and they began to be genuinely worried that he wouldn't be able to make their wedding. If he wasn't working, he had the media hounding him for interviews and it got to the point where there was a small gathering of press outside the Earl's Court house one morning. They were out of luck as the celebrated pilot was away on a long-haul and his two lodgers were in Suffolk so it was the neighbours who called the police who moved the half-dozen or so people on and told them not to come back.

Jean-Guy had booked the register office for ten o'clock in the morning of the first of August and he and Kathy had had several phone conversations with Gisela about the handfasting. Their biggest problem was who to ask to represent the four elements at the ceremony as they didn't think they knew enough people willing to do it. Piers had been an obvious choice, and Danny had agreed a bit more reluctantly. Not sure who else to ask, Kathy approached Emma and Sarah. She wasn't surprised that Sarah wanted nothing to do with anything so pagan but she told her mother, who spread it round the village, and the consequence was that Daisy Hollinger got in touch and said she'd be more than happy to be one of the four if there was still a vacancy. Kathy was even more delighted when Emma said she'd never done anything like it in her life but she would give it a go, even it did mean she'd have to bring husband, toddlers and baby to the farmhouse as she felt she had left them out of things a bit too much recently.

"Our wedding party is growing," Kathy remarked to Jean-Guy as she checked the calendar in the kitchen and realised she was going to be getting married in slightly less than three weeks. "Why do I even look at this thing? We never know where he is these days and I think half the time he doesn't either. Can you actually remember the last time we sat down as a trio and played music?"

"I think we've played together maybe twice since your sister's wedding."

They paused and listened to what sounded like the Aston Martin being lined up to back into the car port.

Kathy looked at the calendar again. "Can't be. According to this he should be on a scheduled Concorde run."

So they listened in case one of the neighbours had got a new car but unmistakeably the Aston was backed into their car port and Kathy flung the side door open with perfect timing just as Piers had got his key out.

"What the hell happened to you?" she shrieked.

To her profound relief he gave her a smile. "Bought myself a cup of tea in the coffee shop. It was a bit hot."

"Well, we're happy to see you but please go and have a shower and get that disgusting uniform packed up for the laundry service."

Jean-Guy really wanted to laugh. "You look like something out of a zombie apocalypse film. But I'm guessing it's not funny."

"Not really," Piers admitted as he shut the door behind himself. "Didn't think it was going to be quite so dramatic. In fact, I thought I was all healed as I'd had the tea and it hadn't even hurt, which was a bit annoying. So I just resigned myself to another day in the office, walked into the briefing room and started dribbling blood everywhere with no warning whatsoever. Ambulance got called, I asked to be taken to Charing Cross to see my specialist and I've spent the day there seeing my usual consultant once A and E had done with me. It took them three hours to stop the bleeding and it's still too damaged to get the endoscope down. Dacre was great again and just told everyone it looked like a stomach ulcer then showed the paramedics the tag so they knew what they were dealing with. So I got carted off, they called in the standby pilot and the flight was away pretty much on time."

"So how long have we got you for?" Kathy asked, thinking it was just like him to be concerned about what had happened to the flight he had been responsible for. "We're off to Suffolk tomorrow for a while as we don't have many bookings between now and the wedding."

Piers sat at the table and tried to refocus his eyes, feeling suddenly exhausted now he was safely home. "They wanted to keep me in for a transfusion as I'd lost so much blood but I refused. So, yes, at least a week then I've got to have the endoscope again and then the odds are I'll be cleared to go back to work."

"Unless you drink another cup of tea," Jean-Guy commented wryly. "Seems to me you now have the perfect get-out whenever you want it."

Piers pulled a face. "Emergency use only, as they say. It was all just getting to be too much. Couldn't cope." He stood up and promptly sat down again. "Oh shit. Sorry, don't feel too good. Or are we really having an earthquake and the floor's moving?"

Kathy sat next to him. "Just how sick were you trying to make yourself?" she asked.

He knew what she meant. "Not this bad and certainly not terminal. Give me a few minutes and I'll make it into the shower."

"Use the one down here," she told him. "At least that way you won't have to try and climb in and out of a bath."

"I'll go and get your towel for you," Jean-Guy offered. "Do you have any pyjamas to put on?" He saw the filthy look the other man gave him. "I'll take that as a 'no'. So I will find your robe. Can't have you wandering round the house naked in front of Kathy."

"Oh, I don't know," she remarked. "Are you allowed to eat anything?" she asked the man at the table.

"Water only for twenty four hours to keep the acids diluted then see how it goes. I'll be up half the night peeing at this rate."

Jean-Guy came back with the towel and the robe. "Come on, you. Let's get you in the shower. I'm sure you'll feel better for it." The two of them got Piers into the wet room where he just sat on the shower chair with his eyes closed and looked as though he was about to be sick. Jean-Guy firmly slid the door shut in Kathy's face. "Go and phone the Prof and tell him there'll be three of us coming tomorrow."

As she went back to the stairs she just heard Jean-Guy's remark of, "Well, your uniform is in such a mess I may as well hose you down with your clothes on."

She was smiling as she dialled the number for the farmhouse but she wasn't surprised that the Prof already knew what had happened. He had also guessed it was deliberate and he wasn't best pleased.

"How bad is it?" was his sharp question almost before he and Kathy had exchanged greetings on the phone.

"He'll be fine. Just got to take it easy for a few days. So we'll bring him with us tomorrow."

"Good. Why the hell did he do it?"

Kathy shrugged even though the Prof couldn't see her. "He just said he couldn't face another day at work. Your lot have been sending him all over the world these last few weeks. And I don't care how useful he is. He won't be any use at all if you drive him to kill himself."

"I told them not to push him so hard. He is damn good at it and so many agencies are willing to pay what he charges now. The mercenary streak in our handsome pilot is getting very strong now. But he will get a cut in his wages as I have come partly out of retirement and I will help his handler for a while to make sure this doesn't happen again."

"So does that mean he's off the hook with your lot now?

"Sadly not. But they really do still need him to do one very simple little job while you are all in Prague."

"We're giving concerts and Jean-Guy and I fully intend to treat it as a bit of a honeymoon so don't you dare make him work while he's out there."

"One simple job while you two are more honeymooning than playing."

Kathy could feel she was getting more and more protective of the vulnerable man who had risked bleeding to death because he couldn't cope. "No."

There was a pause such as she had never known before when talking to the Professor.

"What do you mean, 'no'?"

"I mean what I said. Don't you dare. If it's that important I'll do it for him."

There was a definite note of pride in the Professor's voice. "You'd do that for him?"

"I'd do it for him, for you, for Jean-Guy, for Emma. I'm a violinist from Wimbledon. Who'd look twice at me? And if it's that simple a job then why can't I do it?"

"Why indeed," the Professor mused. "We'll talk more when you're all here. I have some calls to make now. But I'm pleased to hear he's not too bad. I'll see you all tomorrow. I must admit I wondered why Audrey has been so odd today."

Kathy put the receiver back on the phone and looked unseeingly at the baby grand piano that hadn't been played for a while. She felt oddly calm, not the slightest bit scared that she was probably about to set out on a totally unknown path. Without thinking she went down the stairs and into the shower room.

Jean-Guy managed to block her view of a very wet Piers who was at least undressed and upright with his back to her, hanging on to one of the grab rails that were still in the wet room. "Whoa," he cautioned her. "Give the poor guy a bit of privacy."

"Sorry," she said genuinely. "Not thinking. But I may have just done something a bit foolish."

"More foolish than charging in here?" Jean-Guy asked.

"Um, yes. The Prof said there was a little job for Piers to do in Prague so I said I'd do it instead. But the powers-that-be may not let me so I'm not going to worry about it. I'm guessing it's tea for two and water for one, then?" She turned to go but couldn't help herself. She half turned back for another look. "Nice butt, by the way."

"Out!" the other two shouted at her.

Kathy drove the Land Rover to Suffolk the next morning with Jean-Guy beside her as he so often was but this time their third was travelling with them sitting quietly on the back seat, not saying much. He hadn't been at all pleased to learn the Professor was going to be working with his handler as it had made him realise he would always be useful working as a courier while he could pass in and out of airports without the scrutiny the passengers had and could then legitimately disappear into the crew areas and other restricted zones where nobody could follow him. His hope had been that it would all go away once the tours of Eastern Europe were over and done with and he found it hard to watch that hope fade away.

But for a while it was like old times. They arrived at the farmhouse in time for lunch, Audrey hung herself round Piers' neck and refused to get off even when the people all sat to eat. Kathy was not the only one relieved to see that Piers was able to eat some lunch very slowly and carefully without any mishaps and then in the afternoon they finally got back to making music. They started with the last movement of the Smetana which they all loved so much and found it a good warm-up piece then, to the surprise of the Prof, who was listening from his study as he so often did, they then settled to do some serious work on the Henze *Kammersonate* which, so far as he knew, they hadn't even looked at for a few years.

He wandered in to listen as he usually did and quietly turned the pages of the piano score but this time the pianist was well able to cope and it was hard to remember how he had struggled with it when they had first tried it just over three years ago. It was more modern than their usual repertoire and there was some discussion afterwards about whether or not they would use it in a concert. Nobody wanted to say out loud that until one of their working lives calmed down a lot their trio wouldn't be giving any concerts at all.

Piers made his excuses soon after the evening meal and went to bed early with Audrey following him up the stairs as she always did, leaving the other three to sit in the kitchen drinking coffee and talking about what was going to happen to them all in the next few months. The Prof was quite well aware that Piers was still hopeful that once the Trio had been to Prague he wouldn't be told to carry on with the unwelcome extra duties as he would have fulfilled his side of the deal that allowed him to travel. Kathy and Jean-Guy weren't surprised to learn that if their third did back out of the arrangement, it would almost certainly mean that he could have problems travelling anywhere. As the Professor pointed out, the Americans could get very spiteful as he had been doing quite a lot of work for the CIA and refuse him the visa he needed just to leave the airport when he was taking Concorde in and out of New York.

"It's a dirty business," he warned Kathy. "And much as I admire your courage in offering to help out, I would very strongly advise you don't."

"And so would I," Jean-Guy put in. "He has years of training behind him. You have nothing to help you."

"Why don't we wait and see where we're all at when it's time to go to Prague?" she suggested calmly. "Who knows, maybe I'll be pregnant by then and if I am then I promise you there is no way I'm getting tied up in your dirty business as you call it. But what I really must do is get back to my flying lessons. I'm so close now to getting my private licence. I'm not sure which would shock my parents more, getting a pilot's licence or getting pregnant before I get married."

Jean-Guy gave her a loving smile. "Well, I think the licence would be less expected and then you could sew your wings onto your wedding dress."

Kathy had the most ridiculous idea. "Maybe I should have a word with Annette and see if I can't borrow the full-on raven wings for the handfasting. That would be pretty spectacular."

Jean-Guy wasn't convinced. "That would be too scary. Please don't do that."

She kissed his nose. "I wasn't being serious. Especially as I'm half the size of the person who usually wears them. I'd probably trip over them."

It was a beautiful morning the next day and Kathy and the Prof were discussing the programmes for Prague over their breakfast when Piers wandered in to join them with Audrey trotting behind. The first thing Kathy noticed was that he had got the nose ring in again and he looked so much better than he had yesterday.

"Breakfast?" she asked him.

"Yes. Thank you. Then I think I'll go for a walk into the village to see Sarah and the brood."

"More cakes at Alison's? Or do you just want a go on her new coffee machine again?"

He sat at the table and contemplated the boxes of cereals. "That seems like a lifetime ago, but it wasn't more than a few weeks. I never did replace the machine at home, did I?"

"True. But the old one hasn't quite fallen to bits yet. Will you be OK to walk into the village?"

"Oh, yes. I probably didn't lose much more blood than if I'd been to a donor session so I'm sure it's all been replaced now."

"Still hurting?"

"No, not really. Why am I even looking at cereals? I can't take the milk."

The Prof gave a shout of triumph. "Ah-ha! You see, I do listen to what you all tell me," he announced and put a carton of coconut milk on the table.

Fortified with cornflakes, coconut milk and a couple of sliced bananas, Piers didn't say anything when Kathy announced she quite fancied a walk into the village too. Jean-Guy had just about come downstairs by this time and opted to stay in to do some work on the Grieg Sonata which he wanted to perfect for Prague as it had been his grandmother's favourite and he wanted to play it in the city of his birth in her memory.

"Is it my imagination," Piers began after they had walked in silence for a while, "or is Jean-Guy disproportionately excited about this trip to Prague?"

"He can't wait. I think he's realised just how homesick he's been since he ran. Do you ever want to go back to Drumahoe?"

"No I bloody don't. Hang on, that's not right."

The two stopped walking although they were still about a quarter of a mile from the village. Where there had once been a field, full of crops in the summer and bare earth in the winter, there was now a wire fence replacing the old boundary hedge which had been ruthlessly grubbed out and there were huge piles of earth everywhere.

"Oh, my God," Kathy remembered. "That must be the thing all the fuss was about. A developer wants to build a couple of hundred houses on two fields. The locals and the council have been fighting it for years."

"Looks like they lost," Piers commented sadly. "Two hundred houses? Seriously? That'll double the size of the village."

"I think the final consent was for a hundred houses but even so, it's going to alter the place beyond all recognition."

Kathy tucked her hand through his arm and the two walked on more slowly and in silence. She felt oddly as though she wanted to cry.

"It won't be the same, will it?" she mourned. "What with the new power station for the other side of our home and now this lot as well."

"It'll bugger up the village. Hope it doesn't stray any further towards the farmhouse or the Prof won't be happy. How much of the surrounding land does he own?"

"As I remember, the house and the cottages actually come with about two or three acres but it's all overgrown with those rhododendrons so I don't think it'll get too close to him but I can't imagine he's best pleased about it."

"And how hard did the developers try to get him to sell too?"

"Oh, they didn't even waste their time trying. What with the sea on one side, the power station next door almost and all the bird lands round us, he's quite safe from the developers. As he says, not many people will want to live this close to a power station so it'll mostly be more second homes and holiday lets and won't be much worse than having a second caravan park. We're still just that bit too far from the A12 for the Ipswich commuters and there's no talk of reopening the railway to get the London commuters back."

Piers was thoughtful and his greeting to his mother-in-law was a curious, "So what's the deal with the new houses then? Good news for the shop?"

"Truthfully, love, I don't know," she replied. "On the face of it, it'll be good as it should mean more customers. But we're struggling to cope now in the summer as we're so busy and with Sarah at home with the children so much we'll have to take on some staff."

He smiled wryly. "As she told me once, I'm a bit worse than useless and she should have found herself a husband who would just help out in the shop. Maybe that's what I should do," he remarked to Kathy. "You've told me yourself that I've been paid so much by Annette and now the film money that I don't need to fly any more. I can keep both feet on the ground and just be a bloody shopkeeper."

Kathy recognised the unspoken subtext that someone who helped out in a village shop instead of flying all round the world would become worse than useless to the security services. "I can't imagine you not flying," she said truthfully. "I haven't done a thousandth of the hours you've done and already I love it so much I'll happily bankrupt myself so I can keep flying."

He gave her one of his lovely smiles, realising that, yet again, this woman who hadn't chosen him still understood him far better than anyone else. "I know. Somehow I just can't cut those ties yet. Still, only a few more years and I'll be getting retired anyway whether I like it or not. But it's got to the stage where Mick and Dacre have noticed that my on-call work is taking me very close to the legal limits and they keep telling me to back off the hours as I can't need the money that much. I think they're a bit worried I'm going to get taken off our regular lines altogether at this rate."

"Is that likely?"

"No. I've told the bosses I want to cut down the on-call and I think they'll listen to me now."

"Yes, I think they probably will." Kathy could see Sarah's mother was now totally confused so she thought a change of topic was the best thing before any questions were asked. "Do you still sell the cakes the lady in the village makes?" she asked. "It's just that I can buy a whole one of hers and take it home for supper."

"Yes, love. I think most people think like you. The café is lovely for the odd slice but not good value for money if you want a whole cake."

"And did you ever sell all the grape jelly?" she asked next. "We ate up the one at the farmhouse ages ago and someone who goes to the States a lot never thinks to bring any back."

"Yes, over there with the rest of the jams. It seems to sell quite well so we keep a few in stock now."

Piers went off to investigate. "Shall I get some more peanut butter too?"

"May as well," Kathy remarked. "I'm pretty sure you and I have scoffed all that too."

Sarah's mother was pleased to see these two were actually doing some shopping for once. "Something else too," she told them proudly. "Another line our Sarah suggested and is selling better than me and her father thought it would. Over there, next to the boxes of cereal."

They both went to look and one of them remembered it wouldn't be a good idea to swear in front of the mother-in-law. "Where the heck did you find almond and coconut milks?" he asked.

Sarah's mother couldn't keep the smugness out of her voice. "Rang up some other suppliers. We've now got about four different kinds of rice, some tinned vegetables I wouldn't even like to pronounce and extended our herbs and spices range. Sarah and Alison have noticed that we're getting all sorts of different people here now so it makes sense to cater for them while they're in the caravans too."

"Couple of good businesswomen there," Piers remarked.

"I know. People have always thought Sarah is a bit soft in the head just because she didn't do well at school, but she's not in the slightest."

"I've never thought that," Piers said defensively while Kathy was thinking that she was one of the guilty ones. In their younger days, she and Emma had often privately poked fun at Sarah for being the stupid, fat shop girl and now she felt really ashamed.

"No, you haven't," the delighted mother agreed. "I don't know why you haven't with all your brains and your fancy job, but you never have.

Anyway, if you give me your shopping I'll get it all boxed up for you and you can pay for it when you've been next door."

The house next door was unusually quiet when the two called out and stepped into the hall. First out to greet them was Dunlaith, toddling precariously along and looking more like her father every day. She let out a delighted bellow that brought the rest of them out. The boys were more-or-less upright although Iarlaith still preferred to crawl as he found it so much quicker and to Kathy's great delight, within a few seconds the father of the brood had all five either in his arms or trying to climb his legs. The two girls had their arms round his neck and Caolan, with a bit of help from Kathy, was clinging on to his father's back just for that short walk along the hall to the back room where the children's mother was tidying up after a messy session with a lot of toys.

Sarah looked up as the others came into the room and couldn't help but smile to see the dashing Concorde pilot so encumbered with his offspring. She remembered the first time she had ever seen him when he had come into the shop with Kathy and they had both been bundled up against the bitter February cold back in 1981. Now here he was, three and half years and eight children later and still in the village. She would never have thought it.

"You've lost some," Kathy remarked, looking round the back room.

"The triplets are nearly old enough for nursery school now so they're on a trial session this morning. If all goes well then they'll be going there three mornings a week in the autumn now they're two and a half and once they're three in the new year they can go all five mornings. Building up to full-time ready to start school in another couple of years."

"You mean those smelly bundles that used to be all over the floor are getting ready to start school?" Piers asked. "Jeez, that makes me feel old." He sat on the sofa where all that time ago Sarah had first shouted at him for having a tattoo, and five children swarmed all over him, yelling and shrieking with delight.

Kathy suddenly felt her own childlessness as a physical ache inside her and sat next to him hoping the pain would pass.

"You OK, Piglet?" came the soft remark.

She smiled as Eachann and Caolan decided she was just as comfortable to sit on and for a few moments she allowed herself the luxury of cuddling a child and inhaling the scent of him. "Yes. Kind of wishing it could be my turn."

"It will be. Did you get yourself a test?"

She nodded and tried not to cry. "Yes. It was negative as I suspected it would be. It's just me getting fat."

"Funny, I would have betted my pay packet on it." He gave her just a small hug of consolation. "I'm sorry."

"I think I am. It would have been quite fun to have a baby less than nine months after I'd got married and then told my mother. But at the rate I'm going Gayle will beat me to it."

"Do you suppose they'll even tell you?" Piers asked kindly. "I seem to remember things didn't end too well at the wedding. Have you even heard from your parents since?"

"Not from them. Thank-you-for-the-gift card from Gayle and Colin but that's all."

"And nothing from the ex?" There was no reply. "Piglet?"

She hugged Eachann close to her chest. "He sent a postcard," she whispered. "I threw it away."

She heard his sharp intake of breath. "Just the one card?"

"Don't," she said softly. "Just let it go."

Piers gently disentangled Iarlaith's fingers from his hair. "Your call," was all he said very quietly. "So, mother of my many children, what's all this about you and your family blatantly profiteering from all the newcomers to the village?"

Relieved that the conversation was now on something she could understand, and seeing from the mischief in his eyes that her husband wasn't totally serious, Sarah had to laugh. "Well, wouldn't you? We've got I think eighty six new houses going up so that ought to make a good few more customers for us. Alison and I have been talking about maybe combining her café and the shop into one premises then she can keep open all year."

"But one of the main attractions is that it's right on the beach," Kathy thought out loud. "You can drink your coffee and watch the waves."

"Yes," Sarah agreed. "The main café would stay on the beach but Alison would like a little subsidiary tea room as part of the shop. She could increase her trade during the bad weather and it would mean she could stay open all year. Just keep the beach hut as a summer thing."

"Is there room in your shop?" Piers asked.

"Oh, yes. Well, sort of. We've been talking about having an upstairs tea room which would be nice as it would have a really good atmosphere. We'll move a couple of our private rooms to the attic and use one or two first floor rooms above the shop for the tearoom so people can still see the beach and the sea."

"You'll need a whole new staircase, and a lift for anyone who can't manage stairs and you'll need to think about toilets. It's not going to be a cheap option. How would you fund it?"

Sarah sat on the other side of her husband on the sofa and gave him a delighted kiss. "Now I know why Kathy calls you the sensible one," she laughed again. "It's all been thought about and Alison and I have written a ten-year business plan for the shop and tea room and we're going to go to the bank for finance." She paused and tucked her arms round him. "I'm sorry but I don't know how to say this without being rude. I don't want any financial help from you for the business. You've set up a housekeeping account for me to spend on the kids and I must be honest and say I'm grateful for that even though you didn't have to do it. I'm not using it much yet but if they want piano lessons or something in the future then the money's there but Alison and I will manage the business between us."

"That's not rude at all," he told her. "The other thing that's been bothering me is how the hell are you all going to fit into this place? You can't keep eight kids in two bedrooms for ever."

"I've been talking about this with Mum and Dad. Well, Mum mostly as it's her house. We're moving up into the attics of the house as well as the shop. We reckon we can get three middle-size bedrooms and a bathroom up there so what with the five we've got already that will give us plenty of rooms. So if you want to put a bit more in the housekeeping account to help with that, that's fine by me as it's for the children. But the business is strictly me and Alison."

"Fine. Send me all the bills for the house conversion work and I'll put the money in the funds."

Sarah looked at him in astonishment. "You don't know how much it'll cost."

His smile was bitter. "And you don't know my net worth. If I look like going broke I'll tell you."

"Funny thing is," Kathy told him, "when I first knew you, you were shopping in Sainsbury's and genuinely worrying about paying the mortgage and the car finance."

"We've come a long way, Piglet. All of us." He smoothed down his eldest son's hair which was as thick and dark as his own and watched it spring back again. "I'm not sure we're any happier for it."

"Well I am!" Sarah and Kathy declared in a rather comic unison.

"Over-ruled, you miserable old goat!" Kathy laughed. "Come on, I'll buy you a coffee at Alison's and if you're lucky she'll let you make it yourself."

As swiftly as his dark mood had come, it was gone again. "You're right. I need to learn to be grateful. Come on then, coffee break. Then we'd better go back or Jean-Guy will be bollocking me again for not being a good enough accompanist."

Bedřich Smetana – *Fantasy on a Bohemian Song* I Sowed Millet *for violin and piano in G minor, JB1:12*

The Professor was as good as his word; Piers' working life settled back more to where it had been and Dacre and Mick were relieved that their regular captain was back with them on their Concorde runs and, just occasionally, didn't have any work at all when he was on-call. The Tuesday Concorde flight on the last day of July had to have a different captain as by that time the more usual Tuesday captain was already in Suffolk trying to stop the bridegroom from having panic attacks.

By the end of the last day of July, the farmhouse was fully occupied and the Prof had promised himself that he would never have another wedding in that house. He had thought it was going to be a nice, simple affair for Kathy and Jean-Guy but then Emma along with Derek and children had arrived. Fortunately the children were young enough to share a room with their parents so that was the large room at the back taken care of. It was when Danny and Gisela also arrived that arrangements got a bit more complicated and the Prof was glad those two had travelled alone and hadn't brought their partners too or some of the guests would have been staying at the pub in the village. As it was, he had to put Gisela with Kathy in her room, give up his own room for the three men to sort out between them as there was really only enough space for two of them, and he moved into the small room at the front which could only accommodate one person.

The guests had decided it wasn't fair for the Prof to be expected to cook an evening meal for eight people and two toddlers, although baby Duska wasn't a problem as Emma was still feeding her youngest herself, so they sent Danny, as he had the fastest car, out for some fish and chips. Emma had named her longed-for daughter after the mother she didn't remember and would ruthlessly correct anyone who tried to pronounce the name the English way. Originally only the baby's grandfather and Jean-Guy had got it right but the others soon learned.

There weren't enough chairs in the kitchen for everyone to sit at the table to eat so Kathy found herself in the sitting room along with Emma, Danny, Jean-Guy and Gisela all eating their food out of its paper wrapping as they had run out of plates too.

Emma finished first and bundled up her wrappings with a sigh of satisfaction. "You know what, considering you only wanted a quiet wedding, unlike me apparently, you've created far more chaos in this house than I ever managed. How are the nerves?"

"Funnily enough, absolutely fine. When I think of the last time…"

"Is that a sensible thing to do?" Emma interrupted.

"Yes," the bride said firmly. "When I think of the last time, I can't believe this is real. There's no white dress, no flowers, no church service and, above all, no parents." She saw that Gisela was now deeply puzzled. "I was engaged once before. Then the day before the wedding I found out just what a total bastard he was and I ran away. I'm only grateful I found out the day before the wedding and not the day after it. But then I was on my own as he'd driven all my friends away, apart from Emma. Now I'm surrounded by all of you and I don't care if it pours with rain all day tomorrow and we have to have the handfasting in the kitchen."

Jean-Guy gave her a cuddle and couldn't believe it was really going to happen at last. "Aren't you forgetting the small matter of the register office in the morning?"

She gave him a kiss and waved a dismissive hand. "Oh, that's just the legal nicety to keep our mothers happy. The real ceremony is when we have all our friends here and the spirits to bless the union of our souls."

"And you have one heck of a lot of spirits in this house," Gisela told her. "It's giving me a headache just being here. How on earth does Piers cope with them all?"

"Knowing him," Danny snorted, "he just told the whole tribe of them to sod off and leave him alone."

Gisela looked at Kathy. "It's his cat, isn't it? She protects him."

"Don't start going all weird on us again," Danny requested. "Save that for tomorrow. Right, I can't eat another chip so I'm off into the garden for a smoke. Want one?"

"OK," Gisela agreed. "As Samuel isn't here to remind me I'm supposed to be giving up." She gathered up all the paper wrappers and the two went off to the kitchen and out into the back garden.

Emma got on with the business of feeding Duska now she had finished her own meal. "No news on the baby front then?"

"Sorry, no," Kathy said regretfully, watching her friend feed her third child and wondering what it must feel like.

Jean-Guy took her hand. "We can go and talk to the doctor sooner if you want to," he told her softly.

Huge blue eyes looked at him and he fell in love with her all over again. "I want to," she whispered. "I really want to."

"But get tomorrow out of the way first, huh?" Emma laughed.

What Kathy was not expecting was for Gisela to be about the loudest snorer she had ever heard. At four o'clock in the morning she gave up all hope of sleep and went downstairs to make herself a cup of tea. She went into the dimly lit kitchen and somehow wasn't surprised to see Piers cradling a mug of tea and quietly looking out of the window into the back garden, where it was almost daylight but the sun hadn't cleared the horizon.

"You too, huh?" she asked him softly.

He smiled but was still watching the garden. "I've heard less noise when taking off in Concorde. How the hell does Samuel sleep with that racket going on?"

Kathy made herself some tea. "Maybe it's not every night. What are you looking at?"

"There's someone in the garden," he replied.

"What?"

"Oh, just some old lady or another. It's quite fascinating. And harmless from the look of it. Some kind of ritual going on. Never seen her before but she seems to know the place."

Kathy joined him and looked too. "Oh, that's Daisy. The one who made our rings. What on earth is she doing?"

"I've been watching her for a while. Saw her come into the garden but she didn't look like a burglar so I just watched. First she seemed to be talking to the tree and then she walked around a bit and drew a circle on the ground with a stick with that old stone seat at one side of it. Then she just kind of started prowling in the circle. And every so often… yup, just like that."

Kathy watched as Daisy stood facing away from the house towards the sea with her legs apart and her arms and face raised skyward. "I worked out she's at least as much of a pagan as you when I saw all the moons and pentangles and stuff in her studio but, you're right; it is kind of fascinating. She's probably sussing the place out ahead of today's ceremony."

"Is she your priestess? I thought that was Gisela."

Kathy looked again at the woman in the garden as she bowed first to the sea in the east, then to the apple tree in the south, then to the house in the west and finally towards the power station in the north. "I think we've been rumbled," she remarked as Daisy looked straight at them and smiled then beckoned them out. "Should we make her a cup of tea?"

"I'll do it. You go and tell her she's trespassing."

"Hmm. Having watched her little ritual I think I'm the one who's trespassing. She takes it black with a spoon of honey." Kathy went out into the garden which felt fresh and cool in that odd light from the early dawn. "Hi, Daisy. Piers is just making you a cup of tea."

"Kathy, happy wedding day. Can't you sleep? I'm not surprised, the spirits are strong today. They're gathering already to celebrate with you. Have I met Piers?"

"No. He's the one you saw at the window with me. Tall bloke. Dark hair and blue eyes. His family never got round to giving up their Pagan faith and he's going to be my air element at the ceremony as he flies aeroplanes for a living."

Daisy looked as though something had suddenly made sense. "Odd, I thought you were at the window alone. He must have been out of sight behind the curtains. I knew I could feel the power of the faith of someone here which is why the spirits are so strong. Is he a priest or a celebrant?"

"Um, no. I mean he keeps the festivals as best he can and he's explained to me about the Wheel of the Year but mostly he keeps his faith to himself as people don't understand it. I don't understand it if I'm honest."

Daisy nodded thoughtfully. "Yes. Most people can't cope with Paganism. They just think it's all about getting naked and dancing round fires. They can't respect our beliefs but we have to respect theirs. Anyway, let's not get too intense on your wedding day. But the spirits of the house must be more settled now there's a believer here."

"So it really is haunted? Sarah is terrified of the place."

"Sarah Strowger? She would feel them too but as a child she always tried to deny her family's past. Her great-great grandmother was one of the most powerful witches in the county and they say the bones of her ancestors are buried beneath this garden. It was Sarah's great grandmother, the daughter of the last witch, who took the family over to Christianity to stop the persecution."

Kathy felt she finally understood the deep connection between Piers and Sarah. "She's Sarah Buchanan now. She and Piers got married just over three years ago. They've had eight children in that time as they first of all had triplets then did even better and produced a set of quins."

"Yes, I'd heard she'd got married a few years ago. How did he break her protection?"

Kathy guessed Daisy wasn't talking about condoms but really wasn't sure what to say.

Piers came wandering out of the house with two mugs of tea and offered one to Daisy. "Black with honey. Or so Piglet tells me. Hope that's right?"

Kathy was used to seeing him ambling about only half dressed and almost didn't notice the tattoos and rings any more but Daisy stared at him for a few moments before taking the tea.

"Yes, perfect, thank you," she said, still looking intently at the raven on his front. She took a welcome sip of the hot drink. "I wasn't expecting such hospitality."

"Saw you arrive, you looked harmless so I left you to it. What were you doing?"

She gave him a hard look. "You, of all people, will know what I was doing. More to the point, what were you doing?"

"Giving up all hope of sleep as we've got someone in there snoring like a jack-hammer." He was not expecting this odd but harmless woman to touch the head of the raven and instinctively stepped back.

"You would have been more than welcome to worship with me," she told him and smiled at the couple in front of her. "You have welcomed Lugh to this place on his day," she said. "Why are you two having a handfasting when you are already bound?"

Piers and Kathy looked at each other. "Pardon?" Kathy asked first. "I'm not marrying Piers. His wife is Sarah, the mother of his eight children."

Daisy looked rather embarrassed. "Oh, sorry. It's just that I can see the bond fusing you and I have never seen one so strong before. But, it makes sense that you have married a witch."

"Did you just call Sarah a witch?" Piers asked defensively.

"Oh, not in that way," Daisy assured him. "But it's only someone like you who would have the strength to let her accept you." She finished her tea and handed back the mug. "Thank you for the refreshment. It'll be a joyous occasion for you today."

"Can I ask you something?" Piers began hesitantly, not wanting to upset the visitor, although he had a feeling he already knew the answer. "Just how much of a priestess are you?"

She smiled then, clearly amused that someone of the faith was unaware of her reputation even though she knew he could sense her skill. "Oh, pretty high, you know."

Piers knew then he had been right, even if he hadn't recognised her personally. "Sorry about this, Piglet, but can I make a suggestion? Why don't you swap Daisy and Gisela over and have Daisy as your priestess and Gisela as your fourth element?"

Kathy looked at the older woman and saw the joy and hope in her eyes. "Would you like to? I don't know what your fees are though."

The smile on Daisy's face seemed to light up the whole garden. "It will be my honour and my privilege. And no fee. It has been a long time since I have had the blessings that I can feel today. But can I ask one thing in return?"

"What?" Kathy asked.

"I would like to take your Lugh into the inner circle with me. Do you have someone else who could stand in for Air?"

"Derek probably would. Sarah said she'd come and babysit anyway while we're outside having the ceremony as he wanted to attend. His wife is my oldest friend Emma and she's going to be the Fire element so he'll already have a good idea of what's involved."

"Perfect. So, Lugh, which name do you go by? No, don't tell me. I did my research into Viola fashions when Annette asked me to design for her. I believe you prefer to be known as Samildánach? And your animals are the raven and the lynx?"

He let her touch the head of the raven this time. "Only when I'm working."

Daisy just smiled again. "What time are you at the register office in the morning?"

"Ten o'clock," Kathy told her. "We won't be there for long and it's only in Woodbridge so we should be back well before eleven. Just in time for a quick coffee then I get my wedding dress on ready for the handfasting at noon. Gisela isn't going to the register office so she'll be here to help you get set up if you'd like her to. She's got all the things she needs and she was going to use that old stone seat for an altar as she reckons it's already in a good place."

Daisy looked at the stone bench that was on the seaward side of the garden and which was always in the way when the grass was cut but it was too heavy to move. "That's because it already is an altar," she told them. "Have you written your words the two of you?"

"Yes, and Gisela's had a look at them and says they're fine."

"Did she ask you to bring the hoop and the wand?"

"She mentioned it, but Jean-Guy wasn't keen."

"Ah. Well, if you want me to be your priestess then I must insist you bring them. I will give you the eternal fastening which your friend Gisela probably wouldn't do and I will bind in the hoop and the wand. Then when your hands are free you can keep the binding with them in it for ever. What are you using for the binding?"

"We've managed to get a silk ribbon. There's a local spinner and weaver that Sarah's mum knows. So we went to see her and she made us a gorgeous yellow sash and her husband made us a hoop and a wand which we weren't expecting at all. I think he said they're made of hawthorn wood. It's almost a shame to tie it all up in knots."

"Oh, yes, I know them well. They're another family who are becoming interested in the old ways." Daisy looked at the sky and the three could see the first tinges of light in the east. "It's going to be quite an occasion. How many people will you have attending?"

"Including you there'll be eight. Sarah and Professor Mihaly don't want to join in so they'll be in the house with all the children. We didn't invite anyone from the village as the Professor doesn't encourage people to come in. But we've said anyone who wants to can listen in from the coast path."

"Good. This is a very sacred place. Has been for many hundreds of years and needs to be respected as such."

"So who was the original Dead Man it's named after?" Piers asked curiously.

"Anyone and everyone," Daisy told him quite matter-of-factly. "Up until the eighteenth century this was marshland and anyone who lived on it was at extreme risk of dying of marsh fever as it used to be known. A kind of indigenous malaria." She took their hands in farewell. "But it's a happy place now. Blessed be."

Kathy and Piers watched her slip through the gap in the hedge onto the coast path.

"That is one seriously weird lady," Piers announced.

"Says the man with the Pagan tattoos all over him."

"Piglet, shut up or I won't give you your wedding gift."

Kathy was quite touched. "You got us a gift? That's so sweet. We weren't expecting anything. Thank you."

"Yours is a bit corny, so I'm sorry about that. But I ran out of inspiration after I'd sorted out the one for Jean-Guy." He had to smile to see her happy, smiling face looking up at him. "No, you wait. I'm not embarrassing myself in front of everyone so you may not get it until tomorrow. By the way, how are the flying lessons coming on? You never mention them and I don't like to ask too often. You must have used up the original ten by now."

She laughingly tapped his nose. "Now it's your turn to wait." She turned to look across the garden as they reached the doorway. "Going to be a beautiful day," she remarked and sighed happily. "Blessed be, as Daisy said earlier."

Kathy and Piers didn't bother going back to their beds after their meeting with Daisy in the garden but took themselves off to the sitting room where the Prof found them a few hours later with Kathy fast asleep on the sofa and Piers and Audrey in an armchair with man and cat also contentedly asleep. Smiling as though at two innocent children, the Prof went off to the kitchen where the clatter of the kettle on the Aga was enough to wake up the one with the cat.

Gisela was also an early riser and she joined Kathy in the living room with a cheerful, "Sorry, was I snoring again last night? I always know when I've been doing it at home as I find Samuel on the sofa in the morning too."

"I'm actually glad you were," Kathy told her sleepily and tried to remember that this was her wedding day. "I had a strange encounter with a priestess in the garden. Or maybe I dreamed it. Is Piers awake?"

"Yes, I can hear him in the kitchen with the Prof. One of the lads has gone into the bathroom too. So either Danny or Jean-Guy is on the move."

Kathy clambered stiffly off the sofa. "Come with me," she invited. In the kitchen the Prof was making a huge pan of porridge and Piers was trying to find enough bowls and spoons to go round so nobody had to try and eat porridge off a plate using a fork.

"Happy wedding day," the Prof greeted her. "Not sure why I found you asleep in the same room as someone who is not your bridegroom but you were both spark out."

"We had a bit of an odd encounter with a priestess in the garden," Kathy started but Piers wouldn't catch her eye and back her up. She saw the look of annoyance on the Prof's face. "It was Daisy Hollinger. I guess she's come up to the village ready for her part in the ceremony. Thing is, Gisela, would you mind if Daisy took over as celebrant and you took over as her element?"

"You have got Daisy Hollinger as your priestess? How the hell did you manage that? I know you told me you'd got your ring-maker to be an element but if you'd told me it was her I'd have handed over the ceremony to her there and then. You do know she's pretty much the leading authority on all things pagan in this country, don't you?"

"Actually, no, I didn't. So I'm guessing you won't mind helping her get things set up this morning while we're at the register office?"

"You kidding? People pay fortunes to work with her. What about the actual ceremony? She usually works alone."

"Ah. Today is Lughnasadh and she has invited Lugh himself to join her in the inner circle."

Gisela looked straight at the man who had triumphantly tracked down just enough crockery. "You?"

"Yes," he admitted, not sounding best pleased. "Me. How the hell do I let myself get talked into these things?"

"What have you agreed to now?" came Jean-Guy's voice from the doorway and he exchanged a kiss with his bride. "Are we supposed to be seeing each other this morning?"

"Bit hard to avoid each other with the house so crowded," Kathy laughed. She looked at Piers. "Can I have my present now?"

"Oh, alright then," he said grumpily. "Gisela, would you mind looking after the porridge for a few minutes while I take these into the sitting room?"

"No problem. Just don't blame me if it goes lumpy."

Kathy and Jean-Guy were a bit surprised that the Prof was being included in this but he had a quiet smile on his face so they guessed he had long been privy to whatever the secret was.

On top of the piano were a small tortoiseshell cat and two gift-wrapped parcels. Looking rather sheepish, Piers handed the smaller one to Kathy and the larger, flat one to Jean-Guy. "Open yours first," he told Kathy. "It's the boring one. Sorry."

Baffled, Kathy opened the parcel and was not expecting to see a pair of knitted mittens. She knew the design was Latvian and the colours were a cheerful mix of yellow and white. "They're beautiful," she told him, thinking it a very odd wedding gift.

Jean-Guy laughed. "It is a Baltic tradition to knit wedding mittens. Who told you that one?"

"Kerryanne. She helped with the design."

Kathy suddenly worked it out. She raised astonished eyes to Piers and could have sworn he was blushing. "Did you…?"

"Yes," he confessed. "I made them. I did ask Kerryanne if she'd knit them but she made me do it instead."

"Oh, my God!" Kathy shrieked and gave him a hug. "That is so not boring at all. I can't wait for it to be winter now." She put the mittens on anyway and could feel the comforting warmth already. "I thought you and Kerryanne had had a falling out?"

"Not personally," he smiled. "Just professionally. And physically, if you get my meaning."

Kathy was somehow pleased to hear that. "Go on, Jean-Guy, your turn."

Jean-Guy opened his parcel and looked in deep puzzlement at some music. He wasn't quite sure why he had been given a copy of Smetana's arrangement of the Bohemian Song which was such a well-known violin piece.

"Look inside,'" the Prof advised him.

So Jean-Guy looked and inside the piano score, beautifully written by hand, was the violin part arranged for the cello.

"It took me weeks," Piers admitted. "But, don't worry. The Prof has checked it and he says it's fine. I asked Sarah to write it out neatly for you to save you from having to read my scribble."

Jean-Guy shook his head and the other three could tell he was getting quite emotional. "You have so much money you could have bought us stupid, extravagant things we didn't need. But you have chosen with your heart and ... and I don't know what to say. You have given me a beautiful Czech work in time for me to learn it to play in Prague. I can take it home. Thank you."

Piers had got used to the way Jean-Guy would award him spontaneous hugs and had learned not to mind too much. "You're very welcome," he just about managed to say before the other man was squashing the air out of his lungs.

"One from me too," Kathy declared and joined in.

"Remind me," came Danny's amused voice from the doorway. "Which two out of you three are getting married today? Gisela says please come and eat the porridge or she's afraid the cats are going to get it all."

The Registrar had been expecting more people to turn up for his ten o'clock but there were only six people in the waiting room. He called in the bride and groom and was even more surprised to hear that they only wanted the bare legal minimum. They hadn't prepared any vows and there weren't any rings to be exchanged.

Kathy had never thought she would enjoy a register office wedding. For a long while she had thought she would never trust a man enough to marry him but that beautiful August morning she did. She knew that her past would always be there, the 'hunting' with Emma, the brutality of the treatment by her ex, the wild, crazy fling with Danny as she learned to move on with her life. That morning it never even crossed her mind that maybe she was marrying the wrong man. This was her lovely Jean-Guy. The man who had taken her hand and led her further along the path to recovery. He would probably never offer wild excitement, would certainly never take her flying above the clouds. But he was the one she loved more than all the others. Their wedding wasn't the end of her journey, it wasn't the beginning. But it was a huge stride as she walked the path beside him.

The ceremony took about ten minutes, the witnesses were Emma Mihaly and Piers Buchanan and the only other people in attendance were the Prof and Sarah. Kathy hadn't planned on taking more than the two witnesses but both the Prof and Sarah had asked to be excused the pagan handfasting, so Kathy had talked with Jean-Guy and they had agreed it was only fair that they should be invited to attend the civil ceremony instead. After that was over, Kathy put the certificates in her bag, Emma took a few photographs as she felt it wasn't right not to mark the occasion somehow; then Kathy drove her new husband and her oldest friend back to the farmhouse leaving Piers to bring his wife and the Prof back in the Aston Martin.

"So that's it?" Emma asked incredulously, hardly able to believe her oldest friend had got married in her Laura Ashley dress that was a few years old now and her groom wasn't even in a suit. "That's all you have to do to be legally married in this country?"

"That's it," Kathy laughed. "Total cost less than twenty quid and that was for the licence. And it's just as legal as your extravaganza that cost hundreds."

"Ah-ha!" Emma exclaimed. "But what is this afternoon's ceilidh costing you?"

"Not as much as you would think," Kathy told her. She looked across at the man in the passenger seat. "You OK?"

"I'm really not sure," he admitted. "I don't feel any different. I have waited years to be able to marry you and now I feel nothing."

"Oh, you will," Kathy promised him darkly. "Trust me, you will."

"Kath! You tart!" Emma laughed.

Kathy hoped Jean-Guy was feeling a lot more than nothing as he stood next to her in the outer circle in the garden that afternoon. She had changed her floral dress for the beautiful blue from Annette, and Jean-Guy looked equally resplendent in one of House of Viola's suits in that shade of dark red that looked as good on him as it did on Piers. Jean-Guy had unquestioningly accepted that the woman who was now his wife was open to the ideas of spirits and souls far more than he was with his atheist, communist upbringing. Neither of them was quite sure there was supposed to be a small tortoiseshell cat in the inner circle but there Audrey was, keeping her usual close eye on things and there were at least five other cats in the outer circle too. Kathy had to admit that Daisy looked impressive with her long grey hair and her long grey robe with its pagan priestess regalia, and Piers seemed quite resigned to the fact he was going to be spending a large part of the afternoon with his tattoos on display and at extreme risk of sunburn. He wasn't wearing his caduceus tag but instead had a pendant on a short leather thong and it wasn't until he led the bride and groom into the inner circle that Kathy noticed the pendant was a complicated knot that had what looked like tiny bones and black feathers woven into it. He had matching bands on his wrists, and smelled slightly of coconuts from all the sunblock he had put on his pale Irish skin.

Kathy felt the change in atmosphere as Daisy and Piers called in the spirits of the elements and the sudden silence in the garden pressed on her ears like a physical force. Finally Daisy called on the goddess and Piers called on the god and then the embodiment of Samildánach brought the bride and groom to the centre of the circle and there they made their vows they had chosen so carefully and written from the heart, pledging their lives and souls to each other for eternity. Daisy had placed the rose gold rings she had made on the altar and first she picked up the one for Kathy and invited the goddess to guide and bless the couple. The ring was passed to Jean-Guy and he repeated his pledge of love to his bride as he put it on her finger. The ring felt warm as it had been in the sun for a while and Kathy felt so much emotion in her, she nearly dropped the ring for Jean-Guy when Piers passed it to her. Daisy called on the god to bless the ring for Jean-Guy and Kathy pledged herself to him again in front of all their friends and the spirits and she felt the silent tears on her cheeks.

Kathy thought she couldn't get any more emotional but then Daisy asked Samildánach to bring the left hands of the couple together and it wasn't lost on Kathy that just for a split second the yellow ribbon touched all three of them before Daisy slid the sash between the hands of the couple getting handfasted, and Samildánach stepped away. Daisy spoke to the god and goddess again as she bound the couple's left hands in an intricate figure-of-eight method. Three times she went round with the yellow ribbon which felt oddly warm in the sunshine; once for the goddess, once for the god and once for the eternal love of the couple. She bound in the hoop and the wand they had brought with them and knotted the ribbon both on top of and below their hands. It felt the most natural thing in the world for the priestess to offer them the earth, the feathers and the water to touch and so skilfully skim the candle flame below their hands. Then she led the thanks to the god and the goddess and to the elements and made her final blessings. Daisy gently helped the couple to extract their hands from the ribbon so they were left with an intricately tied sash with the hoop and wand bound in to it for ever and Kathy was sure she felt the breath of the god and goddess as they left their sacred place.

  The garden was suddenly hot in the August sunshine and Kathy was now aware there were birds singing, Sarah had released a swarm of children from the farmhouse which had made the attendant cats scatter, and the Prof had come outside to offer his congratulations to the newlyweds.

  Those who hadn't joined in the ceremony in the garden had put out the food that Alison had prepared as her gift to the couple and it reminded everyone more of a standard wedding as the guests, children and cats all seemed to be all over the kitchen and garden at once although there weren't really that many people there. Kathy wasn't surprised that Piers put a shirt on as soon as he decently could and she really hoped he wouldn't get sunburn, but he was still wearing the pendant, visible above the fastened buttons.

Daisy was the first of the party to leave the farmhouse, more than content with the way the ceremony had gone and feeling very blessed as the Professor had said she was welcome to come and pray in the hallowed garden any time she liked so long as she didn't share the place with anyone else. One priestess he could cope with but he didn't want a whole coven in his garden.

Derek, Emma and their children also left the house early in the afternoon as they were spending the rest of the weekend with one of Derek's old work mates who had retired to a small hamlet on the outskirts of Oxford so it meant they could break the long journey from Suffolk to Somerset. Alison called by in her van at about five o'clock and took away Sarah and the children piled illegally in the back of the van which they all thought was such fun. An hour later Danny and Gisela left in his red Saab to catch the overnight ferry from Harwich and suddenly the old house was quiet again. The four left could hear the clock ticking in the sitting room and there was a cat purring on top of the Aga.

They sat at the kitchen table as they had done so often before, idly chatting over cups of tea as everyone was too full up with Alison's feast to want any more to eat. The Prof and Piers had to smile to themselves to see how the newlyweds kept looking at the shiny new rings on their fingers and then gazing so fondly at each other.

Eventually Piers could stand it no longer. "Please just go upstairs and shag each other witless," he told them. "If you're not back down for some food in a few hours I'll bring you up a tray."

Jean-Guy reluctantly stopped snogging his bride for a few moments. "In a minute," he said. "The last thing I must do on my wedding day, well nearly the last," he admitted with a smile, "is to go into the sitting room and try to play the piece that Samildánach so kindly wrote out for me for his special day."

"Good idea," the Prof approved. "It looks as though Piers has arranged it perfectly well but I am not a cellist and would like to hear it."

"And I suppose you'll want an accompanist?" the arranger asked.

"Of course. Did you alter the piano part much?"

"Had to change the key to make it fit. But I can still read it off the printed score."

"Good, just don't forget and start playing in the wrong key. I shall sight-read, you have been playing it for months transposing in your head as you go, so we should be well matched."

"You cheeky sod. Just because it's your wedding day. What are you going to do, Piglet?"

Kathy looked at the others with her and let in the realisation that she had actually got married both legally and spiritually and now she was sitting at the kitchen table in a strapless dress of the most beautiful midnight blue. "Me? I'm going to take a bath then go to bed wearing nothing but my new mittens. But I'd quite like to hear the new piece too first."

So they went into the sitting room where Jean-Guy got his cello out, Piers and the Prof sat at the piano and Kathy and Audrey settled on the sofa.

"Do you realise your cat gatecrashed my wedding?" Kathy asked Piers as Jean-Guy tuned his cello and got the music ready on his stand.

"Yup. Hope she behaved herself."

"She just sat there watching it all."

"It's what she does best. Watching."

"True. Did Daisy give you that jewellery?"

"What? Oh, yes. Forgotten I was still wearing it. It's a bit macabre as apparently it's real raven bones and feathers in it. She made it years ago and never found anyone to give it to and nobody wanted to buy it. The raven was a bit of road kill she found somewhere and preserved."

"Suits you. Another secret to hide under your uniform?"

"Hmm. Think not. I've already got one thing round my neck most of the time. OK, Jean-Guy, what speed are you going at?"

Jean-Guy clicked a beat with his fingers. "I will count you one bar in, please pay attention."

Kathy and the Prof listened very critically as the cellist so beautifully sight-read the arrangement that had been written for him and had to admit that Piers had made a good job of it. Both were surprised when the cellist came totally unstuck in the cadenza just before the end.

"Seriously?" Jean-Guy asked as he made a hash of it for the third time. "You have given me either an awkward cross-string jump or you are asking me to play stupidly high on the D string."

"Play it on the D and that high note you should be able to hit as a harmonic," the arranger told him.

"I'm sorry. What?"

"D string. Harmonic. You're about the best bloody cellist on the planet, what's your problem?"

"My 'problem' is that I didn't know you knew anything about cellos and harmonics."

"Try it. I'll give you your cue into the cadenza again."

So Jean-Guy worked his way up the D string and with a final flick of the wrist hit the top harmonic perfectly. "How the hell did you work that out?" he asked. "It's not in the violin part."

"Oh, no. the cadenza was written just for you. I've been watching and listening over the years and got to work out what you like playing and what you don't. The Prof had to make some corrections to it, but I think we got there in the end." He glanced at the older man and didn't add that he had found out the Prof had been a bit of an amateur composer himself in his day and had been quite flattered to have been asked for help.

"It's bloody perfect," Jean-Guy declared and ran up the string to the harmonic again. "Even I wouldn't have thought of doing it that way. I would have gone for the cross-string jump. Anyway, once more cadenza to end and then I think that will be enough for one day. At least we should all sleep tonight without Gisela making earthquakes."

"You won't get any sleep," Piers told him. "It's your wedding night."

Jean-Guy looked across to Kathy and saw she was smiling at him as she playfully pulled at the laces on the front of her dress. "Oh, yes," he agreed vaguely. "I suppose it is."

Franz Liszt – *La Campanella for piano solo, No 3 from* Six Grandes Études de Paganini *in G# minor, S. 141*

Kathy was almost disappointed that marriage didn't make the slightest difference to her life. Jean-Guy was still busy with his solo work, she had plenty of ensemble bookings and Piers was happy now he was re-established on his regular Concorde lines and the on-call shifts had become more manageable. As they had done for quite a while they flitted between Earl's Court and Suffolk although Kathy and Jean-Guy were still out on the coast far more frequently than Piers whose work kept him so much in the capital.

Piers found it a bit unsettling these days when he was in the house on his own as he missed the company of the other two but as he turned the calendar over at the beginning of September he realised it was only another ten days and then they were all off to Prague. Thinking it was about time Kathy got her private pilot's licence and wondering if she already had but hadn't told him yet, he went to pick up the post having heard the rattle of the letter box.

He sifted through the usual junk mail, opened his credit card statement only to realise he hadn't actually used the card that month so didn't owe them anything and then he noticed the postcard. It was a standard, touristy photo of Snowdonia and he flipped it over without thinking twice.

My Darling, I am so happy to hear you are finally married. I hope you enjoyed your honeymoon,

I look forward to hearing all about it when we meet. All my love, R

At first he thought it was maybe for the neighbours and had got mixed up, then realised it was addressed to Miss K Fairbanks. So he read it once more and swore softly under his breath. He checked the calendar again and noticed that Kathy was due in Earl's Court tomorrow morning, about two hours before he had to switch his pager on. Calmly resolute he went upstairs to the phone and rang a number that was listed only in his memory.

"Oh, hi," he responded to the pleasant woman's voice that answered the phone after a couple of rings. "I need to arrange an extra rubbish collection."

There was a slight click on the line that told him what he needed to know. "Of course, sir," the lady said perfectly calmly. "Is that general rubbish or recycling?"

Piers hesitated. Now the time had come to flex his new muscles he wasn't sure he could take it to the limits. "Recycling, please," he replied and his voice was quite steady.

Kathy arrived at Earl's Court the next morning expecting to find Piers still in bed as he was due to switch his pager on at mid-day which meant he wouldn't get up until about 11.50. She went in through the car port door and stopped short to see him at the kitchen table with a mug of coffee cooling in front of him.

"Thought you'd still be in bed," she greeted him and took her coat off.

"I need to talk to you," was his curt reply.

Kathy sat at the table with him. "OK, you're in Wing Commander mode now. What's the matter?" She looked as he showed her the message on a postcard but didn't let go of it so she could take it. "Ah."

"Is that all you're going to say?"

"Yes."

He waited silently. Didn't offer to make her a coffee and didn't offer any small talk.

Kathy wasn't sure whether she was more relieved or annoyed that her latest secret had been rumbled. Jean-Guy had been sympathetic and supportive when he had learned what had happened to her, but now it was Piers who was with her and he was far more unpredictable. "They've been arriving ever since Gayle's wedding," was all she was prepared to say until she had judged his temper.

His voice was emotionless and gave nothing away. "Gayle told me he gets your address off your parents as they write to you which is how he followed you around the last time. And I assume it's him who has now started phoning here? I've had two calls recently where as soon as I answer whoever it is hangs up." He looked at her but she wouldn't lift her gaze from the table and he could tell from the way she was sitting so stiffly that she was far from happy she had been found out and that annoyed him although he tried to stay calm. "When were you planning on telling anyone? Like your husband, for instance?" Her only response was an incoherent mumble and calmness was forgotten. "What?"

She now knew that Piers was angry. Probably mostly at Richard for coming back into her life but also with her for not telling them. She was terrified of what Piers might do, fear somehow morphed into anger and she raised her head with her eyes blazing. "I said 'butt out, it's none of your business'."

Piers could sense her fear under that anger and he consciously reined in his own temper rather than let the situation escalate out of control. "I'm sorry, but I disagree. He is sending loosely veiled threats and you haven't said a word so it's just carrying on. Letting him rule you again, as he did all those years ago. Do you want to have to start running again?" He got no reply from the woman at the table with him but he could see the strength of her feelings was making her shake, and he wanted nothing more than to take her in his arms and comfort her. But there were things he had to find out first before he let her relax and believe her nightmare was over. "How many has he sent you since the wedding?"

"I told you, it's nothing to do with you."

"And how long before he's knocking on the door?"

"He won't come here. He's met you and Jean-Guy now. He wouldn't dare."

Piers slapped the card down on the table, refusing to give in to her stubborn temper. "I want to make sure you're safe, not avenge your murder, or worse. Give me his address."

"No."

"Why the hell are you protecting him?"

"I'm not," Kathy finally admitted and the tears started. "I'm protecting you and Jean-Guy. He says he's written a letter and if one or both of you go round there and do anything at all to him, whether you warn him off or stick a knife in him, either of which I can believe you at least are perfectly capable of, then it'll be you under arrest and in prison. Not him."

He gave her a hug then and felt some of the tension leave her body. "Oh, Piglet. Is that what he told you?" He felt her nod against his chest. "Just give me the address and don't tell me you don't know it."

"I don't know it. Not unless he's still in the flat in Hounslow and I doubt that."

Piers realised that somehow this man was still controlling the woman who was now crying softly in his arms. "Doesn't matter. I know people who can find out. And please don't worry about what happens to him next. A gentle warning from the right people will see him off once and for all."

Kathy began to understand how the raven was still protecting her. She felt the comfort of his brief kiss on her temple, and his voice was much softer now. "Thank you."

"Now, if you'll excuse me I'm going to ring the council and then you can give me all the village gossip. Like how did the triplets cope with their first morning at nursery?"

Kathy sniffed a bit. "That's next week, silly. And why are you going to phone the council?"

She saw nothing odd in his reply. "Bin men must have forgotten us. I need to arrange an extra collection. Talking of your ex has reminded me."

She managed a smile. "I wondered why there was still a pile of papers in the car port. But now you really are being silly. You should do it more often."

Two more scheduled Concorde flights and one irritatingly unexpected on-call to Nairobi and the airline captain whose behaviour had been impeccable since the nose-ring incident, much to the mock-chagrin of his regular crew, was released on annual leave again and this time it was common knowledge he was crossing the iron curtain to go to Prague to play some piano music. It hadn't even been Dacre who had rumbled him this time but a passenger on his way to be the guest conductor with the Boston Symphony Orchestra who had recognised the name of the captain when it was given over the PA system as he was in the middle of reading a record review in the music magazine he had bought at the airport. So he had checked with the cabin crew, who had checked with the flight crew and the astonished passengers had heard the delighted howls of laughter from the first officer and the flight engineer as the door to the cockpit had been left open.

It was with a profound sense of relief that Piers parked the Aston in the car port and went into his house knowing the other two were already in Suffolk and he was expected there tomorrow as Jean-Guy wanted to cram in extra practice sessions for their two recitals. He wasn't sure whether to be offended or not. The phone stopped ringing just as he closed the side door and his instinct was to check his pager but it hadn't gone off.

He was half way through a cup of tea when the phone rang again but he managed to race up the stairs and answer it before it stopped.

"Is Kathy there, please?" came the formal, phone voice of Mrs Fairbanks.

Something that wasn't quite excitement began to niggle in his veins. "No, sorry, she's is Suffolk. Do you want me to give her a message? I'll be seeing her tomorrow."

"No, don't worry, thank you. I don't have a number in Suffolk for her so I'd be grateful if you could ask her to ring me as soon as she can." There was a short pause. "I just wanted to let her know that Richard has been badly injured during a burglary at his house."

"Oh, sorry to hear that. How badly is he hurt?"

"They don't know yet," Mrs Fairbanks said abruptly and Piers could tell she was deeply upset. "He's had quite a bad head injury. I wasn't going to tell her but apparently when he first woke up he was confused and thought she'd been with him and had been attacked too."

He let a decent pause elapse as excitement imploded into an odd kind of fear. "Well, I wasn't expecting that," he managed to say and he heard the truth in his voice. "When did it happen?"

Mrs Fairbanks had forgotten just how well-mannered this man was, even if he was Irish. "Yesterday. Gayle's just rung me as Richard's mother has only just told Colin."

"Did they catch the burglars?"

"According to Gayle, the police told Richard's mother that the attackers caught him in his hallway when he'd just got home late at night after he'd been out for the evening. They think he must have disturbed them as all they took was his wallet and his house keys."

He kept his voice politely sympathetic. "Sounds bad. Anything else missing?"

It never occurred to Mrs Fairbanks that this man was being anything other than genuinely polite and wanted to know what had happened so he could explain it to Kathy. "No, but Colin's had to see about getting the locks changed for him. But they left a postcard with him."

"Seems a funny thing to do. Oh, well, maybe there's some evidence on it."

"I don't know much. Poor Gayle was in quite a state as she and Colin had just been to see him in hospital and said his face is so damaged it was hard to recognise him. But the police told Richard's mother that the postcard didn't have any fingerprints on it except his so they thought it was one he'd bought and the burglars dropped it when they ran. Gayle said it was a picture of Stonehenge which is odd as, so far as they know, Richard's never been there."

Piers could hear that Kathy's mother was getting more and more upset and wasn't surprised when she continued bitterly, "If only Kathy hadn't abandoned him like that he'd have been coming home at a decent hour to be with her and wouldn't have been out at gone midnight. They would have been so happy together. I'll never know why she did what she did. He was so kind and understanding, did everything for her. But, no, she threw it all away on a whim. So they didn't agree on something, I have no doubt it was something quite trivial, and off she went. She should have got over it and married him as she was supposed to do and she wouldn't be living like she is now with that dreadful man."

Piers felt as though he was getting dizzy from the rant coming down the phone at him. He knew he needed to stop this outburst before the distraught Mrs Fairbanks lost control altogether. "Would you like me to tell her for you? She might hear it better face-to-face. I'm sure you're right and she would like to know and then at least Gayle and Colin can tell him that she knows. But please don't expect her to write to him. She may, but she and Jean-Guy are married now so she can't be too friendly with an ex."

To his relief, Mrs Fairbanks calmed down a lot at the sound of his quiet, level tone. The words said in the cadence of the airline captain trained to deal with a crisis no matter what he was feeling inside. He didn't fail to notice that Kathy's mother made no mention of her daughter's marriage, even though she knew it had happened.

"Would you? Thank you."

"Of course. And please do let us know how he gets on?"

"Yes, yes, I will. And thank you again."

Piers hung up the phone then went and played the last few bars of *La Campanella* far too fast on the Broadwood piano. "Thank Christ for efficient bin men," he said to the teddy bear sitting on the sofa.

Piers gave Kathy the news as soon as he saw her while she and Jean-Guy were sitting at the kitchen table with the Prof, just finishing their breakfasts.

She didn't seem particularly upset. Shocked, but not upset. "When?" was all she asked.

"Day before yesterday."

"And where were you?"

"Hey, hold on. I don't like that implication. If you must know I was in New York as nine air crew and several hotel staff can confirm."

"Sorry," she said sounding genuinely contrite. "It's just a bit of a shock, that's all. It's something I used to pray for but now it's happened I'm almost sad."

"You must have loved him once," Piers remarked not unkindly. "I've asked your mother to let us know how he gets on. Not that any of us cares but it may be useful to know where he goes when he's discharged."

"Oh, OK. Well, I'm sure you told me better than my mum would have done. Just give me a minute to get over the shock and we can go and play some music."

"Want any company?" Jean-Guy asked but Kathy shook her head and went off into the sitting room, closing the kitchen door behind her.

"Didn't think she'd be that upset," Jean-Guy commented.

"It's a funny thing, something like that. Yes, it was what she hoped for, maybe even planned in her mind, when she was running from him but you still don't expect it. And in spite of what she says, it would be a good idea for you to be with her." Piers waited until Jean-Guy had left the room and it was just the two of them and a few cats in the kitchen. "Go on then, say it."

The Professor knew what he had to do and was relieved Piers wasn't going to try to get out of this one. "Where were you and what did you do?"

"Anyone who needs to know will find out I was in New York when it happened."

"Good," the Professor approved. "And if they listen to your phone calls?"

"The line's not tapped."

"No, but if they check your calls for the last week?"

"Call from Piglet's mother. Couple from our agent Jane and two calls to the council refuse department as they forgot us last week. And one call about two hours long which was Piglet and Emma gossiping. I'm adding the cost of that to this month's rent."

"And if they cross-check the numbers?"
"They'll all check out."
"No tracks?"
"None at all."

"You're good," the Professor told him bluntly. "We always knew you would be. Now tell me how it made you feel? No, don't look at me as though you don't understand. I know perfectly well that you gave the order for that accident."

Piers remembered the tangle of emotions that had gone through him as he had orchestrated the assault. "It wasn't what I was expecting," he admitted.

The Professor caught just a flick in the other man's eyes and realised this was someone unaware of the power he now had. "What did you say when you rang them?"

"I just asked for an extra bin collection, they secured the line and I gave them the details they needed."

"Did you ask for general waste or recycling?"
"Recycling. I just couldn't go anything more than that."

"I'm guessing you didn't know what the consequences would be?"

"No, not really. I had an idea that it wouldn't be fatal. Was that too naïve of me?"

The genuine humility reassured the cynical Professor. "You have very powerful contacts now. Perhaps this time you didn't realise what would happen but now you do. You don't call the bin men out lightly. Just don't ever abuse that power again."

Piers had never liked being told what to do. He had been shaken enough by what he had started and didn't want a reprimand from the man who knew so much better how these things worked. "I didn't abuse anything. Piglet was under direct threat."

"Kathy is not taking the ridiculous sums of money to do the work you do." The Professor realised he was at risk of mishandling the whole situation as Piers suddenly went on the defensive and his former humility looked more and more like a sham.

"She's happened to be with me on at least two jobs. She was under threat. Would you call that abuse?"

The Professor gave the younger man a cold, hard look but there was no repentance and no remorse in his expression, and he knew the warning had to be given. "Don't ever pull a stunt like that again. And even more don't you ever, and I mean ever, put Kathy in the firing line. Just remember that you make one tiny slip and all those agreements you signed will come down on you like bricks. You're not the innocent you were three years ago when I told you off for staying out with Sarah, you probably have more power now than I do but just remember I can still call in the same request if I think I need to. And I know exactly what the result of that call will be. Yet still I am prepared to do it if I think you are a threat to us. We live in a dirty world." He gave Piers a charming smile. "Well, that is all I have to say on the matter and I am sure you know I was given my instructions to talk to you. Now drink up then go and show Jean-Guy that you're not going to let him down in Prague. Are you with Sarah tonight?"

Piers got to his feet, thankful the incident would now never be spoken of again. "Should I be?"

"Up to you, but your three eldest are starting at nursery in the morning and it may be nice if you are there to walk along with them."

Piers wrinkled his nose. "Nah, I'll just get up early."

Sarah had barely opened the shop the next morning when the bell on the door pinged and her husband came in.

"Well, hi," she greeted him and rushed across so they could have a kiss and a cuddle. "Wasn't sure if I'd see you today."

He hugged her close. "Wouldn't miss it for the world. Your mum sorting them out?"

"They're all still asleep. I actually quite like being able to come and open up again these mornings. If you're not dashing off back to the farmhouse after the walk to school, I'll take you upstairs and show you what's going on. We've got all our planning consents and found ourselves a builder so we hope it'll all be starting fairly soon. Have you had breakfast?"

"Not yet. Word on the street is you've changed your bakery supplier and you get in things like croissants and brioche now. So I thought I'd get here in time to grab a couple. And, sorry, but I will be dashing off. I'll have a proper look when I'm back from Prague."

"We've had to adapt our stock a lot recently. But we're doing nicely out of it."

People stared and tongues wagged in the village when the Buchanan triplets were walked to the nursery school by both their parents. Most of the residents remembered when the mother had been telling everyone the babies were on the way and then in the next breath that the father had gone back to his first wife. It was also widely known that the first wife had subsequently passed away and opinion had been divided as to the exact relationship between husband and first wife. Had it been a compassionate gesture to a dying woman or had it been a deliberate snub to Sarah? Nobody could ever quite decide but there was no doubting that he was back. Not very frequently, but definitely back.

There were a lot of families moving in as the new houses were completed and several mothers on the same school walk couldn't help but stare at the man with at least one giggling triplet hanging on to him at any one time. How the hell, they said to each other, did that frumpy, fat shop girl ever get herself such a looker? So they asked about a bit and upgraded their question to how the hell did that frumpy, fat shop girl ever land herself a drop dead gorgeous Concorde pilot? Not that he looked much like one in his scruffy jeans and with a ring in his nose but his wife and children clearly all adored him and every one of those women who seethed with envy couldn't help but hope that if he had dumped the second wife once, he may be tempted to do it again.

So the envious ones watched as the triplets eagerly shot off into the nursery school without even a backward glance and their parents wandered back through the village with their arms round each other.

When they got to the shop, they exchanged a kiss and Sarah said,

"Well, see you when you get back from Prague then."

And he set off alone along the coast path heading determinedly north walking swiftly on those long legs as though he would go for miles.

Lunch was early that day, then Kathy picked up the keys for the Land Rover and said to Piers, "You coming?"

"I don't know," he said in bafflement. "Am I?"

"Yes, you are," Jean-Guy told him. "I'm not, still cramming in last minute practice and the Prof's not, still cramming in last minute teaching, but you go. It'll do you good because when today's little trip is over you're really going to start work."

"Oh, all right then. Are we going somewhere nice?"

If he had thought about it, Piers was not expecting to be taken to Ipswich Airfield where Kathy was clearly making a lot of new friends and he found himself in for a lot of good-natured ribbing from all those who had seen the film. And there weren't many who hadn't. Pete Finch was still there and he let Piers walk across to the hangars with them even though he wasn't flying that day. He went into the tiny briefing room with Kathy and Pete who then finally decided to let him in on the big secret.

"Well, today's the day. All tests passed and today's flight is scheduled to be just under two hours at the end of which you'll have logged up enough hours to get your private licence."

"Go, Piglet!" Piers almost yelled and picked her up to whirl her round. "Bloody hell, woman, you've put on some weight."

"I'll let you off for that, just this once," Kathy laughed. "Oh, and to stop you getting bored while you're waiting, Pete has said you can borrow a plane too if you like. There are a few available as it's a weekday."

"Uh-huh," he replied without much enthusiasm.

Kathy sighed, took him by the elbow and towed him to the window of the briefing room. "He thought you might like to try that one," she said, pointing out of the window.

He had to laugh. "Which museum did you get that from? It's nearly as old as I am."

"Don't be silly," Kathy told him. "It's just about ten years old. And it's perfectly sound and maintained. Oh, and it's for sale."

Piers shook his head. "You just don't give up do you? I haven't flown a Lear Jet since the late seventies."

"Test flight?" Pete asked with a huge grin on his face. "We're thinking of buying it for the club so either people can train on it or they can hire it."

"Is it a training craft?"

"That one is. Want to give it a spin?"

Piers sighed, suddenly regretful. "Can't. Sorry."

"What do you mean, you can't?" Kathy wanted to know.

"Sorry, Piglet, but I got an on-call to Nairobi and that has put me close to my limit and I really don't think I've got the concentration left. I'll take it up when we're back again if you like."

"What's your total for the week?" Pete asked solicitously.

"At the moment twenty nine hours and forty five minutes flying time so factor in the admin and all the rest of it and I've just come off a seventy-hour week. In fact I'm pretty close to my annual flying limit already which is why I've now got two weeks off. They pushed me up to the limits week after week earlier in the year and now I'm running out of hours."

"Silly bastards," Pete sympathised. "OK, let you off this once. Maybe pop back for half an hour or so next week?"

"Be after Prague now. Go on, Piglet, or you'll lose your flight path. I'll take you up for a spin in the nice jet another day." He gave her a kiss on the cheek. "I'll go and find a book to read in the lounge. Have a good flight."

Kathy and Pete watched him set off back across the airfield with the sure steps of a man in his home environment. "I can't imagine flying so many hours. That's nearly as many in one week as I've done in the whole of my career," she mused. "He must be exhausted."

"That's why there's a very strict limit for commercial pilots," he told her bluntly. "Come on then, let's get you airborne. Still enjoying it?"

"Loving it," she sighed happily.

Later in the afternoon, Jean-Guy and Piers walked Kathy along to Alison's café so they could buy her a celebratory tea and cake but she just took one look at the cakes and suddenly dashed round to the staff toilet where she was violently sick.

"Should I be offended?" Alison half-laughed.

"OK, so she hurls at the sight of cake and she's put on a heck of a lot of weight," Piers thought out loud. "Think there's something she ought to be telling us? Well, you as her husband first."

Kathy came back feeling wretched and saw the way they were looking at her. "What?" She guessed what they were thinking. "Oh, piss off the pair of you. That was my time of the month starting again. Alison, don't suppose you've got any supplies I can use, please? Wasn't expecting it just yet."

With a sympathetic smile Alison handed over a small bag from the handbag she kept under the counter. "Sorry, I knew you were really hoping this was it." Kathy took the bag with miserable thanks and went back to the toilet. "She missed her period last month," Alison told the two men. "You'll never understand."

"How do you know these things?" Jean-Guy asked.

"Because she talks to me and Sarah. We're the only women friends she's got round here. And much as you are the cosiest threesome I think I've ever come across, sometimes there are things you want to keep among your own sex. Now are you ordering anything or are you just cluttering up my café?" She and Jean-Guy watched as a slight scowl crossed Piers' face then he walked off to the toilet too. "What's up with him?"

"Do you know, I have given up wondering about those two. I'll have my usual Americano, please."

Kathy was sitting on the toilet trying not to cry too loudly when someone hammered on the door. "Go away!" she shouted as loudly as she dared.

"Piglet, let me in or I'll kick the door down."

"I said go away!"

"Three seconds and I start kicking."

If there was one thing Kathy had learned about Piers it was that he didn't make empty threats. She clicked back the bolt and let him have a good look at her tear-streaked face with its puffy eyes and red nose. It was a bit of a squash in there but he sat on the closed toilet, she sat on his lap with her arms round him and just howled against his neck.

He let her sob for a while then picked the sodden hair off her face. "Have you told him yet?" he asked as kindly as he could and felt her shake her head. "Sorry, Piglet. It comes hard. I kind of know what it's like. But you have to tell him."

"How?" she asked breathlessly. "There are two people in the world who know what happened to me. Emma and you."

"You managed to tell me. Can't you tell him now? Alison told us how you missed last month so he's out there right now worried sick about you."

"I... I don't know how."

"Tell him the way you told me," he suggested, still speaking calmly and gently. "You found the words to tell me, so I'm sure you'll find the words for him."

"Yes, I maybe will. But you're different. I haven't married you and you're not hoping I'll have your kids. What if he walks out on me?"

"Then I'll grab him by the scruff of the neck, bollock some sense into him and send him right back to you."

"I could lose him."

"You won't. I won't let him treat you like that."

"He'll never understand."

Piers thought for a moment. "Piglet, we're going round in circles. Either you tell him right now or I'm going out there and bloody well doing it for you. You need to be open and honest with your husband and then go and see a bloody doctor about it."

Kathy knew he was right but sitting on his lap in the stuffy, cramped staff loo she felt her courage draining away. "No,"

"No, what?"

"I don't need to tell him."

"Yes, you do."

"He'll walk out on me."

"Oh, for Christ's sake!"

Kathy was quite alarmed when Piers bodily lifted her up like a baby and carried her outside where he put her on the ground. "No, let me go back in there. I'm safe in there."

He didn't speak but took a firm hold of her and walked her round to where Jean-Guy was sitting at an outside table.

Jean-Guy was startled to see his wife looking terrified and with tear-tracks still on her face. He was about to demand to know what Piers had done to her to upset her like that but the other man's voice was cold.

"You, come on, we're going for a walk."

Jean-Guy didn't argue but got to his feet, leaving his drink behind and walked on Kathy's other side down the beach towards the sea. He thought for one terrifying moment he was expected to join the other two and wade out into the sea but Piers stopped just at the edge of the waves. The beach was deserted and silent as they were far enough away from the café for the conversations round the tables not to be heard.

Kathy couldn't speak. She half-fell, half-collapsed onto the shingle and barely acknowledged that the other two had sat beside her. Piers still had a hold of her so she knew she couldn't run away or even try to make a swim for it but the words were stuck in her throat and all she could do was weep quietly.

"Is she sick?" she heard Jean-Guy say.

From the feel of it, Piers had pulled Jean-Guy's arm across her shoulders so both the men were hugging her now. She didn't want to hear what he said. But he said the words quite calmly. Not making a fuss. Telling a story of something bad and horrible. It was hard to recognise herself as the main character.

"Her ex. When he did that final atrocity on her, he didn't use a condom. One thing else he controlled. He was going to decide what happened to her body."

The comforting arms held her more tightly.

"There was a baby?" Jean-Guy gasped and he sounded more scared than anything else.

"No," Piers replied for her. "There was a termination. Emma went with her. It was done very early on but Piglet is now afraid that it's done some permanent damage and the pair of you won't ever have kids."

There was a long silence.

Kathy didn't even try to stop herself from crying when the lips that kissed her so softly were those of her husband.

"Kathy," he breathed in her ear as he brushed her hair back from her face. "Why couldn't you tell me?"

"She wanted to," Piers assured him and Kathy heard him get to his feet. "Now you know the worst, I'm going to leave you to hear the rest of it. Going home now. You don't want me around for this."

Kathy heard him crunching away across the shingle and she finally managed to look into Jean-Guy's eyes. "I'm so sorry," was the first thing she managed to say. "Piers found out by accident and he's been telling me for ages I need to tell you. But I couldn't. I was too ashamed."

Jean-Guy lovingly tilted her face up by the chin and kissed her lips. "You have nothing to be ashamed of."

"And you're not going to leave me?"

"No I'm not," he assured her quite firmly. "In fact I'm going to make sure you go and see a doctor just as soon as you can."

"I know I should. But not just yet. Please."

"Then when?"

"When I'm ready," she whispered and leaned into him.

Alison looked across from the café as she cleared the outside tables and saw the two of them sitting so cosily with Jean-Guy cuddling Kathy very close and their heads together as they looked out to sea. From the way they were sitting, something wasn't quite right. A customer called for her attention and she turned away from the couple grieving on the beach.

Gabriel Fauré – *Élégie in C minor for cello and piano, Op. 24*

It was a cold, wet and blustery day when the Dodman Trio flew to Prague and two of the three couldn't help but notice their third was not nearly as relaxed as he had been on the flights to Berlin. They were expecting him to refuse any food that was offered but he was jumpy, and snappy with them although not with the ground or cabin crew. They were met at Prague-Ruzyně Airport by a member of staff from the British Embassy, with no sign of Jean-Guy's parents as there had been in Berlin, and were whisked straight to the embassy in a diplomatic car which didn't give Jean-Guy much time to look out at the city. The Ambassador, they were told, was currently on a diplomatic mission in Tallinn and they would be staying in the embassy rather than in the expected hotel as there had been a 'security incident'. They were shown to a suite of rooms that included a double bedroom and a twin room each with its own bathroom and a shared sitting room. The windows looked out from the back of the embassy across a car park to the backs of the buildings in the next street. There was no coffee machine or even a kettle to make a cup of tea and there certainly wasn't a piano.

"Well, that's screwed up my plans," Piers announced. "I was hoping to go exploring the city and now we're stuck in here. Do you think your parents will be allowed in?"

"God knows," Jean-Guy replied and dumped his cello case in the middle of the sitting room floor. "Should we be worried?"

"Not especially," was Piers' recommendation. "It all sounds quite plausible. We just need to find out how we're expected to get around the place and then take it from there."

Kathy could feel how disappointed Jean-Guy was that Prague had turned out to be so unwelcoming. "Well, we're going to need to get to the concert venue pretty soon as you'll need to suss out the piano if nothing else."

"Then I suggest we treat this place as though it is a hotel, we get ourselves ready to go out and then see what they offer. I expect your parents have gone to where we should be and know that's where we're not so they'll go to the concert venue too. As, I'm guessing, will Nikita as we're supposed to be meeting up." The other two looked at him. "He's on secondment here for three months."

"But…" Jean-Guy started.

"Yes, I know he's a Cultural Attaché for the Soviet Union. He also married into my family, the silly sod, and it's in that capacity we're going to be polite and have a drink together while we're both in the same city. Now get yourselves ready and we'll see what they're going to do with us."

What they were not expecting was to be loaned a car for them to drive round the city. A small, quite unremarkable but very old Ford with British diplomatic plates on it and left hand drive so Kathy promptly nominated Piers to drive it. It had been a while since he had driven anything with a left hand drive but with Jean-Guy as navigator they got successfully across the city to the concert venue where there was quite a reception committee. Jean-Guy's parents were indeed waiting for them and there was a joyful round of hugs and kisses again but this time the greetings also included the Soviet Cultural Attaché who, it turned out, had already met Jean-Guy's mother several years ago when he had been in Prague before and she had visited the Soviet Embassy to renew her Russian passport. They had somehow discovered at the time that she had a son who was beginning a promising career as a concert cellist and he was married to an Irish singer so they had music in common. Kathy was welcomed lovingly as the daughter-in-law Jean-Guy's parents had always wanted but he said something to them in Czech which she didn't understand but guessed at as nobody asked when they hoped to have any children.

She noticed that Piers and Nikita were talking together a little apart and were having a few initial communication problems as his English was nowhere near as fluent as his wife's Russian but they found out they had some kind of French in common and were managing to get along in a polyglot language that they somehow both understood. She wondered if it was odd to acquire a brother-in-law after thirty years of not knowing he existed and then find you couldn't even talk to him, which, she realised, applied equally to both men. But they seemed to be getting on well together.

As far as Karel and Anna knew, the man who stayed with them to listen while the Dodman Trio had a quick run-through was nothing more than the husband of a distant relative of Piers although he had been her accompanist in the past. They sat together in an otherwise empty auditorium and those who had heard the three playing together earlier in the year had to admit that the sound was even better, and they had thought it was superb even then.

"They have improved so much since I heard them in Suffolk, it must be three years ago now," Nikita mused to his companions. "I thought they were good then. But now, I don't know of another trio like them. I wonder if they could be persuaded to play in Moscow."

"I don't see why not," Karel Dechaume replied. "They played East Germany earlier this year and were well received there. Ask them for the contact details of their agent and see what she says."

On the stage, Kathy and Jean-Guy were listening to the piano and thought privately that the sound of it wasn't nearly as good as the Blüthner in the music room at home. But they had got used to its warm, mellow tones and anything else sounded hard and bright by comparison. They ran quickly through a movement of the *Dumky* just to check the acoustics then left it at that.

"Don't like that one, huh?" Kathy asked Piers as he pushed his feet back into his tatty brown boots.

He shrugged. "It's OK. It's ever since that bloke mentioned it in Berlin, I miss the piano at home and nothing seems quite right. Just me getting picky in my old age. So, where to now?"

"I have no idea. Shall we ask the native for a tour?"

"Pity his family don't still live here. It all seems to be hotels these days."

"True. Have you got any plans?"

He guessed what she was hinting at. "Don't ask," he cautioned. "And, no, Niki has nothing to do with it."

"Good. He seems really nice."

"Yes," Piers said vaguely. "Roisin could have done a lot worse."

Their first night in Prague, they played as a trio, the second was a cello and piano recital and Kathy got to sit in the audience with her parents-in-law and just listen to the musicians on the concert platform. She was grateful to have the translations from her mother-in-law from the printed programme, which she kept to add to her collection, and more especially when it was time for the demanded encore and the cellist spoke to his audience in Czech. Even before he played a note there was a round of ecstatic applause then the entire audience settled in silence to listen.

"He said he is going to play the Smetana *Bohemian Song* which your friend Piers has arranged specially for him as a wedding present," Mrs Dechaume explained.

"It was rather unexpected," Kathy admitted. "He knitted me some mittens too."

Mrs Dechaume smiled in reply. "A talented man by all accounts. He is lucky to have someone of Jean-Guy's calibre to accompany."

"True," was all Kathy could think to say, and to feel again that sad ache inside that it wasn't yet her turn to be a proud mother.

The *Bohemian Song* nearly brought the house down. Kathy had heard many noisy audiences in her time but seldom had she heard such appreciation as they acknowledged the superb musicianship of the Czech cellist playing a well-known work by a Czech composer in the capital city of their country.

Jean-Guy's parents were staying with friends in the city and they invited the trio to join them in a post-concert meal in the flat where the newlyweds honoured the Czech tradition of sharing bread and soup and Kathy was quite touched that their hosts had thought of such a thing. The three musicians didn't get back to the British Embassy until the small hours of the morning when there was only a very sleepy security guard on duty to welcome them back and to ask how the concert had gone.

The next day was their one free day of the visit and Kathy and Jean-Guy were grateful but not surprised when Piers told them he was proposing to go for a walk along the river and leave them to have their honeymoon in the city for the day. He had his walking boots on his feet, he had a map and they were pretty sure he was armed under his old waxed cotton coat which he still hadn't thrown away. They all breakfasted together in a nearby café then he went off for his walk leaving the native of the city to show his wife the sights.

Kathy thought that Jean-Guy had been quite right. Prague was a beautiful city and they crossed Charles' Bridge to wander the streets of the old town, barely remembering they needed to stop for lunch at some point.

Lunch was a simple bowl of soup and some dark bread in a small café where the only language Kathy could hear was Czech and she was glad to have a native speaker with her.

"So what do you think of Prague?" Jean-Guy asked her as he broke his bread and dunked a piece in his soup.

"It's beautiful," she told him truthfully. "If only there was a way we could find for you to live here if only for part of the year."

Jean-Guy so nearly told her. She had told him so much as they had cried together on the beach and he could understand how she had felt when she had been scared to tell him her secret. At that moment, it would have been the easiest thing to take her hand, look into her eyes and tell her that while Prague was perhaps the most beautiful city he knew, it was also the city of his nightmares. This was the place he came to in those night terrors that never quite woke him but he knew he had disturbed the woman sleeping next to him with his kicking legs and his useless, clutching fingers.

"You alright?" Kathy asked softly. "You look as though a lump of bread has got stuck in your throat."

"I have a strange relationship with the city of my birth," he began but the rest of the words wouldn't follow and he knew his smile was weak. "As I am sure you do with Wimbledon. It is where I have known good things and some things not so good."

She just knew he was desperate to tell her something but he couldn't. Whether he was afraid of stirring up bad memories, afraid she would walk out on him or just didn't know the right words in English, although that was unlikely, she didn't know. So she reached across and took his hand. "If you don't want to think of the bad times today that's OK. There are times when I don't want to let bad memories in either. But, please, don't sit there and be unhappy. You know you can tell me anything, don't you? I won't mind. You listened to me when I needed you to."

"I have bad memories sometimes," he faltered. "I don't like to speak of them. Like Piers and his life in Ireland."

She squeezed his hand and felt the tears at the back of her eyes. "Then don't speak of them now," she whispered. "Tell me another time when we are alone and it's quiet and if you want to cry then you can. Perhaps we should sit on the beach again when we are home. But if you want to keep your secrets for now, I understand."

He nearly cried then anyway to hear the warmth in her voice. "Will you promise me one thing?"

"Well, I'll try," she offered, wondering where this was going.

"Promise me you will never lose your dreams?"

She smiled fondly at him and was glad to see his dark thoughts had passed. "I'm sitting with one of my dreams now, aren't I?"

He leaned across the table and gave her a gentle kiss, thinking, as he so often did, that he was the luckiest man on the planet. "You are right," he told her. "This is not the time for my bad memories. We are still on our honeymoon day and I am going to take you along Golden Lane. Are you going to finish your soup?"

"I'm not really very hungry," Kathy admitted. "I'm sure I'll eat tonight."

Jean-Guy finished the soup off for her as, he explained, food was hard to come by sometimes in Prague and it would be rude to waste any. Kathy had a feeling he missed the tastes of his homeland and was filling up on them before all he had left were memories again.

"Your parents think it would be a good idea if our trio went to Moscow," she said to him as they left the café and resumed their walk through the old town.

"Well that's not going to happen, is it?" he asked and sounded a bit resentful. "Not unless we take another pianist."

"Don't see why not. He's done their little errands for them and they don't seem to have been particularly onerous so I'm sure he'll be obliging for just one more trip."

Jean-Guy remembered the way he had unsubtly been herded from the kitchen so the other two could talk about Richard's accident and he knew there were things rumbling in the background. "OK, so he plays the game for that trip. Then they ask us to go to Budapest or Beijing. When does he stop?"

"Take your point," Kathy conceded. "OK, so what's in Golden Lane that's so special?"

Jean-Guy put his arm round her waist and hugged her close. "Wait and see."

They returned to the Embassy in the late afternoon and already it was starting to get dark so they were relieved to find that Piers was safely back in their suite even if he was still in his scruffy walking clothes and was fast asleep on one of the beds in the twin room. Kathy, as always, thought he looked quite adorable when he was that deeply asleep with a slight flush on his face and his eyelashes so dark against his skin.

Jean-Guy softly closed the door to the twin room. "Well, as we're on honeymoon today maybe I should help you wash your hair like I did once before?"

"Doesn't that seem an age ago? I wasn't planning on washing it while I'm away but how can I refuse such an offer? I'll go and run the bath. Only don't you dare tell me I've got fat like Piers did."

"Wouldn't dare," Jean-Guy assured her. He looked at her and caressed her as they relaxed in the hot water together and he felt a bit treacherous as in a way he had to agree with Piers. But then, he was putting on the inches too so he wasn't going to say anything. They weren't particularly quiet in the bath and weren't surprised to find their third was half awake and sitting on the edge of his bed when they went to see how he was getting on.

"Good walk?" Kathy asked him brightly. "How far did you go?"

"No idea," Piers replied and yawned. "This fresh air's a killer. I walked right off the map you gave me anyway. Then found somewhere for lunch, turned round and walked all the way back." He looked at his watch and did some mental arithmetic. "Guess I walked about twenty miles. Knackered now, haven't done that for ages. How was the honeymoon?"

"Lovely," Kathy sighed.

"And my parents have booked a table at a local restaurant for our evening meal today," Jean-Guy added. "Are you going out like that or are you planning on having a shower?"

He looked up at them from his seated position and smiled. "I'm guessing the shower option is the right one?"

"Correct," Jean-Guy laughed. "Anyway, we will leave you to make yourself all beautiful to go out."

The restaurant wasn't far from the Embassy so the three set out in the city twilight to walk there with Kathy in the middle as she so often was.

"What do you think of Prague?" Jean-Guy asked Piers as they both instinctively grabbed Kathy's arms when her heel snagged in the cobblestones.

"Nice place. Maybe one day you'll be able to have a flat here or something a bit like Roisin does in Moscow. Piglet, why are you wearing those ridiculous shoes? Couldn't you have looked out of the window and seen what the streets are like?"

"I'm not wearing walking shoes with my posh dress."

They were still teasing Kathy about her unsuitable footwear when they got to the restaurant where Jean-Guy's parents were waiting just outside for them.

"Did you have a nice walk?" his father asked Piers.

"Yes, thank you," he replied, a bit surprised.

Karel Dechaume smiled. "I saw you setting off. I was in the bakery queuing for bread when you went loping off on those legs of yours."

"It's a beautiful city," Piers offered in response. "I just followed the river until lunch time then came back the same way."

"Yes, I sometimes wish I hadn't agreed to move to Moscow. But my placement there was only ever meant to be temporary. I have the option to move back to Prague in the next year or so and I think I may take it."

Jean-Guy had overheard. "Really? You will move back home?"

"Your mother and I would like to. Are you sure you won't move with us?"

"Please don't ask me that," Jean-Guy requested.

"I have been assured that there will be no problems and no questions. Kathy will soon pick up the language and she can get work as a freelance musician here too, although it may be easier if she joins one of the orchestras instead."

Kathy had a feeling deep inside her that there was something very wrong with this proposal. "Maybe one day," she offered. "But Jean-Guy and I are booked into work for about the next three years and I at least would hate to let people down." She saw the way all the others were looking at her. "I'm just saying I'm not dismissing it out of hand. But not yet."

"You really are the most incredible woman," Jean-Guy complimented her.

"You're an idiot," Piers told her.

She looked at him and knew that he was probably the only one who would understand. "I can feel it. Smell it almost. One day Jean-Guy and I will be here and we will be happy and free. One day we will stand on Charles' Bridge and watch the tourists eating at the pavement cafes where the people aren't afraid to waste food as there may not be any tomorrow." To the bafflement of her parents-in-law she gently touched the chest of a man who wasn't her husband. "And the raven will fly free."

Jean-Guy glanced at his parents. "I think maybe Kathy didn't eat enough lunch and is feeling a bit hungry." He looked at the other two members of the Dodman Trio and knew he had lost them again.

Piers gave Kathy such a sad smile. "Oh, I think it's been caged now, don't you? And somewhere the key got lost. Come on, Piglet. Let's get some food down you."

Jean-Guy felt his mother taking a firm hold of his arm to hold him back while his father took the other two on ahead into the restaurant. "What was all that about?" she asked in her native Russian.

Without thinking he dropped into the same language although he hadn't used it for years. "It's just Kathy and Piers. I don't understand most of it."

"Is she unfaithful to you with him?"

He was genuinely shocked that his mother would even think it. "No, not at all. I trust the two of them implicitly. He's married anyway."

"I think the sooner you and Kathy join us here in Prague and leave him behind in England the better it will be for you and her. Nikita Fyodorovich told us he is married to Roisin Thompson who is related to Piers which is how they know each other, and they spend time in Moscow and time in England so maybe you and Kathy would like to do something like that? You have the nationality you need and I'm sure it would be possible but only if you admit you shouldn't have run and you agree to come home."

Jean-Guy could sense an urgency in his mother's voice. This wasn't the same woman who had fought so hard for him to get out of the country. This was one scared of the consequences of what had happened. Or maybe even one being blackmailed. "You heard what Kathy said. We have so much work in England at the moment, I would like to honour those bookings at least. And I will never find a pianist who suits me better."

Her grip tightened on his arm, and her eyes and her voice pleaded with him. "Come home of your own free will, Jean-Guy. Before you don't have a choice in the matter. Please."

The evening meal was a protracted affair and the trio were late back at the Embassy again much to the amusement of the night security guard. Once in their suite, Jean-Guy closed the door rather harder than he needed to and demanded of the others,

"What the hell was all that about tonight? All that crap about freedom and ravens? You two made me look a right idiot in front of my parents tonight and now they think I'm not only playing music with a couple of lunatics but I've married one of them too."

Kathy gave Piers a shove towards his room. "Go to bed. You've done a twenty mile walk and I'll deal with this one."

He didn't argue. Just wished them a good night and went to his room, quietly closing the door but the other two were perfectly aware that if he wanted to he would probably hear every word they said.

"I'm sorry if we've upset you," Kathy began softly to Jean-Guy. "You know we would never do anything to hurt you." She put her arms round him and was glad he returned the hug.

He gave her a gentle kiss. "Please tell me the absolute truth. Have you and he ever slept together? I won't blame you, or criticise you. I just need to know now, although once I didn't. You could tell him secrets you can't tell me. I leave you two alone together so much and I have seen how the women are with him."

Kathy knew the question was asked out of love and she smiled fondly at him. "No, we haven't. As I've said so many times before, he's like a big brother to me and I think you're right, he would kill to protect me." A thought so shocking suddenly occurred to her she looked up into Jean-Guy's dark eyes and almost forgot to breathe. "Did he... did he have anything to do with what happened to my ex?" His hesitation didn't console her. "Oh, God. Tell me he didn't. Please. Tell me he didn't."

Jean-Guy had had his own conversation with Piers on that one. "You heard what he said. He was in New York when it happened. It was a burglary gone wrong. The police are satisfied that is all it was."

"Truthfully?"

"I have never lied to you in all the years I have known you."

Kathy knew that was the best she was going to get and didn't ask any more, but she went to bed that night wondering.

The trio split up again the next day even though Jean-Guy wasn't happy about it, but his parents wanted to spend time with him and Kathy and although Piers was always welcome, he wasn't family so he laughingly went off alone to explore the city. Jean-Guy and Kathy guessed he had his own agenda for that day and they knew not to ask but he was safely back at their rooms well before their evening recital which was just the cello and piano again. Then all Jean-Guy had left was the concert with the orchestra the next evening with a rehearsal in the morning, and after that he would leave Prague again. It was still the most beautiful and the most menacing city he knew but it wasn't home any more and he had few regrets that his stay had been so short.

Jean-Guy had chosen to start the programme, unusually, with a slow work and Kathy thought the two of them had seldom played Faure's *Elegy* so well. She was again sitting with her parents-in-law but Nikita had got a work commitment that evening so he gave his apologies and said he probably wouldn't see them again during their stay but, like his wife, he hoped to be able to welcome them to Moscow one day in the not-too-distant future. Kathy had got quite fond of Prague in the few days she had been there and she spent a lot of the recital just dreaming of living like Roisin, half the time in one country and half the time in another. It sounded just a bit too perfect and she couldn't help running through her conversation with Jean-Guy which had frightened her more than she would ever let him know. There was something dark and bad in Prague for him which he wasn't going to let her know about just yet.

Jean-Guy finished his recital with a perfect performance of the Chopin and then, for the second time on his visit to Prague, enchanted the audience by playing the arrangement of the *Bohemian Song* for an encore.

Kathy wasn't surprised that both men were in much happier moods than they had been the previous day when they got back to the Embassy, not too late that night, and didn't think anything of it when one of the staff held Piers back but told the other two to go on ahead to their suite.

They had got ready for bed and were settling for the night when the door to their suite slammed so hard they were convinced the walls shook.

Kathy looked at her watch on the bedside table. "Goodness. What on earth have they been talking about? He's been gone for over an hour."

"You want to face him in that mood?"

"I'll face him in any mood. He doesn't scare me."

"You're braver than I am."

Kathy pulled on her nightdress and a cardigan then went and knocked on the door of the twin room. On getting no reply she called out, "Let me in or I'll kick the door down." Still there was silence. "Three seconds and I start kicking."

"It hasn't got a lock on it, you daft woman."

Kathy went into the room. "I know; I was being dramatic. It worked when you did it. What happened? Are you in trouble again?"

"Just a bit," was the sarky reply.

"Airline again?"

"Nope. Prof's lot this time. It's come to their attention just how close I am to a certain Soviet Cultural Attaché to say nothing of Jean-Guy's parents and their connections with the Communist Party."

Kathy sat next to him on the bed. "But they knew all that before they recruited you."

"And now I've been un-recruited."

"What?"

"Sacked. Fired. Whatever you want to call it. That lot have decided I'm too close to the enemy and I'm just bloody lucky they're satisfied I'm not passing on some of the stuff I carry to the wrong people. I have been slung off their books and all records deleted. They have taken away my diplomatic papers which means my British passport is suspended until a new one is issued which apparently may take a few months so I am travelling home on my Irish passport. Fortunately I often use it when I'm working so all the visas are up-to-date or I'd have lost all my international flights with the airline too."

"Wow. What about your weapons licence?"

"Nothing they can do about that as the licence was issued by the Metropolitan Police. Although they can recommend it's revoked."

Kathy was oddly relieved to hear he was being relieved of those duties he had never wanted and hoped that maybe, underneath the anger at being dispensed with so abruptly, so was he. "So what are you getting so stewed up about? You never wanted to work for them in the first place."

He looked at her then and she saw the temper leave his eyes. "Oh, Piglet, you have your own way of looking at the world." Without warning, he took her face in his hands and kissed her on the lips. "Don't ever lose it. Now, go away, I'm going to go to bed. It's our last day here and you and I have an evening off while he plays with the orchestra."

She had forgotten just how good a kisser Piers was and the desire rocketed through her so hot she nearly grabbed him by the hair and kissed him straight back. But she also knew she had been dismissed so she went to the door but paused and turned back with one hand on the handle. "So why are you so upset about it?"

He had turned away from her to pick up his bathrobe from the end of the bed and didn't look round. "Because I don't believe one single bloody word of it. They want me for something. And I have a bad feeling it's going to be something I won't want to do."

Gustav Mahler – *Lieder eines fahrenden Gesellen*

Neither Kathy nor Jean-Guy was surprised Piers chose to remain in London when they returned to Suffolk after their trip to Prague although he had three days to go before he picked up his Tuesday line on Concorde and wasn't going on-call until the Thursday.

They walked into the farmhouse through the back door and a disappointed Audrey skidded to a halt in the middle of the kitchen floor, gave them the filthiest look she could muster then stalked off to the sitting room where she spitefully scattered every single piece of music that was on top of the piano onto the floor.

"Why?" Kathy asked as she dumped her bag and violin case on a chair without even greeting the man who had come into the kitchen from the study to join them.

"It had to be done," the Professor said. "He's had his wings clipped, that's all. And I'm sure you will both understand when I say it's not up for discussion. I suppose he is sulking in London?"

"That's putting it mildly," Jean-Guy remarked. "I think he is very worried he will lose his job with the airline too."

The Prof looked at the clock and decided it wasn't too late to make some coffee. "He won't."

"Sure about that?" Kathy asked.

"Positive. He could turn up with ten rings in his nose and all they would do is up the fine until he learns not to do it. We need him to stay with the airline and they have their instructions. But he doesn't need to know that or we will only encourage him and we really mustn't talk about it any more. Tell me about Prague. Did the recitals go well?"

"Perfect," Jean-Guy replied. "My father and Piers' brother-in-law feel it may even be possible to get the Trio into Moscow for a couple of gigs but after what happened in Prague I think we may not be able to take our pianist with us."

"Why don't we all wait and see what happens. How did the *Bohemian Song* go down?"

"Couldn't have been better if we'd played it for years. Audiences loved it and Piers has finally agreed that he and I will record together and that will be one of the tracks. I've already got Jane to book us a studio somewhere. At the moment the plan is to cut the master this side of Christmas."

Kathy was glad to go to bed that night in the familiar room where Emma had slept as a child and where she had found a sanctuary when she had needed it. It was even better these days as her husband cuddled up against her and softly kissed her neck.

"Did you enjoy Prague?" he asked. "In spite of all the dramas with the other one?"

"Oh, he's always creating dramas one way or another. Life is never dull with him around is it? Yes, I loved Prague. I would move there any time with you if you wanted to go."

He didn't reply for a while. "I don't want to go."

"Oh," she responded, genuinely not understanding. "I thought from what your parents said it would be alright for you to go back now."

"That is what they want me to think. But nothing really has changed has it?"

"I don't know. What was it like before?"

"Much the same. Do you think Alison will still be open tomorrow?"

Kathy knew that meant he didn't want to revisit those memories of the darker places of his youth that had bubbled so close to the surface in that little restaurant in Prague Old Town. "Yes, I'd think so. We're only in mid-September now and the weather is warm enough so I'd guess she'll be open for a few more weeks."

The weather was still good the next day so they walked into the village as they had done so many times before along the coast path. The new houses were still being built but hadn't gone any further north towards the farmhouse and seemed to be spreading westwards away from the sea. It still gave Kathy a jolt to see them and the village was certainly busier with more cars and people in it even at that time of year.

They went to the café first of all but Alison wasn't there as she was over at the shop working on getting her new tea room set up so she would be able to open for that winter season. Out of politeness Kathy and Jean-Guy stayed long enough to have a coffee but Kathy didn't want to eat cake and Jean-Guy wouldn't eat alone. After that they crossed the street and first of all went into the shop but it was Sarah's mother at work, now helped by one of the local village ladies as trade had increased so much. Thankful the shop was busy so they weren't held up too long, Kathy and Jean-Guy went and knocked on the door of the house next to the shop then stepped into the hall and Kathy called out for Sarah.

She came out of the back room and realised Kathy wasn't with Piers this time. "How was Prague?" she asked and tried not to look disappointed.

"Lovely," Kathy told her. "But being Eastern Bloc we couldn't find any souvenirs for you."

"That really doesn't matter one bit," Sarah smiled. "Piers not with you?"

"Not this time. He's back on the airline in a few days and I think he just wanted a bit of a rest in some peace and quiet without Jean-Guy nagging him to be an accompanist all the time."

"Yes, we can be a bit much," Sarah agreed. There were loud banging noises from upstairs and she pulled a face. "Builders. We've got going on the loft conversion and it's going really well. I'm afraid the money is going to get used more as we'll have to furnish them when they've been built but he hasn't said anything about it." There came a cacophony of infant screaming and wailing from the back room. "Excuse me, quins don't like all the noise. Come on in anyway if it won't hurt your ears too much."

All five children were walking by this time at nineteen months old and they were at the age to be enchanted by the visitors who sat on the floor with them and joined in with the toys. They especially liked the man who would talk to them in a funny language they couldn't understand and then when they tried to imitate what he was saying, he would laugh and change to another language which in turn made them shriek with laughter even though they didn't have a clue what he was saying.

Sarah looked at Kathy's face and said to her, "Shall we leave him entertaining the children and go and make some coffee?"

"We've just had some, thanks," Kathy replied without thinking.

"Then come out to the kitchen and help me to make mine, please."

"Oh, OK." Safely alone in the kitchen with only female company, Kathy stopped pretending. "Does it show that much?"

She was not expecting Sarah to pause with the kettle in her hand. "Are you pregnant?"

"What? No! Why do you and Piers keep thinking that? I wish you'd both shut up about it. You've got babies on the brain, the pair of you."

Sarah switched the kettle on. "I'm sorry, I didn't mean to upset you."

Kathy remembered what Daisy had said about Sarah's great-great grandmother being one of the most powerful witches in the county and wondered just how into that kind of thing the great-great granddaughter was. "It's OK. I know the two of you are madly in love with each other and with your army of children. I'm sure Jean-Guy and I will get round to it eventually."

Sarah made herself some instant coffee and didn't speak for a while. "I never thought I would find a man to marry me. And I had given up hope of ever having children. Then this, I don't know what you'd call him, let's say extraordinary man, walked into my shop with you and I just knew he was going to be the one who would get through to me. And then he took his gloves off and held my hand and I felt as though a wall had fallen down round me and he told me before we had the quins that he felt exactly the same thing. I'm sure you've heard about my mum's family history? This shop goes from mother to daughter. Has done for hundreds of years. It's never been owned by a man. One of my ancestors was taken out of here to be burned as a witch on the marshes near your home. There are supposed to be bones of them under the garden where you had your handfasting and the ghosts in your house are those of the people put to death there. That is why I am scared of your house. I was too scared to do the handfasting with Piers as my mum warned me we would combine some really old and strong powers. Melanie and Dunlaith are like me and Piers the most."

Kathy wasn't sure why the other woman was telling her all this, but it was incredibly fascinating.

"Which is how," Sarah finished, "Piers and I are the ones who can sense the life inside you. When did you last see a doctor about it?"

Instinctively Kathy put her arms defensively across her belly. "I haven't."

"Not even after you thought you had lost it?"

"Why do you say that?"

"Alison had her suspicions that time you bolted into her loo then sat on the beach for ages with Jean-Guy. So, doctor?"

"No. What was the point?"

"The point is that if you did have a miscarriage you may not have miscarried everything and you may have bits of placenta left behind which can become infected. And that can stop you ever having children."

Kathy hadn't been expecting that and realised Sarah had learned a lot about pregnancy and babies and perhaps she ought to listen to the wiser woman. "I didn't realise."

"So make an appointment with your GP and get yourself checked. Are you registered here or in London? I'm happy to come with you to the surgery here if you want me to. It can be hard getting the men involved when it comes to things like this although you and Jean-Guy seem able to talk about most things."

"Um, I'm not actually registered anywhere," Kathy had to admit. "I don't really know which place I call home. If I'm registered anywhere it's with the Queens Road practice back in Wimbledon but that hasn't been home for years."

"Your home is here," Sarah told her kindly. "Your element is the water of the sea. That is why you wear a ring of pearls. Piers is the air and I am the earth."

Kathy smiled wryly. "And Jean-Guy who once worked in a foundry is the fire?"

"I knew you would understand. Yes, you and he are the water and the fire and you complement each other perfectly. Piers is the air which can be the blessing of a gentle breeze or the destruction of a hurricane and I am the earth which can help seedlings to grow or split the land as an earthquake. Jean-Guy can provide the warmth and comfort of a hearth or the force of a volcano and you are always the water who can calm the fire but you also have the strength of a tidal wave. Water and air are what we all need to survive which is why you and Piers are so strong together, but water and air can also mix to create a fog which is thick enough to cause a ship to run onto the rocks. It can be a dangerous mix so you two must be careful when you are together or you could do great harm."

Kathy wasn't sure what to say but she heard her voice speak. "Is that why his tattoo frightened you? Is the flower on his back really you, the earth that grows the flowers, and you could see it was destroying the butterflies who were in the air?"

Sarah drank her coffee for a while, leaning against the kitchen work surface with her eyes focussed somewhere out of the window that looked across the back garden. She hardly seemed to hear her children still shrieking and laughing in the back room. "It is a very strange design. Even if it was a drawing on a piece of paper and not a tattoo, I still wouldn't like it. I don't know why he had it done. All he will ever say is that he lost a drinking bet and that was his punishment. But he did tell me he made up the design himself, it wasn't one he picked from the tattoo lady's book." She finished her coffee and cradled the empty mug in her hands. "He lies to me about all sorts of things and tells me things that are maybe half true."

"Do you trust him?" Kathy asked, wondering where all this was going.

"Not always. But he is too clever for me and I can't catch him out. I know he will never hurt me although Alison says he has a temper, I've never seen it. He gets a bit cross with me sometimes but that's because I'm so slow."

"Do you know what he once told me?" Kathy asked, hating to see Sarah look so sad. "He told me he doesn't know anyone as warm and kind-hearted as you. And that's what he loves about you. And you know he worships your children."

Sarah put her empty mug in the sink and almost smiled. "Yes, but he is a beautiful wild animal. So are you. And all Jean-Guy and I can do is hope we can keep you. My grandmother would have said he is Herne the Hunter, or John Barleycorn. And you? I think perhaps you are the spirit of the sea. A gentle naiad come to live with us for a while." She rinsed out her mug and dried her hands on the roller towel, suddenly practical again. "Anyway, you need to get along to the surgery and get yourself registered. Today would be a good day. They're open until at least five." She looked at the stubborn expression on Kathy's face. "For the sake of your health?"

Kathy's mind was still distracted my Sarah's lapse into the mythology of woods and the sea. "I'll go tomorrow."

"Promise?"

"Probably."

Sarah walked quickly past her into the back room where her children had got Jean-Guy pinned to the floor and were tickling him mercilessly. "Come on, kids. Leave Jean-Guy alone for five minutes."

They reluctantly abandoned their game and he sat up, brushing carpet fluff off his sleeves. "I don't mind. Really. They're good fun your quins."

"They are their father's children, more so than the triplets. 'Quicksilver' my mum calls them. Are you registered with the GP here?"

He deftly fended off Eithne who launched herself at his chest but allowed himself to be felled sideways by a joint onslaught of Eachann and Iarlaith. "No, I registered with one in London soon after I moved into Earl's Court. And a dentist."

"What about Piers?"

"He's with the same practices. I asked him where he went so I could register too. It was a new experience for me to get free health care. Fortunately I haven't needed it. Why?"

"Because your wife isn't registered anywhere and I have advised her to get checked out in case she really did have a miscarriage and it wasn't just a late period."

He turned startled eyes on the woman standing a bit sheepishly in the doorway. "Kathy, is this true? You must go to the hospital. I didn't realise nobody had made sure you are alright."

She bent down and picked up Caolan who had always adored her the most and had grabbed her by the leg so she would give him a cuddle. She sat on the sofa with him and finally admitted, "I don't want to know."

Sarah and Jean-Guy looked at each other and knew no persuasion would change her mind when she was being that obstinate.

"Then promise me one thing?" Sarah asked.

Kathy defensively held the child close against her. "What?"

"Next time you see Piers you will ask him to listen."

"I don't understand," she said genuinely.

"You know what his hearing is like. He can hear if there is a heartbeat. He used to wind me up when I was expecting the quins and tell me he could hear at least ten. If he hears the heartbeat then you will know that he and I are right. So then you will know, but either way you must promise me you will go and see a doctor?"

Kathy looked at her husband and saw there the hope and the fear that she felt inside. "Yes, alright. But he won't hear anything." She reached out and took Jean-Guy's hand. "Then I think it may be time we looked into the tests, don't you? We've waited long enough."

He smiled to see her so protectively guarding the child on her lap and wished it was one of their own. "Yes," he agreed. "I think we have."

September was cooling rapidly by the time Kathy and Jean-Guy went back to Earl's Court and they were pleased to find Piers had reset the Aga so the central heating had already kicked in for the winter and the house was toasty and warm. He wasn't at home and the Aston Martin wasn't in the car port but a check of the calendar told them he was on a Concorde charter to RTW. They hadn't quite got him out of the habit of using the short codes for airports and had no idea where RTW might be. Probably somewhere they had never heard of, but he was due home that day.

"If we're lucky," Jean-Guy remarked as he put the kettle on one of the hotplates of the Aga, "he won't have had to go too far and will come back not so tired he can't play the piano. I'd like to get our recording programme sorted out. Anyway, first I get my music sorted, then we will go along to the doctor and get you registered."

"I was going to register in Suffolk."

"So you said, but you didn't. Now I am going to be as bossy as you and tell you that we will go to my doctor today and register you and we will make an appointment together. I am teaching most of tomorrow but we will see what they say."

By the time the two of them sat down to their evening meal they knew they had an appointment with the GP the day after tomorrow at five thirty in the afternoon and they were both silently wondering and worried about it. Kathy knew she was going to have to tell her sordid story all over again but at least this time she would have Jean-Guy with her and to reassure her he understood. To their unspoken relief they heard the Aston Martin being backed into the car port just as they were about to start the washing up.

Kathy made the mug of tea and had it ready on the table when Piers came into the kitchen. "Oh dear, you do look worn out. Been anywhere nice?"

Piers sat at the table and downed the mug of tea in one go. "Just hopped across from Portugal. Got any food in? Or do I need to go to the shop?"

"We went shopping this afternoon so all stocked up. What would you like?"

"Anything, don't care. Thank you."

Jean-Guy carried on washing up as Kathy opened a tin of soup as something quick to organise. "Just a hop from Portugal?" he asked. "You look too tired for such a short flight. Did you go there from somewhere else?"

"Istanbul," came the surprising reply. Piers went to the pantry and found himself some bread to go with the soup. "While you two have been living the lazy life in Suffolk I have literally been round the world. Two full crews, chartered Concorde for sixty passengers, most incredible trip I have ever done in my life. Six continents, twenty three take offs and landings between us. Seen the polar lights, two meteor showers and flew over the top of a Pacific hurricane. If I never flew again I think I could die happy. Anyway, clocked up so many hours all of us on that little jaunt we're none of us working again for a whole week. But in the meantime it's food, bath and bed in that order."

Piers still hadn't emerged from his bedroom the next morning when Kathy got up to keep Jean-Guy company at breakfast before he went off to Trinity College for the day.

"Reckon I'll see him for lunch?" Kathy asked idly.

"Maybe, but he did look very tired. I'd bet you'll see him again when he gets hungry and the pains in his stomach wake him up."

Kathy looked at the kitchen clock. "Well, he's been in bed for about twelve hours so he'll be hungry soon enough."

"You'll see him for lunch then," Jean-Guy agreed and kissed her as he got up from the table. "And I'll see you this evening. Try to get him to practise the Prokofiev. I'd really like to get that one on disc."

As they had guessed, Piers turned up for his lunch and Kathy was pleased to see he was eating sensibly.

"How was the airline food?" she asked him as he made himself some tuna mayonnaise.

"Surprisingly edible. But on a trip like that there wasn't any option, and it was Concorde food. We all of us ate in the cabin and slept on the seats at some point so I think it'll take me the week to get the kinks out of my back."

"And you'd do it all over again tomorrow?"

"In a heartbeat."

He made Kathy remember what Sarah had told her to do but she shied away. "Any plans for the rest of today?" The smell of the fish turned her stomach but she didn't say anything.

"Not really. Probably ought to do some work on the piano but really can't be bothered. I may just head out for a walk somewhere. Want to come? We can go up to the park and eat ice cream."

"You don't eat ice cream."

"Well, I'll suck a lolly then. Come on, it's a beautiful day."

After lunch they meandered slowly along to Hyde Park and sat in the autumn sunshine eating their ice creams and Kathy felt so sorry for Jean-Guy stuck in stuffy recital rooms all day. But he did enjoy his teaching days and came home full of praise for the enthusiasm of his students even if their playing hadn't always been up to his expectations.

They were later getting back than they had intended and were a bit surprised that Jean-Guy wasn't home ahead of them. Kathy went up to her room to find a cardigan to put on and left Piers to make a start on the evening meal. She was still trying to decide between a rather shabby Aran she had knitted when she had still been at school, or the much newer beige mohair that tended to make her sneeze, when she heard the phone ringing in the sitting room. To save Piers having to run up the stairs she went across the landing and answered the phone.

"Oh, hi," gushed a female voice. "This is Tamzin from Trinity College. Is Jean-Guy there, please?"

"No, sorry. He's not back from teaching yet. He's been with you all day."

"Oh. Well that's a bit odd. It's just that we're all about to lock up and go home for the day and he still hasn't come back to pick up his cello."

Kathy's legs almost gave way under her and she crashed onto the sofa hard enough to make it skid on the wooden floor. "What do you mean?"

"A couple of men called for him and took him out to lunch so he left his cello in the office and said he'd be back for it in an hour or so but he didn't come back. Do you want us to keep it here for the night now? There'll be someone here for about twenty minutes or so if you want to come and get it."

The room was whirling round her and Kathy swallowed the bile rising in her throat. "I... I don't know. I don't think I can get across to you in twenty minutes but he won't want it left overnight."

"Piglet?" asked a worried voice in the doorway. "What's going on?"

Kathy put her hand over the mouthpiece. "Can you get to Trinity College in twenty minutes?"

"I can make it in fifteen if the traffic will let me. What's happened?"

"Jean-Guy's left his cello behind and they want to lock up and go home."

"Silly idiot. OK, I'll be back in about half an hour. Where is he?"

She managed a smile. "Tell you later." She heard the bang of the side door and the roar of the Aston leaving the car port in a hurry. "It's OK, someone's popping across to get it. He's got to drive in from Earl's Court but he'll be as quick as he can."

"OK, thanks. I'll get all locked up and wait just outside for him."

"He'll be in a black Aston Martin."

Tamzin half laughed. "Quite easy to spot then?"

"Yes, hard to miss. Thanks for ringing."

"No problem."

Kathy hung up the phone then shot into the en-suite and was sick in the toilet. Feeling washed out and suddenly very weary, she rang the Prof in Suffolk. She managed to keep her message coherent but wished he would say something to break the awful silence on the phone line.

"What did you say to Piers?" the Prof asked eventually.

"Nothing. I just said Jean-Guy had left his cello. I didn't want to worry him just yet in case there's a perfectly simple explanation."

"Do you think there is?"

"No," she confessed and started crying. "What's happened to him?"

"Kathy, just listen to me. I need you to pack bags for the both of you and then you and Piers need to come out here again. As soon as he is back. Get the Land Rover packed and the house locked so as soon as he is home you can come. I will make some phone calls."

She hadn't heard such urgency in his voice for a long time. "You think it's something sinister?"

"Do you think Jean-Guy would ever leave his cello?"

"No," she howled and dropped the phone receiver back into its cradle.

It felt odd to go into Piers' room with a suitcase and choose some clothes for him but she guessed he wouldn't be needing anything smart and he didn't have much for her to choose from. So she hurled a selection into the case, just about remembering his bathrobe and some underwear although she didn't like doing anything as personal as going through his underwear drawer. As there was still space she added his concert black and a grey Viola jacket, not that she expected him to need either of them. After thinking about it for a few minutes, she collected the small key that was kept in a whole tin of odd keys in a kitchen drawer and went down to the cellar where the gun cupboard was screwed to the wall. She really wasn't sure whether handling the gun was better or worse than delving in her landlord's pants drawer but she did remember to pick up a box of bullets from the cupboard too. She didn't need to pack much for herself as she already had clothes at the farmhouse, and by the time she had packed two cases, collected her Guarnerius and Jean-Guy's Rugieri and got it all in the Land Rover, the kitchen clock told her Piers had already been out of the house for over half an hour. She added her blue duffle coat and his waxed cotton coat to the things in the car and then went systematically round the house as she had done before when leaving it for any length of time and by the time the Aston Martin got back she was ready with the Land Rover out of the car port and parked in the road.

Piers knew better than to ask any questions. He grabbed the cello from his car which he then locked and without saying anything he added the cello to the items in the back of the Land Rover, and climbed in the passenger seat.

"Guess we're off to Suffolk then?" he remarked as Kathy pulled away from the kerb.

"Yes. I spoke to the Prof and he said we were to go there now. I hope you don't mind but I've packed a case for you."

"Well, that's me looking like a scarecrow for the next few days then," he laughed and Kathy was glad he could be so reassuring.

"What did they say at the college?"

"Not much. I met up with a young thing called Tamzin who was waiting outside with the cello but she hadn't seen the men who took Jean-Guy out to lunch and she didn't think to ask anyone. What's the Prof up to while we're travelling?"

"I have no idea. Making phone calls and planning as he always does. I put your gun in the glove box. Wasn't going to leave that behind." She watched as he instinctively ran through the safety checks on the weapon then pushed it into the back of his jeans. "You see people doing that in the films. Aren't you worried you'll shoot your bum off or it'll slip down your trouser leg?"

"Silly. The safety's on and it's not going to move."

"I need to be silly or else I'm going to panic. Tell me all about your round-the-world trip to keep me sane."

So he spun her stories about the myths of the Northern Lights and what the eye of a hurricane looked like from the edge of space and she concentrated on her driving. They made good time to Suffolk although it was dark by the time they arrived.

The Professor was waiting for them in the kitchen but he hadn't made a start on the evening meal yet.

"Sit," he told them peremptorily.

"Tea," Piers replied. "I can listen while I make. She's had me telling her fairy stories all the way up here and I have no spit left."

"Then please make for all of us. I haven't got far with my questions but there are others asking more questions now I have made my report. I haven't found anyone who saw the men who took Jean-Guy to lunch but the Metropolitan Police are making their own enquiries and they will find the member of staff Jean-Guy spoke to when he left the cello. Our contacts are checking as best they can all ferries and flights out of the country."

"Will he have left so soon?" Piers asked as he made a pot of tea and put it on the table.

"I believe so. He won't have put up any sort of resistance to keep you two, especially Kathy, out of any danger. That is why you had to leave London. You also must not be seen in the village and after we have had our tea I will take your car and get rid of it. I have already arranged the meeting and it will be replaced with one with untraceable plates in case you have to run on again somewhere."

"Where is he?" Kathy asked and her voice cracked.

"I believe they will take him to Moscow. I also believe that by tomorrow my plans will have worked out and within a few days you will be there too."

Kathy saw he wasn't looking at her. "You can't send Piers in. He's been fired."

"That wasn't my idea. I said we needed someone we could trust that close to the Russians and nobody listened to me. Well, now I have been proved right. You have been fully reinstated, all channels are open to you and our witty friends who run these things have decided to give you the code name of Havran which, in case you're wondering, is the Czech word for a raven. Introduce yourself as that in any phone conversation and you will get immediate top level clearance."

"Bloody hell, I have been moved up the ranks." Piers added some water to his tea so he could drink it. "And, yes, I promise to behave myself. What about Piglet?"

"What about her? She will be safe here."

"I'm not going without her."

"I think you'll find you are."

"No, she and I and Jean-Guy all work together. You know that more than anyone. I'm not leaving her behind. Either we both go or you send someone else in."

Kathy felt a lovely warmth inside but she knew what she had to do and laid a cautionary hand on his arm as he sat at the table with her. "You're so sweet. But what use would I be? Yes, I would love to come and help you but I think I'll be more of a hindrance than anything."

"Has Sarah ever told you her story of the elements?"

"Yes. But I didn't know you knew it too."

"Oh, it's one of her favourites. Go on, tell it to the Prof. Well, just the bit about the two of us."

Kathy saw the older man was now quite baffled and had to smile as she explained. "Sarah told me she is the earth, Piers is the air, I am the water and Jean-Guy is the fire. All four of us have powers both of life and creation but also of destruction. If you put air and water together you create a fog dense enough to make ships run aground. It sounded better the way she said it."

"And on a more practical level, Piglet now has her PPL, anything else I can teach her as we go, and she knows where we can hire ourselves a Lear Jet which could be very useful."

"Do you know how this will work?"

Piers smiled. "I have an idea that a certain mezzo singer based in Moscow may suddenly need an emergency accompanist. That will get me into the country."

"Correct. On your Irish passport. How are you going to work Kathy into that?"

Piers thought about that just for a few moments. "Only one way I can think of. Not sure if you'll like it, Piglet. Could you pretend to be my girlfriend and page turner? We can't risk taking you in as Jean-Guy's wife as they'll guess we're the rescue mission. And on a much more selfish note, it makes me less of a target as if I were going in as some kind of operative then I would be travelling alone. I can't go in as aircrew, not to the Soviet Union unless you happen to have got a contact in Aeroflot which I very much doubt so I am going in as a musician. And Piglet is coming with me."

The Professor looked at the woman trying not to cry into her mug of tea. "Do you want to go?" he asked not sure if he approved of the scheme but also not sure he could think of a better one. "Could you go through the charade with Piers?"

Kathy glanced into the eyes of the raven. "Yes," she whispered.

The Professor spoke sharply to the other man. "And will you be able to go through the charade with Kathy?"

His voice was professionally calm now. "Yes."

"Then I think Moscow needs to check its weather forecasts as there could be a heavy fog coming down. How soon can you get Kathy ready to fly out?"

"Give me a week. She'll need to learn to handle a jet and brush up on her night flying. I doubt if there are many people booking the Lear so we should be able to monopolise it for the next few days at least. If anyone else has booked it then I'll just up the fee I'm willing to pay for it."

The Professor nodded, impressed by the other man's planning. "Good. I will get things moving with Roisin and those I work for. Kathy, I will ask you once more and then you are committed to going. Will you?"

Kathy looked round the kitchen and felt something almost like homesickness mixed with fear and eagerness. "Oh, yes. Can't wait."

They flew out of Ipswich barely a week later. Kathy hadn't done much night flying, but while they waited for the security services to get things in place, Piers had done as he had promised and taken her up in the Lear Jet in the daylight and the dark, thankful it was a training craft. Kathy found him an unorthodox and unsympathetic teacher but she learned her lessons and he was satisfied. She didn't have any certificates to show she could fly it but he told her that could come later when they had time to do things properly. The Lear Jet may have been old but it was nimble and well-maintained and Kathy felt quite calm when Piers said to her,

"OK, that's our course set. We're cleared to Vnukovo which isn't an airport I know, only one I've ever visited in Russia was Sheremetyevo and that was when I came across with Kerryanne in 81. Right, you take control now and I'll call them up and let them know we're coming."

Kathy just nodded and tried to remember all that she had been taught. "I just wish I'd had time to do more night flying."

"I love it. Just keep an eye on the instruments and you know the beacons we're looking for to check our path. Don't worry if we wander off, some control station or another will send us back to where we belong. I really can't believe we've got the call sign of Catpaw."

"I know. I thought it was a bit daft too."

"And here we go," Piers half laughed and turned his attention to the radio. "First of the stations wondering what the hell we're up to. This is Catpaw," he confirmed. "And good evening to you too," he said cheerfully into his headset. "Yes, confirm our destination is Vnukovo and we have clearance to cross Berlin air space." He listened for a while. "Weather reports all good, we have a tail wind so no problems anticipated." Another listen while Kathy hardly dared breathe she was concentrating so hard. Conversation over, Piers turned to his co-pilot. "You alright, Piglet?"

"It sounds funny," was the best she could manage.

"That's because you're not used to hearing a jet engine. Sounds OK to me." He checked the charts again for her. "We should be well over the North Sea by now so keep an eye out for the next beacon. They'll probably call us up soon just to check on us."

"It's quite busy up here, isn't it?"

"You have no idea. At least the RAF have gone to the bed for the night so they won't be bothering us."

"Oh, I don't know. Might have been quite spectacular to arrive with a military escort."

"There you go, they're calling us now. You can talk to them."

"What are you going to do?"

"Me, I'm going to sleep."

Kathy looked across but didn't know whether to believe him or not. "This is Catpaw," she confirmed to the voice on the radio.

By the time Piers was calmly dealing with the ATC at Vnukovo Kathy had quite a headache from all the concentration and she laughingly declined his suggestion she should take the landing. They were directed to a quiet part of the airport away from the big international airliners and Piers systematically took Kathy through the post-landing checks before giving her a hug.

"Well done, Piglet. Great flight. Don't forget to write up your log tonight before you forget it all. All set for Moscow?"

"I think so. Where do we go now?"

"I have no idea, but I can see someone over there who will." He pointed out through the windscreen and Kathy saw the welcome sight of Nikita and Roisin waving at them from a nearby building.

Aeroplane shut down and locked for the night, the two pilots went across to the building where the Soviet authorities checked their paperwork without any trouble as there was a Cultural Attaché helping with the translations, their passports were stamped and they were cleared to go.

Roisin was finally at liberty to give her brother a hug of welcome. "See, I said I'd see you in Moscow, didn't I?"

"You did indeed," he smiled. "Any news?"

"He's here," she confirmed. "Just started teaching at the Conservatoire. I passed him in a corridor only yesterday. They're not allowing him to go out and about to concert venues but he is living with his parents again and he is allowed to teach now but very heavily supervised. It's not going to be easy to get access to him. Anyway, let's get you home. I'm sorry you'll be sharing a room but we've only got a two-bed flat now the children have all left home."

Kathy was suddenly very tired and she could feel a tugging in her belly as though her period wanted to start again. She was glad she had remembered to pack some sanitary protection for the trip.

Piers tucked her hand through his arm. "Hang on, Piglet. Nearly there then you can crash out and go to sleep. Maybe now you'll understand why I always fall asleep all over the place."

By the time Niki had driven them to the flat he shared with his wife, Kathy was battling to stay awake and desperate to get to the toilet as her period pains were getting quite bad now. She didn't even care that she was sharing a room with Piers as there were two narrow beds in the room with quite a lot of space between them and she declined Roisin's offer for there to be a swap round so the women were in one room and the men in another. She was too tired to bother with a shower or to eat but made her excuses to go to bed early. She managed to make some kind of entry in her log book then fell asleep lulled into a dreamless slumber by a gentle rendition of Mahler's beautiful *Songs of the Wayfarer* performed so exquisitely by Roisin and accompanied by her brother as they had a preliminary run-through for their first recital together in nearly thirty five years.

Ludwig van Beethoven – *Cello Sonata No. 3 in A major, Op. 69*

It was the burning pain in her abdomen that woke Kathy in the small hours and she couldn't help but gasp with the suddenness of it.

"Piglet? What the hell's the matter with you?"

"I don't know. But it really hurts." She screwed up her eyes as Piers switched on the lamp between their beds.

"Where does it hurt?" he asked quietly.

Kathy put her hand on her belly. "Everywhere. Do you think I've got appendicitis?"

"Wrong place."

The pain subsided and she felt a bit foolish. "Oh, it's gone." It was comforting somehow to have Piers feel her forehead and her cheeks as her mother used to do when she wasn't feeling well as a child. "Sorry, must just have been a touch of indigestion."

"Uh-huh. 'Scuse me, but this is something I should have done months ago."

Kathy squeaked a bit as he pulled her nightdress up under her breasts and carefully lowered the bedcovers to a decent level then knelt beside the bed, put his arm across her belly and settled his left ear against her skin. His touch was oddly warm for him and his hair tickled. "But…" she started.

"It's not you I'm listening for. Just stop babbling for a few moments."

So she held her peace, not liking to mention where he had put his elbow as he gently repositioned his head a few times. Another spasm shot through her and without thinking she moaned again and grabbed his hair.

"Ow! Get off! You trying to make me bald? I thought I had it then."

"Had what?" she panted as the pain went away again and she let go.

"Just that," he said softly. "Hush."

Kathy had an idiotic thought that they would have looked quite absurd if anyone had come into the room. She was lying there with her belly all exposed while a tattooed man wearing nothing but a borrowed pair of pyjama trousers was kneeling next to her bed with his ear nuzzled against her and his touch and his breath were warm and soft on her skin.

Piers sat back on his heels and pulled her nightdress down and the bedclothes up. He was silent for a few seconds then gently took her hands. "Piglet, there's no easy way to tell you this. I can hear a heartbeat in there and you're about to give birth."

"What? No. Don't be ridiculous."

"I'm not. I don't think I've been more serious for a long time. I'm guessing you have no idea how far along you are?"

"I didn't even know I was."

"OK, best case scenario is that I was right all those months ago in Berlin in which case you've gone pretty much full term. Worst case," he paused and got control. "Worst case is what you had wasn't a miscarriage but this one is about to be."

"But you heard a heartbeat."

"Yes. Not a very loud one but that depends where your baby is lying."

"I have a baby?"

"Yes."

"And after I got in such a state over having to tell Jean-Guy what I'd done?"

"Yup, pretty much," was the rather brutal response. "I'm going to wake Roisin and Niki up. Give me a minute."

Suddenly panic-stricken, she grabbed his wrists. "No, don't leave me."

"Less than a minute," he promised her just as someone knocked gently on the door.

"You alright in there?" came Roisin's anxious voice.

"Not really," her brother replied. "Come in a minute, we've got a bit of a problem."

Roisin took one look at the woman in pain again in the bed and shouted for her husband. She yelled something in Russian which the other two in the room didn't understand then turned to her brother. "There's an airing cupboard in the hall and there are some old towels on the top shelf, you're tall enough to reach, go and get some for me. Niki will get an English-speaking doctor for you." She took Kathy's hands. "How far apart are the pains?"

"No idea," Kathy managed to say as another wave caught her unawares.

Piers came back with an armload of towels. "What are we doing with these?"

"Giving the poor woman a bit of privacy and saving the sheets at the same time. Go and wash your hands at least. Kathy, are you OK for him to stay in the room?"

"I really don't care any more," she said truthfully and she gave Piers the best smile she could manage as she remembered how he hadn't wanted to be with Sarah when she had her babies. But now here he was, as always, looking after her again. And she loved him for it.

In the background they could hear Niki was speaking to someone on the phone but Kathy had to admire the way brother and sister worked together without really talking to each other. Roisin found her an old shirt of Niki's to put on instead of her nightdress and helped her to change while Piers swapped bedclothes for towels as discreetly as he could and he was in the middle of doing this when, with an almighty yelp, Kathy felt something leave her body and she was suddenly soaking wet.

"Sorry," she panted to him. "What just happened?"

"Your waters broke," Roisin told her.

"All over me," came the grumble, but he didn't sound as though he meant it.

"Sorry," Kathy said again as she felt an unfamiliar touch on her belly and guessed it was Roisin.

"Where the hell is the baby?"

"In there somewhere, I heard it." He crouched beside the bed and had another listen but this time Kathy was ready for the feel of it. "It's still there, moved a bit so guessing it's on the way." He moved quickly away as Kathy curled up with the pain and almost screamed in his ear.

Again she felt something leave her body and then an oddly overwhelming sense of relief. "What happened?" she gasped but nobody answered her straight away. She looked down beside the bed and saw Piers on his knees bent over something that looked a bit slimy and purple in his hands. First he seemed to be scooping it out with his fingers then he breathed into it. Kathy watched without realising what was actually happening as he flipped the bundle over on his arm and started rubbing it. Three times he repeated the breathing and rubbing routine then there was a faint mewling cry from the bundle he was holding against his chest. All Kathy could acknowledge in her mind was the head of the raven apparently watching over this tiny thing that was getting a bit louder.

Piers looked up then and smiled at her. "Congratulations, you have a daughter." He looked down again as the mewling bundle waved a tiny fist in the air. "Well, you're a funny wee thing, aren't you?"

Kathy struggled to sit up in the bed and watched as Roisin handed across a clean towel to her brother who wrapped the bundle with the dexterity of a father of eight and then he gently settled the bundle in her mother's arms. It was all totally unreal to her. All she could think of was how she had got so angry with Piers and Sarah for telling her she was pregnant. The failed test. The monthly bleeds and that awful time in Alison's staff loo. The unnecessary confession to Jean-Guy while they sat on the beach. Now here she was, looking at the tiniest baby she had ever seen with a few mousey wisps of hair on her head and then the baby looked at the mother who hadn't known she was there and Kathy knew what Piers had meant as the baby stared at her with one blue eye and one brown.

"Why didn't you tell me?" she whispered to her child, her heart more full of love than she had ever known before. "I had so much to give you, so many little things I could have done for you before you came. A nursery to get ready for you. And you never told me." She looked at the brother and sister now sitting on the bed with her and took Piers by the hand. "Thank you," she said. "You gave her breath, didn't you? How did you know what to do?"

"Lessons from Sarah's midwife in case she dropped hers a bit early."

There was a quiet knocking on the front door and the three in the bedroom heard Niki open the door. There came a short rattle of Russian before a woman carrying a medical bag came into the room.

"Seems I'm late for the party," she remarked in a cheerful accent that could only be from the Deep South of America. She pulled on some surgical gloves and clamped and cut the umbilical cord. The baby was passed across to the man she assumed was the father. "OK, take your child out to the kitchen and give her a bath while I check Mom over. You might like to clean yourself up a bit too. Cool tattoos by the way. Grandma you can stay if you like." She was a bit confused that the two in the room who weren't the mother were laughing about something as they took the baby away for her bath.

"He's not the father," Kathy pointed out. "He's a friend and that's his sister."

"Oops. Not Pop and Grandma then?"

"Nothing like."

"OK, got that one wrong didn't I. When was your due date? Baby is very small, but then so are you."

Suddenly it was all too much and Kathy started crying. "I didn't even know I was pregnant."

Kathy looked at the baby feeding so greedily from her breast. "She's got my appetite," she remarked idly to the other person in the room. "Where are Roisin and Niki?"

"Niki's gone to work, Roisin has gone back to bed to sleep for a couple of hours."

"Which is probably what you ought to do. Dr Penn was telling me I've had what's known as a cryptic pregnancy. Apparently they're quite rare."

"Trust you. Now all we have to do is get a message across to the father then stand back and wait for fireworks."

"How will you do that?"

"Roisin and I are off to the Conservatoire later this morning as she's giving her recital there tonight and we're going to track down Jean-Guy's father if we can't find the man himself. Got a name for the little suckling?"

"Ravenna Jean Fairbanks. I can't give her Jean-Guy's name yet. When we're home again I'll change it. Don't give me that raised eyebrow look. She's having Jean as it looks like her father's name even if it sounds totally different and I saw the way the raven was guarding her and bringing her life. I think the raven was guarding her all the time she was growing and I was denying her. I can't believe I did that. How could I not know?"

Piers yawned. "Don't beat yourself up about it. She's here now. Sorry, bit of a disturbed night. Would you and Ravenna mind if I had a snooze for an hour or so?"

"Not at all." Kathy looked at him fondly as he rolled wearily into the other bed in the room and, as he always did, fell asleep in seconds. She kissed her daughter's head and still couldn't believe it was all real. The baby finished her feed and Kathy rubbed her back as Sarah had shown her with her own children and Ravenna, full and sleepy on her first day in the world, slept peacefully in her mother's arms.

Niki was back in the flat just after the other three had finished breakfast. He proudly dumped a packet of cloth nappies on the table and told his wife, "Got some in the dollar shop. Nothing locally, of course. No baby clothes anywhere but I called at our neighbour as her daughter had a baby a few months ago and she said she will see if there is anything we can have."

Roisin translated then explained to the puzzled visitors. "It's what Niki calls the shops that only the Westerners ever visit as you have to pay in US Dollars. Russians don't go in there as they haven't got the currency. We're lucky in that we can bring dollars back from the UK with us which gives us a much better standard of living than our neighbours. We help out and share what we can but even in the dollar shops you can't always get what you need."

"I wish we'd known," Piers remarked. "We could have packed out a whole aeroplane with stuff for you."

"It was all a bit of a rush this time," Roisin smiled gratefully. "Maybe next time? I can't imagine this will be your last trip out here now we're playing together again."

"To business," Niki told them in his broken English, and poured himself some of the rather bitter coffee from the pot on the table. "Kathy, you have birth paper from doctor, yes?"

"Yes, but I didn't understand it as it's all in Russian."

Roisin again explained to save her husband having to struggle with his English. "Dr Penn has issued you with a letter certifying the date and time of birth. We need to get Ravenna's birth registered. She will have a Russian birth certificate and you can have a Russian passport for her or we can go to the British Embassy and get her put on your British one. Or she can have both. I gave up my British passport when I married Niki but I am now joint Russian and Irish. Ciaran and I must go to the Conservatoire for an hour or so in a minute but we'll sort Ravenna's paperwork out this afternoon. We can't leave her unregistered." She turned to her husband and there was a chatter of Russian between them. "As I suspected, Niki has told his work what has happened and they have agreed he can have some holiday time for a few days. Fortunately for you he works in what we call the Foreign Office so he knows what to do about the birth. As will your Embassy. So, have a good rest this morning because you're going to be busy in the afternoon. Ciaran, we must go or we'll miss our bus. And I must remember what you're called these days."

"Please do."

"You're going on the bus?" Kathy asked him and smiled.

He shrugged. "No choice. This is Moscow. There's not a lot of petrol around so it's bus or Metro while we're here."

"Good luck," Kathy wished him.

"Think I might need it. See you at lunchtime."

While Kathy and Niki learned how to communicate with each other and slowly made friends, brother and sister took their bus ride to the Conservatoire and Roisin led Piers along the corridors to the room where they would be giving their evening recital. She stopped and chatted with a few people on the way and Piers started to wish he had got Jean-Guy to teach him Russian. But then, he had never expected to need to be able to speak it. He picked up the names of Karel and Jean-Guy Dechaume and also of someone called Paddy but that was as far as he got. By the time they got to the recital room, he had also picked up the words for "hello" and "goodbye" and had heard how the Russian speakers struggled with Gaelic names like Roisin and Ciaran. He gave up trying to correct his big sister. So long as she didn't call him by their old Maloney name, he would live with it for now.

"Here we are then," she told him and paused just outside the door. She leaned close to him and spoke very softly. "I've spread the word that you're looking for Jean-Guy as you played with him in a couple of recitals in London and Prague and would like to say 'hi'. I'll warn you now if he does get to join us he won't come alone and he will come with at least one person who can understand English. Oh, and watch what you say as there are almost certainly microphones running in this room." She opened the door to the room and raised her voice so anyone listening in would hear what she said. "Right, there is your piano. I'll let you get familiar with it while I do my warm-ups. But I daresay you remember the routine well enough?"

Piers just nodded and put up the lid of the piano before kicking his shoes off.

"Ciaran... I mean Piers! Shoes?"

"No chance."

She gave him a spontaneous hug as he started his warm-up exercises. "I have so missed you, you have no idea. I haven't seen you for so long. And now look at you, all grown up with a ring in your nose and tattoos all over the place."

He gave her one of his lovely smiles. "And I have so not missed having a bossy mezzo to play for."

They got on with their warm-up exercises, each subconsciously listening to their own music as well as that of the other person. Roisin wished so much she could openly acknowledge the man at the piano as her brother but she knew that time would probably never come.

The door to the recital room squeaked open and closed and they looked round to see Jean-Guy had arrived in the company of an older man who was not his father.

"Hi," he greeted the man at the piano in English. "Heard you were in town. How are you?"

"I'm doing OK, thanks. I've got a work permit to keep me here a month so let me know if you want a half-decent accompanist for a change."

"I just might." Jean-Guy had been told that Roisin's new accompanist had been shipped in from England with his girlfriend, "You still dating that blonde violinist?" he asked and sounded genuinely nothing more than politely curious. He thought he'd managed that quite well but was totally unprepared for the reply he got.

"Oh, we're good, thanks. She's come on this little trip with me actually. She had a baby girl in the end."

Jean-Guy never knew how he kept his tone light and conversational. He remembered how Piers and Kathy had duped Marianne and, as then, he knew he had to be very careful how he spoke or the wrong questions would be asked not only of him but of this visiting pianist too. "Didn't know she was expecting."

"Nor did she. Quite funny really. Ravenna Jean."

Jean-Guy didn't know whether he was going to shout with laughter or have to rush off to the toilets to be sick. Either way he knew he had to get out of there and along to his father's study which was one of the few rooms in the building that didn't have a microphone in it. "Nice name. Anyway, you're busy and so am I so maybe catch you later? Perhaps we can have a coffee in Paddy's? Roisin can tell you how to get there."

"Sure. Maybe tomorrow, I don't have much time today. Paddy's at ten?" Piers didn't look up from the keyboard as Jean-Guy agreed to the proposal and the door squeaked behind him again. "And that is not how you tell someone he's just become a father," he muttered softly to himself before saying more clearly to his sister. "Right, what are we playing?"

Roisin explained about Paddy's International as brother and sister travelled on the bus back to the flat. "It's a small coffee bar not far from the University buildings and you can't miss it. Looks a bit shabby and got its name in green writing over the door with a shamrock for the apostrophe. It's run by an Australian of Irish descent and his one rule is that nobody is allowed to speak Russian in there, including the staff. It's popular with embassy staff, university students, especially the ones visiting from overseas, all sorts." She had the grace to look a bit sheepish. "I got banned years ago when the twins were young as they were misbehaving and without thinking I told them off in Russian so that was it. I've not been allowed back in since. It's only a short walk from the Conservatoire, I'll walk you there tomorrow at ten but don't expect me to be allowed in."

"I can't imagine you getting banned from anywhere," Piers had to laugh. "That's the kind of thing that happened to me."

They were chatting with an easy familiarity that neither had thought would ever happen again when they went into the flat.

"Oh, memories," Roisin said as the first thing they heard was a baby yelling at full strength of her lungs.

Ravenna calmed down a lot after a nappy change and a feed and the adults all sat down to a plain lunch of bread and cheese with some fresh tomatoes and some apples for dessert.

"Did you see him?" was the first thing Kathy asked.

"Yes," Piers confirmed, sounding a bit grumpy as he didn't dare eat the cheese with a recital that evening. "Roisin spread the story that I'm here with my violinist girlfriend and that had got back to him by the time he found us and he now knows you've just had an unexpected baby girl. It was a bit brutal the way I had to tell him but so far as the world at large knows all we are to each other is soloist and occasional accompanist. We're meeting at Paddy's tomorrow at ten. I don't know if he'll get to the recital tonight but I'd suggest you and Ravenna have a quiet night in if you want to come out with us tomorrow."

Roisin was horrified. "You can't take her on the bus, she's only just had a baby."

Piers smiled at his sister who clearly didn't understand. "I am going to meet her husband. If I don't let her come with me, even if I have to push her and the baby there in a wheelbarrow, she will find a way to get there. I've learned over the years that once Piglet sets her mind to something then all we can do is help her or get out of the way."

Roisin held up her hands in the same gesture Kathy had seen so often in Piers. "OK, I give in. You'll have to take the bus though as she can't walk that far from here. Niki's going to drive us to the various people this afternoon but we don't have any spare petrol for joyrides out to Paddy's. I'd suggest you get some sleep as last night was a bit traumatic and you'll be back in your white tie and tails tonight."

"No I won't."

Kathy looked from brother to sister and knew this was the chance she had been waiting for. "What is it with you and the tails? I've known you give up the gig and the fee rather than go into tails."

"Yes, and I will do the same again today. I don't need to do your recital now we've got the meeting arranged at Paddy's. So I go on stage in full black if you're formal."

"That is so disrespectful to the audience," Roisin told him sharply.

"Your call. You want me on stage with you?"

Brother and sister reached stand-off watched by friend and husband.

"Tell me the story," Kathy prompted as kindly as her burning curiosity would let her. "Then maybe I can offer a solution."

Roisin silenced her younger brother with a well-practised glare. "He was fifteen the last time I ever saw him in the white tie and tails. And it turned out to be the last recital we ever did together. The then British Prime Minister had come across to the Province on some kind of political visit and it had been arranged that I was to give a private recital in some titled woman's home in Coleraine and the PM would be attending. That upset the pair of us to begin with as we've never held with the titled English helping themselves to chunks of Ireland."

"Yes, Piers has made that quite obvious."

Roisin almost smiled. "So our father saw a way to get rid of a lot of enemies as he saw them. He had it set up so that when the recital was over and we were being presented to the Prime Minister a bomb would go off and take out the PM and God knows who else besides. My instructions were to meet the PM first, shake his hand and then get the hell out while Ciaran took his turn. It was all set up, all the wires laid and our father had the remote. And then the PM had to cancel at the last minute as he had to go back to London unexpectedly so mercifully although the recital went ahead nobody died that night."

Kathy was appalled that a father would ever put his children in such danger. "You mean he'd wired up the piano or something?"

"No," Roisin explained. "The piano would have been checked before we arrived as our father had quite the reputation for blowing things up. Would have been a pity anyway as it was rather a good Yamaha as I remember."

Kathy realised this could explain why Piers didn't like Yamaha pianos and she glanced across at him but he wasn't looking at her. To her horror, he sniffed a bit and wiped his eyes on his cuff. "Not the piano," he said huskily. "He'd wired me."

Jean-Guy Dechaume managed to get in to see Roisin Thompson's recital that evening and he had to smile to see that her accompanist wasn't in the white tie and tails that would have been expected but was in full black with the top shirt buttons undone to expose a leather and raven-bone pendant as well as a silver caduceus tag sitting perfectly just below the hollow of his throat. He had his dinner jacket on over the shirt and very classy links in the cuffs of his black shirt but his shoes were out of the way under the piano stool and there was definitely a ring in his nose. It amused him even more to hear what the two young women behind him were whispering to each other before the music started and he wondered if he ought to tell Piers that in Russia you wore your wedding ring on the right hand. His own rose gold ring was still on his left hand and he had no intention of moving it as Kathy had put it there when it was still warm from the sun in the garden. Less than two months ago. It seemed as though a lifetime had passed.

The recital itself was exquisite as Roisin performed so beautifully the songs of Mahler and Prokofiev in German and in Russian none of which challenged her accompanist in the slightest. He didn't miss any notes out as he still sometimes did with their instrumental work when he was being lazy as the piano reduction of the orchestral score could be extremely challenging, but Jean-Guy could tell that the piano player was unhappy. This was a quiet, unobtrusive pianist sitting in the shadows, almost asking not to be noticed and just occasionally he flinched slightly as though at the memory of a physical pain but the music was never less than perfect. He didn't have a page turner but Jean-Guy watched very carefully and realised that the accompanist still knew large parts of those works by heart. He didn't need Kathy's intuition to know that was a pianist tortured by memories and just wishing the recital would end. Jean-Guy hoped the people sitting near him thought it was the unbearable sadness of Mahler's *Kindertotenlieder* that had got him so emotional, but it wasn't the music that was breaking his heart.

   Jean-Guy got his emotions under control as he caught the Metro back to the flat where he was now forced to live with his parents. He didn't even try to go backstage to talk to Roisin and her incredible accompanist as he could see there was a group of some of the Conservatoire's leading soloists already wanting to make use of the man who could play like that so effortlessly. Only his mother was at home as his father was in Prague for a few days, getting everything in place for the whole family to move back in less than a month. Even Marianne was going to be with them again although she had been living in Leningrad for a few years now.

   "Did you get in to Roisin Thompson's recital?" Mrs Dechaume asked, fully expecting her son to growl at her again as he so often did these days.

"Yes. It was good," he replied. "Some news got through to me today." He searched his mother's face for any flicker of treachery but if anything she looked a bit sad. "You're a grandmother."

Her eyes opened wide and she audibly gasped. "Kathy?"

"Has had a baby girl. She has named her Ravenna Jean and didn't even know she was pregnant."

For a long while his mother didn't speak. Then she said quietly, "We have to get you out again. I just don't know how. They watch you so closely now." It saddened her to realise that her own son no longer trusted her completely. He had given her his news as he knew it would delight her but he made no further comment. "Are you teaching tomorrow?"

"No. But I am going to Paddy's at ten. Roisin Thompson introduced me to her new accompanist and I'm meeting him there to see if he may join me for my recital in the Kremlin next week."

"Oh. Is he good?"

"I watched him at her recital this evening. I was impressed but I'll see how well he knows the Beethoven as that requires a very high technical level from the pianist."

"I didn't think you were going to play that in your recital."

"If he knows it I think I will change the programme."

"Did you catch his name?"

"It wasn't given out but Roisin definitely called him Ciaran a couple of times. He wasn't the accompanist she should have had I do know. She should have had the one I used last week and he wasn't up to the job at all."

His mother had to smile. "You still have a bad reputation with accompanists. I think your friend Piers is the only one to have survived more than three recitals with you. Did you have any news of him?"

"No. Roisin and Kathy seem to be keeping in touch now but he didn't come up in the conversation."

"Do you want anything to eat?"

"No, thank you. I'm not hungry." Jean-Guy felt a sharp stab of homesickness as he remembered the way he or Kathy would wait for the other one to come home from a concert. Sometimes they would raid the pantry, sometimes they just went to bed. But there was always a lot of giggling and mock-fighting over the food and trying very hard not to be so noisy they disturbed their landlord sleeping two floors up when he wasn't out flying round the world.

"Do you have any dollars to spend at Paddy's?"

"I still have some sterling left. Unless his prices have improved I'll only be buying a very small coffee. But I may get yet another accompanist out of it. I must find the Beethoven and I'll take it with me to show it to him. Then I think I may as well go to bed."

"Good night then," his mother said and watched him wearily go to his room. If she had known a way to get him out of the country again, she would have laid down her life to make it happen.

Jean-Guy saw the two of them as soon as he walked into the steamy, fuggy atmosphere that was

Paddy's International on a cold, wet September day in Moscow. Piers still looked annoyingly handsome and Kathy still hauntingly beautiful as they sat side-by-side, heads together and looking like an ordinary couple in love. Jean-Guy couldn't see any obvious signs of a baby but there was definitely something new about Kathy's face. A softer light in her eyes and a gentleness in her smile as she talked with the man sitting next to her. He was her husband, and yet he felt he was the intruder.

Kathy had been almost bouncing with excitement from the minute she had got up that morning and Piers had had to remind her several times that when they met at Paddy's she had only met Jean-Guy briefly before when the two men had played together. No matter what her emotions were inside, she had to maintain a cool friendliness towards him when they met. So she sat quietly next to Piers, trying not to stare at everyone who came in and glad he distracted her with the game of guessing which people were genuine customers and which were the secret service personnel keeping an eye.

She hoped she didn't visibly jump when, at about ten past ten, the door opened letting in a squall of cold rain. The wind caught it and blew it shut with a bit of a bang so everyone in the coffee shop looked anyway and Kathy saw Jean-Guy had finally arrived but, as Piers had warned her, he wasn't alone. With a supreme effort of will she didn't leap to her feet and rush across the room to embrace him but she clasped her hands a little more tightly round the shawl tied to her front.

"Piglet!" Piers hissed urgently in her ear. "Give me your ring."

"What?"

"Your wedding ring. Take it off. He's still wearing his and you match."

Kathy didn't want to do as she was told but she saw the sense of it and before the two new arrivals reached the table, she pulled the ring from her finger and discreetly dropped it into the pocket of Piers' old waxed coat. She felt oddly naked without it.

"Hi," Jean-Guy greeted them, slightly formal. "Are you Roisin's new accompanist now? Brilliant recital last night by the way."

Piers got to his feet and offered a greeting hand. "Thank you. We have played together in the past so I don't think I count as new, but it has been a long time since we last played together. You remember Kathy, don't you? And inside the shawl on her front is Ravenna."

Jean-Guy knew that once again one wrong inflexion in his voice could blow this whole thing apart and he was proud of himself for sounding so casual. "Good to see you both again and congratulations on Ravenna. This is Ilya Nikolayevich, one of the viola tutors at the Conservatoire. He speaks perfect English so don't worry that he won't understand. Anyway, I see you have got your coffees, so just give us a minute and we'll get ours. In the meantime, please would you look at this Beethoven and I'll ask you what you think."

Jean-Guy tossed the Beethoven score onto the table and walked off to the counter while the impassive Ilya sat opposite Kathy and just glared at her as if wondering why on earth she had brought a baby into the coffee shop.

Kathy checked inside the shawl but Ravenna was still sleeping off her breakfast and just moving slightly as she slept.

"All OK in there?" Piers asked her.

"Yes, she's fine."

"How old is she?" Ilya asked, trying to be polite.

"She was born yesterday," Kathy told him and couldn't help sounding rather proud of herself.

Ilya digested that for a while and the other two wondered just how good his English was. "Your baby is one day old and already you are out?" He looked across the café and saw Jean-Guy was about to be served by the rather beautiful young American woman at the bar. "Excuse me," he said and went off to do as he had been instructed and make sure the cellist behaved himself in the company of foreign nationals.

Ravenna started getting fractious and Piers peeped inside the shawl. "She's probably getting a bit hot, take her out for a while."

"Do you think I should?"

"Well I've seen notices saying 'no dogs' but I haven't seen one saying 'no babies' so go for it. The worst they can do is sling us out and I've been slung out of worse places than this. Mind you, the coffee's so bad I think being slung out would be a blessing."

"Silly," Kathy said softly as she gently extracted her baby, who calmed down now things were cooler for her. "So glad your eight children have got you trained."

"Hush. Remember where and who we are."

Suitably chastised, Kathy looked over Piers' arm as he did as he had been asked and looked at the

Beethoven. "Looks a nice work. Lots to do for the pianist."

"That's what bothers me too. What do you want to bet he comes back here and asks if I can perform it in the Kremlin in about three days' time?"

"With the Soviet President in the audience," Kathy added for fun. "Good job it's not still Brezhnev, he'd probably remember you."

Jean-Guy and Ilya joined them. "I saw your recital last night," the viola tutor suddenly challenged the man looking at piano music. "Do you only accompany Roisin Thompson? You look a lot like her."

Piers didn't even blink. "We are related, complicated family tree, not sure exactly how it works myself. And, no, I'm not exclusive, which is why I'm willing to negotiate with Jean-Guy so he can use me while I'm here."

"She calls you Ciaran, same name as her dead brother."

"Common name in the family. Professionally and personally I'm known by my middle name of Piers but I think Roisin still misses her brother so she will insist on calling me by what was also his name. Which I find kind of irritating. And I'm definitely not a Maloney as he was. "

Ilya knew when a topic was closed and tried another tactic. "You have a very small baby."

"She has a very small mother. OK, Jean-Guy, this piano part is playable. When is your recital?"

Jean-Guy could barely stop looking at the baby in Kathy's arms. "Four days' time, in the

Kremlin." He wondered why Kathy and Piers exchanged a look and seemed about to laugh.

"Well, I'll need at least two rehearsals with you to make sure you're up to standard. And I don't know if Roisin told you what I charge for accompanying?"

"Um, no, she didn't. I'm sorry, but Ilya is quite right. That is a very tiny baby. How old is she?"

"Born about 5am yesterday."

"My God," Jean-Guy breathed. "And you have brought her out?"

"She's tough, like her mother."

Kathy looked at her husband and hoped her love for him that she just knew was all over her face, would be translated by Ilya as love for her child. "I didn't even know I was pregnant," she explained. "It was all so unexpected. We flew in to Moscow in the evening and she was born less than twelve hours later. At least I didn't have her on the plane. And now she's already visited the British Embassy and the Soviet Foreign Office and she has her own passport. I think the passport's bigger than she is."

"I don't think I have ever seen a baby so small."

"Would you like to hold her? She has eyes that don't match."

Jean-Guy looked almost scared. "I don't think I dare. I might break her."

Piers was clearly bored with the baby-chat. He got out a packet of Winston cigarettes and offered them to the other two men. Only Ilya accepted so Piers lit the cigarettes for both of them and casually blew his smoke away from Kathy and the baby. "Jean-Guy, I charge six hundred pounds for a three-hour rehearsal and nine hundred pounds for a recital, assuming the recital lasts no more than two hours total playing time. After that it's four hundred per additional half hour or part half hour. All fees to be paid in pounds sterling and wired direct to my British bank exclusive of any transaction fees. I wear my own choice of concert clothes and must insist there is a supply of iced water available for me as I am prone to throat infections. Those are my terms. In return you will get a bloody good accompanist who doesn't take any crap from the soloist. Oh, and if the rehearsals are public then I charge as for a recital. Your call."

Jean-Guy almost forgot there was a viola teacher sitting next to him who would understand every word. "That is immoral to charge so much. You are some mercenary."

"I know my worth. What do you want to do?"

Jean-Guy shrugged. "I can't afford you. Give me back my music and I'm sorry I wasted your time."

Piers looked decidedly less than happy and put the pack of cigarettes and matches on the table closer to Ilya than to himself as if tempting him. "Look, as a gesture of goodwill between us, I'll offer you an hour's run through without charge. But I'm not backing down on the recital fee. Who's paying yours?"

"This is the Soviet Union. It doesn't work like that. I am paid now by the Conservatoire and my recitals such as the one coming up are expected of me as part of what I do. I'm not freelance like you."

Piers leaned back in his chair. "OK, I'll be honest with you. You have a reputation as a great cellist but a total bastard to work with as an accompanist. I like the look of the music and I like a challenge. Make me an offer?" He smiled when no offer came, took a twenty dollar bill out of his jacket pocket and gave the awestruck viola player one of his most devastating smiles. "Ilya, do me a favour and get us some more drinks, please. Just make sure you tell the American lady not to burn the beans this time. She has the water far too hot. Mine's an iced black and Kathy likes a hot chocolate. Thank you."

Overawed by the handsome man who smoked American cigarettes so stylishly, Ilya meekly took the money and went off to the counter thinking he'd never met anyone who talked so nonchalantly of pounds sterling in the hundreds like that and was so casual with a twenty dollar bill.

"Neatly done," Jean-Guy approved. "Bloody hell but the Prof was right, you are damn good at your job. Now what?"

"Now while he is away we negotiate that as I have no piano where I am staying and as you don't like public rehearsals, you are going to invite me round to play your dad's piano this afternoon. Any chance Ilya will tag along too?"

"Unlikely as my father will be back from Prague by now and my mother is also at home. The authorities trust my parents."

"Do you?"

Ilya suddenly realised he had left Jean-Guy alone and came hurriedly back to his seat. "American lady says she will bring drinks over. What have you decided?" He put some dollars on the table. "Here is your change."

Piers deliberately didn't touch the money. "Nothing really. Did you tell the lady not to burn the beans?"

"I did, I think she was a bit surprised. So, decisions?"

"We seem to have reached deadlock. Got any ideas?"

"Me?"

"Uh-huh. I'm expensive and Jean-Guy is poor. What's the solution?"

"You should be like Jean-Guy and paid by the State to do their work. It is not right to charge so much money."

Jean-Guy hoped that was Kathy's foot tickling his leg. He glanced across and saw she had a deliciously wicked smile on her face as she watched the verbal battle going on.

"I'm not a communist. Never pretended to be or wanted to be. I'm here as a guest in your country."

"So, you are guest. You should live by our rules."

"Good point. Would the Conservatoire like to employ me in that case?"

Jean-Guy knew when to take his cue. "Now you are being silly. Why don't you come to my flat now? I'm sure my mother will be able to offer you some lunch and we can have the free run-through you offered. If it goes well then maybe the Conservatoire will help out with your fees."

Ilya didn't look very happy. "You can't take him to your home."

"Excuse me," an American voice said right next to the table. "Did you just speak Russian?"

The four at the table looked at the beautiful American girl with her long dark hair and her large dark eyes and saw she was glaring at Ilya over the tray of drinks she was carrying.

"No, not a word," he pleaded.

"Paddy!" the American girl yelled across the café. "We've got another one."

A stocky man who looked to be in his mid-fifties came barrelling across the room. "Which one was it?"

"Guy with the glasses."

"I didn't. I was speaking English," Ilya protested. "Wasn't I?" he appealed to the others at his table.

"Don't ask your mates to back you up," the man said in a strong Australian accent. "If Jess says she heard you speaking Russian then that's enough for me. I'll make your coffee to go."

The other three watched as Ilya was escorted out of the café by Paddy while Jess calmly put the tray of three remaining drinks on the table. She scooped up the change that Piers had left there as well as the cigarettes and matches and gave him a lovely smile when he discreetly added another couple of twenties.

"Thanks, Jess," was all he said.

"You're very welcome," she replied. "Paddy will see he's out of the way." She turned her dazzling smile on Jean-Guy and was clearly vastly amused. "Hey, I know exactly what it's like to have some guy hit on you like he was. Glad to have helped. Want your drinks to go too?"

As Jean-Guy wasn't quite sure how to respond, Piers just laughed and said, "We'd better. Just in case that pest finds a way back in again."

"OK, I'll go sort these out for you."

Kathy and Jean-Guy looked at their third when Jess had left them again. "Set it up with Jess when we arrived," Piers explained. "Said we were meeting you but you'd got this ex who wouldn't leave you alone and when he came across and told her not to burn the beans it meant he was being annoying and I asked her if she'd help get rid of him. I guessed you'd be with a bloke given the situation."

Jean-Guy shook his head. "Oh, you're way better than good."

By the time Jean-Guy and Piers settled to have a run-through of the Beethoven, baby Ravenna had been cuddled and totally adored by her father and her grandparents; she had had her lunch and her nappy change and was happily asleep in an armchair with her doting grandmother keeping an eye while grandfather sat on the page turner's chair and listened in just as the Prof had done so many times. Kathy, exhausted after being out and about so much with a newborn baby, was sleeping in her husband's bed, lulled into a deep sleep by the reassuring scent of him and the sound of the cello and piano in the other room.

The piano in Karel Dechaume's flat was nowhere near as good as the pianos Piers was used to at home but it was good enough for a trial run through of Beethoven's third cello sonata.

Jean-Guy looked at his father when they had finished their performance. "Well?" he asked in English.

"You two are the perfect match. I thought so from the first time I heard you. I also thought the Conservatoire might have phoned by now."

Piers ran through one of the piano cadenzas again trying out a slightly different fingering which suited him better. "We were tailed to the flats. They know where we are. OK, what's it to be? Public rehearsal and then the recital?"

Jean-Guy looked at him. "You mean you'll walk into the Kremlin?"

He half-laughed. "Why not? Been there before. Different President in those days. You do seem to be getting through them since Brezhnev went. Is there any chance you've got a recital coming up in Leningrad in the next few weeks?"

"No, sorry. Why?"

"Because Leningrad is a hell of a lot closer to the Finnish border than Moscow is."

"What do you suggest we do? Ski?" Jean-Guy asked rather sarkily.

"I'll deal with the transport, you just get yourself into Leningrad before my work permit runs out."

"I think I may be able to arrange something for you there," Karel remarked. "What will you do from there?"

Piers flicked back through his score and marked in his preferred fingering. "Ski?" he suggested lightly.

Kathy was torn. Piers had asked her if she wanted to come to the Kremlin and be his page-turner, but there was no way they could get baby Ravenna in as well. So she either had to stay with her baby or be with her husband any way she could. Shattered by new motherhood and emotionally fragile after the way she had given birth, she was more reluctant to leave her baby so she sent Piers on his way with lots of love to Jean-Guy and just hoped nobody would suspect that Piers was anything other than a pianist brought into the country by Roisin Thompson and now commandeered by Jean-Guy Dechaume. She didn't make any remarks about the penguin suit now she knew the awful truth and privately thought he looked much smarter in his full black than Niki did in white tie and tails. Nikita was going to the formal function in his capacity as a Cultural Attaché and both Roisin and Kathy were consoled to know that Piers would have somebody with him in case of crisis as although he was picking up words and phrases in Russian with an enviable ease, there was no way he could have carried on a conversation.

The flat was quiet after the two men had gone out to the recital and Roisin looked in the tea caddy in the kitchen.

"Well, I think we just about have enough tea to make us a pot if we don't mind it too weak. And we have no milk, but is that alright for you?"

Kathy was learning that life in the Soviet Union was hard, even for those like Roisin who had access to many things the Russians didn't. "Perfect, thank you." She took some cups and saucers from the kitchen cupboard. "I wish we'd known, we could have brought you some tea and biscuits if nothing else."

Roisin smiled. "We're fine. It would almost certainly have been confiscated at the airport anyway and sold on the black market. We seem to be in England more than we are in Moscow now, especially as all our children are settled away from the Soviet Union. I have quite a busy autumn and winter lined up with concerts and recordings in London so probably we will be off to Wimbledon about the time Ciaran's work permit runs out and you all have to go too. Any developments on that front?"

"Not really. We need to find a way to get us all to Leningrad."

"Oh, that's an easy one. I have a couple of recitals there in a fortnight and I can easily tell them I'm changing the accompanist. Jean-Guy, I don't know. I can always invite him along too, the authorities may be happy as he will be with Niki. Or I suppose one or other of his parents could accompany him. I wish we could get them out too as if he defects for a second time it won't be very pleasant for them. But they have no reason to travel outside the Soviet Union and will be moving to Prague in less than a month anyway. Does he know you flew here in a private plane?"

"No. Piers isn't letting out any information about our travel arrangements. In fact he's going to tell Jean-Guy that we're on a scheduled flight to Leningrad which will coincidentally be fully booked so, if you can organise it, Jean-Guy can travel with you and Niki on the real scheduled flight and we'll just hop across on our own."

"He always was a devious child. That's our father's upbringing. The lies he would tell not just our parents but his teachers and anyone else as well. Evil, wicked lies too, not just funny little white lies to get him out of a scrape. Our grandmother told him many times he had sold his soul to the demons so he was beautiful but he was damned." She shook her head at the memory. "I was so glad to get his letter saying he'd joined the military. It was either going to be that or prison the way he was going."

Bedřich Smetana – *Prodaná nevěsta (The Bartered Bride)*

In the end it was Jean-Guy's mother who came up with the perfect solution. She too had been invited to her son's recital at the Kremlin and she watched him as he played so well with his Irish accompanist. Unlike the other accompanists who had tried to work with the cellist, this one was neither overawed by the soloist nor was he so full of his own skill that he thought he could outplay the other. Their Beethoven was a perfect match and Anna Dechaume knew that her son had to be sent back to the freedom of the West no matter what the cost was.

She thought about that as the pair finished their recital with the famous Fauré *Elegy* which they both played from memory and nearly left their audience in tears. It was a bit of a squash in Nikita Fyodorovich's car with five people and a cello in it, but he had offered them a lift home and it would have been rude to refuse.

"I have been thinking," Anna announced in English as the only language the five in the car had in common even though she didn't use it much herself. "Jean-Guy, your sister is coming to live with us in Prague and I think it may be good idea if you go to Leningrad to help her get packed for her journey. Don't you?"

There was a short silence in the car as they all realised the basic simplicity of such a plan.

"Just for few days," she put in. "You won't need to take your cello as you are not playing and if we can time it right you will be able to go to Roisin Thompson's recital while you are there."

"Perfect," he agreed. "And as I now have a new accompanist I hope it will be alright if I give you a few scores of music to look at before we are next playing together."

"Hey, I've seen the size of your library and please remember luggage is weight restricted on flights."

"Just a few of my favourites."

"Well, OK then, but just a few."

The five were all planning in their heads as the car crossed Moscow in the quiet, late evening streets.

"I have a thought too," Karel said into the silence. "I think maybe, Anna, it is time you and I went to see my brother for a while. It has been a few years now and I believe the opera house is staging a revival of *The Bartered Bride*, which is my speciality."

"You mean Uncle Ferdy?" Jean-Guy half laughed. He explained to the two who didn't understand. "My Uncle Fyodor took up a post quite a few years ago now. With the Santa Fe Opera. And, yes, I do mean Santa Fe, New Mexico."

Piers was quietly impressed but also rather cautious. "And you think you'll get travel permission while Jean-Guy's in the country and likely to do another runner?"

"Jean-Guy has shown no inclination to run," his father pointed out. "He came across quietly when he was asked to, he has taken up his teaching post and he has just done a perfect recital in front of the President."

"Yes, and if I was in charge of homeland security that would all make me very suspicious. Why would he so willingly give up his freedom?"

"Maybe because going to the West was a big mistake on my part?" Jean-Guy suggested. "I could bring that up in some conversations with those who are always with me."

"Yeah, right. Like they'd believe that one. You went off with nothing but a cello and a cold and came back voluntarily leaving a wife and a strong career behind? I wouldn't trust you for one minute."

"So what should I do? I thought if I just lived quietly then they would lose interest in me."

"Try having a couple of those conversations. Test the water and see what kind of reaction you get. You have to tread a very fine line between being too quiet and too pushy. Either way will attract suspicion. First thing you need to do is ring the British Embassy and ask how you can get your marriage dissolved."

"What?!" Jean-Guy almost shrieked at great risk to the hearing of all those in the cramped car.

"You have to be seen to start cutting the ties with your life in the West. Then you need to write to the Prof and ask him to send your cello out to you. Or we have to stage a very public conversation where you ask me to arrange it for you when I go back to the UK. What is the cello you're using now?"

"It belongs to the Conservatoire. I miss my two back in England."

"I'm sure you do. But don't ask to have the Rugieri shipped out as there's no way the UK will agree to that being exported. Your old one will do as it has the family ties."

"I can arrange a piano practice room for you at the Conservatoire," Karel offered. "I think you will need one as Jean-Guy is going to need practice sessions with his new accompanist before he goes off to Leningrad to help his sister pack and your work permit runs out. I may even use you in one of my classes too. I have watched you a few times now and I can say quite truthfully that you do everything I tell my students not to do."

"So how does it work so well?" Jean-Guy wanted to know and the conversation swung onto musical topics for the rest of the journey.

Kathy was already in bed when Piers and Niki got back from their recital but she was sitting up and looking at her baby who was asleep, snug and secure in the drawer from the bedside table which had been pulled out and put on top of the cupboard for her and the lamp was now on the table the other side of Piers' bed.

"How is the little suckling?" Piers asked quietly as he dropped the music he had been given onto his bed and took off his dinner jacket.

"Perfect. I still can't believe she's real. And I still can't believe Sarah and Alison coped with five of them in one go. Roisin's neighbour called by earlier with some baby clothes that her grandchild has grown out of so at least Ravenna has some proper clothes to wear." She watched as her room-mate calmly stripped down to his underwear with his back to her then put on his bathrobe.

"It's a funny thing," he told her as he fastened the belt then neatly folded his smart concert clothes. "People who have so little are always so willing to share. I have a net worth of eight figures and these people put me to shame. It's been a humbling experience."

Kathy was silently astonished that he should have amassed such a fortune. "Know what you mean," she agreed. "Like that time you let me have the biscuits. You were on your basic salary, a darned good salary compared to what I was on, but you were bankrupting yourself to pay the mortgage and you'd just come home from that awful trip to Greenland and wanted a custard cream with your cup of tea. I bet you wouldn't be so generous now."

"No," he admitted sadly. "I probably wouldn't. Somewhere along the way I got lost and I got greedy and I'm glad to have been reminded. Do you know what Jess charged me for her help in our little charade in Paddy's?"

Kathy smiled slightly. "Well, it looked to be about fifty dollars and a packet of American cigarettes."

"She asked for twenty dollars. She is a student at the University, she's being paid pennies to work in that café and she has nothing in the world with her except the clothes she packed and a return flight to Seattle at the end of term and all she asked for was twenty dollars and a bit of fun behind the coat rack to wind Paddy up. I'd have charged a few hundred minimum."

Kathy really wanted to laugh now. "You mean, all you had to do was give her twenty dollars and let her give you a snog and a grope in front of Paddy and that was it?"

"Yeah, pretty much. But before we go home I am going back there and I am going to pass on my lessons from Alison and show Jess how to make a half-decent coffee, even with those godawful beans they use."

"Wow. You'd better hope Kerryanne doesn't find out you've been making out in Moscow."

Piers had been on his way to the bathroom to get ready for bed but he paused in the doorway. "Kerryanne and I haven't been lovers since I was single and she was out to get me." He knew he owed her the courtesy of the truth. "OK, I'll give you the full story and then you can stop bugging me. Yes, we had, call it what you want, a bit like Danny said you had with him. Sex off the scale and that was it. When I look back I can see she got me into bed for information. We never loved each other. She got what she wanted out of me for her novel then she dropped me like the proverbial hot brick in the bedroom but we've kind of struck up some sort of a friendship now and we've met from time to time when I've been in the City. So, yes, probably more like you and Danny than you realise except she got what she wanted out of me, made her millions and moved on." He fiddled with the collar of his bathrobe and shrugged. "Unlike Sarah, who got what she wanted out of me and refused to let go."

Kathy hadn't realised this man knew so much about her past life but she was also extremely pleased to hear that sentence. "Go on, say it."

"Say what?"

"You're madly in love with your wife and you couldn't cope with having a mistress as well."

He gave her one of those smiles that had made Annette so rich. "Might, if it was you."

She was tempted to throw a pillow at him but was afraid of disturbing the baby. "Just go and clean your teeth," she told him. "And get those smutty thoughts right out of your head. Are you Bobby's father?"

He stopped smiling. "No, I'm bloody not."

"So who is?" she asked, not sure she totally believed him and now consumed by curiosity.

He looked at her over his shoulder and the smile was back. "Piglet?"

"What?"

"Shut up and go to sleep."

Petr Mihaly was in the middle of reading through the proof copy of a very long and meticulous book on the chamber works of Johann Christian Bach when the hotline phone rang on his desk. He picked up the receiver but didn't speak.

"Call for you. Havran from the Irish Embassy in Moscow. Clear to talk?"

He turned on the machine that would scramble their conversation. "Clear to talk." There were a couple of clicks on the line then he heard Piers' voice quite clearly.

"Hi, Prof, haven't got long. I'm just here to update my travel papers. We're moving on to Leningrad in a few days. You are going to get maybe a letter but more likely a phone call from Jean-Guy asking you to ship out his cello. Please agree to his proposal as lines will be tapped and all letters will be intercepted. Arguments are OK and I think you will find you have problems getting export clearance for it which will delay the sending of it."

"Understood."

"Oh, and before I go, you're a grandad again. Piglet had a baby girl the day we arrived here. She says you can pass it on to Emma if you like but you've got to remember every word she says in reply."

It was as though the other three were in the room with him, and oddly he felt a sense of relief to realise there had been a perfectly rational explanation for Kathy's emotional behaviour over the last few months. "I think she will say lots of words and many of them will be rude. How are mother and child?"

"Both doing well. The doctor called it a cryptic pregnancy so nobody knew what was going on. Ravenna Jean, weighed in at just over five pounds according to Roisin's kitchen scales. Not a lot of hair, one blue eye and one brown. Born at about 5am on September 28th which pleased Jean-Guy as apparently that's some kind of Czech festival day. And that should be enough information to keep Emma happy."

"Nothing will keep Emma happy where baby-talk is concerned. Are you coming home soon?"

"Hope so. Jean-Guy's parents are flying out to New Mexico tomorrow as Karel's got a brother out there. Something to do with an opera revival so they've got permission to be out of the country for up to a month. Roisin and I have a couple of recitals in Leningrad in about a week after which she and Niki are booked to fly to the UK anyway as she has a lot of work there for Christmas. The three of us will be the last to go. Sorry, four of us. Mustn't forget Ravenna."

The Professor closed his eyes and hoped this half-trained operative would pull it off. "I can only wish you luck."

"Thanks, we're going to need it. And, don't forget; argue with Jean-Guy if you think that's the right thing to do, then give in but do nothing."

"Of course."

"Better go, I said I'd only be five minutes. Piglet sends her love."

"And mine to all of you."

The line clicked again and was silent. The Prof looked round and wasn't surprised to see Audrey was sitting on his desk although all the cats had learned they were never to go into the study.

"Yes, Audrey. That was your crazy human. I'm sure he sends you his love even though he didn't say so."

Audrey was satisfied. She gave him a loud chirrup then went to see if there was any more music she could throw off the top of the piano.

"I don't understand," Jean-Guy said for the tenth time. "Why the hell are you two flying Vnukovo to Rzhevka when the rest of us are going Sheremetyevo to Pulkovo?"

"Because, as we've told you a hundred times already," Kathy replied, "We are going on some tiddly little plane that Piers found out about and you and Roisin and Niki will be on the Aeroflot monster with stewardesses and food and all the luxuries."

Jean-Guy was almost certain she was lying to him but they were in a public coffee shop and he had been allowed out without a direct chaperone for the first time and knew better than to stage any kind of a scene. He looked across to the counter where Paddy, Jess and Piers were in a deep conversation at the coffee machine and one of them at least was treating it like the flight deck of Concorde and making adjustments to the controls.

"And there are really no spare seats on your flight?"

"Apparently not. It's something Piers managed to arrange through the Irish Embassy when he went there to sort out his travel papers. We weren't originally cleared to go to Leningrad. We only had permission to go to Moscow."

"Well, I suppose he has his reasons," Jean-Guy admitted grudgingly. "I just wish you could tell me what they are."

Kathy looked towards the counter too. "Shall we just say air and water are creating a bit of a dense fog and we can't risk the fire burning it off."

He smiled as though at an old memory. "Ah, yes. Sarah and the elements."

"Exactly. Oh, and that's another thing. He had to go to work with Niki yesterday and he's now got a USSR visa in his Irish passport which means he can come and go to Russia for the next ten years. It's something Roisin got set up for him as he's not eligible for a Russian passport or anything like that and she's planning on using him a lot in the future. So looks like this is the first trip of many to Moscow, for him at least."

Jean-Guy was momentarily distracted. "I can't imagine he was best pleased about that. I got the impression he doesn't enjoy recitals with her."

"Too many memories. But I do now know the history of the tie and tails and he's said I can tell you, because he never will, but it's not a story for a public coffee house." She saw what was going on at the coffee machine. "Honestly, he really can't stop himself, can he? Paddy's going to throw him out soon if he doesn't stop misbehaving with Jess. Did you know she's a full-blooded Chinook?"

Jean-Guy was in a way relieved to know that there was probably a perfectly rational explanation for Piers' refusal to wear the penguin suit but he was also now totally baffled. "Isn't that a kind of helicopter?"

"Native American. Apparently she's hoping to have a career in politics fighting for the Chinook cause and is out here for a term polishing up her Russian as part of her languages degree from UCLA."

"Smart girl."

"Very."

"And are she and Piers…?"

"Oh, no, not what you're thinking at all. She's just fed up with Paddy putting his hands all over her so she asked Piers to help wind him up. Part of her fee for helping you get rid of Ilya."

"But she must be nearly thirty years younger than he is. Who's going to fall for that?"

"She's twenty two."

"Jesus! How the hell does he do it?"

"Do you really want me to answer that question?"

Jean-Guy looked at the annoyingly handsome man of forty eight who was being caressed and kissed by an annoyingly beautiful twenty two year old, both of them playing their parts quite shamelessly, and then looked at his wife and child sitting at the table with him and knew he didn't envy the other man in the slightest.

"I had a letter from Petr Mihaly yesterday. He is arranging to have my old cello shipped over to me but it will go to my Prague address as he said it will take a while to organise the British export licence. He sent the message to the Conservatoire so of course several people there read it before I saw it but never mind. At least I will have my cello back."

"I'm sure you miss it," Kathy agreed politely as a man they didn't know sat within earshot with his coffee. "Right, I must go and round up Piers and remind him we have a plane to catch tomorrow. What time is your flight?"

"I need to be at the airport at ten."

"OK. I think we're flying at about the same time so might see you in Leningrad tomorrow? Where are you staying?"

He half-smiled. "I am at the Czech Embassy."

"Ah, yes, I suppose you would be. We're at some hotel or another, can't remember what it's called. Maybe we could invite you for a meal there before you come home?"

They were both well aware that the man at the next table was listening in to every word.

"Maybe. But I'm not there for long and Piers will be busy as he has two recitals with Roisin and I have to help my sister get her belongings all boxed up for the move. We'll see."

"OK." Kathy got to her feet and offered a formal hand in farewell. "Maybe see you in Leningrad. I'll contact you at the Embassy and let you know which hotel we're at."

"Thank you. It will be good to discuss some more recitals now he has clearance to travel."

Jean-Guy watched as his wife walked calmly over to the counter and hailed the man who was supposed to be her boyfriend. "Oi! Time to go."

He, unrepentantly, let Jess give him a heady kiss on the lips and a very familiar smack on the behind.

"Go on," she told him. "See you when you get back. 'Bye, Kathy! Have fun in Leningrad."

She just laughed. "Oh, I will. And I promise I'll keep him hot for you." The regulars in Paddy's who had got to know the couple loudly applauded her reply.

The man sitting at the table next to Jean-Guy leaned a little closer to him and spoke in French. "Take care, Comrade. Don't get too close to them. They are a dangerous couple and they are being watched."

Jean-Guy looked at him as though he was mad. "Are you joking? I use that man as my accompanist as he must be the best I have ever played with. That is it. Nothing more. I want nothing personal to do with someone so degenerate. And I am certainly not planning on meeting them socially in Leningrad." He downed his coffee then left the café as though genuinely disgusted with the whole idea.

"We didn't think this through, did we?" Kathy said to Piers as they got into the Lear Jet and realised they didn't know what to do with a tiny baby. There was no sort of seat she could use and they couldn't risk flying with her not strapped in.

He had to laugh at the sheer absurdity of it all. "Well, if we'd known we were going to be flying on with one extra we'd have sorted something out. Just stuff her in the shawl for take-off and we'll see where we go from there."

With a bit of help from Piers, Kathy got the five-point harness adjusted round the bundle tied to her front. "OK, all set."

"Good. Call up the control tower and let them know we're on our way and need runway clearance. You know the drill by now. You've had enough lessons and watched me do it on the way out here."

"You want me to take control?"

"Yes. This is a training craft so I can always take over if you look like going off the end of the runway. I trust you, Piglet."

"But I've never taken off from a proper airport like this one. There are a lot of other aeroplanes around and they're all bigger than us."

"Got to be a first time. Off you go."

To the unspoken relief of the experienced pilot, the novice made a perfectly good take-off and set course for Rzhevka Airport, just a short hop away for a fast jet like the Lear. Kathy tried not to think of Roisin, Niki and Jean-Guy enjoying the luxury of on-board refreshments as her ruthless tutor took the baby from her so she could concentrate on flying the plane.

It seemed like no time at all that Piers tucked the baby inside his own jacket and adjusted his harness round her. "OK. You've got your runway clearance so start your final approach. Bit more air speed, you've got a Jet Star up your backside and you need to get down and get out of the way."

"What? Where?"

"Circling for landing behind you. So get yourself down and follow the ground crew signals. Poor sod looks like he's got a malfunction."

Just then they heard the ATC radio calling them. "Catpaw, this is Rzhevka, go around, please.

We have malfunctioning craft behind you and need runway clear."

"Pull up," Piers instructed her sharply and to his relief she did as she was told. "Bank left, he's coming in from our right." He was watching what was going on below. "Good kid. Circle to your left, keep circling. They'll call us in when it's our turn." He didn't stop watching below. "Shit, that's a hell of a messy landing. Stand by, there's crap all over the runway. They're probably going to send us on to Pulkovo."

"But that's…"

"Just where we didn't want to go. Yup, here we go."

"Catpaw, come in, Catpaw. This is Rzhevka. We have debris on runway. Abort landing and proceed to Pulkovo. We have told them to expect you and they will waive your landing fees as you have paid here."

Piers got the charts out. "This is Catpaw. Received and understood, Rzhevka. Hope the pilot's OK?"

"He has walked away."

"Good landing then. ETA Pulkovo what? About quarter of an hour?"

"Five minutes in your craft. Thank you, Catpaw. Safe landing."

They flew on for a few minutes with Kathy following Piers' directions and it made her think oddly of the first time they had run from London and she had had to direct him to the farmhouse from the A12. Kathy was getting used to the feel and sound of the Lear by this time and didn't need any prompting when Pulkovo called them to guide them in.

Her first jet landing at an international airport wasn't the best it could have been but the pilot sharing the cockpit didn't say anything just calmly folded up the maps and charts and stuffed them away in their cubbyhole leaving her to follow the directions of the ground crew. Again they were guided to a part of the airport away from the big airliners but this time there was no Roisin and Niki to greet them. Post landing checks completed and plane shut down, they grabbed their luggage and followed the pointing arm of one of the ground crew.

"What's your Russian like?" Piers muttered to Kathy as two very unsmiling officials stopped them when they arrived in the building.

"A lot worse than yours," she had to admit having heard how Piers seemed almost to be soaking up the language by osmosis.

"Papers, please," one of the men greeted them in English. He checked all the documentation and even made sure they had the baby with them as she was on her mother's British passport. He stamped their passports and suddenly smiled. "Welcome to Leningrad. This gentleman will take you to your hotel now."

The second man showed them a US diplomatic identity card. "Just come with me, please. We heard you'd been diverted here. We'd like to ask a favour while you're here."

"Uh-huh? So long as it's not asking us to take an extra passenger or three. Not risking that without full paperwork in place. And we're not carrying any extra freight without full documentation either."

"Nothing like that. I'll give you full details before you leave."

Piers and Kathy knew that meant the man wasn't going to say anything as long as she was with them.

"Here, take your child," Piers said to Kathy and handed across the baby who was getting a bit smelly and fractious by this time. "Is it far to the hotel?"

"Half an hour in the car. I didn't realise you would be travelling with a baby."

"No, nor did we."

They went through a door and came into the main concourse of the airport, just as the flight from Moscow cleared immigration and baggage reclaim. Any hopes they may have had of escaping from the airport unnoticed were thwarted by Ravenna who had had enough by now and voiced her extreme disapproval of being flown wrapped in a jacket and then handed across like a piece of baggage.

Kathy's best attempts to hush her child were useless.

"Keep your head down and whatever you do, don't look across," Piers advised her quietly.

"There's no way they won't see us."

"I know. Keep walking. We'll sort Ravenna out in a minute."

It was Roisin who recognised the baby's cry even in the bustle of the airport concourse and she looked across to see Kathy and Piers in the company of a man who looked like an immigration official. She nudged her husband and nodded towards the little group on the other side of the airport and Jean-Guy saw what she was doing.

"What the hell are they doing here?" he wondered out loud, speaking Russian out of habit as he had been using it so much recently. "Kathy quite clearly told me that they were flying in a small plane to Rzhevka. Where are the other passengers from their flight?"

"Their flight could have been diverted for any number of reasons," Niki told him quite calmly. "I think it best if we just ignore what is going on as they seem to have been picked up by immigration although I don't know why as all their documentation is in order, even Ravenna's."

They weren't expecting to be stopped by a rather glamorous young woman. "Mr Dechaume, I'm from the Czech Embassy," she greeted them in Jean-Guy's native language. "We have a diplomatic car waiting for you outside." She switched to perfect Russian. "May we offer you two a lift to your hotel? It seems pointless you taking a taxi when we are going into the city anyway."

Jean-Guy couldn't help but think it was all very civilised after the cold unfriendliness of Moscow. His room at the Embassy wasn't large but it was clean and he had his own private bathroom and even a coffee machine and a water cooler. His guide had told him to make himself comfortable and if there was anything he wanted he only had to pick up the phone and ask. His sister, he was assured, was still at work but would be joining him later in the afternoon. He realised his parents had never told him what Marianne was doing to earn her living these days. The last he had heard of her, she had been a violinist in one of the orchestras in Prague but he had no idea what had happened to her after her failed attempt to bring him home. And now here he was, just where she had wanted him to be. And so, somewhere, was Piers.

He picked up the phone. "Is it OK if I pop out to see Nikita Fyodorovich and his wife now? We talked about having a meal together tonight."

"Yes, of course," he was assured. "We'll arrange a car and a guide for you. Please come down in about five minutes and your escort will be ready for you."

"No, don't worry. I'll wait for Marianne now. Perhaps tomorrow."

He put the phone down and realised that nothing had changed. He was still in prison. It was of some comfort to know he had friends somewhere in the city but right now he could see no way out. He looked up as a plane flew over, its lights flashing and winking as rain clouds started to gather over Leningrad and he could have sworn there was a light fog coming down in the distance. He leaned his face on the cold glass of the window and smiled to remember Sarah's story about Piers and Kathy combining to make a fog so powerful it could make ships run aground. He wished.

Somehow Roisin and Niki weren't surprised to find Piers and Kathy checking in to the same hotel. There weren't that many in Leningrad considered suitable for Westerners and as Roisin and Piers were on Irish passports, Kathy was on British and Niki travelled everywhere on diplomatic papers it was quite likely they would all end up together.

"You got diverted then?" Roisin hailed her brother.

He smiled warmly in greeting. "We did indeed. How was your flight?"

"Pretty good. Yours?"

"Uneventful until we got to Rzhevka. Are we having a run-through at any time before tomorrow's recital?"

"Not really time, but you know the programme and we can go to the venue early for you to try the piano. But you are in Leningrad. You must promise me that both of you will go and look at the Hermitage while you are here?"

"Sometime," he agreed and took the room key from the receptionist. "Well, this is us. 207. Drop by when you're ready and we'll all grab a meal somewhere, but give us time to sort the baby out first."

"Is this what your working life is like?" Kathy asked her travelling companion as they went into their room, thankfully noticed there were two single beds and an en-suite and each instinctively threw their cases on the beds with Kathy taking the one closer to the door and Piers the one closer to the window without a word being said. "Out of the plane, reams of paperwork, taxis and hotels?"

"Yup, not forgetting to update your log book. Going to be an interesting entry for today. And then you can do it all in reverse to go home."

"Think I'll stick with playing the violin."

"I would if I were you. But get Ravenna fed and changed first, huh?"

Jean-Guy was getting quite hungry by the time his sister came to meet him at the Embassy. She hadn't changed, he noticed. Her dark hair was still kept short, her blouse was low cut and her skirt was short. This time she did give him a hug in greeting.

"How are you?" she asked politely in Czech.

"Hungry," he replied honestly. "Are you my official escort for the evening to make sure I don't mix with undesirable foreign nationals?"

She just smiled. "Come on. I know a really good restaurant where there is no chance you will meet any foreign nationals."

He knew what she meant as the café she took him to was well off any kind of tourist track in a part of the city where no foreigner would want to go.

"How do you know about this place?" he asked as the two dined on cheap wholesome food that finally satisfied the hunger that had been nagging him for most of his time in Moscow.

"I work not far from here," she told him. "You've been out of touch too long. I work for the State now, broadcasting on long-wave radio to Western Europe speaking in French and English."

"Propaganda broadcasts?"

"Yes, if you like. I'm glad you saw sense and came home. Are you getting work with your cello still?"

"I'm mostly teaching at the moment. But our parents said you're coming to join us in Prague. I'm glad you said I could come and help you get sorted. We parted so strangely back in England."

"Why couldn't they come?"

Jean-Guy realised his sister, who broadcast propaganda in French and English, didn't know that their parents were now well out of the way in Santa Fe. "Papa is very busy at the moment getting ready to move back to the Prague Conservatoire and tidying up all his classes and students before he has to leave them. What will you do? Will you broadcast from Prague instead?"

Marianne stopped eating. "I'm not moving."

Jean-Guy began to get worried. "So why did our parents ask me to come and help you to pack?"

"Because until yesterday I was all set to come to Prague and play happy families with you all."

"Oh? What happened yesterday?"

"I got engaged."

He looked at her then as this information slowly registered in his mind. "I didn't even know you have a boyfriend. Congratulations."

She tapped his left hand with her fork. "I guess you married Kathy then? I knew I was right about the two of you. What happened to Piers?"

"He made his peace with Sarah and they now have eight children."

"No. They haven't had time."

"Triplets then quins. But never mind about him, you lost him when you pulled a knife on him. Was it likely he'd trust you again after that? But the more I know him with our music, if I am truthful, the less I like him and I am glad you and he didn't get married. And I have already been in touch with Kathy and told her I want to dissolve our marriage unless she agrees to join me here. So I don't want to talk about her. Or him. Tell me about your boyfriend. As my flight to Prague isn't for five days maybe I'll even get to meet him."

Marianne was satisfied and chatted happily with her brother as the evening got late and cold, then she walked back to the Embassy with him and took her leave with a kiss on his cheek. "Tomorrow, then?" she checked with him.

"Tomorrow," he confirmed and went into the building, hoping his rescue party was making more progress than he was.

The next day he met the man who would become his brother-in-law in less than a month. Part of him was glad that his sister had found her own kind of happy ending and another part of him was resentful that she was making her own life now while he was trapped, separated from his wife and child and had no idea what would happen next. He knew Piers and Roisin had the first of their two recitals that evening and wished he could have gone there. But enquiries at the Embassy had just given him the news that yes, Roisin Thompson was doing two recitals in the city but they were private performances and there were no public tickets available.

Not far away in the same city, Kathy was also fretting against the rules and regulations that kept her away from her husband. She had had nowhere to leave Ravenna so she had spent the evening in the hotel with her child, thinking of the lovely music and wishing she could have been there. Her watch told her it was gone eleven by the time Piers got back.

"Good concert?" she asked.

"Not really. I mean the concert was good but Roisin got a message just now when we got back. Her daughter has rung to say one of the twins has had a road accident and is in hospital in London. Got knocked off his motorbike somewhere near Chancery Lane so she's cancelled her second gig and she and Niki have gone straight off to catch the red eye to

Amsterdam, should just make it, and going on to London on the first morning flight. I asked her to ring us when she gets home to let us know how Ruairi is."

"Did it sound bad?"

"Don't really know. Siobhan could only leave a message and when Roisin tried to ring back there was no reply. I told her not to bother stopping off at our room but just to go. You have no idea how tempting it was to come and get you and fly her and Niki back tonight. But we may not be allowed in again and I'd like to see a bit of Leningrad while we're here."

Kathy realised their room was almost certainly bugged and Piers was being very careful with his words. "So what happens now?"

"We have to go home, got no reason to stay as Roisin has gone and I have no official bookings with Jean-Guy. Right, I'm taking a shower and then in the morning we'll work out a flight plan. But while our papers are still good for a few days we may as well be good tourists and I've long wanted to see inside the Hermitage."

Kathy watched him go into the bathroom still fully clothed and heard him turn on the shower. She was not expecting him to come out again and take her by the wrist into the bathroom so their muttered conversation was disguised by the sound of the running water. "Tomorrow we get the hell out of here. Roisin should be in Amsterdam in a couple of hours and she said she'd ring if they have any problems so unless we hear from her we can assume we're OK to go in the morning. They'll be suspicious if I don't go pretty much straight away now she's gone and they will be expecting us to go back to the UK as I have no reason to stay here."

"Well, that gets us out, but what about Jean-Guy?"

"Wait for it, Piglet. Thanks to my other job I have a couple of contacts in the CIA we can make use of so before we go to sleep tonight, we plan a perfectly acceptable flight plan to Ipswich. We daren't offer to take Jean-Guy back to Moscow as there'll be an escort waiting for him so we're going to have to risk it and run for Finnish air space straight from here with an unlogged passenger on board. We have one of the fastest civilian aircraft we could but they'll send the fighter jets after us as soon as they realise we've taken their cellist with us."

"Fighter jets?" Kathy queried and could feel the fear starting inside. This was getting way too serious now.

"Standard procedure. They'll make some excuse to get us to return to Pulkovo which we can probably ignore for a few minutes, but they'll try to force us back to where we should be long before we've crossed over into Finland."

"So what happens?"

He laughed without humour. "We fly as fast as we can and we pray. We've got enough fuel to get us home, we're sticking to our fight plan. We've just got a passenger on board that we're not supposed to have. It's the easiest solution. Now, unless you want to see me wet and naked I suggest you go back to bed and start planning a flight. No, Piglet, that wasn't an invitation. Oh, for Christ's sake, piss off."

Kathy started. "Sorry. Thinking. Wasn't planning on staying. Honestly. How can you be so calm about it all?"

He treated her to a lovely slow smile. "It's what I spent years training to do. Literally flying in the face of the enemy. And a very large part of me is looking forward to finding out if I can still do it."

Jean-Guy got up the next morning and the cold, damp fog that hung over Leningrad suited his mood. He almost smiled to think that maybe Kathy and Piers had worked out a way to wreck the ship that held him captive. He had arranged with Marianne that she would call for him at about ten thirty as she planned on taking him along to the radio station where she worked. He knew the idea was just to keep him supervised at all times and wasn't surprised that he had been told he would be brought coffee and a cold breakfast in his room at eight. He looked at his watch and saw the time was barely seven thirty and jumped when the phone in his room rang.

"Good morning," a cheery voice greeted him. "We have a Mr Buchanan downstairs. He says he's your accompanist and he's come to take you out to breakfast."

"Oh, OK. Is he allowed up? I'm not dressed yet."

"He can wait down here for you."

Jean-Guy couldn't remember the last time he got dressed so fast. Without any regrets at all he left behind the few clothes he had brought with him from Moscow but he shoved the Russian passport he had been given into his coat pocket and picked up the pile of music he had been planning on working through that day as he had nothing else to do. He had found his old copy of the Rachmaninov *Sonata in G* and he was determined Piers was going to learn that one. Its passionate storminess was in his mind as he ran down the stairs to meet his accompanist and hoped this was the start of the rescue party, although he couldn't see how.

He was taken aback to realise Piers wasn't with Kathy and Ravenna but was accompanied by a very unsmiling gentleman and he hoped the man wasn't a policeman and this whole thing was yet another trap.

"Hi," he greeted Piers quite cheerfully. "Glad you're here as I've been thinking about works we can use at our next recital. I have brought the scores so we can look at them over breakfast."

Piers looked at the armful of music the other man held and had to smile. "You certainly believe in making your accompanists work hard. Come on, we're having breakfast at the US Embassy so I hope you like waffles."

"Love them. Where's Kathy and the baby?"

"Already eating her waffles and then we're going to the Hermitage after breakfast. Don't know if you've ever been? The Americans will be escorting us today, it's been cleared with the Czech authorities so you can be a tourist too."

Jean-Guy instinctively glanced at the security guards at the door but they just nodded rather sourly. "Sure. Thanks. I've never seen the Hermitage. But I can't be back too late as my sister will be expecting me."

The three men stepped out into the street where a large black car with the Stars and Stripes on its bonnet was waiting for them. Jean-Guy got in without protest and was surprised to find Kathy and Ravenna were already on the back seat.

"What the hell?" he asked.

Piers got into the back seat with them and the unsmiling gentleman got into the front passenger seat. With just a gentle purr of the engine the car pulled away from the kerb.

"Say 'hi' to Jim from the CIA," Piers invited. "He's giving us breakfast at the Embassy, then it's a tourist trip to the Hermitage and finally a lift to the airport."

"Um, hi. Why are the CIA involved?"

"Shall we just say we're doing each other a favour and leave it at that?"

"If that's how you want to put it, then that's fine by me."

Kathy could feel the nervous excitement growing inside her all during that day. The American breakfast was wonderful but she had no appetite and the Hermitage was as fascinating as she had thought it would be. But all the while she was aware that there were eyes watching them. Eyes that wanted to make sure they did as they had been cleared to do and didn't go anywhere or do anything that they shouldn't.

They walked out of the Hermitage, aware that those watching were within earshot and Kathy wasn't surprised when Piers said perfectly normally to Jim, "Any chance we can drop by the airport, please? I need to pick up some paperwork from the aircraft as we're planning on flying out today." He spoke loudly enough for the watchers to hear and then turned to Jean-Guy with just a slight smile. "Want to have a look round a rather elderly executive jet? You don't get many of them to the pound these days."

Jean-Guy felt as though he was walking on a knife edge. "I would be curious to see inside," he admitted. "But I am meeting with my sister for lunch."

"No problem," Jim assured him warmly. "You can just have a quick look inside the plane if you like then these two will be off and I can take you back to your Embassy in time to meet your sister. OK with you?"

"Yes, thank you," he managed to say and really, really wanted to grab Kathy by the hand and hang on to her for ever. But he knew this wasn't the time or the place.

Kathy didn't even dare look at Jean-Guy and she was grateful to Piers who tucked her hand through his arm as he was, after all, supposed to be her boyfriend, and gave her a lovely smile. "You're flagging, Mum. Come on, let's get you back to the aeroplane and you'll be home in time for tea."

It was a silent ride to the airport and it all got very unreal for an anxious Jean-Guy. He was just glad he was being looked after by a very experienced pilot who calmly logged a flight plan to Ipswich. He understood the conversation between Jim and the Russian authorities when the American promised that the cellist was just going to have a look round the executive jet and they had clearance to do a loop round the local air space before bringing him back. The flight was expected to last about ten or fifteen minutes and Jim finished by pointing out he would wait for Jean-Guy to return and then drive him back to the Embassy where he was expected to be meeting his sister. All their documents were checked and security grudgingly cleared them to go to their aircraft. They clearly weren't happy that Jean-Guy had been invited to have a look round the extravagantly capitalist private jet but as he had a member of the US diplomatic service with him they didn't protest too much. Jean-Guy began to feel he could almost breathe again but he didn't dare say a word in case he jeopardised what was clearly a very well-planned operation. He could feel his mood lightening by the second as he carried his baby daughter to a part of the airport he didn't know existed and Piers opened the door to a small, sleek jet aircraft.

"One executive jet," Piers told him. "Hop in. Piglet will be showing you round while Jim and I deal with the last minute necessities. You can help her get the baby sorted out while you're in there. At least we've got a proper seat for her this time."

Jean-Guy looked round as he followed Kathy up the short flight of steps she had pulled down from the side of the aeroplane and realised they were being watched very carefully by a couple of men dressed as ground crew. He doubted they would have a clue what to do with a plane if anyone asked them. But then he was inside the plane and he genuinely stopped to look at the luxurious interior.

"Hell of plane," he said out loud.

"Bit old fashioned now," Kathy assured him and the two of them got Ravenna organised in her baby seat.

They both strained their ears to hear what was going on outside and could hear Jim and Piers were obviously talking to the ground crew men.

"When did he learn Russian?" Jean-Guy asked.

"Oh, picked up a few words here and there. What are they saying?"

"He's telling them he's got permission to do a lap of the airport to give me a ride in the plane. They're not happy. But I think even they aren't going to argue with the Americans right now."

"Good."

Jim followed Piers into the aircraft and helped stow their luggage and a box of food which had been thoroughly checked by the airport staff and cleared to go with them. He then went and stood in the open doorway so the men in overalls would hear them and said he would wait there for them to bring Jean-Guy back in a few minutes and wished them a safe onward journey. He went down the steps and shut the aircraft door for them, and Jean-Guy watched as his wife so efficiently checked the door and then kissed their baby daughter on the forehead now she was settled into an infant seat which had been strapped in to one of the standard seats.

"Seat belt on," she told Jean-Guy and gave him a soft kiss too. "We'll be over Finnish air space in less than half an hour as Piers is flying this morning."

"Why do I get the impression that's not as good news as it should be?"

The sides of her mouth lifted in a humourless smile. "The Russian Air Force can catch us in twenty minutes. Piers won't be doing too many aerobatics but it'll most likely be a rough ride so you might like some of these." She handed him a pile of sick bags and did smile then. "I've got my own supply in the cockpit. If we cross into Finnish space safely, we'll fly straight to Ipswich as that's logged as our destination after your sightseeing lap."

"How can you be so calm about it? Look at me, I'm shaking. And we have our baby with us. Are you risking her life too?"

Kathy smiled into his terrified eyes and gave him what she hoped was a reassuring kiss. "We have to have blind faith in our pilot who, as he told me yesterday when I asked him the very same question, has been highly trained for such circumstances. Just keep your seat belt fastened for the whole trip. OK?"

The twin engines whined into life and Jean-Guy dutifully put his seat belt on, not feeling much better about the whole thing but realising that there wasn't a choice. "Are you really that little blonde mouse I met at Ipswich station?" he murmured softly.

Kathy leaned down and gave him a hug. "Not any more. I am the, oh I don't know, snarling tigress that popped out of the mouse's skin. Try not to be sick too loudly, you'll upset the baby."

A short, hard kiss and she joined Piers in the cockpit but left the door latched open so they could talk to Jean-Guy.

"Ready, Piglet? Want to take the take-off while I chat up ATC?"

"I have control," Kathy confirmed and didn't know just how proud her husband was of her at that moment.

"Good morning, Pulkovo. This is Catpaw requesting take-off permission. To confirm, we'll be doing a couple of circuits for our passenger then returning to let him out before getting on our way to Ipswich."

"Catpaw, you're cleared to go and logged through to Ipswich. Take care on your circuits as we have heavy traffic at the moment. Have a good flight. Please proceed to runway."

Jean-Guy had never flown in such a small plane before and found the whole take-off experience quite exhilarating. Suddenly he understood why Piers didn't want to give this up for the earth-bound existence of a pianist. Kathy's second take-off in a jet aircraft at an international airport was even better than her first and she banked the plane right then straightened it out.

"Catpaw, this is Pulkovo. Advise you seem to have damage to your rudder. Please abandon your scheduled circuits and return immediately for a maintenance check."

"You absolute bastards," Piers muttered under his breath. "Just for a minute I thought they'd let us go." He spoke perfectly calmly into his radio. "Sorry, Pulkovo, we don't have any indications on the instrument panel but we'll keep an eye. Just getting out of your traffic lanes for our circuit. Thanks for the warning."

"Catpaw, return immediately. We have reason to believe your plane is malfunctioning."

"Give us a couple of minutes to run our checks as everything looks good here. We'll get out of your air lanes and check. Thanks, Pulkovo."

Kathy looked across, fighting down the rising panic and saw Piers was calmly fiddling with the radio. "What are you doing?"

"Breaking the law. Want me to take over now? Great take-off by the way. We really will have to sort out your licences though."

"Thank you. She's all yours."

"I have control. Want to go and see if our passenger is still awake?"

Kathy looked over her shoulder and gave her husband a wave. "He's fine." She listened to the sounds coming through the radio. "What is that awful noise?"

"That's the sound of a scrambled military radio. And if it's scrambled that means they're flying."

She gasped at the flagrant breach of aviation law. "You can't hack in to military wavelengths."

He gave her one of his wicked smiles and spoke into the radio. "This is Catpaw calling. We'd like to invite Brer B'ar and Uncle Tom to lunch. We have beetroot soup on the menu."

"Identify yourself, Catpaw?"

"This is Aunt Harriet, but without the hat."

"Bloody hell. Thought you were a bus driver these days."

"I am."

"Good to hear from you. Brer B'ar can be with you, Uncle Tom is at a wedding but we'll send Fannie Cottontail to join you. Advise position and flight path, please?"

Kathy listened to the chatter on the radio waves and realised Piers had called up some old buddies from the RAF. She was just about to be astonished that he would ever dare do that when the radio went silent.

"What's happened?" she asked.

"Some bugger's jammed our radio. We're on our own now, Piglet." He took a split second to glance at his watch. "We'll cross the border into Finland in about twenty minutes."

"And the Russians?"

"Will be with us in ten." He looked out of the window over his left shoulder. "Or maybe slightly less."

Kathy's stomach lurched as Piers suddenly pulled the plane up and right before pushing it as fast as he dared until the engines were howling.

"Yup, that's confused them but now they know we're running for it. Can you adjust the radio for me until you hear a lot of Russian swear words, please?"

Kathy tried but the radio remained stubbornly silent. "It's not working."

"Bastards have well and truly jammed us. Sodding Russians always did play dirty. At least the RAF would challenge you before they started shooting."

"Shooting?" Kathy gulped.

"Finnish border in ten minutes. Didn't know this old girl could fly so fast. And here we go again."

Another stomach lurch as Piers savagely banked hard right and dropped several hundred feet ignoring the warning light that lit up the control panel.

"Terrain warning," Kathy reported.

"Yup. It thinks we're losing height too fast but we've got a couple of hundred feet to play with." Piers was scanning the skies round their plane but all was ominously empty. "They've gone behind us. Hang on tight, you lot. They're going to try and box us in."

"How many are there?"

"No idea, can't see them. I'd guess we picked up two at take-off but we've probably attracted four by now. They'll try to box us in to force us back to Pulkovo."

Kathy couldn't believe that he was still so calm.

"Yup, there they are. I can hear them now. So we let them come alongside. Just like that. And off we go. Thank Christ for Red Arrows training, even if it did make me lose my lunch on a regular basis. Sorry you three, it's going to get a bit unpleasant now, but I don't want to risk them firing warning shots at us."

Kathy had barely registered there was a very aggressive-looking fighter plane next to them before Piers pulled the jet up again and they soared away from the chasers. She watched the altimeter and knew Piers had pushed that little jet to within a hundred feet of its known limit but that wasn't high enough to lose a military jet. As the fighters rose up to join them, Piers put their plane into a twisting, rolling dive at great risk to his digestive tract and circled the Lear Jet behind the others. The other pilots were clearly confused by his tactics and Kathy saw there were indeed four of them. The pilots weren't fooled for long and two of them circled and got behind again.

"Feel sick now," Piers remarked and sounded it. "Hate aerobatics. Finnish air space in five minutes. And here comes the lunch party."

Kathy jumped as two jet fighters with British markings went screaming past them going the other way and then the silent radio came back to life.

"Hey, Aunt Harriet. What the hell kind of bathtub is that? You need to get yourself a proper machine. Oh bugger, I think we're trespassing. About turn, Brer B'ar or we'll be getting beetroot soup all over our noses."

The two arrivals peeled round in a beautiful example of formation flying and raced on ahead, hotly pursued by two of the Russians.

"Two minutes," Piers intoned and calmly dropped left and went under one the fighters that had been pulling alongside again.

Then it was the Russians who banked and turned away. To Kathy's astonishment the Russian pilots all dipped their wings to the little Lear Jet as a mark of respect to the one who had out-run them.

"Is that it?" Kathy asked and heard her voice shake.

"That's it. We're out of Russian air space now. Oh, hell, they're back. Must have got permission to fly in Finnish space."

The two RAF jets fell into formation with the Lear, one each side and so close Kathy felt she could have jumped from one wing tip to the other.

"Hey, Aunt Harriet. Nice co-pilot. You little sod. You haven't lost it have you? Nobody else could have taken a bathtub like that and out-flown four bloody MiGs. When are you going to come back to flying proper aeroplanes?"

"When you retire. Thanks for the escort, but I'm sure you've got better things to do with your flying time than babysit us."

"Oh no you don't, you bugger. You've got a military escort and you owe us at least ten pints each. Where's your destination?"

"Ipswich."

Loud howls of laughter came down the radio waves. "Oh, sweet Jesus. Is there even an airfield at Ipswich?"

"Yes. And it's got a bar."

Loud cheers over the radio. "Come on then, Catpaw. We'll take you home."

Johannes Brahms – *Wiegenlied Op. 49 No. 4*
(Lullaby)

"It was like something out of a crazy film," Kathy laughed as she settled comfortably back against the sofa cushions and took another thankful mouthful of tea.

Emma was still looking at the tiny baby now in a Moses basket on top of the piano in the sitting room of the farmhouse. "How could you not know you were pregnant?" She came and sat next to her oldest friend. "Sorry, you were saying?"

"It was like a crazy movie. I mean, can you imagine two RAF fighter jets landing at Ipswich airfield? It was a neat landing too, I'd swear there wasn't more than inches between the planes although there must have been. And then we all went into the club lounge and Piers and his RAF buddies had a quick catch-up although how they knew what each other was saying I have no idea as they all seemed to be talking at once. Then Brer B'ar and Fannie had to be off again as they were expected back at base and we just got in the car and drove back here like we'd been out for a picnic for the day."

Emma was far more interested in Ravenna. "Well, I thought I was being brave going for a home birth with Chas but I think you've outdone me. And your baby already has two passports?"

"Well, kind of. She's on my British one, but she has her own Russian one. She had to have my surname as I couldn't give her Jean-Guy's but we'll change it as soon as we can. And don't pull faces at me like that. I know your three have Czech papers as well."

"True," Emma agreed and thoughtfully sipped her glass of chilled rosé wine. "Where are the other two?"

"Well, I'm here," Jean-Guy announced as he came into the sitting room with his own mug of tea. "Last I saw of Piers, he was heading off to have a bath. Emma, please tell me you didn't drive all the way across the country just to see us? You are one mad woman if you did."

"Hey," she laughed. "I get a phone call from Dad to say my oldest friend has had a cryptic pregnancy, dropped her first sprog in the back bedroom of a cockroach infested Moscow flat and you expect me to sit at home in a crumbling pile in Somerset and not come over here with lots of leftover baby stuff for you?"

Kathy was so tired she felt as though she had drunk even more wine than Emma had. She gave her friend a hug. "Well, I'm glad to see you. Do you know if your dad has heard anything from Roisin?"

"Mmm. Apparently it was quite a nasty accident her son had but he's in hospital and the surgeons have managed to salvage his legs but he'll be in a wheelchair for ages. Professionally she's cancelled most of the gigs on her calendar as he's the only one of her children who hasn't got a partner so she and her husband are pretty much living at the hospital and will take him home to Wimbledon to convalesce. The only booking she's got left is a charity concert about Christmas time and from what Dad told me, she's booked her brother to be her accompanist. Is it safe for them to be seen on a concert platform together?"

"I think they both feel the time has come. If anyone says anything they're going to admit to being related but they're not making any grand public statements about who her 'new' accompanist is and, of course, neither of them uses the Maloney name but they are so perfect together musically. Such a shame there's this massive thirty year gap in their professional careers."

"Shame for who?" asked a voice from the doorway and Piers came in with a wriggling towel-wrapped bundle in his arms. "Idiot cat fell in the bath," he said and sat in one of the armchairs so he could rub an indignant Audrey dry. The cat wasn't the slightest bit grateful for the help and clawed her way out of the towel then shot out of the sitting room howling her outrage as she went. "So, Jean-Guy, quite recovered from your little trip to Mother Russia?"

"Not yet," he replied honestly and wondered how the other man could calmly inspect a bleeding scratch on his arm and appear to be so relaxed about it all. Piers looked as annoyingly handsome as usual even in scruffy jeans and with the sleeves of his unironed checked shirt rolled up. "To speak the truth, I don't think I ever want to leave this house again." He saw the others were looking at him. "They took me once, how can I be sure they won't try again?"

"They'd be idiots if they did," Emma laughed. "Bloody hell, we scrambled the RAF to come and get you and from what Kath says your escape flight featured a few Red Arrows stunts for good measure. What more proof do they need how hard we're going to fight to keep you?"

"Technically they were flying anyway," Kathy pointed out. "If they hadn't already been in the air, I doubt if they would have got to us in time before the Russians started getting heavy-handed with us."

"Can we not talk about it, please?" Jean-Guy asked. "I am not as tough as you two and would like some time to remember I am safe again for a while." He half-smiled. "But I have to admit, you are one crazy army the pair of you and I wouldn't like to get in your way."

"Very wise," the Prof agreed as he put his head round the door. "Is anyone going to eat tonight? I thought we'd just have something light. And what is the matter with Audrey?"

"She found out she can't swim," Piers laughed and got to his feet. "Well, I need to eat. Moscow rations have been playing hell with my stomach acid. But at least by some miracle I managed not to be sick on the flight home. Came bloody close to it though."

So they all went into the kitchen where Audrey, clearly in a foul mood, was sitting on top of the Aga and still very damp. Kathy thought rather idiotically that it was quite surprising the cat wasn't steaming as she dried out.

Kathy left the doors open so she would hear if Ravenna made a sound while they were in the kitchen and went to the dresser to get crockery and cutlery for their meal. "What are you thinking of cooking?" she asked. She reached to get down some plates and knocked off a music manuscript book that had been balanced rather precariously on top of a pile of newspapers on the dresser. "Oh, sorry. Must be more tired than I thought, I'm getting clumsy."

Emma picked the book up and looked inside. "Dad," she said slowly. "Have you been composing? You haven't done that for years. Probably since I was about twelve and you composed something based on *Lavender Blue* to encourage me not to give up the violin."

"Technically I have been arranging," he smiled. "I thought if a Concorde pilot can make a go of some Smetana then I can have a go at some Brahms." He looked at the other three. "I have arranged his *Lullaby* as a little birth-day gift for Ravenna. Maybe more of a theme and variations I suppose. You can try it tomorrow when you have all rested. None of the parts is easy."

He exchanged a smile with his daughter as the three members of the Dodman Trio bunched round the book and looked at the music he had arranged for them.

"Shouldn't it have been a violin and cello piece?" Piers asked as he looked at a horrendously complicated variation played on the piano with the strings accompanying with a simple pizzicato background.

"I understand Ravenna has been extra blessed as she needed the help of a third party when she was born. All three of you gave her life and that is what I wanted to celebrate. You know I don't believe in your ghosts and mysticism. But I have had you all under my care now for a few years and even I have to admit there is a strong bond between you. Something I couldn't name. Something I have never known among other people. As Jean-Guy has said, you all breathe as one and Ravenna is the embodiment of that breath."

Kathy thought that was beautifully put and she looked at the violin part which she could see was going to present its challenges. She saw what the Prof had written at the top of the music.

Brahms' Lullaby, *arranged for the Dodman Trio by Petr Mihaly. For my extraordinary musical family and Ravenna Jean who took us all by surprise in Moscow 28th September (Wenceslas Day) 1984.*

"And you really wrote all this in the couple of weeks since Piers rang you from Moscow?" Kathy asked.

"I have been working on it for a while now. Making it more and more difficult as your playing improved. I think now it is not perfect but it is where it should stay. So I have put in the dedication and I am now trusting you with it."

"You realise I'm quite envious, don't you?" Emma laughed as she helped her father get a cold meal ready for them all to eat. "He hasn't written anything for any of mine." She gave Kathy a hug. "And I really don't mind. I've seen the early versions of that stinker he's written for you three and I'll be quite happy to sit in the audience and listen to you all make a pig's ear of it."

Kathy looked across at Jean-Guy. He had put the cello part out of the way on top of one of the kitchen cupboards. "We'll have a look at it tomorrow," she agreed. "But I wouldn't like to promise when we'll play it out." She tried to catch Jean-Guy's eye but he had turned away and she knew that her husband still hadn't shed the chains that had trapped him. But he was home, he was safe, and he was smiling as he went out of the kitchen to find out why their daughter was demanding attention.

The story continues in *Dark Sonata*

Historical notes for the sake of the storyline:

1) *Although Moscow does have a famous Conservatoire of Music and the "dollar shops" were real in the 1980s, Paddy's International doesn't exist except in the imagination. At least, not yet.*

2) *Imogen Holst (1907 – 1984) conducted her father's works on several occasions but the concert in Ely Cathedral is purely fictional.*

Printed in Great Britain
by Amazon